A HERO RISES

MORONI & THE BATTLE FOR MANTI™

AUTHOR:
JASON MOW

ILLUSTRATOR:
GABE BONILLA

A Hero Rises: Moroni & the Battle for Manti
Author: Jason Mow
Illustrator: Gabe Bonilla
Graphic Design: Nicole Bonilla

ISBN 978-0-9905953-0-4
First English Edition, May 2015
Printed in the USA

DEDICATION

This book is dedicated to Nicholas and Rachael.
So you will know who my Hero is.

Love Dad.

Table of Contents

PREFACE

The War Chapters Series of books are based on characters appearing in the Book of Mormon—a volume of scripture of The Church of Jesus Christ of Latter-day Saints. In our book, as in the Book of Mormon, the characters frequently affirm their faith and commitment to the Savior, Jesus Christ. We think the messages of faith, honor, courage and sacrifice in these stories are universal and should appeal to everyone, regardless of religious belief.

While we hope this book contains insights that will help the reader in their effort to better understand the great messages contained in the Book of Mormon, this book is a work of fiction by its author. It is not produced, endorsed or aided by The Church of Jesus Christ of Latter-day Saints, or its leadership, in any way. While the author is a faithful member of the church, this book should not be used in the place of true scripture study, prayer and reflection. These books are meant to serve as catalysts to inspire readers in their efforts to further study the war chapters in the Book of Mormon.

There are plenty of theories as to where the Book of Mormon lands were located. There is not, as of yet, a definitive location acceptable to the majority of historians. We are not endorsing any of these theories. While we are using the actual place names from the Book of Mormon, there are also some fictional places the author has created for the benefit of the story. Any geographical similarity to existing locations is purely coincidental.

The label "War Chapters" is often used to describe the long period of war, civil war and social upheaval that is described in the book of Alma, chapters 43-62, in the Book of Mormon.

INTRODUCTION

600 years before the birth of Christ, in a land far, far away, a rich but humble man named Lehi lived with his wife and four sons in the great city of Jerusalem. For many years, Jewish prophets of the time had been warning the people that God would punish them and allow them to be enslaved if they did not turn from their evil ways and remember Him.

One night, while he was sleeping, Lehi had a divine vision in which a heavenly messenger warned him the time of God's wrath was at hand and that he must take his family and flee the city. Lehi woke and told his wife and children about the dream. Believing the warning, Lehi told them to gather what they could carry and prepare to leave their home forever. However, Lehi's older sons, Laman and Lemuel, did not believe him and argued against going, thinking he was a fool and Jerusalem was too great a city to ever be conquered. Lehi's younger sons, Nephi and Sam, believed their father and supported him. Because Jerusalem at that time was governed by Mosaic Law, children were required to obey their parents or they could be taken to the gates of the city and stoned to death. Therefore, Laman and Lemuel reluctantly fled with their family, leaving all their worldly treasures and possessions behind.

After a few days of traveling in the wilderness, God again spoke to Lehi in a dream, telling Lehi to send his sons back to the city and obtain the "Brass Plates" from a man named Laban. The Brass Plates were a record of the lineage of the people of Israel, and they also contained a copy of the laws and commandments of God that had been handed down from father to son from the time of the exodus from Egypt. Laban was a very rich and powerful man. He commanded a large group of armed men, and he was responsible for the records of the people, including the Brass Plates. But Laban was also a very wicked man who used his power and riches to influence others to do evil and to make himself more wealthy.

The sons of Lehi returned to the city and tried to obtain the Brass Plates from Laban. First, they asked if they could have the plates and he flatly refused, laughing as he sent them away. Next, they returned to their own house and gathered up all the gold and other possessions they had left behind. They brought the riches to Laban and offered to trade the family fortune for the plates. When Laban saw the wealth laid out before him, he refused to trade for the Brass Plates and, instead, ordered his own men to kill the boys so he could keep Lehi's wealth for himself.

The boys fled the city while being chased by Laban's guards. Once outside the walls of Jerusalem, the boys hid themselves in a small cave while Laban's men searched the countryside for them. Laman and Lemuel decided to return to their father empty handed. Nephi believed his father had talked to God and refused to go without the Brass Plates. Laman and Lemuel, angered by Nephi, started to beat him with sticks. Suddenly, an angel appeared before them and told them to stop trying to hurt Nephi. The angel told them Nephi would rule over them because of their wickedness. They were commanded to return to the city to obtain the Brass Plates and told that God would deliver Laban into their hands.

The angel departed, and Nephi told his brothers to be strong like the great heroes of old. He told them to hide themselves outside the gates of the city while he went to confront Laban alone. Waiting until dark, Nephi slipped back inside the city and went to Laban's house. He did not know what he was going to do or say when he confronted Laban, but he trusted in his God.

Just outside Laban's house, Nephi found a man lying in the gutter, passed out from drinking wine. As Nephi approached, he discovered the drunken man was Laban and that he was alone in the dark. Nephi saw Laban had his great sword with him, and Nephi drew it out of its sheath. The Sword of Laban was a mighty weapon, with a large blade and jeweled handle, and it was quite heavy. It took both hands for young Nephi to just lift it up.

As Nephi admired the massive weapon, the spirit of God spoke telling him to kill Laban. But Nephi was just a young man. He had never killed before and could not understand why God wanted him to kill Laban. The spirit told him that the Lord slays the wicked to bring to pass righteous purposes and it was better that one man perish than an entire nation dwindle in unbelief. Nephi remembered God had said that, without His commandments and statutes, his seed could not prosper in the land. Those laws and statutes were written on the Brass Plates, and Laban was the only man standing in the way.

Nephi understood his responsibility and, having trust in God, cut off Laban's head. He took Laban's garments and armor and put them on. Dressed as Laban, Nephi walked into Laban's home and told a servant to get the Brass Plates. The servant, Zoram, saw Nephi in the armor and clothing of Laban and, thinking it was his master, retrieved the plates. Nephi ordered Zoram to follow with the Brass Plates as Nephi walked out of the house and toward the gates of the city. Once outside the gates, Nephi went to the place where his brothers were hiding. When they saw a man wearing Laban's armor approach, they got scared and tried to run, but Nephi called them back. When Zoram realized who Nephi was, he also tried to flee. Nephi captured him and took the Plates away from him. To save his own life, Zoram made a pact to remain with Nephi and his brothers when they returned to Lehi and their mother, Sariah, in the wilderness.

After some time, Lehi commanded his sons to again return to Jerusalem and find a man named Ishmael. Ishmael had many daughters and Lehi wanted his sons to marry and have families of their own. The sons of Lehi spoke to Ishmael and told him about their father's vision and the danger he and his family were in if they stayed in Jerusalem. Ishmael's heart was softened by the spirit of God, and he agreed to join Lehi's family with his own in the wilderness.

The two families wandered in the wilderness for several years, being guided by the spirit of God. The sons of Lehi married the daughters of Ishmael and they had children of their own. After some time, they came to the edge of a sea and God told Nephi to build a ship. Nephi followed God's commandments and, with divine aid, he and his brothers built a large ocean-going vessel.

Trusting in their God, Lehi and his family left the old world behind and sailed across the water. After many days at sea, they landed on the American Continent or, as Nephi called it, "a choice land of promise."

Shortly after their arrival, Lehi died and Nephi was appointed the family leader as well as their spiritual guide.

Now that they were living in a strange and foreign land, Laman and Lemuel were finally rid of the old customs and Mosaic Law they felt were keeping them from their rightful destiny. They refused to follow Nephi because he was their younger brother. They felt that, by right, Laman, who was the first born, should be the king and rule over the entire family.

This was a desperate time for Nephi and his family. To avoid any trouble, Nephi and those who supported him, along with their wives and children, split from the rest of the family and started a new life far away from Laman and Lemuel.

From this action, two great civilizations emerged: the Nephite civilization, named after their first king, Nephi; and the Lamanites, named after Laman. For the next 500 years, both families grew in population and eventually covered the face of the land. They built great cities, roads, and large urban areas with farming, agriculture, industry, and religion.

There were wars and contentions between the two peoples. God's prophets walked among them warning both Nephites and Lamanites to remember they were a choice and blessed branch of Israel, and that the land they now possessed was the land of promise from which the laws of God would go forth to all men. They had kings and powerful men rule over them. When the kings were honorable, the people prospered. When the kings were evil, the people suffered.

About 92 BC, a good and just man, wise King Mosiah, king of the Nephites, abolished the practice of kings and noble ruling bloodlines and established a system of "Judges" or representatives appointed by the voice of the people to govern the land. With a new representative republic as their system of government, the Nephites continued to wax strong and grow in the land. The Lamanites refused to follow the Nephite example and held to the traditions of their fathers, becoming a more warlike and ferocious people.

In 76 BC, a great and destructive war was fought between the two peoples near the land called Jershon. The Lamanites were defeated in a final epic battle and thousands were slain on both sides. The Lamanites were eventually driven back to their own lands, and peace was once again established among the Nephites.

About 74 BC, the Lamanites' hatred toward the Nephites was kindled again by a Nephite, a descendant of Zoram named Zerahemnah. Zerahemnah was an antichrist. He hated the godly ways of the Nephites and rebelled against the leaders of God's church. Zerahemnah used cunning and lies to stir up the anger the Lamanites felt toward the Nephites. Taking command of their armies, Zerahemnah marched the Lamanite army to a staging area just outside the Nephite lands in preparation for a massive invasion.

The Nephites were still recovering from the previous war. Their lands and several cities were decimated and many of their great war chiefs had been killed in battle. They were not prepared to face this new and overwhelming threat from the Lamanites.

What was needed now was a strong military leader to guide the Nephites to victory and save the very fabric of freedom, their religion, and families— someone they could all rally around, a man who was larger than life and could inspire greatness from his soldiers, a leader who feared God and was pure in heart, mind, and deed.

What they desperately needed was a Hero.

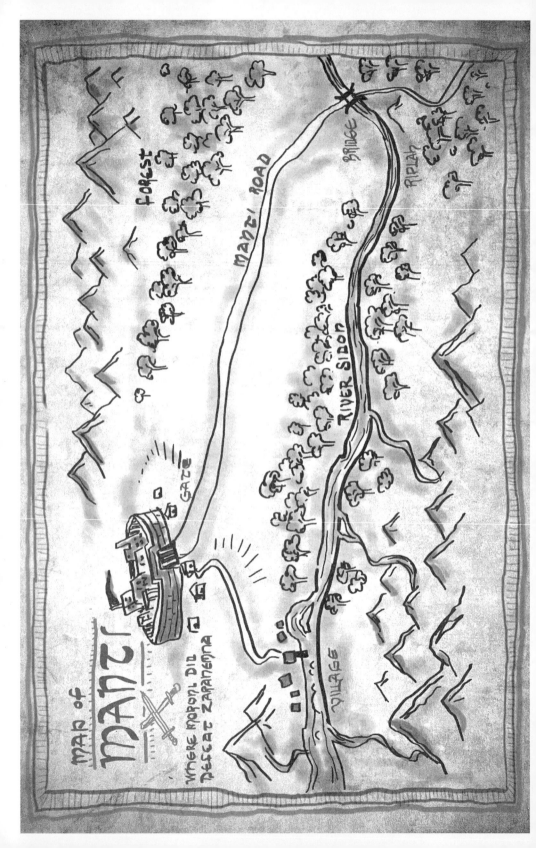

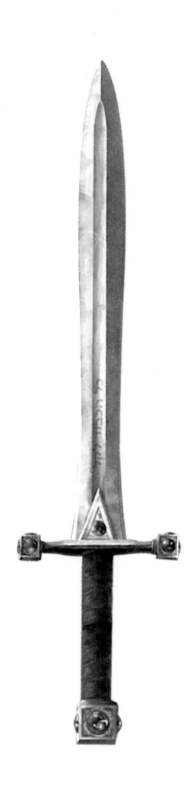

RUMORS OF WAR

A light afternoon breeze blew through the trees and across the wide valley nestled beneath the lush dominant mountains surrounding it. It sent waves of welcome fresh air across the bustling Nephite military encampment growing in the valley. The smoke from hundreds of cooking fires started to clear away, and the almost unbearable smell of human and animal waste was flushed by the cool, sweet aroma carried by the wind from the jungle-covered mountainsides.

The loose ends of the tarp opening rustled against the side of the large Nephite command tent strategically positioned on a small hill overlooking the camp. Nephite soldiers working around the tent felt the effects of the cool wind against their sweaty bodies, and they all stopped their labors to enjoy that simple pleasure.

From the distance, a horse galloped up the worn path that led to the command tent from the camp below. As the rider approached, he was confronted by the sergeant of the guard force that was standing vigil at the top of the hill and around the large tent. Although the sergeant recognized the rider, Nephite military protocol demanded he stop the soldier and ask him for the password before allowing him to get any closer to the important person inside the tent. The young commander sitting inside the tent heard the sergeant ask for the password, and then heard a familiar voice responding correctly. He continued to listen as heavy footsteps approached the tent opening.

"Amiha!" the commander called out from inside. His voice sounded unsteady, revealing his frustration over the day's events. Things were not going well for the Nephite army, and he knew the rider was not bringing any better news.

"Yes, sir!" barked the Nephite warrior as he rushed into the command tent. He was dressed in the battle armor of a chief captain, with the red sash of the aide-de-camp to the commanding general wrapped diagonally across his chest plate.

"Yes, my general?" Amiha asked, as he took off his helmet and snapped to attention. He stood in front of a large, wooden table covered with map skins of the surrounding area. He clicked his heels together and rendered an overly exaggerated hand salute and a slight grin broke across his face. The imposing figure behind the desk was not amused with the extremely theatrical display of Nephite military customs and courtesy.

"That's enough," the dark-haired giant of a man said under his breath, without looking up from the maps spread in front of him. "I'm not in the mood for your showmanship. Please see if you can get the back of the tent open to let some fresh air in ... it's as hot as dragon's breath in here."

"Yes, sir," Amiha said soberly. He blinked several times, lowered his salute and began to move slowly toward the back of the tent, feeling somewhat disheartened over the response to his jovial entry.

"Amiha?"

"Sir?" Amiha turned to face the young general.

"Sorry about snapping at you like that, my brother," Moroni apologized. "It's been a long week." The boy general looked up from his maps to face his lifelong friend.

Amiha paused awkwardly, gazing into the tired blue eyes of the most powerful military man the Nephite nation had ever known. "I'm sorry, too, Moroni. You are right; it has been a long week. Can I get you some food? You've been fasting for almost two days now."

"No, thank you." The general leaned back in his chair and rubbed his eyes with the palms of his big hands. "A long week indeed ... any word yet?" General Moroni asked, but he already knew the answer. Without waiting for Amiha to respond, Moroni got up from his seat. He had been sitting behind that desk and studying the maps for some time. Amiha watched as the young military commander slowly walked in circles, shaking his hulking arms and legs trying to get the blood flowing to his aching limbs. Moroni stretched his arms over his head and arched his back. Reaching for the canvas ceiling, he yawned for several seconds and then brought his hands down and rubbed the bulging muscles on his neck and shoulders to relieve the tension he felt.

"No, no word yet, Moroni, but the scout teams have only been out one day," Amiha spoke as he moved to the water basin for a drink. He poured two goblets of water and walked over next to the general, who stared blankly at the map of Jershon. Even after all these years together as friends and brothers in arms, Amiha was still amazed at how big Moroni really was. Amiha himself was no slouch. He was a big man, well over six-feet tall, with hard, lean muscles developed from living a soldier's life. "But Moroni," Amiha thought as he stood next to him, "he is big." Standing next to each other, Amiha's head came only to Moroni's shoulders. Amiha had not met anyone who was taller, broader, or stronger than Moroni. Amiha offered one of the water goblets to Moroni, who reached out for it and lifted it to his lips, the muscles in his arm rippling and bulging with the slightest movement. "Massive" was the one word that crossed Amiha's mind.

Moroni took a long drink, and then pointed to a section of the map marked in red. It was labeled "Antionum."

"My gut still says he's there," Moroni said. "It's his home city, there is plenty of food and good drinkable water, and the north road runs right through it." He paused, and then asked, "What do you think?"

"That would make the most sense, but what about this war makes any sense?" Amiha said in a low tone.

Moroni took another drink of his water and wiped his chin with the back of his hand. "Zerahemnah is no fool," he continued, pointing the goblet in his hand toward the map. "He will not go far outside his power base until he has control over all the Lamanite armies. Only when he has the support of the great Lamanite chiefs can he make his war."

Moroni walked away from Amiha and stood in the opening of his command tent, looking out over the growing sea of humanity under his command below. He emptied the rest of the goblet of water into his mouth, swallowed and spoke, "How can one man hate so much?" he breathed out. "He has set all of this in motion to will see the destruction of so many of God's children and for what? What unseen evil would drive a man to cause so much pain?"

Moroni stood in the tent door, motionless and silent, lost in the thoughts that only a veteran soldier can have of the impending horrors of war. He could feel the breeze now. It was cool and refreshing against his skin. The sweet smells from the jungle carried on the wind stole his thoughts for a moment, and he closed his eyes and inhaled deeply, flashing back to happier times, but only for a moment.

"We yearn to live in peace with them ... yet, they come," he whispered loud enough for Amiha to hear. "We give them the gospel of Christ and messages of hope from Alma the Great and his sons ... and, still, they plan for battle. We give aid and comfort to their brothers and sisters and, yet, they pledge to enslave us," his voice got louder. "Even the loss of so many in combat at the river near Jershon two years ago does not stop them from again taking their blood oath. I fear this will be a war like no other."

Amiha was caught up in the moment and the words of his best friend and commander. He could feel the love and concern Moroni had, not only for the people he had pledged to protect and serve, but for the Lamanites as well. Amiha knew that Moroni did not want this war. Only a real soldier could understand the true price paid for war, and Moroni was a soldier's soldier. Amiha put his empty goblet on the map-covered desk and moved next to Moroni at the tent opening. The two stood in silence, looking at the camp below in the dusty haze of the afternoon sun, both lost in their own thoughts, and both certain that what lay ahead would be dark. They both knew death was coming.

FLASHBACK

The two friends seemed to shake their inner darkness at the same time and moved back into action and planning.

Moroni faced his friend with a determined resolve. "I need better intelligence, and these maps are ten years old," the general said in disgust, waving his left arm at the tent and the desk scattered with maps.

They walked together back into the middle of the tent. In addition to the maps spread on the desk, hanging along the inside of the tent were several other maps with colored markings on them. A second large table stood in one corner. It held an ink quill and a reading lamp, burning over a growing list of the Nephite troops and supplies that were arriving. In the opposite corner was Moroni's extra-large sleeping cot. A large, wooden trunk stood next to the cot. The open trunk revealed that it contained changes of clothing and Moroni's personal items. Standing upright near the trunk was an oversized, metal washbasin resting on a wooden pedestal. Next to that was Moroni's armor stand, a large, handcrafted piece of wood and metal, shaped like a cross, where Moroni could hang his body armor and helmet to air dry or for when they needed repair or cleaning. On the floor of the tent were several large area rugs. Every evening the camp attendants took these rugs out and hung them on a rope strung between two large trees. They struck the rugs with long rods to get the dust and dirt out of them.

All together, these were simple living conditions in contrast to Moroni's extremely high military rank. He would have it no other way. He was a soldier first and refused the trappings, pomp, and privileges that came with his high rank and leadership responsibilities.

"Give it time, sir," Amiha said, moving over to one of the chairs by the table filled with maps. "Perhaps the intelligence you need will come tomorrow. The bulk of Captain Lehi's troops is expected to arrive any day, and we are hoping for another shipment of supplies from the people of Ammon."

"More sweetbread and honey, I hope," Moroni said, patting his stomach. "That would be a great way to break my fast."

"Any more sweetbreads, my general, and we are going to need to get you a bigger horse."

Moroni spun around and tossed his empty goblet at Amiha, playfully shouting, "Get out!"

"Yes, my general." Amiha laughed as he blocked the goblet with his hands and knocked it to the ground. He backed out of the tent opening, bending over at the waist with his arms stretched out like an obedient servant preparing to leave the presence of a dictator.

"Now you are really in trouble! You know you don't bow to me, even in jest. I am a soldier, not a pompous king. Watch out or I will put you on cooking duty for a month." Moroni smiled and extended his right hand toward his boyhood friend.

Amiha straightened and his smile took on a more serious look as he shook his friend's hand. "For liberty," Amiha said.

"For liberty," the general replied.

As the two warriors broke their grip, a deep, booming voice could be heard coming from the camp below. Even over all the noise, confusion and activity in the camp, the distinctive gravelly voice could be heard shouting orders and verbally reprimanding some poor, unseen soldiers.

"Sounds like the sergeant major found a new victim," Moroni said. He and Amiha both strained to find the exact location in the camp of the voice.

"Yep, I would recognize that voice anywhere," replied Amiha. "That is one mean old crow you've got there."

"That is true … I'll be sure to let him know how you feel about him at the next staff meeting."

"Don't you dare!" Amiha hissed, his voice laced with concern.

Moroni tried to maintain his serious composure but could no longer hold back his smile. "Who's the brave soldier now?" he laughed.

"Nice," Amiha replied sarcastically. "By your leave, my general … I have a camp to run." This time, Amiha rendered a proper, less theatrical, salute to his commanding officer and made his way down the rise toward his waiting horse. He took the reins from the hand of the guard who had been holding his horse outside the perimeter of the tent and gracefully climbed into the saddle.

"Tell the sergeant major I need to see the updated troop rosters, and find the camp quartermaster. I want a report on the progress of the supply issues before sundown," Moroni shouted as his friend began to ride away.

"Yes, sir!" Amiha called over his shoulder and saluted again. He gave the horse a quick jerk on the reins and rode down toward the camp. The dust from his horse stirred in the afternoon breeze and wisped past Moroni's giant frame. Moroni watched the dust settle as Amiha rode out of sight. Alone again, he looked out over the camp below. He dropped his shoulders slightly and took in a large breath of air, holding it for several moments. The responsibility of it all was almost more than he could bear. By his command, the lives of all Nephites hung in the balance. Moroni was smart enough to know he was going to need help. Slowly, he exhaled, letting the outgoing air pass over his nearly closed lips. Shutting his eyes, he whispered a quick prayer.

"Mighty Father, please give me the strength to do Thy will."

Moroni opened his eyes and stood still to again feel the sun on his face and the cooling breeze coming off the mountains. His current predicament weighed heavily on his mind and he silently wished he could stay where he stood.

After a moment, he hesitantly opened the tent flap and stepped back inside.

"That knucklehead never got the back of the tent open," he said. Letting out a sigh, he walked to the back of the tent. In the dim light, he used his hands to search the tent wall, found the opening, and pushed the flap aside, letting sunlight pour into the dark recesses of the tent.

Moroni struggled to secure the open end with a piece of rope to a stake in the ground just outside the tent. The guards and camp attendants standing around the back of the tent were shocked to see their leader step out of the back and do something so beneath his high rank as to tie down the tent opening. Clamoring over themselves, they moved quickly to assist Moroni, but he waved them off and smiled to reassure them they were not in trouble. Moroni walked back inside, brushing dust off his tunic.

He paused in the center of the tent, feeling the cool breeze blow through.

"Much better," he said to himself. Knowing his day was far from over; he sighed and moved with the weight of the world on his shoulders through the large tent toward his desk to get back to the battle planning.

Passing his cot, Moroni caught a glimmer of sunlight dancing off a metal object lying on top of the blanket. He blinked and forced his eyes to focus on the object that was reflecting the light. He felt a familiar tingling across the back of his neck, across his shoulders, and down his arms. Just as it had many times before in his life, the feeling was followed by a warm rush of emotion that surged through his entire body, ending with an all-encompassing sense of peace and reassurance.

"I feel your spirit, Lord," Moroni whispered. Taught from the time he was small, he recognized God's presence when he felt it. This had been confirmed to him when he met with the High Council of Chief Judges and Alma the Great many weeks before. His thoughts drifted back to the great hall of the judges, near the holy temple, in Zarahemla. It was there, those long weeks ago, that Moroni became the first Commanding General of all the Nephite armies. In his mind, he was taken back to that time and remembered kneeling before Alma the Great, Prophet of God and High Priest of His church.

"For the first time in our history, all Nephite military forces are now under one commander," Alma had said before placing his hands on Moroni's shoulders. When Alma's hands touched Moroni, Moroni had felt the same warm feeling pass through his body.

"The Council of Judges has spoken and the will of the people is done. You, Moroni, now wield power never before known to the Nephites. If you trust in God, obey His commandments, and lead with humility, He will bring you to victory." The old prophet's words echoed in Moroni's mind as, now in his own tent, he again experienced the same feelings he had felt as Alma had continued to speak to him.

"Do you now feel God's spirit upon you?" Alma had asked.

"Yes, sir," Moroni had gasped, fighting to hold his emotions in check.

"Remember those feelings and trust in the mercy of heaven."

After Alma had finished speaking, Chief Judge Nephihah exclaimed, "Take up your father's sword, young Moroni." He pointed to the giant weapon lying on a table behind them. "This is the very same sword passed down from our father, Nephi, the very same sword that your father used so expertly to defend his lands, his clan, and his kin from the Lamanites."

The chief judge handed Moroni the sword and continued, "I knew your father. We all still mourn his death. I know his wish was to unify all the Nephite clans to make us stronger, but that dream went unfulfilled in his lifetime."

The chief judge had walked around Moroni to address the gathered crowd. Moroni saw that his mother, sitting in the front row of the hall, was wiping tears from her eyes.

"Now, with this new form of government, the will of the people can finally be heard and our forces can at last rally to one standard, your standard, Moroni. The people have spoken and this council has appointed you Commanding General of all the armies of the Nephites. Lead them well, young Moroni."

Although he could still almost hear the cheers of the crowd, everything else about that event seemed so surreal, so dreamlike that, deep down, he wondered if it had been real at all. However, nothing could change the fact that there, lying on his cot, was the ultimate symbol of Nephite military authority, the great mantle of leadership, the power to make war in God's name.

"The Sword of Laban!" Moroni said in a reverent whisper.

Every Nephite soldier, Christian or not, knew the legend of that mighty weapon. It was an expertly crafted sword made by master craftsmen in old Jerusalem and used by father Nephi to cut off the head of Laban and secure the holy Brass Plates. The blade was almost four feet long and made of thick, polished steel, sharpened on both edges to a razor-like finish with a round tip. The blade of the fine sword and the handle—which included the guard, the grip, and the pommel—were one solid piece of forged metal made of the finest steel in all Israel. The guard was a long, straight bar at the base of the blade that protected the hand of the sword bearer from his opponent's blade. This guard was of a straight, perpendicular design, rounded off with a four-sided, block-shaped tip on both ends. The grip was long enough to allow a warrior to hold the weapon with both hands. The pommel was also block shaped, but was slightly larger than the two tips on each end of the guard. Beside the sheer size of the sword, its most stunning feature was the twelve large imbedded jewels on the sword, one jewel on each of the four sides of the blocks on the tips of the guard and pommel—twelve different precious stones, each representing one of the twelve tribes of Israel. Inscribed on each side of the base of the blade were the words "Glory to God," in Hebrew on one side and in Egyptian on the other.

The sword had been handed down from generation to generation and carried by the Nephites' mighty leaders at the head of marching armies. It was a symbol of freedom. Because of its size, most men would have trouble wielding it. Because of its size, it had usually been carried only as a symbol of freedom, but for Moroni, who was taller and stronger than anyone else he knew, the sword felt completely balanced in his hands.

More events from his past flashed before him. He recalled the teachings from his earliest instructions as a young squire in the service of his father, the great Nephite warrior and chief captain of legions of soldiers. He remembered sitting by his father's side at campfires and feasting after a victory, or training with his father's legions. He remembered walking across a vast training ground where young recruits received training in the arts of war from his father and the officers under his command.

He had listened to old warriors talk of great battles and glory won through feats of marshal skill and high honor, all for liberty and the defense of freedom. He could still hear his father speaking to young army recruits about the importance of self-sacrifice and their duty to protect God's children from any power that would seek to take away the rights of self-government from the people.

"Never forget, my sons," his father said, addressing the soldiers warmly, "that you are all that stands between liberty and everything that is evil in this world. If you do not stand for what is right, just, honorable and true, then lesser men will fail and your family will be in bondage. Be like father Nephi, and stand ready with the Sword of Laban to fight for justice and peace!"

His father would then hold the mighty weapon in its scabbard with two hands above his head, and the gathering of young soldiers would all stand and shout together in celebration of freedom.

"God himself knows of this sword," his father would continue. "It was the voice of God that told father Nephi to pick up this very sword, to slay Laban and to secure the Brass Plates to ensure our religion, our freedom and our rights as humans. This sword and those holy records are the only things that remain with us from the old world. It is never to be unsheathed except in the defense of God's children. It should always remain as a symbol to us of our Heavenly Father's guiding hand in all we do!"

Moroni's mind suddenly returned to the present. He walked toward his cot, drawn ever closer to the sword of power by an unseen force willing his feet to move forward. With every step, the images, sounds and events of the past again flashed in his mind. Enveloped in the moment, his mind was whisked to a time not so long before, as vivid, heart-wrenching memories came crashing into view.

THE BATTLE OF JERSHON

"Father! … Father!" young Moroni shouted, while galloping across the open battlefield. He reined his horse to a stop and held up his right arm to halt his companions galloping behind him. The horse, sensing his master's emotions, shifted nervously, huffing and spinning as Moroni tried to keep it steady enough to hear a response. The fighting, noise and confusion of this skirmish in the great battle of Jershon was over, but the battle raged on not far away. Both armies had moved down river, and all that remained was oppressive heat and hundreds of wounded and dead soldiers. Both Nephites and Lamanites lay together in death, scattered across a large open, grassy area more than a mile wide. This was the outer edge of the massive land battle, the largest and most destructive thus far in the greatest war that anyone had seen since father Lehi had come out of Jerusalem.

Young lieutenant Moroni was desperate to find his father, the chief captain over the Nephites, who fought in this section of the battle. Hearing no response, Moroni spurred his horse across the field of battle. The troop of Nephite cavalry he commanded followed closely. Moroni stopped a short distance later to survey the incredible sight of carnage before him. Everywhere he saw death and destruction—men and boys slaughtered, wagons broken, animals slain, weapons and armor of all kinds discarded and scattered, left to rot under the unforgiving midday sun.

This was not Moroni's first view of death and war … but it certainly was the worst. The young leader observed a group of Nephite men off in the distance to the right, searching among the dead for wounded soldiers. Should they, by luck or grand design, find any of their fallen brothers still breathing, a large wagon pulled by two oxen stood in wait, ready to transport the wounded to the physician's tent. The oxen were indifferent to the carnage before them as they pulled at the grass and chewed. Hoping for news of his father, Moroni spurred his horse forward to speak with the men.

As he got closer, he could see that the men in the detail had removed their armor and markings of rank; their only weapons were swords strapped to their sides. They wore only light tunics that were soaked through with the blood of those they were trying to help. Working in pairs, the men of the medical detail walked slowly, looking for any sign of life—gasps, a movement, a cry out for help—anything to give them hope that they could save another man.

Moroni rode up to the man sitting in the wagon holding the reins. The young leader averted his eyes, trying to avoid the sight of the cleaved bodies of men and boys in the wagon. He swallowed hard, nearly gagging on the taste of bile that rose in his mouth.

"Where is the chief captain?" he asked the teamster. Moroni turned his head a little more, trying to keep from being distracted by the sight of so many injured and bleeding soldiers. The sounds of their screams and cries for help were harder to ignore.

Moroni could see utter exhaustion in the wagon driver's eyes as he worked to stand and render a proper salute to the young cavalry officer before him. Moroni wanted to wave to the young soldier to sit down, but he knew from his father's instruction that during extreme times, like combat, discipline must be maintained to ensure order among the troops. The soldier gritted his teeth and, supporting his weight by leaning on a spear he carried in the wagon with him, he stood and saluted.

"At ease," Moroni said after returning the salute.

"The chief captain is over there, sir." The driver tried to pivot his body and pointed to a small grove of trees farther up river.

Moroni could see the wagon driver was young, probably close to his own age, but physically much smaller. A band of cloth, stained dark by sweat and dirt, kept his light-colored hair out of his eyes. He did not have a sword but carried a large knife tucked into his belt, in addition to the spear.

Noticing that the driver was neither bandaged nor bleeding, Moroni asked, "Are you wounded?" while gesturing to the spear the soldier was leaning on.

"I'm not hurt by a weapon, sir; something is wrong with my knee. I fell during the first charge at sunrise yesterday, and it has not been the same. I can't march any more so my sergeant put me with the medics to help pick up the dead and wounded … been picking up bodies for two days straight now." The young wagon driver was almost numb from the experience. His eyes were hollow and void of life. Moroni had seen this lack of feeling before. He knew everyone responded differently to the stresses of battle. Some got angry, some cried, and others reacted like this young soldier, trapping their emotions deep inside themselves. Moroni always took courage from seeing his father's example in past battles. He watched again and again as his father seemed to thrive during conflict while others cowered or shrank from their duties. "Most of them are not cowards," he would say to young Moroni when they spoke about how some men acted during war. "They are just now warriors."

Moroni looked in the back of the wagon and saw the price of this war. "All dead?" he asked.

"No sir," the young driver said. He was so exhausted that even blinking his eyes was a challenge. "I think one or two might make it back to the surgeon alive."

"Why are you not taking the wounded back as soon as you find them?" Moroni said with anger in his voice as he spurred his horse toward the back of the wagon. "Give them a chance!"

The soldier shrugged and his voice caught when he tried to speak. "Sorry, sir, but we only have one surgeon and a very few medics for our entire legion, and they are completely overwhelmed. They have been working harder and longer than anyone out here. The wounded are stacked like firewood outside the medical tent. Either they wait out here or outside the doctor's tent, it just doesn't matter. It's going to be at least a day before anyone can see to them." The young soldier looked away. Moroni could see the tears leaving streaks in the boy's dirty face. He was finally starting to break down. This was not his fault, but Moroni could see the driver was bearing pain and guilt over the gruesome task to which he was assigned. Moroni's heart ached for him and for the wounded. He knew the young wagon driver was right. With Nephite medical resources spread too thin, only the truly strong of mind and body could survive severe wounds after a battle of this magnitude.

"You are a good soldier," Moroni commended.

The driver looked up and wiped the tears from his eyes.

Moroni added, "Remember your ethos. You do your duty with honor and courage. The Lord sees this, as do I. I will personally tell the chief captain of your bravery."

The driver's eyes gleamed and a smile broke across his face.

Moroni took out his own rations pack, bandage kit, and some water skins and tossed them to the driver. "Tend to the wounded the best you can … at least give them a chance." Several of the other horse soldiers followed their young leader's example and dropped their water and rations at the back of the wagon.

The driver carefully climbed down from the wagon and limped to the back. He picked up the supplies and, with them, he gathered a fresh dose of courage as well.

Moroni clicked his tongue and his horse moved toward the grove of trees where he hoped to find his father.

"Sir!" the teamster called out as Moroni rode away.

Moroni stopped and turned to face the Nephite warrior.

"Did we win?" he asked in a painful, and yet almost sarcastic, tone.

"It rages on down river," Moroni shouted back, pointing down the riverbed.

The Nephite returned no expression or gestures; he just paused for a moment, nodded his head and went back to tending to the wounded among the dead.

Moroni guided his horse forward in the direction of the trees, with his soldiers following closely behind.

"There must be a better way to care for the wounded." He spoke to no one in particular, but loud enough for his whole troop of soldiers to hear. A horse trotted up next to him. Moroni looked to his right and into the eyes of his best friend, Amiha.

"We should find a way," Amiha responded with a wisdom far beyond his years. "But now is not the time."

"Agreed," Moroni said. He signaled to the small band of Nephites, and they broke into a gallop toward the distant wood line.

"Here, boy!" Moroni heard from a distance.

It was the booming and unmistakable voice of the chief captain. Moroni knew instantly where to find his father. He dismounted and led his horse into the small grove. Moving around a large tree, he found his father under the shade of a small, rectangular tarp stretched out among some of the smaller tress.

"Father!" Moroni's voice revealed his concern. He handed his reins to a soldier and approached the mighty Nephite chief captain. "Are you all right?" A medic, his face lined with exhaustion, was kneeling next to Moroni's father, tying stitches across a deep wound on his father's muscular left arm.

"I will live long enough to need to explain this to your mother," the older man said, smiling and jabbing his right thumb toward the wound. He winched in pain as the medics pulled the last stitch closed and cleaned the wound with water. Not wanting to be the one responsible for causing the commander any more pain, the medic nervously rubbed a clear ointment on the wound and left. Recovering quickly, the old but very powerfully built warrior jumped to his feet and began to laugh aloud.

"That will teach those godless Lamanites to attack a lonely chief captain with only ten men," he shouted. He turned back to face Moroni and spoke with a slight grin and a twinkle in his eye.

"I fought off nine of those dogs before the tenth one slashed me from behind and then fled like the dirty coward he was." He flexed and moved his left arm and, when he spoke again, it was softer and less aggressive. "What news from your reconnaissance, my boy?" he said as he wrapped his good arm around Moroni's shoulder and shook his son while squeezing. He had done this since the time Moroni was a small boy. It always raised Moroni's spirits when his father did that. It reminded him of the more carefree days of childhood.

One of the cavalry officers stepped in under the shelter, shouting loudly, "The whole army is falling back to the edge of the river. If we don't move now, we will be cut off and caught behind the battle lines and on the wrong side of the river!" Moroni shot the man an angry glance. He knew the soldier was concerned for everyone's safety, but it was completely unacceptable to interrupt a senior officer like that.

"Why are we retreating?" the mighty captain bellowed. He turned and snarled toward the group of young men still on horseback. Most of them, out of instinct, pulled back on the reins of their horses and tried to make some distance between themselves and their angry leader. They all knew and deeply respected the chief captain's fighting abilities. His fiery temper was legendary and, even wounded, they knew he was more than a match for any man in a fight. They all know the chief captain was not personally angry with them, but they were not about to take any chance.

"Sir," Moroni spoke as he pushed his way past the other mounted soldiers, "most of the other chief captains have been killed. Captain Lehi is fighting a rear guard action at the river. He is trying to hold the crossing so what remains of our army can get safely to the other side before our lines collapse. You are the only field commander left anywhere near the entire front line!"

"WHAT?" he shouted and spun around to face his son. He walked quickly in a semicircle, looking into the eyes of every man there. There was a long pause as the men around him began to back farther away from their leader. They could see his face turning purple and then a crimson red as he took in several deep breaths. They feared bearing the brunt of his anger.

"COWARDS!" the old warrior shouted as he drew his sword and started to walk out of the grove and toward the distant sounds of the war drums.

"Father, wait!" Moroni exclaimed. He ran to his father, grabbed him by his sword arm and looked into his eyes. Moroni had seen that look before. He knew his father was serious and would walk alone right up to the front ranks of the entire Lamanite army if he could.

"Sir, I have discovered a way for us to turn the tide of this war." There was a pause as Moroni let his good news sink in with his father. Swallowing hard he continued. "While conducting my reconnaissance, I observed that the Lamanites have collapsed their left flank just over that rise." Moroni pointed toward a small, grassy knoll northwest of their position and about two miles away. "They left their main supply camp unguarded and exposed to a counterattack." Moroni felt the tension in his father's arm relax.

"In the valley just beyond that hill lies the command center and supplies for the bulk of the Lamanite army. It is now largely undefended. Only a few old men and wounded troops remain." Moroni paused for a moment to let his father process what he had just said. His father turned his head toward the battleground. "Are you sure of this?"

"Yes, sir. Most of the Lamanites have joined the main push to the south as our army retreats," Moroni continued. "If we gather what soldiers we can and attack their rear area now while it is unprotected, we can destroy their supplies and kill or capture any of the Lamanite command staff still in the camp." Moroni took a step back as the old soldier spun back to look at him.

"Father," Moroni made a slicing motion with his hand. "It's like cutting the head off of a snake. If we destroy their command center, it will end their ability to continue waging war."

The mighty chief captain blinked several times and paused as if contemplating deep thoughts.

He started slowly, and the speed of his words soon increased. "While the whole of the Nephite army is in full retreat, you want to charge into the heart of the enemy and attack its headquarters with a few wounded men who are caught behind enemy lines? … HA!" The chief captain laughed. Moroni felt a sudden pang of shame. His father was a brilliant military tactician. Of course he would see the weakness in Moroni's daring battle plan. He dreaded letting his father down and, now, in the heat of battle, he has presented to his commander a flawed plan of attack.

The chief captain slid his massive sword back into its sheath and moved closer to where his son was standing. Moroni tried not to look his father in his eyes. He knew he had disappointed him and did not want his father to see the acknowledgement in his expression. The old captain put his hand on Moroni's shoulder, looked him in the eyes and said, "My son, it would be my great honor to join you in this suicide mission." A flood of emotions and relief came pouring out of Moroni as he realized his father approved. The chief captain brought Moroni's forehead against his own. He patted the back of Moroni's neck and softly whispered, "My son."

The tender gesture lasted only a few seconds, but Moroni basked in the warm feelings, letting them fill his being, and he stowed them away in his mind, where he hoped they would remain. He loved his father, and he knew his father loved him.

Not wanting to delay any longer, the chief captain turned back toward the grove. "Sergeant Major," he shouted.

"Sir?" a gravelly voice snapped in response, and a tall, lean man more than twice Moroni's age walked out of the shadows of the grove. Moroni instantly recognized the man as his father's oldest and most loyal soldier. Moroni knew the sergeant major and his father had been brothers in arms long before he was even born. They had shared many adventures together and the sergeant major was the only person, other than his mother, Moroni ever heard call his father by his given name, Joshua.

"Sergeant Major, gather every boy and man who can still wield a weapon, arm them all and form them into ranks."

"Yes, sir!" the old soldier smiled. "Once more into the fray, my Captain?"

"Yes, my old friend," a tired smile formed on his face. "Once more."

The old chief captain turned to his son, "So, what are the details of your battle plan?"

With the sounds of the sergeant major barking orders in the background, Moroni pulled a long dagger from a sheath on his belt. He knelt down and traced in the ground a map of the surroundings and the location of the enemy camp as he explained his plan of attack.

"We place what archers we have left here, at the maximum distance from the camp." He poked the ground at a location away from the camp. "Have them all concentrate their fire on the enemy supply wagons and sleeping tents with flaming arrows. We strip down the infantry for better mobility, have them drop their packs, carry weapons and armor only, for a full charge right down the middle of the camp. At the same time, we split the cavalry in two. I command one group and you the other."

He looked up at his father. "When the camp is set ablaze by the arrows, we charge in from opposite sides while our infantry charges at the center—a simultaneous three-pronged attack to confuse and disorientate the enemy. Once we are in the camp, we all fight toward the middle and regroup there. The archers and our walking wounded will then move to the south of the camp … here." Moroni stuck the ground with his dagger to show the final location of the archers in relation to the Lamanite camp. "They will form a skirmish line to stop any Lamanite survivors who try to flee. They also will warn us if any Lamanites return to camp from the battle down at the river." He then drew a long S-shape in the dirt to show the location of the river on his map. "We kill all who resist and take the others prisoner. Take what supplies we can carry, burn the rest and then meet back here to regroup and move toward the river at first light."

Moroni waited for a moment; letting the old warrior process the plan of attack just presented. The younger man held his breath, hoping for his father's approval.

"It's a sound plan, my son. Only one thing to change though—I will be leading the infantry charge."

"But, father … I …"

"No," Moroni's father held up his hand to cut him off. "I will lead the infantry from the front where everyone can gain courage from my example." Moroni's father stood and grabbed him by the arm. He walked Moroni past the rest of the troops and out of earshot. "Our lines broke today, and the soldiers who remain are all ready to turn and run." He sounded uncharacteristically sober. "The only thing holding them here is their faith in me and their loyalty. Remember my actions here today, Moroni." He poked Moroni in the chest with his massive finger. "One day you will command men and armies. You must never falter or show fear in the face of the enemy. Remember, my son, you are destined for greatness."

Moroni felt his father's strong touch on his chest, and when he looked into the older man's eyes, he saw deep kindness reflected there. He knew his father's soul was that of a true hero. Here was a man who strongly defended his beliefs and would willingly give his life for any one of his men.

Under his father's gaze, Moroni searched his own heart, wondering if he would do the same.

As if his father could tell what Moroni was thinking, he said, "Moroni, you must at all times trust in God and keep your honor. Never forget your warrior ethos, my son. Remember that there are things worth fighting for … there are things worth dying for—your family, your God, justice, peace, liberty and freedom are all worthy of an honorable death." Nearly overcome with rich emotions of love and respect, Moroni instinctively looked down. Even though he was the oldest son, he felt unworthy to stand next to such a good man. The old Captain saw his son look away and grabbed him by his shoulder. Moroni looked back up when his father said, "Now go and gather what officers I have left. Quickly now, we have much to do and not much time to do it."

Moroni walked away a few paces, then stopped and turned.

"Yes, Lieutenant … you have something to say?"

"For liberty, my Captain!" he said, rendering a flawless hand salute.

"For liberty, my son!" He saluted back.

Moroni trembled, barely able to control his emotions as he walked back to the edge of the grove and mounted his horse. He spurred his mount into the grove and shouted, "All officers and soldiers above the rank of platoon sergeant to the medical tent, rally around the chief captain for your orders, men."

A number of men picked up their weapons and moved from the wood line. Moroni joined them at the medical tent where a command meeting was held involving all remaining soldiers who could lead the men in a fight. The sergeant major made short work of rounding up soldiers fit enough to carry weapons. Before long, he had assembled nearly two hundred foot soldiers and forty additional cavalry, along with several soldiers who could help shoot the fire arrows and then support the attack with logistics and medical aid.

The old sergeant formed the soldiers into ranks and, when the command meeting had concluded, the chief captain took precious time to conduct a rank and file inspection of the attack force. The sergeant major ordered the men into a formal inspection formation and, with young Moroni following behind, the chief captain walked up and down each row. He stopped several times along the lines to congratulate individual soldiers on a job well done during the day's fighting, to comment on a fresh wound, inquire on family matters, or even to crack a light joke.

Moroni could see firsthand the effect it had on the warriors' morale to have a great leader like his father among them at that moment in time. The chief captain was not a leader who sat far behind the battle lines ordering men to their deaths. This man never watched from a hilltop under shade tents, complaining that things were not going as planned. He would never enjoy a good night's sleep and hot breakfast while his troops were up all night fighting without food or water. No, he was a true leader of men, willing to share the pains and sorrows of a soldier's life with his men.

Moroni watched his father walk up and down the rows of warriors. He could see the admiration the men had for their chief captain. They all stood a little taller and held their chins up a little higher when the chief captain was near. He also clearly felt the love his father had for the men under his command. At that moment, Moroni felt like he was truly among a band of brothers with those men in the formation. He even considered abandoning his responsibility to lead the cavalry and join his father in the infantry charge down the hill into the Lamanite camp, but he had a duty to fulfill.

The inspection ended and the chief captain called for a prayer. Respectfully, the men each removed their helmets or head covers and bowed their heads.

"Almighty Father, the master of life," the Old Captain called out. "We, your humble servants, who only wish to live in peace, call on Thee for mercy this day. We only attack now in defense of our families and our way of life and ask you, great Lord, to guide our hands. Be merciful and grant us victory that we may return to our homes and live to worship thee for the remainder of our days. But if this be our last day, Father, grant us the strength to die with honor facing the enemies of freedom in combat. We pray that our children may come to know what took place here today and what their God did for them through his servants, these fine Nephite men. All glory and honor is yours, Father, and we seal this prayer in the name of your Son, the Christ, Amen."

The prayer ended and the mood quickly changed. It was time to be soldiers again, and each man prepared himself for the coming battle. Moroni and the men around him all knew these could be their last moments on earth, and a mood of somberness fell over the formation.

Moroni put on his helmet and mounted his horse. The helmet, made of fine steel, covered his head and came down the back of his neck and flared out to protect his neck and upper spine without hindering his ability to turn his head. The front of the helmet formed around his cheeks and was cut back away from his eyes so as to not impede his vision. A strip of metal came down the bridge of his nose and just past the tip. Ties under his chin held the helmet on his head. His helmet was well adorned. From the top, running down the back in a straight line, lay a large strip of leather threaded with long horsehairs and dyed red and white. This denoted that he was a cavalry officer of some rank. His armor was light, but effective, designed to protect him from the glancing blows of sharp objects and strikes from stones and small fiery darts. Because he was a horse soldier, he did not need the heavy armor protection of the foot soldiers, who were expected to slug it out toe to toe with the enemy on the ground. His job was to sweep in fast as a shock troop from the flanks or behind the lines, cutting his way through enemy troops or clearing a path for the large war chariots. He had on a leather shirt and chaps with leather boots that had metal foot and shin guards attached by leather and cloth wraps. His arm gauntlets were also made of metal that wrapped around his forearms and went from his wrist to just below his elbow. The chest piece was only two large plates of metal, one covering his chest and one his upper back attached by cloth ties that went over his shoulders and under his arms. The chest piece was uncomfortable and made breathing difficult after only a few moments of combat. The plates offered some protection, but Moroni was displeased with the design and had been working on a new type of armor before the war broke out. He adjusted the chest piece with his hands and grumbled something under his breath.

"What did you say?" Amiha asked as he rode up next to his friend.

"I said this armor is giving me a rash!" Moroni responded. "There must be a better way to protect soldiers." He shifted in the saddle, nervously gazing first to the right and then the left.

"Be grateful for what you have, my friend. Most common soldiers could never afford such protection."

They both looked at the gathered men preparing to move toward the enemy camp.

"Look at them, Amiha. Some don't even have helmets."

"Moroni, not everyone is the son of a famous soldier who can afford to outfit his family with the best armor."

"Or give hand-me-down armor to his son's best friend," Moroni shot back with a grin.

"I do look good in this, don't I?" Amiha said sitting up straight in the saddle and lifting his chin up like a proud warrior.

"Humph," Moroni scoffed and shook his head. He turned to look again over the gathering of Nephite soldiers behind him. He knew some of them would die tonight, and it was his plan that would be leading them to their doom. He could see them making final preparations for the attack. Some were eating a few morsels of bread or drinking water, some bowing their head in contemplation or prayer, some adjusting their armor. Others stood motionless, staring off in the direction of the unseen enemy. His thoughts returned to the question of armor and he focused on what the soldiers before him wore. A few were well-equipped and well-protected with adequate body armor, helmets and heavy shields, and they had an array of expertly crafted weapons. Some were sons or family members of rich noblemen or merchants who could afford to personally support a soldier. Moroni was saddened, however, to see that most in the gathered band had only pieces of precious metal armor, mostly helmets, or a garment of a heavy leather cloth with strips of metal or studs wrapped around vital parts of the body. The poorest of soldiers had nothing but a tunic and leggings with a bright-colored piece of cloth tied around his head or around his bicep to help identify his clan or the city he where he lived.

Every soldier had a spear or long pike. This was a standard weapon for Nephite infantrymen and, for those who had the privilege of attending a military training academy or school, it was the first weapon on which they trained. Yet, even something as simple as a spear showed a social class distinction. Some of the spears were made of strong hardwood and had a thick metal blade attached to the point, with eagle feathers or colorful cloth streamers adorning it. The well-made pikes were long, wooden poles, two- to three-inches thick, some taller than a man sitting on a horse, with a small, broad ax blade and a metal spike or hook on the tip. Sadly, only a few were of this well-made variety; most of the spears the soldiers carried were only long pieces of wood with the tips shaved to a rough point. Moroni could see that not all the soldiers carried swords. Some had axes or maces, or several long knives tucked into their belts. Some even carried large, wooden clubs with metal spikes sticking out of them.

One particularly large and strong-looking Nephite soldier stood transfixed, gazing in the direction of the unseen enemy. He was holding a huge, dangerous-looking club in his large, powerful hands. The jagged spikes on the club were stained with blood. The soldier was slowly swinging the club back and forth in front of him. He had an evil grimace on his face. The other soldiers gave him plenty of room. Moroni shivered inside as he envisioned that giant man smashing through the lines of enemy soldiers and crushing their bodies with that monster club.

"I'm glad you're on our side," Moroni said to the big Nephite.

Without taking his eyes of the horizon, the man let out a throaty grunt and nodded his head.

"How can this be?" Moroni thought to himself. "As prosperous as we are as a people, why do many of our defenders go into battle hungry and poorly equipped? If the day ever comes that I have a say in the decisions regarding this army, I will see that they are well-supplied and well-armed."

He looked back at his father, who was standing in front of the mass of foot soldiers. The chief captain was busy fitting on his helmet and trying to hold a large, wooden arm shield with the still-fresh wound affecting his ability to grip and hold the shield. Three physically smaller soldiers were attending to the chief captain and buzzing around him like nursemaids. They all tried at once to tend to him and advise him on different ways to hold the heavy shield without it affecting his wound. After putting up with their over attention for several moments, the chief captain showed his annoyance by shouting at them and swatting them away like flies. The movement hurt his arm and he winced. "Cursed thing!" he said in disgust of the fact he was hurt and frustrated by his inability to wield the shield. He tossed the shield to the ground and shouted, "My spear! Give me my spear."

Moroni worried about his father's decision to leave the shield behind, but he knew there was no arguing with the chief captain. A young boy ran up to Moroni's father and handed him a large, wooden pole with a long, flat metal tip. Grabbing the spear with his uninjured arm and holding it high in the air, the old leader faced the crowd of warriors and shouted, "For liberty!"

"For liberty!" the mass returned with a shout in unison, all thrusting their weapons in the air.

The captain lowered his spear and pointed the tip of it at his son.

"Lieutenant Moroni, you have until dusk; get your horsemen into place and wait for my command. The flaming arrows will be your signal to charge the camp!"

"I will see you in the middle, sir!" Moroni saluted, and then nodded at Amiha. Amiha, who now commanded the other cavalry element, winked back at Moroni and rode off with his cavalry soldiers following. Moroni took command of the horse soldiers who remained. As they moved past the edge of the grove, Moroni saw the sergeant major standing next to some wagons and making final preparations for the attack. He wanted to say something to the sergeant major before he rode away. The old man had been in his life from the day Moroni was born. He was afraid they might never meet again, but he could not think of anything meaningful to say.

"Sergeant Major," Moroni stumbled with his words. "Please look after my father down there. He is going to need more than luck tonight, I think." Moroni knew it sounded corny, and he felt a bit ashamed for even asking. Of all the people on the field of battle, the sergeant major understood the risks.

"That's funny," the old soldier replied with a broken grin. "Your father asked me to do the same for you."

Moroni turned in his saddle to face his father's friend and saw the large grin on his face get wider.

"Luck in battle boy," the sergeant spoke under his breath as he saluted the young officer. Moroni returned the salute, smiled back and spurred his horse toward his destiny.

Moroni looked down at the large Lamanite camp from his vantage point on top of a small hill more than a half mile away. He and several of the horse soldiers with him had left their mounts and crawled through the tall grass to a point just over a small rise. There, unseen, by enemy guards, they could observe the Lamanite encampment. "They left this area unguarded," he thought to himself, and he intended to make them pay for that gross tactical error.

Even though the sun was setting, he could still clearly see people moving around in the camp. They looked busily occupied with the battle continuing downriver. Moroni could see them loading food and supplies into wagons and unloading wounded Lamanites. The number of fires lit told Moroni there were probably more enemy soldiers there than he had first calculated.

"See that massive tent in the middle, surrounded by banners?" he said to the other soldiers with him. "That is the final objective point. Fight your way to that point and regroup. It's there that we will link up with the others. Understood?" There were no questions. Moroni and the others crawled back down the rise and returned to their horses.

As he was mounting, a burst of movement off in the distance to his left caught Moroni's eye. In the fading light, he could just make out Nephite archers slowly and carefully moving into place through scrub trees and tall grass. After a few moments, a wisp of black smoke arose. Almost in unison, the Nephite archers rose to their feet and pulled back their bows. Moroni could see each bowman had a flaming arrow loaded and ready to fly toward the large camp.

Some unheard command was given and all the archers, in unison, launched their arrows. Moroni traced the smoking path of the arrows arcing across the darkening sky and watched almost transfixed as they found their marks. A cry went up from the Lamanite camp as tents and wagons suddenly burst into flames.

"Now?" one excited soldier asked Moroni, as he rode up next to the young lieutenant's horse.

"Wait for one more volley," Moroni said.

A second barrage of burning arrows went flying toward the camp, and instantly more tents were set ablaze. Moroni moved to the top of the hill and saw the camp was alive with frantic activity. Panicked soldiers, without giving thought as to what started them, scrambled to put out the fires or save the animals and supplies. From his position, Moroni could see that no one from the camp was looking in the direction from which the arrows came. The war horses that the Nephites were riding sensed the coming charge and began to stomp and snort, ready to be unleashed. As his horse reared up, Moroni held his spear in the air and shouted.

"For liberty!"

The soldiers with him held up their spears and replied.

"For liberty!"

Moroni could now barely control his excited mount. He shouted "Charge!" and spurred the beast forward down the hill.

As if of one heart and mind, the group of horse soldiers charged down the hill behind him in a line formation at a full gallop with their spears pointing forward.

AUDACITY

The flaming arrows and the element of surprise had the effect on the enemy that Moroni had hoped. In the confusion and chaos of tents and wagons suddenly bursting into flames, many of the camp's occupants focused on trying to save whatever they could from catching fire, while others tried to douse the flames and stop the fires from spreading to other things within the camp. The diversion worked so well that no one in the enemy camp saw Moroni and his horse soldiers come over the rise of the hill at a full gallop or the second charge of Amiha and the other horse soldiers from the opposite direction.

A lone guard finally saw the advancing cavalry and tried to sound the alarm, but by then it was too late. Death was coming to the Lamanite camp.

Aware that his cavalry attack had been spotted, Moroni thought aloud while smiling under his helmet, "As long as they focus on us, no one will see the advancing infantry." With his crimson war cloak snapping in the rushing air and the hollow sounds of his breath ringing inside his helmet, Moroni spurred his horse forward, every galloping step of his mighty war horse drawing him and his brave men closer to the now fully alarmed camp.

As he advanced on the enemy, the warrior spirit rose within him. His perception of time slowed, his hearing muffled and his sight fixed on the camp while surges of hot blood pumped throughout his entire body. His senses were alive and his mind and body prepared for the events about to take place. He shouted and charged toward the enemy.

Moroni had calculated that the three attacking Nephite units would strike the camp at almost the same time. It looked as if all was going according to his plan. Moroni and his soldiers had closed to within one hundred yards of the camp and were moving at tremendous speed. With the evening turning to nightfall and the sky now almost dark, Moroni could see the fire-drawn silhouettes of a few Lamanite soldiers forming defensive ranks and preparing to shoot arrows at his charging team. To counter, and to protect his men, Moroni raised his spear and shouted, "Wedge!"

Their vigilant training and experience kicked in and, without question, the horse soldiers broke formation and reformed into a giant V shape, with Moroni at the point. They reached the edge of the camp as Lamanite arrows shot out at them. Always perceptive of what was happening around him, Moroni noticed one of his soldiers go down from the arrows, but he did not stop to see who it was. Moroni's men plunged like a giant spear into the small rank of enemy soldiers who had tried to hastily form a defensive line to ward off the surprise attack.

For Moroni, everything now felt surreal and slow-moving. He could see the faces of the enemy and the utter fear in their eyes. After crashing through the first line of Lamanites, Moroni guided his horse toward two more Lamanite soldiers. As he drove past them, both were violently knocked down by the overwhelming power of his animal. Fighting his instinct to look back and see if his men had made it through the enemy's defensive line, Moroni drove his mount forward toward the big command tent in the middle of the camp. Disorientated and scared, Lamanite soldiers were now running in all directions. Moroni and his men were killing them at will as they drove deeper into the camp.

Moroni pressed on, guiding his horse around empty tents and burning wagons. An enemy soldier stepped out from behind a stack of liquor kegs. He held a large battle ax in his hand. When the two made eye contact, the Lamanite screamed and raised his ax to strike Moroni off his horse. Moroni instinctively rode past the Lamanite and, with perfect form, plunged his spear into the Lamanite's chest before he could hit Moroni with the ax. With his spear left sticking out of the dead Lamanite's chest, Moroni pulled his sword from its scabbard and continued toward the command tent. His mighty sword strokes cut down the enemy soldiers he faced before they knew what was happening. Using his horse as a weapon, Moroni rode down rows of tents, trampling over anyone who got in his way. The men in his small troop struggled to keep up with their young leader as Moroni drove hard toward the center of the Lamanite camp. The power and sheer audacity of Moroni's actions caused the other Nephites with him to look to him in awe and find fresh courage to push forward.

The few Lamanites who managed to make a stand were quickly dispatched by Moroni and his brave soldiers. Lamanite resistance was weakening fast.

As the group led by Moroni reached the middle of camp, they came upon a vicious hand-to-hand battle waged between several of his father's infantry and what appeared to be special guards for the command tent. The special guards were greatly outnumbered, but they were putting up a valiant defense. These Lamanite guards were not like the regular soldiers Moroni's troops had just faced. These soldiers were much larger, well fed, had better weapons and, surprisingly, they wore armor. Each also wore a red sash around his waist.

The surprise attack Moroni had planned, followed by the valiant efforts of his fellow Nephites, was a perfect combination. This was about to become a Lamanite slaughter. Although numerically he commanded a much smaller force, they caught the enemy completely unaware and total victory was almost at hand.

Moroni dismounted and, with his sword drawn and shield in hand, moved forward toward the large tent opening. "Clear the tent, follow me!" he shouted as he approached the opening. Those soldiers next to him moved to follow their young leader inside. As he tried to enter the large tent, Moroni was challenged by more of the special guards as they rushed out of the tent to face the Nephite attackers. Moroni moved toward the Lamanite guard closest to him. That guard let out a war cry while holding his sword high over his head. He charged toward Moroni, looking as if he would cut Moroni in two from head to toe with one powerful stroke. Moroni waited until the last possible second and sidestepped the blow by spinning clockwise away from the enemy's downward swing. This caused the Lamanite guard to miss his target and his momentum made him stumble forward, bouncing his sword off the ground. A second guard joined the fight and slashed his sword at Moroni's head. Moroni instinctively dropped to one knee, causing the blade of the second Lamanite to miss his head by inches. In a quick and powerful move, Moroni brought his sword up and sliced the second guard across his stomach, almost cutting him in half. Moroni stood up and quickly maneuvered to face the first guard he had encountered, surprised to find the soldier had recovered so quickly and was poised to try to strike again. Moroni raised his shield to protect his head from the enemy's sword but, instead of striking Moroni, the guard paused, his motion suspended in mid-stroke. A look of shock crossed his face and the Lamanite dropped face first, dead, at Moroni's feet.

Moroni could see a spear sticking out of the back of the fallen guard and Amiha standing behind where the fallen guard once stood.

"That's two you owe me!" Amiha said, pointing at Moroni and smiling. Moroni smiled back and spun to face any remaining challenge from the Lamanite guards blocking the entrance. The attack on the camp was intense and brutal. Lamanites fought valiantly to defend their camp, and the special guards around the command tent were skilled warriors, but Moroni's surprise attack and his soldiers' valiant efforts were too much for the defenders, and suddenly the battle was over.

Gasping for air and holding his sword in front of him, Moroni looked around for any additional threats as his men rallied around him. Slowly, Moroni lowered his weapon and looked at his exhausted soldiers. They were looking back at him, their eyes blazing in the light of the remaining fires. Moroni held his bloodied sword high over his head, filled his lungs with air and shouted, "Victory!"

With their own weapons raised high in the air, the Nephite warriors shouted with him in a joyous celebration.

The celebration continued as the sergeant major broke through the crowd and shook the hand of the young lieutenant.

"Well done, young man, well done," he said.

"My father," Moroni begged, "have you seen him?"

"We were separated near the wagon depot," replied the old soldier.

At that moment, a woman's scream was heard from inside the great tent.

"There are more people inside!" Moroni shouted and cursed to himself for not finishing the assault and clearing the tent before he proclaimed victory. He knew that was a big mistake and he was mad at himself for his lack of focus. He and the old sergeant rushed to the opening with several other soldiers following closely. They burst their way through a small chamber, killing two more of the special guards, and rushed into a large room in the center of the tent.

They were totally unprepared for what they found inside. It was richly decorated with heavy dark wooden furniture and thick carpets on the ground. Burning oil lamps made of precious metals cast uneasy shadows on the room's occupants. Bolts of fine silk and cured leather were leaning against the tent wall and a large chest full of rare gems and gold coins was open for all to see. At the far end of the room, several older Lamanite warriors with the markings of leadership held their weapons out in front of them. Behind the old warriors, several well-dressed royal attendants huddled together in one corner, weeping bitterly. The warriors had formed a half-circle, with their backs to a young and very beautiful Lamanite woman, who was crying over the body of an old Lamanite man, sitting slumped forward on a large wooden throne. The old Lamanite man was dressed in a leopard skin wrap and had a golden crown of jewels on his head.

"That's their king," the sergeant major said softly in Moroni's ear. He pointed with his sword to a growing pool of blood forming on the carpet beneath the throne. "Looks like he's killed himself. Did you know he was here?"

"No," Moroni answered in a puzzled tone.

Moroni looked closer at the king and saw his right hand holding the hilt of a long knife that had been plunged into his own belly. "It seems the king has taken his own life to avoid the shame of being captured or defeated in battle," Moroni whispered.

The young woman stopped her sobbing long enough to look up and see the giant Nephite warrior standing in the room with a bloody sword in his hand. She panicked and screamed, holding her hands in front of her face. She cried out in her native Lamanite tongue, but in a dialect Moroni did not know. He could make out "please" and "mercy," but not much else. As he looked down at the sobbing girl, a burst of compassion shot through his heart

Moroni looked into the eyes of the remaining Lamanite officers. He saw resolve; they were not going to back down. They were ready to die where they stood rather than allow the young woman behind them be to be harmed. He sensed the Lamanites' muscles tensing, gripping their weapons tighter. Behind him, he could feel the Nephites edging closer and closer as more of his warriors entered the tent.

Moroni knew he was about to lose control of his men. He had to do something and do it quickly. The pause in the battle had cooled his bloodlust and he remembered his ethos and training. "Stop!" he barked. The tension was thick, the moment of no return was close. Too many of his friends and fellow soldiers had already died tonight and he desperately wanted the bloodshed to end, now.

Moroni faced his men. "Put your weapons down," he ordered. Slowly the Nephites behind him lowered their weapons. Moroni faced the Lamanite high commanders. He flipped his sword over and drove the tip into the ground in front of him. Standing fully upright, his massive presence commanded everyone's attention.

"Do any of you speak my language?" Moroni asked in an even tone as he took off his helmet.

"We all do," replied the most senior leader among them. With a snarl on his face and pointing his sword, he spouted at Moroni, "By our own blood, you will not harm the daughter of our king!"

The sergeant major readjusted his stance, readying himself to parry any attack directed at Moroni.

"Your guards are all defeated, your camp is taken. There is no one left to protect you or come to your aid. You are in our hands now." Moroni gestured to the Lamanite king lying in his own blood. "Your king is dead; this war is over." He paused. "No one else needs to die tonight. Make peace with me, I beg you!"

The Lamanites looked stunned at the words Moroni used. Why would he want to make peace with them? There was silence and only the cries of the heartbroken young princess could be heard.

Moroni held his hands out to his sides, palms toward the brave old man.

"I do not wish to harm the daughter of your king," he said. "Tell her, if she will command what remains of her army to stop fighting and lay down their weapons, and if she will make an oath of peace with me here and now, on my honor, she and all Lamanites who remain alive this night will go free. If peace is not what she wants, I will order my men to attack. Every Lamanite left in this camp will be destroyed."

The old Lamanite looked at Moroni, narrowing his eyes. He seemed to regard Moroni like a dangerous animal. "Why would you do this?" He said suspiciously. "A trick, perhaps. Is it because you lack the strength to finish us?"

With one fluid motion, Moroni moved like lighting and pulled his big sword out of the ground. He slashed at the old Lamanites neck, stopping his blade less than an inch from his skin. The Laminate's eyes were wide with fear. He had never seen a man move so fast or wield a sword with such precision.

"If I wanted to kill you," Moroni spoke in an even tone, "I would have already ordered my men to cut you down. I do not want your lives. I want peace."

The old Lamanite soldier searched Moroni's face for any sign of deception. Looking into his eyes, he could see Moroni was not bluffing. Now the Lamanite commander knew exactly what type of man he faced. The old commander's look of mistrust faded and he lowered his sword and dropped it to the ground. He knelt down next to the young princess and spoke to her in a low voice for several seconds. While obviously fighting back tears, she whispered back to the soldier. Her voice had a questioning tone, and she gestured toward Moroni with her hand. The Lamanite leader nodded in response to his princess's inquiry. The young woman looked up at Moroni and slowly nodded her head in agreement. That old soldier stood up and spoke to the remaining Lamanites in a commanding tone. They all slowly dropped their weapons at the feet of Moroni and bowed down before him as a sign of surrender.

"What is your name?" Moroni spoke to the Lamanite commander.

"Lehonti," he replied. 'I am the son of Laman and chief captain of the royal armies of our king." He had sorrow in his eyes as he looked back at the dead man slumped over the wooden throne.

"Lehonti, I am called Moroni, son of Joshua, who is chief captain of the Nephite army in this sector. I speak for the chief captain, and I command the men who are with me. I accept your princess's oath of peace, and we are enemies no longer." Moroni put his sword back into its sheath and extended his right hand in friendship. Lehonti slowly reached out and shook his hand, and then bowed his head as a sign of respect.

"I know of your father," Lehonti spoke as he raised his head up. "His reputation precedes him on the battlefield. He is a brave soldier and a man of honor. I am honored to know his son. I pray his redeeming qualities have passed to his offspring."

"I am my father's son," Moroni reassured Lehonti. "You and your company will be treated with respect."

Moroni nodded to the soldiers behind him. They quickly moved around the giant frame of their leader and gathered up the weapons that had been surrendered by the Lamanite command staff. When they had finished ensuring the Lamanites were all disarmed, Moroni continued.

"Lehonti, please send out riders to your field commanders and inform them of the peace treaty struck here tonight by your wise princess. As soon as I have confirmed that her soldiers have laid down their weapons and are marching back to their homes, then you, the princess, and your company may go in peace." Moroni waved his hand past those standing behind Lehonti. "Until then, the princess and all who attend to her are to remain in my custody inside this tent as my honored guests. Sergeant Major!"

"Yes, sir," the old soldier barked.

"Secure the camp, have our wounded recovered, and please find my father."

"Yes, sir." The old soldier walked out of the tent and could be heard yelling commands as he walked through the camp.

Lehonti was shocked. "Your father, he is here, in this camp?" Several of the other Lamanites behind Lehonti were whispering excitedly to each other.

"Yes," Moroni seemed puzzled. "He commands the forces that raided your camp this night."

"The boldness of your raid on our command center … of course it was him leading the attack. Who else among you has the courage to plan and execute such a thing?" Lehonti smiled and shook his head.

Moroni paused for a moment to let those words sink in. This attack was his plan, and he was the Nephite officer who parleyed for the peace treaty. To think that the enemy considered his actions something so bold that only his father could accomplish it was a great compliment. He yearned for his father to be with him. He could not waste any more time here; he needed to find him.

"Amiha!"

Amiha, hearing Moroni call for him, pushed his way forward past the other Nephites still standing in the tent and moved next to Moroni.

"Yes, sir?"

"Place some of our cavalry around this tent as security for the princess and her attendants. Then prepare some wagons for them to leave as soon as we get the word that all the Lamanite forces have surrendered."

"Sir?" Lehonti spoke in an uncomfortable tone. Moroni guessed it was not easy for him to address someone as his superior.

"Yes, my friend?" Moroni responded to Lehonti.

"The messengers I am to send to the commanders at the front lines to advise them of the peace treaty?"

"Yes, of course. Who will you send?"

"It will be more convincing if I give the word myself."

In the eyes of the Lamanite commander, Moroni saw only truth. Moroni knew Lehonti was not going to try to escape or rally the remaining Lamanite forces for a counterattack. Lehonti was a man of honor and he had given his word.

"Very well, my friend. Amiha, a good horse for this man."

"Yes sir," Amiha replied, "and may I add an escort out of camp and past our archers for his safety?"

"Oh, you're right … yes, yes of course, see to it."

"When you are ready, join me outside." Amiha said to Lehonti, and he walked out of the tent.

Moroni turned and spoke to the remaining Nephites.

"The rest of you, gather up our wounded and get them to the medics. Find what wagons are still useable and load as much of their equipment and supplies as you can. Except this tent. This tent and all who are inside are under my personal protection." He let that order linger for a moment for full effect. "Anyone found violating the peace treaty struck here this night will be put to death. The Lamanites are our enemies no longer."

Moroni bowed his head to the young lady, who was still sobbing and sitting on the ground next to the dead king. Then he turned to walk out of the tent.

A FALLEN HERO

"**G**reat one, please wait," Lehonti asked. "The princess, I fear, in her state of mourning, may not fully understand the respect and grace you have shown to your enemy."

Lehonti bent close to the princess and started to speak in quiet tones. He explained the honorable way Moroni conducted himself and the mercy he extended to her and her army. After hearing Lehonti explain, she wiped her eyes and stood to face him.

Lehonti swung his arm around to point toward Moroni. The giant of a man stepped forward. His gaze was focused directly on the princess, but Moroni spoke to Lehonti. "May I address the princess?"

"You may call me Aiyana. It means 'flower' in our language." The young girl spoke in a shaken tone.

With all the grace of true royalty, she bowed before Moroni's imposing frame and spoke in broken Nephite. "Thank you for … kindness and honorable ways. May I please … attend the body of father?"

"Of course, my lady, I am at your service." Moroni bowed majestically. The young princess attempted a broken smile but Moroni could see that the grief of losing her father was enveloping her. His heart was touched by her sadness and, to keep his composure, he turned and walked out of the tent and into the night.

Several large fires were still raging as Moroni surveyed the damage around him. Broken weapons were scattered around and dead bodies of Lamanite soldiers were strewn everywhere. "We caught them completely by surprise," he thought aloud. Many had fought bravely to defend their lives and their king. Moroni would have been proud to command such men. Surveying the cost of war, he thought, "What a waste." He knew two things kept their nations apart. First was the simple fact that they had been born in different parts of the land. The second was more complex. The two nations were divided because of the traditions of their fathers. The Nephites believed in God, while the Lamanites did not.

As his soldiers moved all around him, Moroni was standing a few paces away from the Lamanite command tent, lost in his own thoughts, when a horse galloped up behind him. He turned to face the rider. It was a breathless soldier from his own company with Moroni's horse in tow.

"Sir, the sergeant major sent me to find you, come quickly. ... It's the chief captain. ... He's hurt!"

Franticly, Moroni jumped on his horse and followed the soldier through the smoldering camp.

Arriving near the camp's wagon depot, Moroni found a large crowd of Nephites standing around one wagon. When they saw it was Moroni who rode up, their expressions showed deep sorrow. Some dropped to their knees to pray, while others wept openly.

The surgeon and his aides were attending to someone in the wagon, where the sergeant major, from beside the wagon, looked on. Moroni dismounted and forced his legs to carry him forward to the wagon. Panic welled up inside of him. He wanted to run away, not get any closer; he dreaded what he might see. Then the agonizing moans of his father echoed from the wagon. Finding his courage, Moroni shouted for men to move out of his way. Moroni staggered toward the wagon and the crowd surrounding the scene parted as he approached. He reached the back of the wagon and his legs nearly buckled when, to his horror, Moroni found his father lying inside the wagon. He was writhing in pain and had three arrows protruding from his left side.

"Father!" Moroni shouted as he lunged closer.

"Easy lad," the sergeant major spoke as he grabbed young Moroni by the arms. "It's a mortal wound," he whispered into Moroni's ear. "There is nothing we can do. It's in God's hands now."

"Boy ... come here," the wounded chief captain called out, half choking.

The surgeon's face was expressionless and gray as he moved out of Moroni's way. He was still clutching the bloody rags he had used to try to stop the blood.

Moroni was numb. He climbed into the wagon, knelt down next to his father, and took off his helmet.

"What news of the battle?" the older man gasped painfully, looking into his son's eyes.

Moroni could see the wounds up close. The arrows were buried deep into his father's side and dark crimson-colored blood was pouring out of the wounds. Moroni had seen many wars and many wounded. He knew his father would not leave this battleground alive.

"The battle," his father barked, trying to sit up. Blood sprayed out of his mouth with every rattled breath.

"The surprise was complete, father." Moroni tried to hold his father down searching his hero's eyes for any sign of hope. "Their camp is taken, the Laminate king is dead, and the enemy has surrendered. The war is over, Father … you have won, the day is yours. We are at peace."

"God bless this day!" the old soldier painfully replied, dropping back down in the wagon and coughing roughly. He tried to sit up again but the pain of his wounds overpowered him. He slumped down again as pink foam gathered around his lips.

"My sword," he shouted breathlessly, with his right hand held out. The sergeant major handed his wounded leader the legendary weapon. The dying warrior took hold of the sword. It seemed as though the very touch of the weapon comforted him, and he clutched it to his chest and closed his eyes.

"Moroni …!" he gasped. It was a painful exertion for him just to breathe. "This is the sword of your fathers. You know better than most what this sword represents." Pitifully struggling for air, he strained to continue. "It is now in your care. I leave it to you to guide these men in righteousness. … Take it."

"No, father, I can't." Moroni desperately tried to choke back his tears. He knew it was hopeless, but he said it anyway, "You must survive!"

With a surprising surge of strength, the chief captain grabbed Moroni by his arm and pulled him close. He was fighting for every gasp of breath and spoke at barely a whisper.

"Don't … argue with me … son, do as I say … Now is your time." He pushed the sword toward Moroni. "You must be a mighty man now and lead these men. They are all depending on you! Take it, son, and trust in God."

Overwhelmed with emotion, Moroni meekly reached for the large sword. In a significant and symbolic moment, the sword passed from father to son, and the dying soldier's massive arm dropped heavily to the floorboards of the wagon.

"Tell your mother," he gasped out his last breath, "I will always love her!"

And then he was gone.

The silence was like death itself as Moroni looked down at the lifeless face of his father. With tears flowing down his cheeks, Moroni ran his right hand across his dead father's open eyes to close them for one final time. He then put his hand on his father's chest.

"For you, father," he whispered, "I will lead these men."

After a few long moments, Moroni composed himself and, wiping the tears from his dirty face, he slowly brought his giant frame fully upright. He looked around at the soldiers present. Everyone was weeping openly at the loss of the great man whose body lay in the wagon bed. He knew they all loved the fallen captain as if he were their own father.

"Sergeant Major, have my father's body prepared for travel. Post his standard here and place an honor guard around the wagon. We will take him home and give him a hero's burial."

"Yes, my captain." he replied, pulling his own tear-soaked face up to gaze at Moroni.

Hearing the title "Captain" from his father's most trusted friend caused Moroni to feel a surreal wave and mixture of emotions. A heavy sadness filled his entire frame, weighing him down with a cold heaviness. Yet, looking around at those gathered by the wagon, he was warmed by the vote of confidence and acceptance from his father's friend and the strength of the men who were now his to lead. Those men were now bowing before him. He realized they were acknowledging the transfer of authority from his father to him. He was now their leader. Moroni felt numb and a bit lightheaded as he nodded to the sergeant major. Climbing down from the wagon, Moroni heard a voice from the crowd of gathered Nephites.

"Sir, the battle ... is it really over?"

Moroni turned toward where he had heard the voice.

"Yes ... it's over." He paused as he looked back at his father's body. "And the victory belongs to our honored dead."

Moroni knew he should say more to raise their somber mood and to congratulate their valiant efforts, but his own heart was too heavy, his mind too filled with questions about the worth of war. Moroni mounted his horse and rode back to the center of camp. He realized this was a defining day for all Nephites.

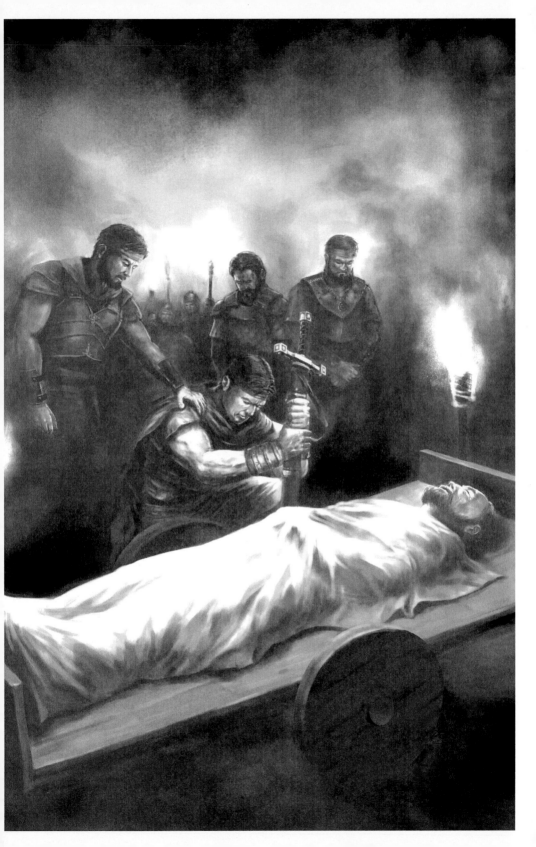

A PLEDGE OF PEACE

With the morning sun fully exposed from behind the lush, greenery-covered mountains, the scorched Lamanite camp was alive with activity. Most of the Nephites working in the camp had removed what armor they had on as the heat of the day started to warm their skin. It had been a long night for Moroni. The emotions of battle and the loss of his father had taken a heavy toll. He was spent, both physically and mentally. He felt as though he could sleep for a week, but there was still much to do and now he was in charge.

Moroni, Amiha and several junior-grade officers stood next to their horses looking down from a small rise just outside the camp. The final preparations were taking place to move wagons loaded full of captured Lamanite equipment and supplies back to Nephite lands. In addition to these wagons, there were several filled with wounded Nephite soldiers, who would be carried back to the main body of the Nephite army. Moroni insisted that the wounded be made comfortable and given as much care as possible. The camp was stripped of all its blankets and even the cushions and pillows from the Lamanite commanders' tents were used to line the wagons to make the wounded more comfortable.

During the night, the Lamanite leader, Lehonti, had spread the word of the king's death and of the capture and surrender of the king's daughter. By sunrise, defeated Lamanite soldiers began to arrive at camp. In small groups and in organized companies, they came to the center of the camp and left their weapons of war in growing piles on the ground. Out of tradition, they bowed to their conquerors and made a pledge of peace, promising to return to their own lands and never again bear arms in anger against the Nephites. From his position, Moroni could read the attitude of many of the Lamanite soldiers. Their faces and body language told him that, for all their promises, he would be fighting them again someday. He could tell that most did not intend to keep their vow and, if given a chance, they would join the next army coming to fight the Nephites. Still, Moroni would be true to his word to let them go if they would pledge to not fight.

After laying down their weapons and making the promise of peace, some Lamanites gathered outside the camp where they formed into small units, marching toward home while singing praises to their fallen brothers. Some just walked away from camp, without looking back or even speaking a word.

By noon, the bulk of the Lamanite army had passed by and surrendered their weapons. Satisfied that they had held up their end of the agreement, Moroni summoned Lehonti, who had returned from the front lines and was now overseeing the weapon gathering and the loading of the princess's personal effects into her wagon.

"You wish to speak to me, great one?" Lehonti asked. Escorted by four well-armed Nephites, Lehonti approached Moroni at the top of the rise, and then bowed out of respect.

"Yes, Captain Lehonti, tell Her Majesty the princess that she has kept her word and, with my compliments, she and those who attend to her are free to leave."

"She will want to thank you herself for your kindness and mercy," Lehonti replied.

"Of course. Tell her I am at her service."

Lehonti hesitated as if he had something else to say.

"Is there anything else?" Moroni asked the Lamanite commander.

"Sir," Lehonti said, then paused uncomfortably, "may I speak to you in private?"

"Of course. Gentlemen, will you excuse us?" Moroni asked the Nephite officers standing near him. The soldiers immediately moved several paces away from their leader, except for Amiha, who remained next to Moroni. Lehonti looked at Amiha, then at Moroni.

"Amiha is my most trusted advisor. You may speak freely in front of him," Moroni reassured Lehonti.

Lehonti took one step closer to Moroni and pulled a small leather bag out from under his tunic. "I knew the mind of my king better than most," Lehonti started. "He was a flawed man, but he did try to be a good king for his people. Even though he and I were your father's mortal enemies, we both held Captain Joshua in the highest regard." Lehonti gently grabbed Moroni's right hand and placed the leather bag in it. "Your father was a man of honor. I am sorry to hear he died during the night. Please see that your mother gets this small token of respect from the treasury of my king. It is to help ease her suffering at the loss of such a great man."

Moroni closed his fingers around the bulging bag and could feel it was full of coins.

"You are very generous, Captain Lehonti. I accept this token with gratitude from my family." The two leaders exchanged a look of trust and mutual appreciation, and neither felt the need to say more about the matter.

"May I have your permission to tend to my young princess?"

"Yes, Captain Lehonti, you have my leave."

They saluted each other, and Lehonti walked back down the rise toward the smoldering remains of the giant Lamanite camp.

As they watched Lehonti walk back to the camp, Moroni sensed another battle. This one was within the heart of his friend, Amiha. For Amiha, losing Captain Joshua was like losing a second father in battle with the Lamanites. Moroni knew Amiha had a deep hatred for the Lamanites, and Moroni could see the great conflict play across his friend's face.

"You are just going to let them walk away?" Amiha whispered past his clenched teeth.

"Yes, brother, it's the right thing to do."

"The right thing to do is find the dog Lamanite who shot arrows at our father and burn him alive!" Amiha was a bit louder now. The other Nephites standing a ways off turned when they heard Amiha bark at Moroni.

Moroni held out his empty hand, telling Amiha to stop. "They surrendered and made a pledge of peace. What would you have me do?"

"You know they will never keep the peace treaty," Amiha shouted. "They will return and, because of your naiveté, more Nephites will die. I say we finish the job now and be rid of them all!"

Moroni had never seen Amiha so upset. He was flush faced and breathing hard. Moroni knew that Amiha did not mean what he was saying; he was in pain and grieving over the loss of his adopted father, the chief captain. Moroni lowered his voice and spoke calmly, "I did what our father would have done." He paused to let those words sink in. He knew Amiha had plenty of reason to be upset, and could feel a boiling frustration rising, but he loved his adopted brother. Amiha had been welcomed and loved by

Moroni's parents as if he were their own son. "I fear our Father in Heaven more than I fear the Lamanites." Moroni continued. "God's laws are very clear on this matter. We only fight for the defense of our families, to liberate the oppressed, and to end war. If we attack out of anger or aggression, we lose the blessings of heaven. If they break their pledge of peace, then they face God's wrath as well as mine."

Amiha stood still with his jaw locked tight. "You are a better man than I am," he hissed. "How can you not be angry? These Lamanite beasts have caused so much sorrow and death and, now, to take the life of our fa…"

Amiha's grief burst open and he choked while fighting back tears.

"We'll get through this with God's help," Moroni said, reaching out to embrace his friend and brother. Amiha nodded to tell Moroni he was right and that he would submit to Moroni's will.

"Let's get this over with so we can go home," Moroni said, clapping Amiha on the back.

"Yes, sir," Amiha sheepishly responded.

Moroni put his friend in a loose headlock and rubbed the top of his head. They both had a quick laugh and then looked back down at the camp below.

The Nephite junior officers, who had wandered back to join Moroni and Amiha on the hill, greeted the sergeant major who arrived on horseback. As they all spoke together, a single horn sounded from outside the Lamanite command tent. A moment later, the young princess stepped out of the tent and into the light of the noon day sun. She was dressed in a brightly colored wrap, fitted about her, and covered with golden, brightly stoned jewelry and a large headdress adorned with colorful bird feathers. Moving slowly and with all the dignity she could gather, she stepped up into her royal wagon. Several attendants followed her and climbed into the carriage as well. The Lamanite army officers who had served her father gathered into a large wooden wagon waiting behind the royal carriage. When they were ready, the driver of the carriage snapped the reins and the two horses lurched forward, slowly pulling the carriage up the rise toward where Moroni and Amiha stood.

The carriage's fabric top had been removed and stowed away for the trip, so everyone in camp could see the princess as she rode by.

"Wow, I didn't realize how beautiful she was," Amiha said.

"Now, there's something you don't see every day," the sergeant major exclaimed under his breath as he and all the other men and boys in the entire camp stopped what they were doing to watch the young, beautiful princess and her royal entourage move past them and toward Moroni.

Moroni had been preoccupied with other things during his encounter with her the night before, so he only now fully realized just how attractive and exotic the young Lamanite princess looked.

It was a Nephite custom for men of honor to remove their head coverings when speaking to a lady. Moroni, and those standing with him, took off their helmets as the beautiful young princess approached. Moroni quickly brushed the long strands of dark hair out of his eyes. Using the end of his war cloak, he tried to wipe dirt and blood off his face and off his breastplate in a useless attempt to improve his gritty looks. Amiha was also trying to groom himself in anticipation of the meeting with the beautiful princess. The sergeant major looked at them both, rolled his eyes and shook his head.

"Youth is wasted on the young," he grumbled as he watched the humorous act of the two of them fussing over themselves.

As she got nearer, the two friends stopped their frantic grooming and snapped to attention with their chests puffed out and their chins held high, both trying to make themselves look manlier in the young princess's eyes. The carriage stopped in front of Moroni, and one of the attendants jumped out. He placed a wooden step stool next to the carriage's side door and helped the princess slowly step down. When she reached the ground, she looked up into Moroni's eyes and gracefully walked toward him, not taking her eyes from his. She stopped in front of him, bowed, then recovered and stared up again into his blue eyes, holding her gaze for several seconds. Moroni could see she had been crying. Her eyes were bloodshot and mournful. Her expression showed the same sadness and concern he had seen on his mother's face so many times when she watched his father leave for battle.

The princess continued to stare up at him with her dark, beautiful eyes and Moroni started to feel a bit uncomfortable. It had been a long time since a beautiful woman had stood that close to him, and she definitely smelled better than the sergeant major. Moroni was about to say something when the princess spoke and gently took Moroni's hand. As her soft hand touched his skin, a shock of warm sensations shot across his body. He blinked several times and felt goose bumps rising on his arms. He looked down at the hand she was holding and saw that she had placed in his hand a long, thin knife with a golden scabbard and a jewel-covered hilt.

"I want give you ... to have this ... as sign of friendship and peace," she quietly spoke in her broken version of the Nephite language.

Moroni fought to regain control of his composure. He was quickly becoming overwhelmed by her scent and exotic looks. He took the jeweled weapon, stepped back two paces from her and bowed.

The princess then signaled for Lehonti, and the entire Lamanite command staff climbed out of the wagon. Lehonti walked up behind the princess. In a soft but commanding voice, Lehonti spoke some words in their native language. All the attendants and soldiers with the princess unbuckled their weapons belts and started to remove whatever weapons they were carrying that had not been not surrendered to Moroni the night before. The princess looked at her attendants, who were disarming themselves. Moroni saw panic and fear forming behind her dark eyes. She lowered her head and slowly made a move to leave when Moroni spoke.

"My lady, please wait … Lehonti." She paused and turned to face him.

"Yes, great one?"

"I don't want my words to confuse her. Please tell your princess that I know a hard road lies ahead for her. Many of her subjects will have questions about this war and why she surrendered. It will be a dangerous time for her and I wish her no harm." Moroni looked directly at her. "Tell her that she and all her attendants, as well as her command staff," Moroni nodded to Lehonti, "may keep their personal weapons as my gift of peace to her. Tell her that, with my blessing, she is free to leave."

Shocked at Moroni's words, Lehonti translated what he had said to the young princess. She looked stunned and, for a few seconds, stood motionless, staring at the young giant of a man. Then, with great poise, she took three steps forward and bowed deeply before Moroni again. She then grabbed his right hand and kissed it several times. With a look of profound relief, she returned to standing. Moroni held out the jeweled dagger to give it back to her. She gently stepped closer to him, while she pushed the weapon up against his armored chest with her right hand. She placed her left hand on the massive upper arm that held the knife and softly stroked her fingers across his rippled muscles. Chills shot up and down Moroni's spine and goose bumps appeared again on his exposed arms and legs. The princess could see the physical effect her touch was having on Moroni. She knew, from life in her father's court, how her physical appearance and the gentle touch of a woman could affect the way a man thought and acted. She looked up again into Moroni's eyes and smiled a broad toothy smile. Moroni, by now, was completely helpless, and it showed in the goofy half smile that formed on his face. The princess had to cover her mouth to keep from laughing out loud. She wiped the tears from her eyes, winked at Moroni, and, still not

taking her eyes from his, nodded. Moroni started to bow, but she quickly grabbed the top collar of his breastplate and pulled his face closer to hers. Catching Moroni completely off guard, she gave him a flirtatious kiss on the lips. When she finished her kiss, she slowly pulled her face away from his and stroked his stubble-covered cheek with the palm of her hand.

"Thank you … great one," she whispered in a thick Lamanite accent.

Speechless, Moroni simply smiled.

She winked and smiled back, then spoke to Lehonti in her Lamanite dialect. He, in turn, barked a command to the rest of the Lamanites. They all picked up their weapon belts and walked back to the royal carriage. The princess climbed in and the carriage began to move toward the Lamanite homelands. As it pulled away, she leaned over the edge and waved to Moroni who, still with the goofy grin on his face, waved back.

Amiha, who had been standing next to Moroni during his exchange with the princess, said sarcastically, "You going to ask her to the winter harvest dance?"

"Huh … what … no … shut up!" Moroni shot back in a confused tone.

"Pretty," the sergeant major said in a matter of fact voice.

"Yes, I guess … I didn't really notice … um, well, ok, let's get back to work." Moroni said, turning away in an attempt to change the subject. Amiha and the sergeant major looked at each other and chuckled while enjoying the lighthearted moment at Moroni's expense. Knowing that they were enjoying this moment, Moroni shook his head and chuckled with them.

"Yeah, she was pretty." He cleared his throat. "All right, gentlemen, let's get back to work." They all turned and walked back down the rise toward what remained of the captured Lamanite camp. In the middle of the camp, Moroni walked past the large piles of spears, swords, bows, cimeters and other weapons left by the surrendering Lamanites. He stood staring for several seconds at the weapons, and he had an idea.

"Sergeant Major," he said, "find out if any of our soldiers need a replacement weapon or a better made one. If so, have each one of them come down and take what he needs from this pile. Start first with the young foot soldiers. When they are all fully armed, the noble sons and officers can have their pick. After that, form a detail and have whatever weaponry is left loaded into the wagons to take with us. There is no reason to leave any quality weapons behind or burn them."

The sergeant major nodded and walked away, shouting commands. Several of the young soldiers ran to form a line in front of the cache of weapons.

Moroni walked slowly toward the wagon that held the body of his father. The slain warrior's battle standard was posted at the front of the wagon and was flying proudly in the breeze. A four-man honor guard was placed at each point of the compass around the wagon, standing a silent vigil over their dead leader. They came to attention when Moroni approached.

"Gentlemen, would you please give me a few moments alone with the chief captain?"

"Yes, sir," the leader of the honor guard responded, and the soldiers marched briskly away from the wagon. Moroni went to the back of the wagon where the gate had been lowered. There, to his surprise, he saw several personal items left as mourning gifts for the fallen hero. There was wine, food, coins, some cloth, captured weapons, and someone had even found a bunch of wildflowers and placed them on top of the white cloth that was wrapped around the body. Moroni stood for several long moments staring at the body of his father. He felt the dagger given to him by the Lamanite princess in his hand and placed it next to the flowers. After a while, Moroni could feel the presence of his father's old friend standing behind him.

"Without the ability to hold his shield, he was defenseless against their arrows. He knew that and still led the infantry charge. Was that bravery or insanity?"

"I don't know, Moroni," replied the old sergeant major. "What I do know is that he was a great man who died on his own terms, a soldier's death."

There was a long pause while both stood quietly in the rays of the afternoon sun, lost in their own thoughts. Behind them a long trail of wagons loaded to capacity with all manner of supplies was forming. A Nephite soldier rode up to the two warriors.

"Sir, we are about ready to move out," he said to Moroni.

"Very good. Sergeant Major, let's ..." but before he could finish speaking, they heard the sound of war trumpets and drums coming from the direction of the river where yesterday's desperate battle had taken place.

"She tricked us," someone shouted.

"She circled around behind us and cut us off from our own army!" another added. All the soldiers in the camp ran to their armor and readied themselves for action.

"I don't think so," Moroni shouted back. "Sergeant Major, a scouting party please."

"Yes sir," he replied. "You two with me."

The sergeant major pointed to two mounted warriors standing close by.

He jumped on his own horse and the three galloped off toward the top of the rise. The three soldiers rode toward the sound of the drums and, when they reached the top of the rise, they all paused for a moment. One of the riders turned and rode back to the camp while the sergeant major and the second Nephite continued over the rise toward the unknown. Amiha rode up to Moroni with his armor on and Moroni's horse in tow. Puzzled, Moroni and Amiha looked at each other silently wondering what was happening. The lone rider quickly returned and reported to Moroni.

"What is it?" Moroni said.

"Sir, it's Captain Lehi. He is coming with his army!" he said breathlessly as he strained to control his horse. "It's Captain Lehi!" he shouted past Moroni toward the soldiers behind him. With the surrender of the Lamanites and now the arrival of Captain Lehi and his soldiers, a cheer went up from the Nephite warriors, who knew now that they had truly survived the great war of Jershon in the fifteenth year of the reign of the Judges.

A NEW WAY

"Sir?" a voice came from behind Moroni.

Moroni blinked several times but didn't break his focus on the sword in his hands.

"Sir? My general?" Again the voice came from behind. This time Moroni passed from the dream state of the past back to present. Breaking through the surreal memory, Moroni realized he was back in his command tent. Still standing, he slowly turned in the direction of the voice and saw one of his guards on the threshold of the tent, standing at attention.

"Yes, Corporal, what is it?"

The Nephite guard noticed the great Sword of Laban in the hands of his commander. In awe of the sword and of the imposing sight of Moroni holding it in his hand, the guard instinctively took two steps back. Without taking his eyes off the weapon, he said, "Sir, the command staff will be gathering soon for the evening briefing."

"Very good, Corporal. ... Have the cooks bring dinner to us here. ... I feel it's going to be a long meeting."

"Yes, sir!" The young Nephite warrior rendered a salute and ran from the tent and to a horse that was saddled and waiting for a rider to carry important messages from the command area to the camp.

The sound of fine steel echoed in the distance as Moroni gently placed the great sword back into its scabbard. As tenderly as a young mother places a sleeping child on a soft bed, Moroni put the sword of power back on his cot. He stood upright and looked down at the weapon lying on his bed. He bowed his head in respect, thinking of the great men who had carried the symbolic weapon before him.

"Great men," he thought as the stories and faces of those who previously had wielded the sword flashed in his mind. From father Nephi, who used the sword to secure the Brass Plates, down the line of heroes to his own father, Moroni had much to live up to. He knew the stakes could not be greater. The lives of those he loved, the liberty of his people, their freedom to worship the God of their fathers, the very existence of the Nephite race, all depended on him, his leadership, his faith and his ability to weld that sword.

Panic and doubt crept into his mind. He felt his blood slowly go cold and his lips dry out, as hot air rushed out of his lungs.

Quietly whispering, a dark thought entered his mind. "You are not a great man like those who came before you." Moroni blinked. "You're just a boy. How can you lead these men in battle?" Moroni felt his pulse quicken, the muscles in his neck tighten and his face flush.

"I am just a boy," he agreed.

"Yes," the inner whisper continued. "They ask too much of you. How can they possibly expect you to command so many? Of course you will fail."

Moroni's shoulders slumped forward as the weight of those words came crashing down on his mind. The whisper became bolder. "If you make terms of surrender with the Lamanites now, you will save the lives of thousands of your countrymen, and there will be peace in the land." The whisper paused to let that statement affect Moroni. "There is no vice in trading liberty for security and peace," the dark whisper gently insisted. Moroni took a deep breath and nodded his head.

"Yes, security and peace is the goal."

"Slaves are made in such ways!" The booming voice of Moroni's father exploded like thunder across Moroni's mind.

"Father!" Moroni shouted as he frantically searched the tent for his inspiration, but no one was there.

"Slaves are made in such ways." His father's voice rang again in his ears, this time slower and less intense.

Moroni spun around again, but still no one was there.

"Slaves … I cannot surrender to the Lamanites. I must not surrender to the enemy. I cannot surrender our rights and privileges as free men." Moroni made his hands into fists and shook them as he spoke aloud. "Never!"

He instantly realized what had happened. The adversary was trying to plant fear and doubt in his mind. This was one battle Moroni knew how to fight. Grabbing the side of his cot, Moroni dropped to his knees and prayed.

"Heavenly Father, forgive me for having doubt and fear. I have been appointed by the voice of your children and anointed by your prophet to lead your army into battle. I beg you to give me the strength and wisdom to keep your people free. I do not want to fight my brother Lamanites, but if I must fight to keep my people free, and then guide me, I beg you, mighty God, to do so in righteousness and with honor. Protect me from the power and influence of darkness I pray. In Christ's name, amen."

Having finished his prayer, Moroni lifted up his head and started to stand. Pausing halfway he stopped and smiled as he thought about his father's warrior spirit watching over him. "And, thank you, father, for watching my back ... again."

Renewed by this sacred experience, Moroni rose and walked out the entrance of his tent and to the edge of the hill where he was camped. The sun was just starting its descent toward the high mountains in the west and the long afternoon shadows began to form at their base. From his vantage point, Moroni could see the entire camp and most of the main road that led into the forest. He could see the stables off to the left of the main camp. There, Captain Teancum was busy overseeing the training of the newly formed cavalry. Moroni observed large groups of mounted soldiers training their horses in battle maneuvers in the open grassy plains outside the camp. Captain Teancum was standing in a large wooden tower built in the middle of the field. Standing next to him were a flag man and a trumpeter sending signals to the training officers, and sergeants who were directing the movements of the horse soldiers up and down the field. All around the wooden tower were the battle flags and pendants of the sub-commanders.

"They're getting pretty good," Moroni thought as he watched squads of cavalry break off from the main group and perform precise movement drills. One group of horse soldiers was moving as a column, the next was moving in a wedge formation. Others were in a line, pivoting left and then right. Some were riding in a large circle around the commanders' tower, while others were at the weapons lane.

Training in the weapons lanes was always Moroni's favorite part when practicing with the cavalry. Soldiers took turns charging down a lane marked with painted rocks and lined with large wooden poles sticking out of the ground at different heights. The horse soldiers charged forward toward the poles with their swords drawn, slashing at the poles, using forward fluid strikes on their sword-hand side. Then, using momentum from the first strike, they crossed their swords to the weak side and strike a different pole with a follow-up slash. The different heights of the poles helped them train as though they were engaged in fighting both mounted and foot soldiers coming at them from different sides and angles.

A second group of soldiers was working on mounted archery skills. They set their horses at a gallop and, as they rode past, tried to hit stationary targets with their arrows. This was extremely difficult because the rider needed to time the gallop pattern of his horse and shoot the arrow when all of the horse's hoofs were off the ground at the same time so as to not disrupt his aim. As the soldiers charged past the targets set at different distances and heights, most of them aimed at the closer targets.

Watching one soldier, Moroni thought, "That would have been an easy kill, but," he reminded himself, "that distance would put them close to the enemies' weapons."

No sooner had that thought passed than a small group of six mounted soldiers let out war cries and took off in a line across the target range at a fast gallop. When in range, the first soldier stood up in his stirrups and shot an arrow at the farthest target, striking it just outside of the red center. A cheer went up from the group watching the display of soldierly skills as the second mounted soldier from the group did the same, striking the same target close to the first arrow.

"That target is fifty yards away," Moroni thought out loud.

The third soldier, following the first two, passed the target with the same result.

"Very nice!" Moroni said while nodding his head in approval.

The fourth rider rode past, striking the same target with a well-placed arrow. The fifth and sixth soldiers took their turns shooting their arrows, all striking the far target near the center ring.

"Well done," Moroni thought. "I hope they can do that when the targets are shooting arrows back at them."

He turned his attention to a different group working on spear and lance skills. This advanced training required soldiers to ride their horses at a gallop while holding a long spear or heavy lance out in front of them. Their targets were man-shaped dummies made out of animal skins stuffed with straw. These targets were placed on the ground or hung from poles by ropes and set at various heights around the training grounds. This made it difficult for the warrior in training to attack the targets and forced him to adjust his aim and learn to guide to horse while setting up for the next kill.

Several training sergeants walked among the mounted soldiers with long cane poles. The trainers tried to strike soldiers on their helmets with the poles while the soldiers practiced their spear handling or swordplay. The cane-pole strikes, which were more embarrassing than painful, were designed to teach the soldiers to use their shields to deflect the strikes and to move their horses to better defensive positions to avoid a follow-up strike.

Moroni was taking particular notice of a short trainer who was on foot and chasing a mounted soldier around the training area with one of the long cane poles. He could hear the other soldiers laughing as the two playfully sparred with each other. The trainee dodged the pole on his horse while the short trainer ran around trying to tag him with the pole. The comical scene continued until everyone heard a long blast from a ram's horn coming from the direction of the training tower. The horse soldiers all stopped what they were doing and turned toward Captain Teancum, who was still in the tower looking out at his men before him.

Holding his own spear high in the air, Teancum let out a war cry. The horse soldiers instantly responded by holding their spears and swords high in the air and screaming their war cry in return. Without any spoken instructions, the horse soldiers guided their mounts toward the far end of the grassy plain and galloped off to a pre-planned destination. At the far end of the open field, near the thick forest tree line, they reformed into a massive line of horses behind their unit commanders.

Teancum climbed down from his tower and mounted his waiting horse. He galloped to where the cavalry had formed. When he reached the impressive formation, the soldiers, in unison, began to shout and wave their weapons in the air. Teancum galloped past the front line of soldiers, shouting and waving his spear in response to the soldiers' zeal. After passing the troops, he galloped back, and stopped, front and center of the line.

Moroni could see that Teancum was speaking to the soldiers but could not make out what he was saying. He could see the soldiers react to Teancum's words by shouting several times and waving their weapons in the air. Teancum then pulled on his horse's reins to direct him away from the line and again held his spear in the air.

Moroni felt his hands turn cold. He knew what was about to happen and chills rushed up and down his spine.

THE OLD WAYS VERSUS THE NEW

S trange sounds coming from the encampment drew Moroni's attention away from Teancum and the cavalry. Moroni saw a mass of soldiers moving from the camp to the area next to the training field. Those who had gathered there had started shouting as well. Some were banging pots and pans together, others were blowing horns, beating drums or waving small bits of cloth. It seemed the entire camp was alive now, shouting and celebrating as the large group of cavalry soldiers formed a giant wall of horses and men at the far end of the valley. The camp's occupants knew it was time for the final practice maneuver of the day, the charge, and they came to watch in awe of the sheer power of so many men and horses moving in unison.

Teancum, now ready and positioned in the middle of the long line of horses and riders, raised his spear into the air and looked over his right shoulder at his men. He made eye contact with the cavalry commanders, shouted "CHARGE," and spurred his horse forward. Teancum's horse rose up on its hind legs and leaped forward as the entire line of horse soldiers instantly responded to the command and dashed forward at breakneck speed with spears, lances and swords pointed forward.

Seeing a massive cavalry charge is awe-inspiring if you're watching it from a distance, but if you are a hapless enemy soldier staring at it coming toward you, it is dreadful. The noise and dust created by hundreds of thundering hoofs moving toward a battle line in a full frontal assault can break the will of almost any army that stands in the way. The very ground shakes as the charging horses approach, and fear wells up inside nearly every soldier, knowing death is rushing his way. It takes true courage to stand your ground and hold the line in the face of such an attack.

For the practice charge, the whole group of soldiers had traveled about two hundred yards when Teancum made two stabbing gestures into the air with his spear. On that visual cue, the cavalry sub-commanders shouted orders and the line of troops quickly changed to a giant wedge, with Teancum at the point.

"Just like at Jershon," Moroni thought, as he watched the charging mass move beyond the encampment and past the base of the small hill where he was standing.

The crowd that gathered at the edge of the camp to cheer the cavalry on ran out onto the field as the horses galloped past. They jumped and shouted through the dust as if they were celebrating a real victory. A cloud of dust from the horses rose up to where Moroni was standing. He blinked several times and tried to fan the dust out of his face with his left hand as he turned to watch the charging horses go past the base of the hill and over a gentle slope on the far end of the open grassy area.

Teancum led his men down the slope and toward the banks of a river that was fed by runoff from the mountain ranges surrounding the Nephite camp. The river had cut a deep enough gorge that the horses moving toward the river's edge were soon out of Moroni's view. Only a telltale column of trailing dust remained.

Moroni stood wondering what Teancum and his men were doing and considered mounting his own horse to go and see.

"No," he thought, "I gave the command of the cavalry's training to him, and I trust him to train them properly. I should leave him be."

Moroni turned to walk back to his tent and was startled to find his security detail standing behind him.

"Sir, we heard a commotion," the sergeant of the guard quickly said. Moroni noticed the sergeant's swift motions and realized he was trying to cover the fact that the guards had left their posts to watch the evening's event.

Moroni felt it wasn't worth a confrontation. He knew they were young but dedicated soldiers and simply said, "I'm ok, sergeant. Return to your duties."

"Yes, sir," the young sergeant responded and quickly saluted, then ordered the men of the security detail to return to their assigned posts.

Moroni took one last look toward the river and saw Teancum leading his cavalry back up the slope and toward the camp stables. He was surprised to see that, for the first time, Teancum had organized the cavalry into small, manageable units, each with its own captain and standard bearer. Moroni knew from this morning's briefing by the sergeant major that the count was 300 horses ready for battle. As Teancum rode closer, Moroni could see that the mass of riders had been broken up into six units. Doing some quick math in his head, he figured that each unit consisted of fifty soldiers in columns of five with ten soldiers in each column. Teancum led the formation, followed by his personal command group and a soldier holding a large, red flag with an image of a galloping horse painted on both sides. The first unit behind Teancum had a smaller, red-colored standard with a large number one painted on both sides. The second unit had a large number two on its standard, the third had a number three, and so on, with the last unit's standard bearing the number six.

The concept of dividing the cavalry into several smaller, more manageable, units was the topic of hot debate during several past command and staff meetings. Captain Teancum's idea, while opposed by some, was to dissolve the long-held tradition of one mass body of horse soldiers charging headlong into the battle lines and engaging the enemy's front.

"This tactic," as he argued it in the past, "made the cavalry lose its advantage of mobility and speed. The old way made the unit nothing more than foot soldiers with horses."

During one such war council several weeks ago, Teancum presented his new tactics to the body of Nephite military leaders assembled. He brought to the meeting several small wooden horse and foot soldier figurines and placed them on a table around a large map skin. He used the them to show how a field commander could exploit a weakness in the enemy lines by employing his forces in a more manageable way.

"Instead of having one large body with only one commander," Teancum explained, "breaking up the cavalry into several smaller and more controllable units will give the battlefield general greater control of the battle. The reaction time to exploit a weakness will be reduced, as smaller units are more maneuverable."

"Here, gentlemen, let me show you," he continued as he moved the figurines on the map. "Suppose this line of soldiers represents the Lamanite front line …"

Teancum unrolled a large map skin on the table and placed four small leather bags full of sand on each corner to keep the skin flat. He also placed several red painted soldier figurines in a line across the large map for all the gathered leaders to see.

"The red soldiers will represent the Lamanites. As we all know, the Lamanite style of fighting is to mass in one large group and charge as one body into our lines. Until now, we had two ways to respond. We could either meet that threat with a mass charge of our own, leaving the soldiers on the ground to hack away at each other until one side overpowered the other, or we could send out our champion to fight theirs and let their personal battle decide the fate of us all."

"That's been the way of it from before father Nephi." A booming voice from outside the tent interrupted Teancum's map display. All the men inside the tent turned to see who made the statement. There was Captain Lehi standing in the doorway of the command tent. A shout of excitement went up and several junior officers moved out of the way while Lehi stormed toward the table that held the map and figurines. He was followed by several dangerous-looking Nephite soldiers, all dressed and armored like Lehi.

Standing just over six-feet tall, with long dark hair, a gray speckled beard and piercing steel blue eyes, Lehi was well into his fortieth year of age. The streaks of grey in his beard gave away the truth of his age, but his barrel chest, arms as hard as steel, fierce gaze, and battle scars proved to all he was a man among men. His exploits in combat were legendary among both the Nephite and Lamanite peoples. He had been called on many times to be the champion who fought for the Nephite army, and he had never lost. There were stories of enemy troops, even some that had greatly outnumbered Lehi and his men, who had surrendered or run away rather than face him in open battle. Lehi was bred for combat. He was born in a military camp and raised in the discipline and duty of a military family. His father and older brothers, uncles, grandfathers and great grandfather were all combat veterans. Lehi spent his early years around other soldiers, training and preparing his mind and body for combat. When it was his time to enlist, he refused a commission to be an officer and, instead, entered the military service as a foot soldier. There, he earned his rank from common soldier to chief captain one battle at a time. This was a source of great pride for him and a point that earned him the greatest respect from both his enemies and the men he commanded.

Reaching the center of the large tent, Lehi stopped just short of running over the table. He dropped a large battle ax on top of the map skin, smashing some of the small wooden toys to bits.

"Captain Lehi, thank you for answering my call to attend the war council," General Moroni said in a calm, even tone.

"I fear no man in battle," Lehi said looking around the room and locking eyes with those in attendance with his burning gaze. The men who entered the meeting with Lehi all shook their heads and grunted in response.

"And I do not agree to change the system of warfare that has seen this people through hundreds of years of combat," he said, while staring at Teancum.

"We all fear change; yet, change we must," Teancum responded as he came around the table to face the challenge Lehi was making to the new tactics. Teancum, who was younger and taller than Lehi, stopped just out of arms' reach of Lehi and stood in a defiant pose. Teancum was no coward. He was covered in lean, hard muscle and looked more like a marble statue than a man. He also was known by both friends and foes as a powerful and feared warrior, with a gift for an unconventional style of combat.

Teancum was born to a life of privilege on a large cattle ranch just outside the great city of Zarahemla. Benefiting from his family's wealth, he had been educated by the great scholars of his time and became a medical doctor. He helped to discover cures for several diseases by incorporating preventive measures like better hygiene and natural cures through herbs and plants. He became very popular with the people of the city and was starting into politics when word came one morning that his wife, two young sons and parents had been killed by robbers who attacked his family ranch. Worst of all, his only daughter was missing. A frantic search was conducted, but the robbers who took his daughter melted into the jungles and mountains outside the ranch and were not found.

Teancum was beside himself with grief and, after the funeral, vowed on the souls of his slain family to find his missing child and bring those responsible to justice. Gathering a few things from the burnt shell of his home, he disappeared into the very mountains where the robbers had disappeared. Some said he went to find those responsible for the murders. Others said he went to find his missing child, and there was even a rumor that he had killed himself. After several months, most just gave up on ever seeing him again. Then, exactly one year to the day of the murder of his family, Teancum returned to the great city. He was twenty pounds lighter and his body was scarred and hardened from combat. With fire in his eyes, Teancum walked right to the center of the city and demanded an audience with the chief judges. He gave them an impassioned speech about justice, true freedom, and the rule of law. When he was finished, he told the gathered that he was unable to save his child, but he took revenge on those bandits responsible and hunted each one of them down. The council of judges was so impressed they granted him a commission as a chief captain. He was charged with raising a force to fight the robbers and Lamanite raiders who had been attacking farms and villages along the frontier.

Teancum sent a call out for volunteers from all over the Nephite lands. While living in the mountains, Teancum had developed new concepts and tactics to hunt down and fight the robbers, and he used those tactics against the men who killed his family. With his new commission as a chief captain, he trained his band of volunteer soldiers in the new style of fighting he developed. They became experts at hunting down the enemy using ambushes, traps, assassinations, stalking and night raids. The robbers and Lamanites feared Teancum's soldiers so much they began to call them Teancum's "Ghost Soldiers" for their ability to move in the jungle unseen, strike without warning, and then disappear without a trace.

"Yes, you are right, Captain Lehi," Teancum continued. "The old ways of fighting sufficed the need of the times, but the battle of Jershon two years ago was so devastating to our armies that we, to this day, have not fully recovered."

Teancum took his eyes off Lehi and walked around the room, looking at the assembled officers in the tent.

"We lost so many men at Jershon that we can only muster a portion of what we need to face this new Lamanite army in open war. General Moroni's bold maneuver against the enemy's king should have taught us all a valuable lesson in the advantages of mobility, surprise and speed."

Teancum turned and pointed at Moroni, who was still sitting behind the great table. "The loss of your father in that fight is a tragedy this people will not soon recover from." Teancum bowed his head slightly in acknowledgement of Moroni, who nodded back.

Moroni leaned forward and put his giant arms on the tabletop. He took a deep breath, let it out and rested his head in his left hand with his thumb under his chin, his first finger running up his cheekbone and the rest of his fingers curled in front of his mouth. He remained silent and turned his head toward Lehi, waiting for a response. In the background, several of the gathered officers started to whisper among themselves in agreement with Teancum's tribute.

Seeing Moroni looking at him, Lehi spoke.

"A great maneuver, was it? More like brash, youthful luck, if you ask me." Lehi snorted in defiance as he stared back at Moroni. Lehi felt he was the rightful leader of this army, not a young upstart boy general. Lehi was the people's champion, and he was twice Moroni's age. He was also the most experienced of all the Nephite chief captains, and he wanted everyone in the tent to know how he felt, especially Moroni.

"While my men were fighting with the bulk of the Lamanite army at the front, young Moroni took on their sick and old by sneaking up on them and attacking at night from behind. Where was the honor in that?"

Some of the gathered soldiers standing with Lehi snickered at his comment.

Amiha, sitting next to Moroni, was outraged by what Lehi said. Flush faced and eyes burning, Amiha jumped from his chair and pointed an angry finger at Lehi. "The honor was found in a great victory for our people, their king dead and a peace treaty struck!" Amiha paused for the effect. "And, if I recall, you were not even there."

Lehi sneered back at Amiha, the muscles in his jaw clenched tight. Amiha's words were true. All Lehi really had was secondhand knowledge of the greatest military achievement in his lifetime. Lehi missed out on the fight against the Lamanite king and his men. He was not there for the capture of the camp and the surrender of the princess. No true warrior wanted that. Lehi understood better than most that a war is won by the efforts of all involved, not just those who parley for surrender, but his pride got the best of him and he had something to prove to Moroni, the soldiers gathered in the tent and all of those in Zarahemla who elected him as a general.

Moroni had had enough. The tension between his commanders was weighing on the emotions of the men. He needed to regain control of the meeting and assert his authority over all of these soldiers. He pushed his chair back and stood, pausing long enough for all in the tent to turn and face him. His size alone was enough to gain the quiet respect of most in the meeting. He put his hand on Amiha's shoulder and gave him a slight nod. Amiha understood the unspoken communication between him and his oldest friend. Backing down from Lehi, Amiha sat down but continued to glare at Lehi and the men standing behind him. Moroni looked over the men gathered and spoke.

"Gentlemen, let us not argue over the fact that we won the war," Moroni broke in and locked eyes with Lehi. "Chief Captain Lehi, your wisdom and experience are desperately needed at this war council. I asked you here to help us now solve this new problem."

He bent over the table and then pounded it with his fist, startling everyone in the great tent. "How do we defend this land from the growing Lamanite threat of invasion?" Moroni took a deep breath and gestured toward Teancum.

"Chief Captain Teancum has been given the floor to explain his thoughts. Please allow him to continue."

There was a tense silence as Moroni and Lehi locked eyes again. Above all, Lehi was a good soldier and he had honor. He did not like it, but the voice of the people had spoken. Moroni was his commander. With a slight nod, Lehi took two steps back to allow Teancum to finish his presentation. Lehi was still frustrated but, for now, he would do his duty and obey a command from his leader.

Teancum moved back to the table. He picked up the massive ax from his map and handed it back to Lehi. Lehi grunted and glared as he angrily snatched his weapon from Teancum. Outwardly unfazed, Teancum brushed onto the floor the small broken pieces of wood from the figures smashed by Lehi's ax. They landed silently on the grass and Teancum cleared his throat to continue.

"As I was trying to say …." Teancum spoke with a hint of disdain for the interruption in his battle planning. "By using surprise, mobility and proper tactics, we can take away the advantage the Lamanites have of their greater numbers. By planning the battle beforehand and using the terrain to our own advantage, we can choose the time and place for the fight and then place our armies in such a way that the Lamanites can only fight with a portion of their army at one time. Let me show you." Teancum took two more small leather bags and placed them on the table. "Let's say that these two bags are mountains and the space between them is a small pass. Now, gentlemen, we have a choice. We can fight the Lamanites out here, in the open area outside the pass, where their superior numbers can envelop us …" He gestured to the area on the map next to the bags.

Teancum pulled several more small wooden figures from a leather pouch. He put them on the table in front of the sand bags and set them up to show the Nephite army surrounded on three sides by the numerically superior Lamanite army.

"… or," Teancum continued, "we can suck them into this small area where only a few of their soldiers at the frontlines can fight at one time." He moved figurines representing the Nephite soldiers into the space between the small leather bags and showed how a few could defend the small section of land. He then moved the Lamanite army figures up to the pass.

"This way, only small numbers of Lamanite soldiers can attack at one time. The rest of them are stuck behind the front rows and cannot engage us effectively, making them useless. We also can put archers on the sides of the

mountains to fire down into the mass of Lamanite soldiers. In this example, the bulk of the Lamanite army will end up stuck in the valley behind their front ranks while our archers shoot at them from above." Teancum paused as the other captains and sub-commanders leaned over the map to see up close what he was demonstrating.

"Gentlemen, this is just one example of a sound strategy concept that General Moroni and I developed. I have learned during my time hunting down mountain bandits and Lamanite raiders that, if we use our superior training, discipline, better armament, and the terrain to our advantage, we can defeat a massive army with a smaller force." There was a moment of silence, and then the group of officers gathered in the room all started to show agreement and discuss the tactics among themselves.

"General Moroni, may I speak? I wish to point out something," Lehi bellowed with a bit of theatrical frustration while looking at the map.

"Yes, Captain Lehi, you wish to add something?"

"Sir, moving whole units with such timing would be impossible," Lehi spoke as he walked around the table. The room went silent as the tension started to rise again. "First, this would require that every officer down to platoon level know every detail of our battle plan. This is an unacceptable risk. We all know that the Lamanites will surely torture any officer they capture to gain intelligence. If even one word of our plan is leaked, the surprise is gone. Second, have you considered how we would communicate with everyone at the same time during the battle to order the movements you speak of?"

Lehi looked at Teancum but didn't wait for Teancum to answer. He continued right on with his rant. "Even if you somehow manage to keep all of our battle plans secure, if even one battalion fails to fall in line when ordered, the enemy can exploit that weakness in the front lines and cause the whole line to collapse. And what of these disciplined Nephite soldiers you speak of, who will perform these flawless tactical maneuvers under fire?" Lehi waved his hands around the room. "We have never been trained to fight using these tactics. And now I hear talk of a possible general military draft of the male population to fight?"

Lehi shook his head and bellowed on. "A common goat herder knows nothing of military operations and cannot be trusted to hold the line under a Lamanite charge. No, gentlemen," Lehi said, looking at Teancum with a hint of disdain in his voice, "we must stand and fight like men in the old ways. I do not fear death, and my mighty men can and will defeat an army ten times our size with sheer brute force!"

The soldiers who had entered the tent with Lehi let out a war cry and cheered when he said these words. Lehi, with a piercing gaze, continued to face Teancum across the table. Teancum, with quiet intensity, met the stare and for a few seconds not even the air moved.

Moroni had heard enough. He was not going to allow his two top field commanders get into a power struggle under his command. Rising again to take control of the meeting, Moroni spoke. "Enough of this, gentlemen," he said with a commanding tone. He paused as he waited for everyone in the room, including his two quarrelling chief captains, to turn and face him.

Moroni went on. "We have much to do to prepare this army for combat and very little time. My orders are as follows." He paused and looked at the gathered men, so everyone understood who was giving the orders. "Captain Lehi, you are to begin a basic training program for the infantry. I want every foot soldier to be outfitted with a complete body armor kit, helmet and shield, a spear, good sword, second handheld weapon of his choice, long knife, bow, and quiver of arrows. Every soldier is to know how to use each of these weapons and how to fight and move in simple formations. You have made a strong argument, Captain Lehi, for the old ways of fighting." The two made eye contact when Moroni said those words. "I feel before this war is over we will need to engage the enemy in the old ways. I leave it to you to prepare the men to do so."

"Yes, sir," Lehi snapped back, bowing slightly with his head. "You found a way to show your dominance over the army and still allow me to save my honor in front of my men," Lehi thought to himself, half smiling at Moroni. "That was a political move I would have expected from a much older man than you. Very interesting."

"And you, Captain Teancum," Moroni continued, "you are to continue your training with the cavalry. The ideas you have for the small unit tactics have merit; continue along your path with them. Also meet with my aide-de-camp and, between the two of you, outline some answers to the justified concerns raised by Captain Lehi."

"Yes, sir," Teancum responded.

"Sergeant Major?" Moroni called out for his trusted sergeant.

"Sir?" the sergeant major said as he walked forward to the table. He had been standing behind Moroni the entire time, in the shadows at the back of the tent, watching the heated debate in silence. No one saw, but he had his hand on the hilt of his sword ready to draw it out to defend his young commander. He knew how Lehi felt and was ready, just in case.

"Sergeant Major, I want this camp in proper working order. I want new latrines dug; the old ones are too close to the mess tents. And we need to make room for the remainder of the troops coming in from the outlying cities. Also, set a watch on the road and about the camp, and send patrols into the wood line. I'm quite confident the enemy has sent spies, and we need to flush them out. Are my orders clear, gentlemen?" Moroni's gaze took in everyone in the candlelit room.

"Yes, sir," was the response.

Although he had finished giving orders, Moroni had more to say. He paused to find the words. "I know quite well that some of you question my appointment as the supreme commander of the Nephite forces," he stated, this time looking only at Lehi. "Some of you think of me as too young or inexperienced to lead. Some of you think I am in this position because of my father. Whatever your thoughts are, understand this, gentlemen." Tapping his index finger on the table, he continued. "I am in command of this army … and I have been given command by the consent of the people through the authority of the chief judges and anointed by Alma the Prophet himself. … While I am in command, you will follow my orders … are we clear?!"

"Yes, sir," the men spoke in unison.

"Now, gentlemen, I'm starving … let's eat." A shout went up as several attendants entered the large open area carrying platters of meats, fruits and bread.

PREPARATIONS

The gray light of dawn was giving way to the piercing red of the sun's first true light. The sergeant major flung open the back door of the command tent and shouted to the sergeant of the guard.

"Boy, summon the trumpeter, and get me a rider who can deliver an urgent message to the City of Zarahemla."

The sleepy sergeant was instantly awake and full of energy. He knew who was in the tent with General Moroni, and he knew what it meant when the sergeant major needed a trumpeter this early in the morning. He ran to the tent where half of his squad was sleeping, while the other half pulled night shift guard duty around the command tent. He kicked the first body he came to. "Get up," he demanded. "Let's go, ladies, we got to move right now … double time!" Clapping his hands, he moved from one sleeping soldier to another, pulling off blankets and kicking cots.

"Go, go, go," he commanded.

Groaning and cursing under their breath, the sleepy soldiers stirred in their cots and slowly grumbled to life.

"Sergeant, my shift does not start for two more hours," one soldier lamented as he tugged at the blanket in his sergeant's hands.

The young leader jerked the blanket back out of the soldier's hands. "The scout just got back," he shouted. "He is in the command tent with the general as we speak. Now the sergeant major is calling for a trumpeter and messengers to ride to Zarahemla."

The men stopped dressing and all looked at the sergeant at the same time. There was a long pause of dead silence in the tent; then a giant smile crossed the young face of the sergeant.

"That's right, boys and girls, we're going to war. So, if it's not too much trouble …." The sergeant paused and picked up a metal shield and spear leaning against the side of the tent. "MOVE," he shouted, banging the spear against the shield. "Formation in ten minutes. Full battle gear!"

The sergeant dropped the shield and spear by the door of the tent and stepped out. He waved his hand at one of the soldiers already on duty near the command tent, motioning to him to come over.

"Yes, Sergeant?" the young Nephite warrior responded.

"Where is the corporal?"

"Other side of the tent by the command stables."

"Go get him and find the trumpeter. Bring them both here right now."

"Yes, Sergeant." The young soldier took off at a trot around the large tent.

The sergeant stood quietly for a few moments, drinking in the morning sun. He listened to snatches of conversations as his men shared their excitement and dread about the coming war. He shook his head, knowing that if the rumors were true about the size of the Lamanite army, the Nephites were outnumbered three to one. He thought about the weeks spent training on Moroni's new battle plans. "Even with all that training," he thought, "will we really have any hope to withstand so many?" His thoughts were cut short by the sound of clanking armor. He turned to see a soldier coming toward him at a dead run from around the tent. Running a few paces behind him was a boy dressed in a light tunic and leggings, carrying a brass horn in his hand.

"You needed us, Sergeant?" a young, fresh-faced soldier spoke breathlessly.

"Yes, Corporal Phan, get your horse and report with the trumpeter to the sergeant major. You are needed to carry a message to the capital." He turned to the boy holding the horn, who had not heard his orders to Corporal Phan. "You go with Corporal Phan and report to the sergeant major."

"The sergeant major?" the young trumpeter gasped with fear in his voice. Everyone in camp was afraid of the old soldier and this scared boy was no exception.

"Don't worry. As long as you don't mess up, he won't kill you." The sergeant held a serious face for several seconds looking at the trumpeter. The young boy with the trumpet looked down at his metal horn, then took a deep breath and walked away toward the command tent. The soldiers snickered under their breath at the joke just played at the expense of the young musician.

"Poor kid. I think he actually believes you," Corporal Phan said under his breath.

"Yeah, but I make it a habit to not cross the old man's path just in case the rumors about him are true," the young leader responded.

The corporal took a deep breath of morning air and nodded to his brother warrior. He took off toward the stables, as a second soldier came up from behind the sergeant.

"What is it, Sarge? What's going on?"

"It's time to earn your pay, Junior. Go pack your gear. Formation in eight minutes!" he shouted back into the tent.

Near the command tent, the sergeant major grabbed a jug of oil and a burning torch from the staff kitchen area. He walked at a quick pace toward a large pile of logs about fifty yards to the left of the command tent. The woodpile was as tall as a man, with logs stacked one on top of another like a log home, with dried leaves and twigs shoved in the gaps. The corporal and trumpeter ran up next to the old warrior and reported for their duty.

"Follow me," he snorted as he briskly walked toward the logs. He stopped about five feet away and tossed the clay pot full of oil at the logs. It popped open and spilled out its contents all over the side of the log pile. Next, he threw the lit torch in the same direction. When it hit the pile, the whole thing instantly burst into flames.

"Sound formation, son, and keep sounding until you see the whole camp moving," the old soldier ordered.

The trumpeter nervously took two steps back and put the horn to his lips. He tried to let out two short blasts from the horn, but it came out sounding more like a wounded duck than a musical instrument. Scared for his safety, he quickly looked at the sergeant major, who was looking back at the trumpeter as though he were the devil himself.

"Lips … my lips were not warmed up," the young musician choked out while he blew hot air past his lips and tried again. Quickly, he made the correct sounds, letting out two short blasts followed by one long blast of the same note. He repeated this several more times, two short, one long; again two short, one long, over and over again until he heard the watchmen within the camp signal back. Fires lit within the camp acknowledged the command to assemble on the training field.

"They're … they're responding, sergeant major," the trumpeter stuttered, relieved that he had accomplished his assigned task.

The sergeant major squinted his eyes, growled at the young boy and walked away.

Realizing that he was not going to be killed, the trumpeter said a quick prayer of thanks and returned to his unit.

In camp, most of the soldiers were still asleep when the lone trumpet sounded. Most soldiers were able to sleep with the typical sounds and movements of the sentries and those on fire watch. For health reasons, the Nephites learned long ago not to keep animals close to the main camp. Even the noises from the livestock, held at a safe distance from the main camp, were not enough to rouse a tired, sleeping soldier. But they were all attuned to hear the trumpet and knew what it meant. In an instant, the entire camp was alive.

Corporal Phan met the sergeant major near the entrance to the command tent. "Corporal, you are to wait here at the command tent for a message from the general. You are to guard that message with your life and deliver it at all costs; do you understand?"

"Yes, Sergeant Major!"

The young soldier turned and walked his horse to the open area in front of the big tent.

The sergeant major rounded the corner behind Corporal Phan when Captain Lehi galloped up and was met by the security detail. He did not have on his distinctive armor, but Lehi never went anywhere without his mighty ax.

"Everyone is inside, sir," the sergeant major spoke before Lehi had a chance to ask. Lehi dismounted and handed the reins of his horse to one of the guards at the security checkpoint. Lehi stomped toward the tent opening, his heavy footfalls kicking up the dust around his strong calves. In several long strides, he was at the door and burst into the command tent unannounced. There he found Moroni, Amiha and Teancum standing around a big map spread out on the table in the center of the room. He also saw a very dirty and ragged soldier sitting in the corner eating bread and cheese and drinking water from a jug.

"Captain Lehi, just in time to join us," Moroni said. "Scout, come, please show us on the map again where the enemy is."

"Like I said sir," the frazzled scout spoke, almost choking on a large bite of bread. "We were watching the enemy camp outside Antionum from the mountainside when we saw them send out several riders in different directions. We assumed it was just a patrol, but then several more riders left the camp and some of them started toward our location. We were hidden well up in the trees and wrapped up in those special bark-colored cloaks that Captain Teancum made, so they could not see us. I overheard them talking as they rode around under us. They were looking for us; they knew that we were watching the camp, and they wanted to find us to keep us from reporting the movement of their army. They searched for a while but could not find us. Then they left and set up a blocking position on the road. It was then that we saw their main force start to assemble and prepare for deployment."

"Which way did they go, boy?" Lehi asked.

"Sir, I don't know."

"What do you mean you don't know?" Quick anger raced across Lehi's face.

"Let him explain," Moroni interrupted. He spoke calmly to the young soldier. "Go on and finish."

"Yes, sir, when we saw that the main body of the army was going to move, we had no choice but to return to camp and raise the alarm. With the road blocked, we figured that fighting our way past the blocking force would leave little chance of one of us getting through to warn you before they could send reinforcements and run us down. If we tried to go over the mountains and not take the road, it would take us several days to cross. The woods we were in were starting to fill up with the vanguard forces so we had to move right then or be trapped there. We slipped past them by crawling through the brush for several hundred yards on our bellies back to where we stashed the horses."

"So, you don't know where they are going, just that they are on the move?" Amiha asked.

"Yes, sir. As you can see from the map," the scout meekly pointed to a location on the map, "the road they were on branches off in several different directions; all of our cities on the frontier roads are in jeopardy."

"You did not think to just fall back and watch them from afar?" Lehi asked.

"Yes, sir, we did just that but we were discovered, and they attacked us. We fought our way out of an ambush and fled. I am the only one who survived. I ran my horse for two days and just now arrived."

"Did you get a count of their forces?" Teancum asked, while looking over the map.

"I started to, sir, but it was then that they found us." The exhausted soldier sat back down and let his arms and legs relax. "I saw at least one legion forming with too many more soldiers still to count. My best guess, sir, is a four-to-one advantage against us."

There was a long, silent pause as those in the meeting looked at each other.

"Very well, scout, well done. Report to your platoon commander. Get some more food and rest," Moroni ordered.

"Yes, sir." The scout slowly stood, saluted and left the tent.

Moroni waited until the tired scout was gone. "Recommendations, gentlemen?"

"Sir, if the scout is right, they could be anywhere within a two hundred mile stretch of the frontier, including a day's ride from our location," Teancum said.

Lehi gave his opinion next. "Unfortunately, at this point I think all we can do is wait and be ready to react when we get better intelligence as to their location."

"We can't just sit here and wait until we get word that they have sacked one of our cities!" Amiha's outburst was filled with frustration.

Lehi shouted back, "Yes, but we can't split what forces we have and send them in three different directions looking for this army either."

The three captains started to argue about what they should do—Teancum logically laying out his plan, Lehi voicing his position loudly and Amiha breaking into a sweat across his forehead while trying to reason with both of them. Before the planning got any more heated, Moroni needed to once again take control. He raised his hand, the three stopped talking and Moroni began, "Teancum, send out three squads of riders. Tell them to ride half a day and wait here, here and here." Moroni pointed to the map three times in three different areas on roads leading out of Antionum. "They are to avoid contact at all cost. Have them observe only and report back if they see any sign of the enemy's movement. Tell them to conduct surveillance until dawn tomorrow, and then come back if they see nothing."

"Lehi, you and the sergeant major are to prepare this army to move. It will take us at least a full day to get ready, and, hopefully, by then we should know the direction we are going."

"Amiha, you are to ride to Zarahemla at top speed and speak with Alma the Prophet. We need the Lord's help. We cannot spread this force out, and we need to know the will of God. Ask Alma what the Lord would have us do. By my reckoning, if you ride hard all night, you should be back here late tomorrow with his message. Questions, gentlemen?"

"No, sir," the three answered in unison.

"Good. Make it happen."

The three captains saluted their general and walked out of the tent, leaving Moroni alone with his thoughts.

The sergeant major met them outside the tent.

"Report," Lehi said to the old soldier.

"The camp's awake and moving, sir."

"Excellent. Have the infantry battalion captains report to me in one hour in my tent."

"Yes, sir," the sergeant major responded and walked away.

The three chief captains looked at each other and communicated in the unspoken words of soldiers facing a battle together. They were not enemies; they all respected and admired each other for the qualities they brought to the fight, but the challenge before them was daunting and they knew that the freedoms of all Nephites rested on a knife's edge. Emotions were running high and personal feelings had been hurt. Somehow they all needed to overcome their biases and hold this little army together. They shook hands and walked off to tend to their duties.

"Are you the general's messenger?" Amiha asked the corporal standing next to the tent holding the reins of his horse.

"Yes, sir. I'm Corporal Phan," the young soldier responded nervously.

"Go and get two additional horses and supplies for two days' hard ride. Quickly now. You and I have a long, hard ride ahead of us."

"Yes, sir!" Corporal Phan said. He swung up into his saddle and spurred his horse toward the camp stables.

ZERAHEMNAH THE ZORAMITE

"Their camp is here, sire." The Lamanite soldier was sweaty and breathless. He pointed to a crude map skin set on a table under the shade of a large cloth tarp. "They make camp in the valley right where this road leads out from the jungle. Exactly where you said they would be."

The Lamanite scout giving his report was dressed in only a loincloth. A knife was strapped to his side, resting against the brown skin of his midriff, and he held a wooden spear in his hand. He was tall and thin, and the long, lean muscles of his arms, calves and thighs gave the impression he had excellent endurance and distance-running skills. He finished his report, wiped the sweat from his shaved head, took two steps back from the table and waited, at attention, for the Lamanite commander to speak.

"Of course they are, I know their tactics well." His commander responded with a hollow and indifferent tone.

The soldier was nervous and tried desperately not to let his emotions show. This was the first time he had been this close to his leader, Zerahemnah the Zoramite.

"The stories are true; he is a big man," the Lamanite scout thought. He stood ramrod straight, staring off into the distance. He dared not make eye contact with the Zoramite but, instead, tried to size him up by looking out of the corner of his eye at the imposing figure sitting in a large wooden chair under the same shade tarp. Zerahemnah was wearing Nephite-style armor, he had a jaguar skin wrapped around him like a cloak, and wore a crown of gold and bright bird feathers on his head.

The scout thought his leader looked like a Nephite with the same skin color, beard, dark hair and clothing. "But there's something different about him," he thought while carefully studying his new commander. Zerahemnah did not act like any Nephite he had met before. "Killed the old army commander with one blow, they say. Marched right into the middle of camp one night and challenged him to a fight for the right to lead the army. One stroke of his sword and he split the old man almost in half, then drank the dead man's blood and swore to kill all those who were enemies to the Lamanite people."

The Lamanite continued to evaluate his leader and the other Zoramites, who formed a circle around the table, looking at the map. Like Zerahemnah, they were all wild men. Loud, drunk and dirty, even for Lamanite standards, they were dangerous and bold. More like barbarians, the Zoramites quickly came to dominate the Lamanites and imposed their will on the people of the land of Nephi.

"Scout, you have seen them with your own eyes. What is the status of the camp?"

"Sire." The scout instinctively snapped back into the position of attention. "They have set up camp in the valley just beyond the forest off of the north road. Training has begun and they patrol the woods."

"What type of training do they conduct?" Zerahemnah asked, as he bit into a large section of juicy melon given to him by a young Lamanite woman dressed in rags. He was paying more attention to the servant girl than his own scout's report.

"They are training with horses, bows and infantry tactics, sire."

"Their numbers?" Zerahemnah inquired as the juice from the bitten fruit dripped down his beard.

"Sire, they have maybe two thousand foot soldiers and a few hundred cavalry."

"Those fools!" scoffed one of the Zoramites standing under the tarp. He, too, was massive, dirty and very drunk. His words were slurred as he said, "We have them at least three to one. General Zerahemnah, we should strike now while they are vulnerable and before their reinforcements arrive."

"Is that the consensus of my command staff?" Zerahemnah asked. The mixed gathering of Lamanite and Zoramite men shouted in agreement.

Zerahemnah reluctantly brushed the servant girl aside. "Scout, what is the quickest route to the heart of the Nephite camp?"

"The main road that follows the river will take you right there." The Lamanite soldier moved toward the map and pointed to a road marked in black. "It intersects with the road we are on here, and is maybe 20 miles away from this very camp."

"Excellent," Zerahemnah exclaimed. He stood and raised a golden scepter. "Inform the army that we move at once. Leave the wagons and baggage trains to catch up. We will travel at double time and attack at dusk. We will kill Nephites all night and eat their food and drink their blood for breakfast!"

A shout went up from the tent and men began to move away, when a voice cried out.

"Sire, may I point something out to you?"

An older Lamanite captain walked through the crowd and stopped at the table.

"What is it?" Zerahemnah said impatiently. He had already had enough delays, and he wanted to get moving and engage the Nephites as soon as possible. With clan rivalry, sickness, and lack of food, Zerahemnah had more challenges than he wanted to deal with. The magnitude of managing this army was proving to be beyond Zerahemnah's ability. He was a much better thief than he was a captain of men and it was starting to show.

The old Lamanite stepped forward. "Sire, our army has been on the move for two days now with little food or rest. A 20-mile forced march will leave them at the point of collapse. The road you wish to travel is heavily wooded with impassable jungle on both sides. Our army will be spread out for miles on the road, leaving us vulnerable to an ambush. I advise that we send out an advance party to secure the way and make sure the Nephites are still there. Also, sire, we should ..."

Before the Lamanite could finish, Zerahemnah raised his hands and smiled.

"What is your name?" he said, his voice sounding much more lighthearted than it had just moments earlier.

"Sire, my name is Shiblon, from the valley of the dark trees."

"My good Shiblon," Zerahemnah said, "I see the problem here."

"Problem, sir?"

Zerahemnah placed his left hand on Shiblon's shoulder and looked into his eyes. "Yes, Shiblon, there is a problem!" He rammed a jewel handled short sword into Shiblon's gut. "It's your lack of faith!" Zerahemnah's words came hissing out of his mouth. He continued to grasp Shiblon's shoulder and watched as the life poured out of him. At Shiblon's last desperate gasp for air, Zerahemnah released his grip and watched as the old Lamanite slid off the sword's blade and landed on the ground, a dead man.

Zerahemnah turned to the remaining men around the table.

"Are there any other cowards in my command?" he shouted. He looked around at the gathered men. No one dared to move.

"No? Then get my army on its feet and ready to move, or you will find your headless bodies lying next to this coward dog," he shouted and kicked the lifeless form of Shiblon. The men quickly moved away from the covered table and began shouting orders to the mass of Lamanite soldiers.

CHAPTER ELEVEN

STRIKE CAMP

"Ride hard, my brother, and don't spare the horses. We must know the will of God. Come back as soon as you have word from Alma the Prophet."

"Yes, sir!" Amiha said to Moroni as he pulled up on the reins and spurred his horse forward. Young Corporal Phan saluted and followed behind on his horse, with the extra horses and supplies in tow.

It was already late morning, and the camp was far from being on pace to march out at dawn the next day. Moroni could see and hear the commotion of men and animals preparing to move the camp. Horses were being shod, cattle and sheep rounded up, water barrels filled at the river, tents folded and packed on the platoon wagons, groups of men moving in formations, all under the watchful eyes of the sergeant major and Chief Captain Lehi. Moroni looked out over the camp and prayed to his Father in Heaven for guidance.

"Father, guide us," he whispered. "Guide us and protect us."

After his prayer, he spent several minutes breathing deeply and standing with his head bowed, his massive arms relaxed at his side. He felt the tightness in his jaw drain away as a soothing and reassuring calm passed over him. Thankful for the quiet influences of heaven, he turned and walked back to where his personal guards were folding and packing up the large command tent into a wagon.

"Leave my armor out here where I can get to it, please," he said to the young sergeant leading the detail.

"Already done, sir." The sergeant pointed toward a large tree several paces away. Looking in the direction his aide had indicated, Moroni saw his armor displayed on its wooden stand with an array of weapons stacked next to it. The great Sword of Laban was nowhere to be seen.

"Sergeant, where is my sword?"

"Here, sir." The young warrior quickly moved to the back of the wagon and found the giant sword wrapped in a red cloth. He picked it up with both hands and carried it back to Moroni.

"I knew you would want it close to you, sir, so I kept it where I could watch over it and give it to you if you needed it. It's very heavy." He struggled under the weight of the sword, continuing to use two hands to hold up the mighty weapon and present it to Moroni.

"Thank you, sergeant. That was good thinking on your part." When Moroni took the cloth-wrapped weapon, he saw a look of disappointment on the soldier's face.

"Have you ever seen the Sword of Laban?" Moroni asked the young soldier.

"From a distance, sir. This is the closest I have ever been to it."

Moroni unwrapped the weapon from the cloth and pulled the shiny blade from the scabbard. He held the large sword out in front of him with one hand.

"Would you like to hold it, Sergeant?" he asked. "Careful. Like you said, it's very heavy."

The young soldier grinned and grabbed at the handle of the sword with both hands. He was still amazed at how big it really was and that General Moroni was so strong he could easily hold it up with only one hand.

"I am holding the Sword of Laban. This is something I will tell my grandchildren. Thank you, sir, for this great honor." The young soldier examined the sword closely and admired the workmanship. "It's just like the stories I heard as a child—jeweled hilt, gold covered handle, and the inscriptions on the side of the blade—it's just as they said it was ... and now it's in my hands. It's unbelievable—just amazing."

He handed the sword back to Moroni.

"Thank you, sir, for that great honor," he said, then added, "I should return to my men and see to our tasks."

"You have my leave to do so, young sergeant."

"Thank you, sir." The soldier gave Moroni a smart salute.

Moroni returned the salute and put the great sword back in its sheath.

He looked up to see the sergeant walking vigorously away toward the other men who were still diligently working. "That young sergeant," Moroni thought, "is close to my age, but I feel so much older."

Moroni watched the soldier return to his men and reflected on the events at hand. "So many good men like him are going to die if this war continues," he thought.

"I need more soldiers and more time to train them, and I have neither." He let out a long, deep breath, and looked up into the sky. A large flock of birds was heading toward the river for their evening drink and meal of bugs before they found a perch for the night. Moroni closed his eyes and tilted his head up to let the late afternoon sun warm his face. He had spent too much of his time lately inside his tent looking at reports and studying maps. He wanted to be outside and enjoying nature, carefree and safe, but he knew it would be a long time before he could go fishing on the coast of the great sea where his father had taken him as a boy or go hunting and exploring the wilds with Amiha looking for evidence of the ancient peoples who lived on this land hundreds of years ago.

Moroni looked back down at the camp below. He felt a heavy ache in his chest, knowing that many of those brave soldiers would not return from this battle. They would never go home to their families. How many would never go fishing with their sons, or spend the day playing with their daughters? The sadness of it all started to creep in again. It weighed heavily on his mind and made his throat tighten. He sensed the darkness returning, but this time Moroni recognized the power of the devil and knew what to do.

With his eyes closed and face to the sun, he prayed again. "Father, protect and guide this army; show mercy on us and lead us to victory. Give me the strength to do Thy will." Instantly he felt better. He knew the battle wasn't over, however. Even as they went to face the enemy, he would have to continue to fight his own internal battle against insecurity, discouragement and darkness. For now, he moved forward with renewed strength and trusting in the God of his father. Looking back down at the camp, he took another deep breath and said to himself, "Still so much to do. I guess I'd better get moving."

CHAPTER TWELVE

PLANNING A DEFENSE

The weathered and tired sergeant took a moment to look at the men under his command. They were part of the reconnaissance teams sent that morning by Teancum to watch the jungle road and look out for any sign that the Lamanite army was moving toward the main Nephite camp.

Huddled together under the exposed and oversized roots of a monstrous tree, they were trying to cover themselves with branches for shade and set up a small camp when one of his men gestured toward sounds coming from the thick brush. The sergeant turned and saw a scout come running up to the tree breathless and excited. This scout had gone looking for a good location to watch the road, and the sergeant knew instantly why the young scout was running. "How many?" he asked as he jumped up from the under the roots and stood to face the scout.

"Thousands, Sarge, as far back on the road as I can see, and they are moving at a dead run! They are almost on top of us. We need to move now if we're going to make it back to camp to warn the others!" the young Nephite scout gasped in a whisper. He moved past the sergeant and into the makeshift camp, hurriedly gathering up his belongings and strapping them to his horse.

The sergeant wiped a small bead of sweat off his forehead. He was having a hard time processing the magnitude of the message the scout just gave him. Slowly he made his way back to the cluster of large roots where three other Nephites were waiting. Everything was surreal for him. The men looked at their squad leader and then at their fellow soldier, who was still quickly gathering up his meager belongings.

"We need to go!" the scared soldier exclaimed, fear sounding in his voice. He finished shoving his bed roll into his pack. The scout's fear was contagious and, one by one, confusion and concern showed on the faces of the reconnaissance team as they were torn between running as fast as they could and keeping their military bearing and waiting for orders from their squad leader.

"Sarge?" one of the young soldiers barked.

The young leader stood in an almost disbelieving trance. He was frozen by the consequences he now faced.

"Sarge, what do we do?"

Still nothing from their leader.

"SERGEANT!" This time their united voices were dangerously loud and demanding.

The pleading shouts snapped the dazed leader out of his mental lock. He faced his men and blinked several times to regain focus.

"Strike camp! Let's move, gentlemen, we must warn General Moroni," the sergeant commanded. He moved to kick out the small cooking fire.

In short order, the small squad of Nephites had their horses ready for travel. "No matter what," the sergeant now spoke with authority, "the message must get through. Our lives mean nothing now; it's the message we carry to General Moroni that means everything. Do not stop, no matter what. That is an order. GO, GO, GO!"

The sergeant mounted. His horse rose up on its hind legs and jumped to a gallop down the trail that led to the main road toward the main Nephite camp. His men followed close behind.

The first volley of Lamanite arrows struck almost as soon as the Nephite squad broke from the trail and reached the main road. Two of the Nephite horses were hit with arrows in the back legs. The wounded horses buckled with pain and their riders were thrown to the ground. The sergeant heard the horses bellow, and he turned around in his saddle. He saw the two soldiers who had been thrown from their horses rise up in the middle of the road and pull their swords and small wooden shields from their dying horses. Being a reconnaissance unit, the team traveled light and did not carry the heavy armor or metal shields that the infantry used. Not far behind them, a mass of Lamanites was barreling down the road, running, shouting and waving weapons in the air. Defiantly, the two fallen Nephite soldiers faced the oncoming Lamanite army that was charging toward them. One of them looked back to see that his sergeant had stopped and shouted, while waving his small sword in the air, "Ride on. Go!"

The sergeant spurred his horse forward as a second volley of arrows slammed into the trees and ground all around him. As his horse galloped away from the advancing Lamanites, he slowed and glanced back over his shoulder one last time and saw his two brave soldiers fighting for their lives as the vanguard of the Lamanite army crashed over them like an ocean wave hitting the shore and wiping the sand clean. The mass of enemy soldiers enveloped the two Nephites and, without pausing, continued their death run toward the Nephite camp. Knowing the message he carried was more valuable than the lives of his men, he tucked in low behind his horse and urged the animal onward.

The young Nephite sergeant pushed his horse to near exhaustion. After running at a full gallop for some time, he could feel the horse's pace start to slow, its breathing labored, but the sergeant pushed his mount on. He lost sight of the others in his squad and hoped the rest of his men made it out alive from the first encounter with the Lamanites. He guessed they were somewhere in front of him on the road and were driving their horses as hard as he was. The jungle flew past him in a giant green blur as his horse continued to gallop down the wide dirt road lined by massive trees and undergrowth. After several more minutes of hard galloping, he could feel his horse start to stumble and the animal strained to continue going at that pace. He pulled up on the reins and brought the horse to a quick walk. The animal gasped for air and saliva foamed around its mouth.

The sergeant reached forward and patted the animal's neck. "If I don't take care of you, I'll never get back." He spied a small stream running just off the path and guided his mount over to it. The horse took several drinks from the stream while the young sergeant dismounted and splashed water on his face and arms. After a short rest, he jumped back on the horse.

"OK, boy, just a few more miles." He guided his hose back onto the road and spurred the beast onward. After another hour of riding, he could see the break in the jungle where the road ran through the center of the valley. There, at the edge of the clearing, and to his joy and relief, he saw his two missing soldiers. They were being questioned at the edge of the tree line by several heavily armed Nephite sentries who were pointing spears at them. As the sergeant galloped up to them, he, too, was challenged. Looking past those soldiers guarding the road the sweaty sergeant squinted under the noonday sun and could see the camp alive with activity as tents were being folded and animals moved amid the sounds of controlled chaos.

"Who goes there?" one sentry shouted.

"Reconnaissance party under orders of Captain Teancum." The sergeant's mouth was so dry the words barely came out. "We carry an emergency message for General Moroni. These men are with me. Let us pass!" the exhausted sergeant shouted.

The leader of the guards walked up to the three riders with an almost bored look on his face. He was older than most others of his rank. Discipline was no longer his strong suit and it showed in his mannerisms and dirty uniform and armor, the very reasons he had been passed over several times for promotion and was now working a less glamorous job like guard duty.

"What is the password?" he lazily spoke to the men on the horses, and took a bite of the piece of bread he carried in his hand.

"Jericho!" the sergeant spat back. "Now, let us pass. Lamanites … thousands of them, coming down the road. Ready your men!"

The sergeant of the guards' demeanor changed almost instantly when he heard the troubling news. Spitting out his mouthful of bread, he asked, "When … when will they be here?"

"Dusk, maybe sooner."

The sergeant of the guards looked back down the road as it disappeared into the jungle. This was his chance to regain his honor and show his men and his superiors he was still a good soldier.

"Corporal," he called to his second in command, "have the men fall in, full battle gear, rally on me right now."

"Fall in, let's go, move," the corporal shouted as he pushed and kicked the other sentries into a formation.

"Go quickly and may God save us all," the reenergized sergeant shouted to the riders. Stepping out of the way of the horses, he watched as the tired and tattered recon squad made their way toward the main camp in the middle of the valley.

The three riders charged through camp at a full gallop toward the command tent. Those in the camp, feeling the urgency, stopped their tasks and watched them gallop past. The inexperienced wondered why three soldiers were racing through the camp. Those who had faced battle before knew instantly that it could only mean one thing, their faces and body language reflected what they knew—war was here.

The riders made it through the camp and started up the slight incline toward Moroni's command tent. Seeing the riders' approach, one of the guards stationed at the door of the tent burst into the command tent and saluted. "Sir, one of the scouting parties has returned," he said.

"Thank you, Private. Have my command staff report here immediately."

"Yes, General Moroni." The soldier ran to summon the camp's leadership, but he could already see Teancum, Lehi and the rest of the command staff gathering at the base of the hill and moving toward Moroni's tent.

Moroni was standing over a sizable table with several large map skins laid open when Lehi, Teancum, and the sergeant major arrived.

"Sergeant Major," Moroni said, "have the scouts come in and make their report."

The sergeant major stood in the doorway of the tent and motioned with his hand for the three riders to enter the tent.

"Report!" Captain Lehi forcefully stated.

"My general," the young scout saluted. He was dirty and exhausted from the ride. Now, in the presence of his commanding general, he spoke meekly, but his face shone as it revealed the pride of his accomplished mission, and the concern, he felt.

"The Lamanites are upon us, thousands of them moving on foot at the double time. No cavalry or war chariots were seen, just a mass of foot soldiers and a few leaders on horseback driving them forward. More enemy soldiers than I have ever seen in one place, with war paint and shaved heads. They killed two of my men like swatting flies. We barely escaped with our lives."

"Where? Show me," Moroni said in a commanding voice and pointed to the great map on the table.

The scout sergeant walked up to the table and took a moment to study the map. He walked around to the side of the table where Moroni was standing and pointed to a spot on the map.

"Here, sir; this is where we saw them, coming up this road. And now, sir, given the pace at which they are traveling, I would say they are about here." He pointed to a second location on the map and looked up at his supreme commander.

"Could you tell who was in command?" Moroni asked.

"No, sir. I saw no battle standards or flags, but I did see what looked like a Zoramite wearing armor on a horse shouting at some of the men in the front of the army to keep moving. Is it true, sir, that Zerahemnah and the Zoramites are against us?"

"It looks like it is so," Lehi responded.

"How were they armed?" Moroni asked as he gave Lehi a hard look. That the Zoramites had defected to the enemy was a war secret and Moroni was not ready to inform the army of that fact. He was not happy with Lehi but he knew it was only a matter of time before the truth was revealed.

"The ones I saw were all carrying hand weapons, swords, cimeters, small hunting bows and spears, but no body armor or helmets. They shot arrows at us, but I could not see how many archers they had."

"Is there any reason to think they are going someplace else other than here to this camp?" The sergeant major looked at the points on the map that the sergeant identified and asked in his usual calm but gravelly tone. He acted almost bored and a bit annoyed. The old soldier had seen more battles and sat in more war councils than anyone else in camp. For him, the thrill of an impending battle had worn out long ago.

"I don't think so, Sergeant Major. There are small trails running off the main road, but no roads large enough to move an entire army between these locations. Also, the way they attacked my two soldiers and tried to move against us ... it makes me believe they know we are here and they want blood. I'm sure they know where we are, and they are coming for us." The sergeant finished his report and slowly backed away from the table. There was a long pause as each man contemplated the sergeant's last words.

"Very well, Sergeant; well done. If there are no other questions ...?" Moroni paused and looked at Lehi, who slightly shook his head to say no. He looked at Teancum, who also shook his head. "Then you are excused. Report to your commanding officer, get some food and rest if you can. You know what is coming so prepare yourself and your men the best you can."

"Thank you, sir," the three scouts said at the same time. They all saluted and exited the tent.

"Options, gentlemen?" Moroni asked. He walked around the table and stood with the other three in the middle of the tent. Teancum spoke first.

"The camp's supplies are not ready to move, if we pull back without taking the supplies, we will avoid the battle, but in less than three days without our supply of food or water, the army will suffer greatly."

"And the Lamanites will have our left-behind equipment to more than support them while they lay siege to any city on the frontier," the sergeant major added.

"Captain Lehi?" Moroni questioned. "What is your opinion?"

Lehi's face showed surprise at being asked his opinion. After the stern look from Moroni he thought he had fallen out of favor with the boy general. Asking Lehi his opinion was the mark of a true leader. "Uh, well ... I think we fight them now or fight them later, it just doesn't matter," Lehi said waving a frustrated hand over the map. "Either way we are outnumbered and on the defensive."

The four men stood in silence, studying the map and pondering the situation. Almost unnoticed, an elderly female servant stooped over from age and wearing a plain homespun apron entered the tent through the back door carrying a tray with four cups and a large jug of fruit juice.

"The refreshment you requested, your Excellency." Her voice was breathy and weathered.

"Just put that over here," Moroni said gently. He pointed to an open spot next to him on the large map table. The sergeant major folded up the maps as the old maid approached the table. It was a security measure to keep the old one from seeing the battle plans. The servant set the tray down next to Moroni and grabbed the jug to fill the cups. Caught up in his thoughts, Moroni stepped back and accidentally bumped into the old servant, causing her to spill a large amount of the sweet liquid on the table. The maid gasped and quickly put the jug down as the men around the table stepped back to keep the splashing juice from getting on their clothing and armor. Moving quickly, she grabbed a large cloth she had tucked in her apron. The servant formed a V with her hands and, using the cloth between her hands, she caught up the juice before it ran onto the folded maps. The old woman then pushed the spilt liquid off the table and mopped up the remainder with the cloth.

Moroni watched with puzzlement as everything the old servant was doing took on a strange, slow quality. Something deep in the back of his mind was telling him to focus on the servant.

"Watch her," a still, quiet whisper crept into his thoughts. "Watch her actions and learn."

For some reason, during this surreal moment of watching the servant move, he was drawn to the V she formed with her hands and the cloth. It quickly struck Moroni that with that one movement she was able to stop the liquid from running onto the maps and all over the table. She then forced the sticky substance off the table. Watching the old woman cleaning the table, Moroni felt a blanket of warmth and peace fall over him.

"I know this feeling," he thought. "What is it Lord? What are you trying to tell me? Is the old one a spy; are we now in danger? No, this is a feeling of peace, not a warning. Am I to learn something from this?" The feeling intensified when Moroni asked that question in his mind.

"My apologies, great one," the old servant lamented. She picked up the jug and, hugging it like a crying baby, she backed away from the table.

"The fault is mine. No harm done. Some juice, please?" Moroni asked, while holding out his cup. Shaking, she slowly filled his cup, then, setting the jug down, she bowed and backed out of the tent. Moroni watched for several seconds as the mortified old woman walked away.

Teancum, Lehi and the sergeant major all looked at each other with puzzled and questioning eyes, wondering what Moroni was doing.

Like a crack of lighting, it suddenly came to Moroni. "Of course," he whispered. "Thank you, Lord." Quickly, he spun back around to face his captains. He drank the entire contents of the cup in one gulp and, in two steps, Moroni was up against the table again. He had fire in his eyes.

"Gentlemen," he smiled, "I have a plan."

The three other leaders moved back to the table and, with a bit of confusion, looked at their young commander. Moroni unfolded the maps and spun the top map around so he could read it.

"Here," he pointed to the map. "This is the road they are coming down, yes?"

"Yes," Lehi answered slowly, a question in his tone.

"Which means, if they follow this road, they will come out of the jungle here, into the open lands where we are camped?"

"Yes," Lehi again responded with a bit of frustration mixed with sarcasm. Lehi looked at Teancum who also had a puzzled look in his eyes.

Moroni smiled and nodded, never taking his eyes off the map.

"What is it? What are you thinking?" Teancum asked.

Moroni formed his hands into a V and placed them right on top of the markings on the map that indicated where the road left the jungle and emptied into the open ground where they were camped. Moroni held his hands in place and looked at each member of his command staff with a giant grin on his face. Teancum was the first to understand what Moroni was trying to say with his hands on the map.

"The jungle is too thick for them to go around in force. They must come out into the open to fight," he said, smiling back at his general.

Moroni nodded in agreement. Lehi quickly understood and added his observation.

"Yes," he barked. "The scout said they are moving at a dead run. Their army could be spread out for miles along the road. They won't have time or the numbers to form battle ranks. They will be too tired to overcome a preplanned defensive trap if it's waiting for them when they get here."

Moroni nodded again in agreement. He and Lehi exchanged a look of understanding. Lehi raised his eyebrows and nodded, giving a look back to Moroni that he thought this just might work. Moroni stood upright and gave his orders.

"Sergeant Major, have all noncombat personnel continue to break camp, get the wagons loaded and ready to move as soon as they can. Make sure they are armed and ready to defend themselves if our lines break, but their job is to square the camp away."

"Yes, sir," the old soldier replied.

"Captain Lehi."

"Sir?"

"I want our combat-ready soldiers fully armored, in battle ranks and waiting at the opening of the jungle road. Form them into a giant V to funnel the enemy into a kill zone. Put our archers behind the ranks and set them up for point-blank fire into the Lamanite ranks as they emerge from the jungle."

"Yes sir," Lehi said.

"Captain Teancum."

"Yes, sir?"

"Gather your Ghost Soldiers. Deploy them in the jungle on both sides of the road. Their job will be to kill any Lamanites who leave the road and try to outflank us by moving through the jungle. If they try to stand and fight with Lehi, there will be a logjam of soldiers on the road. That should make for easy pickings for your men."

"Yes, sir," Teancum spoke with a smile on his face. "Finally, a chance to show the mettle of my men," he thought to himself.

"I will be with the cavalry behind the formations, directing the fight and standing ready to exploit our advantage," Moroni continued. "I will ride them down when they try to run away, or reinforce our lines if needed. Questions?"

There were none.

"Very well, gentlemen, you have my orders. Godspeed, and I pray He will help us all."

"Yes, sir," they responded. The leaders saluted their commander. Moroni returned the salute and dismissed them to their assignments.

Teancum and Lehi exited the tent at the same time.

Lehi glanced at Teancum and then back at the tent. "I see his father in him," Lehi softly spoke.

"You don't think he is ready to lead, do you?" Teancum asked bluntly.

CHAPTER TWELVE

"Do you, Teancum?" Lehi asked in return. "Are you ready to pin all our hopes of freedom on a boy? A sound battle plan does not a victory make. You know better than most what we face."

PREPERATIONS FOR BATTLE

Squaring his shoulders, Teancum moved to look directly into Lehi's eyes. His strength showed, along with the passion behind his words.

"I know this, Lehi: The chief judges and Alma the Great all gave their consent for Moroni to assume complete control over all matters concerning this war. Not at any time—from father Nephi to the time that good King Mosiah ended the reign of the monarchs and established a reign of judges until now—has any one person wielded such power over the Nephites. For all practical purposes, he has been declared king while we are at war. He understands this. He was taught well by his father, and he is willing to listen and heed the counsel of his captains."

There was a long pause as the two men looked into each other's eyes. Teancum and Lehi were two of the greatest warriors the Nephites had ever known. They were men of honor and personal conviction, but times had changed, and they both were dealing with the uncertain future in their own ways.

"Yes," Teancum continued, "I think Moroni is ready to lead. The real question is, are we ready to be good soldiers and do as we are commanded?"

"I am a good soldier, and I will lead my men into battle as I have done for all these years!" Lehi barked. "But know this," he continued, stepping closer to Teancum and speaking in a lower, more passionate voice, "I will not sacrifice the lives of my men or the freedom of my people for the ego of a boy who would be general. He has a sound plan, but we are still outnumbered at least four to one. Those are odds even his father would be challenged to overcome."

Teancum broke the tension with a jovial comment and slightly sarcastic smile. "Well, Captain Lehi," he said, slapping Lehi on the back, "regardless, it looks like by tomorrow night we will both have an answer to this question."

Lehi grunted, put on his helmet and started to walk toward his waiting horse.

"For liberty, my brother." Teancum spoke. He extended his hand to Lehi as he walked past.

Lehi turned. "For liberty," he responded. He took the few steps back to Teancum and shook his hand. They looked again into each other's eyes, knowing that if the enemy struck now this might be the last time they peacefully met in the flesh. Personal feelings aside, both men deeply respected the other, and both knew they only wanted what was best for the Nephites.

"I'll see you on the field, Chief Captain Teancum."

"Godspeed, Chief Captain Lehi."

With that, they parted ways. Lehi mounted his horse and rode down the hill and toward the assembly area with two of his own soldiers following close behind.

Teancum remained outside the large command tent, standing motionless for several seconds with his eyes closed. Using the calming breathing techniques he learned as a young physician and improved upon while hunting his family's killers in the mountains outside Zarahemla, he took several long, deep breaths in through his nose and out his mouth. Tilting his head up, he could feel the warmth of the sun on his face. He focused on the sounds of the birds chirping in the distance. After a short time, he lowered his head and opened his eyes. Now focused, his demeanor had changed. He knew it was time to again be a hunter of men. His eyes were fixed and intense. His jaw line was taut, and he walked with purpose. He reached the edge of the small hill and looked down on the Nephite camp below. Teancum gazed toward a small encampment set a short distance from the main camp. He reached into the large leather satchel pouch that hung over his shoulder and took out a small, oddly shaped piece of wood with a length of leather rope attached to it. On one end of the rope was a loop that he put around his right hand and moved up onto his wrist. Teancum let the piece of wood fall toward the ground and worked to untangle the attached rope. With the rope straightened and the wood piece nearly touching the ground, Teancum began to swing the wood around his head in a wide circle.

As the wooden object gained speed, it created a low-pitched vibrating sound. The faster Teancum swung the object around his head the louder the sound became. Soon the strange vibration was attracting the attention of soldiers in the camp; several of them looked up to the top of the hill to see who or what was creating the noise. Some of the soldiers in the camp knew instantly what that noise was and what it meant. Those soldiers quickly started back to the small encampment outside the main camp. One soldier, who was standing in the middle of the small separate encampment next to a large cooking fire, looked up at Teancum and raised his right hand above his head as if to let Teancum know that he could hear his signal. Teancum stopped swinging the wooden object and raised his right hand in the air in response to the man in camp. Teancum then lifted one finger and made several small circles above his head. He pointed to the encampment, signaling to his Ghost Soldiers to rally to the center of their camp. The soldier by the fire acknowledged the signal and responded by shouting commands to the soldiers around him to assemble. Teancum removed the leather rope from around his wrist, rewrapped it around the small wooden object, replaced the object in his satchel and walked to where his horse was waiting for him.

In one fluid motion, Teancum mounted his horse and quickly rode to the small encampment. As he jumped off his horse, the soldier he signaled to came running up to him.

"Sir, all present and accounted for."

"Excellent, Lieutenant. We haven't much time. I need to speak to the men right away."

They walked together toward the assembled men standing in formation. A mean-looking sergeant, bristling with muscles, called the formation to attention. Teancum stopped and looked out over the band of men before him.

"My Ghost Soldiers!" he exclaimed.

"Sir, yes sir!" was the enthusiastic, unison response.

Standing at attention before Teancum were two hundred of the most disciplined and well-trained warriors the Nephites had ever known, each of them physically fit far beyond expectations for a normal soldier. They were lean with hard, bulging muscles created from tough physical training and extreme combat experiences like no other soldier in the Nephite army. Not just anyone could join the Ghost Soldiers' legendary unit. Teancum had created something special when he organized this group, and the requirements to join were very demanding. Each of these soldiers was a proven combat veteran prior to volunteering for this special assignment. Most held rank in the Nephite army as an officer or senior sergeant. All had demonstrated their abilities in leadership, combat tactics, physical fitness and bravery just to get a chance to try out for the unit.

"My brothers," Teancum continued, "the time has come for us to show General Moroni and the rest of the Nephite army what we all know to be true: That a small unit of well-trained and motivated warriors can engage a much larger force and, using sound tactics, superb training, and better weapons, defeat that larger force and turn the tide of the battle."

A shout went up from the assembled men as they raised their hands or weapons in the air in celebration of the news.

"Men," Teancum shouted. He held up his hands, gesturing to the soldiers to regain their composures. "Men, today we take the fight, our way of fighting, to the cursed Lamanites. We have been given the honor of flanking the jungle road on both sides where it empties into the open ground behind you and attacking the Lamanite army as it bottlenecks near the clearing. The Lamanites will be stuck on the road while fighting a blocking force created by General Moroni and his infantry, and the Lamanites will try to outflank them through the jungle. My orders to you are as follows: Prepare for jungle concealment and fighting and ready the noisemakers for psychological warfare. Take enough food, water and medical supplies and prepare yourselves for at least two days of hard fighting. The rest is to be packed and secured on the wagons and ready to move with the baggage trains. Now fall out and reform into an instructional formation, and I will lay out the plan to you all."

Upon command, the Ghost Soldiers moved from their line formation into a semicircle around Teancum. Those in the front few rows sat down or took a knee so that the soldiers in the back could see. Teancum took a long, thin branch from the woodpile next to the cooking fire and drew a crude map on the ground in front of the soldiers.

"A Company, you are to form a skirmish line on the east side of the jungle road, here; and B Company, you are on the west side. Set your ambush about one hundred paces from the road and your secondary fighting positions behind that. When the Lamanites hit the blocking force, there will be a backlog of enemy soldiers and some may try to out flank the main body by working their way through the thick jungle growth. When that happens, suck them in close to you and kill them quickly. Use the noisemakers as a diversion and try to make them think the woods are haunted. My hope is to cause a panic and force the remaining Lamanites to run back to the main body, causing even more confusion and fear. When General Moroni has the upper hand on the main body, we will move forward and crush them between us and our infantry. Questions?"

On the faces of his men, Teancum saw only smiles and anticipation of the upcoming battle. They nodded in agreement with their leader. These were well trained and disciplined men. They all understood what to do.

"No questions?" Teancum asked again. When none were raised, he went on. "Good. Then we need to be in position as soon as possible. Company and platoon commanders, report to my tent in one hour for final briefing. Sergeants, break down this camp and get your men ready for battle. Dismissed!"

Another shout went up as men began to move away and prepare for the coming conflict.

Lehi was busy rallying his troops, as well. Riding through camp he shouted, "Commanders, assemble on me!" Lehi's shouts were completely unnecessary; all he had to do was have a trumpeter sound the commanders' call to get the leaders of the different infantry units to come to his location, but he wanted to excite and inspire the soldiers in the camp. He knew most of the men and boys before him had never tasted battle. He wanted to show the men he was not afraid, and he hoped they would draw courage from his example. He could see there was still much to do to ready the camp to move. When Lehi reached the center of the camp, several young soldiers stopped what they were doing and came over to him.

"Are you ready for a fight, boys?" Lehi shouted while guiding his horse in a circle around the gathering of young men.

"Yea," was a timid answer from some of the gathered soldiers.

"What?" Lehi shouted back.

"Yes, sir!" the response was louder but still lacked the raw emotion Lehi was hoping to hear.

"Ready or not, a fight is coming and it's coming today. So prepare yourselves for glory, men."

The sounds of galloping horses could be heard as Lehi turned to face the infantry commanders arriving at his location.

"Sir, your orders?" one of the commanders asked.

"Stop whatever you are doing and have all men and strong lads who are able to wield a weapon and carry a shield assembled on the training grounds ready for battle, right now! Those who are not able to fight for whatever reason, have them report to the sergeant major for work details. Make it happen!"

"Yes, sir!" was the response as shouts went out and drums and trumpets were played to sound the alarm. As the alarm rang out, men dropped what they were doing and ran for their equipment and weapons. In a short time, several formations of infantry were assembled on the training ground, armed and ready for a fight.

"Bring me a map of the valley and something to write with," Lehi shouted to one of his men. He dismounted and walked to where the infantry commanders were gathered. Quickly, two soldiers brought him a small wooden table along with a map skin, some ink and a quill for writing.

"Gentlemen, gather around," Lehi ordered his field commanders.

"General Moroni has issued the following directions. Our scouts have spotted the Lamanites moving toward us down the main road. They will be here by dusk." Lehi pointed directly to the part of the road coming out of the jungle and paused to let the reality of the situation sink in to his commanders.

"We are to form our fighting force into a large V shape at the edge of the clearing where the road empties into the valley from the jungle, here." Lehi unrolled the map and marked a V on it using the quill and ink to show the location he was referring to.

"Teancum and his so-called Ghost Soldiers," Lehi said a bit sarcastically, "are to hide in the woods and try to keep the enemy from outflanking us." Lehi marked on the map the location of Teancum's units. "General Moroni will be with the cavalry to support us and plug any holes in our lines created by the attacking Lamanites. We, gentlemen, are to stand and fight. The plan is to catch them unprepared as they exit the jungle and stop them from forming into ranks to attack us. The jungle is too thick for them to flank us in mass and our pre-positioning will mean only a small portion of them will be able to fight at the same time. We want to take away the advantage of their superior numbers. I want our heavy armor and large shields at the front of each formation. Archers are to stand ready for point blank fire behind the formation. We will be at a slight angle to each other, so advise your archers to watch the crossfire."

Lehi looked his commanders in the eyes. "Gentlemen, we will not fall back or regroup because there is no place to go and no one is coming to help. If one soldier goes down, pull him clear and fill the hole with another soldier. Whatever it takes, you and your men must stand your ground. 1st and 2nd Battalions on the right, 3rd and 4th Battalions on the left. I will be the point of the V here." He marked his position on the map with a dramatic flair. "Have your men form up on me. Close up all the gaps in the lines; leave no holes for the enemy to exploit. If even a few get past us, all is lost, gentlemen. We have only two outcomes available to us: victory or death." Lehi looked back up from the map and again into the eyes of his commanders.

"Questions, gentlemen?" The men stood in awkward silence, absorbing what they had just heard.

"Sir," one of the sub-commanders spoke, "this type of fighting has never been tried by this army, only tested. It's still just a theory. Is now the time to try something like this?"

"Time is a commodity we don't have, if the scouts' reports are true. By nightfall we will know the fate of freedom and justice for this land. Listen to me, gentlemen; if this plan fails ..." Lehi paused and gesturing for his commanders to move closer to him, he lowered his voice to just above a whisper. "If our lines break, look to me to assume command of the whole army and follow my lead. We will rally the troops and finish this the old way, our way. Are we clear?"

"Yes, sir," the men said in unison.

"Excellent, you are dismissed to see to your men." Lehi finished as he dropped the writing quill on the map.

Moroni was sitting on a wooden stool under a large shade tree and strapping on the metal shin guards to his leg when the young sergeant who was supervising the guard force interrupted.

"Sir?"

"Yes, Sergeant, what is it?" He answered without looking up to see who was talking.

"General, the command tent and all your belongings are packed. The maps and camp logs are stored in the lock box under the teamster's seat and your personal guards are ready."

The sergeant was dressed in full armor and was leading Moroni's horse as well as his own. Behind him, all of the soldiers who were assigned as Moroni's personal guard were mounted on their horses and fully armed with helmets, shields, body armor, spears, and swords. One soldier was holding up a large, green battle flag with the symbol of a great sword sewn on it. This was the symbol Moroni had chosen for his command flag, to remind all who looked upon it that the commander of the Nephite army was carrying the Sword of Laban.

"Thank you, Sergeant. Give me one moment, please."

"Yes, sir."

Moroni turned his back to his men. The hilltop where he stood was now void of any distractions or from anything blocking the beautiful panoramic view of the jungle-covered mountains. A gentle breeze was blowing his hair and moving the ends of his tunic while he stood and absorbed the scene before him. Moroni closed his eyes and tilted his head back to feel the warmth of the midday sun on his face.

"It's so quiet now," he thought. "Why has it come to this? Am I ready to lead these men into battle?

"What if you fail?" a dark voice rang in his ear.

"Failure?" he questioned himself. "What if I have led my army into a death trap?" Deep in the back of his mind, panic rose and Moroni began to doubt his abilities.

"It is true that I am not my father. I am not prepared to lead a grand army into combat. I am just a boy." Moroni felt panic build in his mind as images of death and ruin flashed across his conscience. Then, suddenly, a warm peace wrapped around him like a thick blanket on a cold night. All time and motion stopped for Moroni and he heard a voice as quiet as a whisper, but with all the command of mighty thunder echoing in his mind:

"Be still and know that I am the Lord."

Moroni's heart burned in his chest and all doubt instantly left.

"Forgive me, Father, for having ever doubted you." He whispered. "Whatever happens is your will, and I am just your humble servant."

Moroni took a long, deep breath. He held it and then blew it out past his lips. He turned to face his men.

"I do not command armies from a distance," Moroni said forcibly. He picked up and donned his armored chest plate. "I lead from the front, and if you men are with me then the front is where you will be. Are you with me?"

A shout went up from the gathered soldiers and Moroni climbed onto his horse.

"My helmet!" he commanded.

A young boy ran up to the side of Moroni's massive horse and handed the large helmet up to his master. While Moroni was putting the helmet on, the boy ran to grab Moroni's shield and spear that were leaning against the tree and handed them to the general.

"Follow me!" Moroni shouted as he spurred his mount to a gallop and charged down the hill and toward Captain Lehi's formations.

TEANCUM DRAWS FIRST BLOOD

The scene was more pathetic than inspiring as Lamanite men and boys struggled to maintain the hard-driven pace set by their Zoramite commander, who was following them on horseback. All through the long formation, soldiers moved at the point of total collapse. Several, who had fallen out of rank completely exhausted, were left lying on the ground without medical aid or water. They were simply left where they fell as the Lamanites were ordered to abandon the fallen and push forward, farther down the mountainous jungle road toward the Nephite camp. The pace of the march, the heat of the day, the distance traveled and the lack of food and water had transformed battle-ready Lamanite soldiers into mindless machines as the seemingly never-ending road continued to wind around yet another bend and over the next hilltop. The enthusiasm and blood lust the Lamanite soldiers felt when they found and killed the two wounded Nephites riders alone on the road slowly gave way to the crushing jungle heat and almost complete exhaustion from the forced march. Those feelings were replaced by a mindless response to commands, and the boisterous shouting had been replaced by the rhythmic sounds of feet hitting the ground and heavy breathing.

Zerahemnah rode near the back of the long formation. Several of the Zoramite sub-commanders followed close behind Zerahemnah. Without stopping, the Lamanite leader took a drink from a wine skin, and then took a bite from a crunchy apple. One of his scouts ran up to him from the front of the formation.

"Report," Zerahemnah ordered, with a mouthful of half-chewed apple.

"Sir," The young Zoramite scout raised his ax and pointed down the path in the direction of the Nephites. "Most of the mile markers along the road have been removed, but by my count, I figure this army has traveled 15 miles. At this pace we should arrive at the Nephite camp in about one hour. I also have been informed by many of the sub-commanders that we have lost close to three hundred who have fallen by the wayside, too weak to continue this forced march."

Zerahemnah angrily spit the remaining bits of apple out of his mouth and all over several Lamanites who were running next to his horse. They were not happy about being showered with bits of fruit and glared up at their leader as he rode past.

"What?" he shouted, wiping his mouth with the sleeve of his tunic. "Those undisciplined dogs. A simple twenty-mile forced march and we lose the equivalent of one battalion because they are too tired!" He snorted as he pulled up on the reins of his horse. "Sound the halt!"

A signalman, who was running a bit behind Zerahemnah and carrying a large horn, responded to the command, lifted the instrument and tried to blow the horn. He tried more than once but was unable to draw enough breath into his lungs or hold up the horn while continuing to run.

"Stop moving, you idiot, and sound the halt!" Zerahemnah exclaimed in anger. The trumpeter stopped running and, with his last bit of reserved energy, managed to sound the signal to halt. When the sub-commanders heard the sound of the trumpet, they shouted the command, "Halt." This command alerted the other sub-commanders' signalmen to blow their horns and tell the army to halt. Within seconds, there was a resounding relay of horns and the shouting from unit leaders ordering the Lamanite army to stop and rest. As the disorganized group came to a stop, many of the Lamanite soldiers fell to the ground from pure exhaustion. Others bent over at the waist or leaned against each other or a tree or rock for support. No one took up security positions or sent scouts into the wood line to ensure that they were stopping in a safe location.

A few of the Lamanite leaders were shouting orders, trying to organize their men and get them back into some kind of formation. They weren't having any luck. The army had simply fallen apart, and all that was left were thousands of men and boys strung out along the wide dirt road who were too physically spent to maintain any sort of soldierly discipline. In fact, the only people moving with any purpose were several of the older, more experienced Lamanite warriors. Their efforts were directed at trying to stop

the soldiers who were blowing the horns and keep them from giving away the position of the army to anyone who could hear the sounds echoing throughout the mountains.

Very near the front of the long Lamanite column of troops, one young soldier was blindly following orders and blowing his trumpet. "Stop you fool!" one older soldier shouted as he pushed the instrument out of the grasp of the young soldier blowing it. "Now every living thing within 10 miles knows we are here!"

The Lamanite soldiers sitting or standing around him looked at the surrounding mountains and saw flocks of wild birds take flight, squawking angrily in reaction to the sudden blasts from the horns. They all quickly figured out the dangerous tactical error they had just committed.

Hoping to cover for himself, the young trumpeter spoke up, "I'm just following orders. Besides, what does it matter if the Nephites know where we are? They will all be dead by nightfall, and I will be sleeping on Nephite pillows, eating Nephite food and drinking Nephite wine."

A half-hearted shout went up from the Lamanite soldiers gathered around him.

"Only a fool will think he has won a war before ever having tasted battle, young one. I'll remember you said such things when this is all over," the older warrior said in a sarcastic tone. Having made his point, the old one let it go at that, too physically spent to continue the debate. Wiping the sweat from his eyes, he sat down on the ground next to his companions. Several Lamanites giggled under their breath at the rebuke he had given the young trumpeter. The older soldier was almost asleep when, in an attempt to save face, the cocky trumpeter responded to the laughing and sarcasms.

"What do you know of battle?" he challenged. "My guess is you all were just pig farmers who got drunk and got lost on your way to market. You joined the army because you were too stupid to find your way home." The boy chuckled, and then looked around for some validation from the soldiers sitting around him. None of them moved or acknowledged his remarks. The forced march had simply wiped them out. Physically and mentally, no one was up for anything except resting, rubbing their tired feet and being still for as long as they could.

After a few more seconds of awkward silence the old one managed to say, "I wish my life were as simple as a pig farmer's life, boy. But I do know two things about war. First, it is never a good idea to announce to the army, you plan to attack, that you are coming. It gives them a chance to ready themselves and the advantage is always for the defense if they are ready for the attack. Second, carrying a horn into battle is much different than carrying a sword."

That rebuke evoked a much louder laugh from the others than before. Embarrassed, the boy blushed three shades of red and angrily stomped off into the jungle in an attempt to distance himself from the laughing men. Just before he reached the edge of the jungle, he turned and spoke loudly to the resting Lamanites.

"The enemy is just around the corner, and you are all too scared or too tired to fight. Well then, just sit there like cowards and rest. I will be back with the head of Moroni before sundown."

"Don't go too far, lad. You will need to sound the horn when it is time for us to eat dinner." There was a roar of laughter as the boy, now flush faced, turned in disgust and walked into the jungle growth. As he walked into the thick brush, he pulled out the long dagger he carried strapped to his waist.

"I'll show them," he spoke in a loud whisper. "I'm going to kill the first Nephite I see and take his sword."

The boy slashed his knife at a large fern, pretending it was a Nephite soldier. "They'll see. When I come back with the trophies of war from all the Nephites I kill, they will stop laughing at me and respect me as a great warrior."

He continued to walk deeper into the jungle, slashing and stabbing at the large ferns. He had walked father into the overgrowth than he thought when, suddenly, the sound of a breaking twig behind him caused him to freeze in place. A few seconds later, a second twig was broken and an icy chill shot down his spine. The young Lamanite realized he was not alone in that part of the jungle. The jungle creatures also seemed to realize it as the noises of the birds, insects and distant animal calls suddenly stopped. Silence surrounded the young soldier, and true panic welled up inside him. Someone or something was slowly moving behind him. He could feel it. He spun around to face the unseen presence, but nothing was there. A quiet whistle came across the jungle from somewhere in front. That whistle was answered by a strange chirping animal noise from very close behind him. Shocked into near paralysis, he forced his body to slowly turn to see what or who was making the noises. What he saw made his horror complete. The image he was facing was something out of a dreadful nightmare. Two jungle demon monsters in human form stood not more than five feet away from him. They held metal weapons in their hands, but their clothing and skin were painted the colors of the jungle itself. Green, brown and black, with branches and leaves seeming to grow right out of their skin. This made it look like they were part of the lush surroundings. Scared completely out of his mind, the young Lamanite shook as he tried to raise his dagger in defense. The two man-shaped jungle creatures slowly stepped forward. The young soldier took two steps backward, unaware that a third creature was quietly rising up behind him from the ground.

This creature, dressed and camouflaged just like the other two, was actually Captain Teancum and the others were two of his Ghost Soldiers. The first two soldiers were slowly moving forward, forcing the enemy soldier to move backwards toward Teancum. The young Lamanite was finally within reach and Teancum took from his weapons belt a thin, braided leather cord that had wooden handholds on both ends. He quickly passed the cord over the head of the young enemy, wrapped the cord around the unsuspecting Laminate's neck, violently pulled the cord tight and, with all his might, cut off the flow of oxygen and blood to the head of the young Lamanite. Teancum held tightly as the enemy soldier dropped his knife and struggled to free himself from the choking effects of the cord wrapped around his neck. The soldier kicked and twisted, gasping for air and trying to claw at the cord, but Teancum held fast. Teancum violently jerked down on the handles at the ends of the wrapped cord, bringing the doomed soldier to the ground flat on his back. Twisting his wrists, Teancum instantly snapped the boy's neck and the body went limp. Waiting for several seconds to ensure the Lamanite was dead, Teancum unwrapped the cord from around the dead Lamanite's neck and stuffed it back into his equipment belt around his waist.

"He is just a boy. What is he doing out here alone?" one of the camouflaged soldiers said to Teancum as he knelt down on the ground and inspected the lifeless body.

"Looks like he was a trumpeter," the second warrior whispered. He bent down to pick up the metal instrument the boy had been carrying. He grabbed the instrument and walked the few paces to where Teancum was now standing. He handed the metal horn to his captain, who took it and inspected it quickly.

"Wars are not fought by only old men. With this, he could have summoned a thousand Lamanites who would have come here and killed us all. He made his choice to support the enemies of freedom. And I made mine to kill him to save the lives of my men and hold this position. Now, cover the body and cover up the scene. We are Ghost Soldiers; we leave no traces."

Both men reacted instantly to the orders from their captain. They brushed away the foot tracks left in the soft dirt and mud then moved the dead body to a shallow depression behind a large tree and covered it with a stack of large ferns and leaves. When the task of covering their tracks was complete, the three men melted back into the jungle growth just as quickly and quietly as they had appeared.

ZERAHEMNAH ATTACKS

When the Lamanites sounded their horns, everyone in the Nephite camp stopped moving and turned toward the mountains and the direction of the sounding trumpets and the flocks of angry birds. A sudden stillness rushed over the soldiers as reality sank in. The enemy was close, almost to the edge of the jungle now. As angry flocks of birds rose higher in the sky, Moroni spun his horse around and looked at Lehi, who was standing among his own group of soldiers. With a sense of urgency Moroni barked out an order.

"We're out of time, Captain Lehi; move the infantry into position."

"Yes, sir," Lehi answered, and then said to his men, "You heard the general, men. Move your troops into battle formations, Go, go, go," he shouted as he clapped his hands together several times. The men with Lehi scattered, shouting orders as the main body of the Nephite army prepared to move toward the jungle road.

The vastly outnumbered Nephite army moved on foot, by battalions, from the assembly area toward the jungle opening about a mile away. Lehi mounted his horse and joined Moroni in riding up and down the line of soldiers moving toward the chosen battleground

"I intermixed the more seasoned soldiers with the raw recruits to help bring balance to the lines," Lehi said to Moroni as they rode past the line of troops. The two leaders continued to talk to each other and to direct the army while it moved in a calm and well-disciplined manner toward the jungle road. The Nephite cavalry was divided into two groups, each with the responsibility of supporting their own side of the defensive line.

General Moroni rode up and down the line, ensuring the formation was set in place correctly.

Long, dark shadows were forming off the western mountains as the sun began its descent behind the ancient rock and earthen monuments.

Zerahemnah had waited long enough. He could not hold back any longer. Rest or not, he knew the Nephite camp was close, very close, and the hour was growing late. He had to reach the camp before dark or risk spending the night on the jungle road. This was just not an option. Every day he went without attacking the enemy was a day he risked losing control of the army. He had been able to hold over his soldiers' heads the promises of looting, pillaging and taking captors as slaves back to their homes as strong motivators for the Lamanite soldiers. After days of constant marching and little food or water, the soldiers were tired and Zerahemnah could feel his iron grip on the mass of soldiers slipping. He moved his Zoramite brethren around the different units in his army and that helped to maintain discipline and keep the Lamanites in line, but even those mighty warriors knew they were hopelessly outnumbered if the Lamanites chose to turn on them.

"They must fear you more than they fear the enemy," he told the other Zoramites long before they started out on this campaign of terror against their brother Nephites. "If we can convince them to do our will, we can get the Lamanites and Nephites to kill each other and, when the dust settles, we will be there to take whatever we want. We will be kings among those who survive."

Now, with only a few hours of daylight left and his entire army physically spent and strung out for miles along this road, Zerahemnah was forced to reconsider his original plans of an all-out attack on the main Nephite camp. The very thought of stopping his campaign so close to total victory was making him quite angry. He looked around at the state of the men under his command. He could see they were all sitting or lying around trying to get out of the sun or find a comfortable spot to sleep. Some were drinking the last of their water from the water skins or slowly eating the last of their rations, while others just sat on the ground or leaned against one of the many trees. Up and down the road as far as he could see, Zerahemnah's powerful army was slowly breaking down.

"I need to get them up and moving," he thought. "We can't stay here for the night; there is no food, water or shelter here. If the Nephites were to get word of the condition of the army, they could sneak in during the night and kill all of us one by one. At the very least, the lack of food and water will bring mass desertions during the night. I must get my army on its feet and move the last few miles to the Nephite camp. Only a blood lust will keep them going now until we can pillage the camp of its supplies."

"Get up!" he shouted. "Get on your feet and move forward." Zerahemnah climbed down from his horse and started to kick the soldiers who were asleep around him. Slowly, the mass of exhausted soldiers around him got to their feet as the message was passed up and down the lines. Zerahemnah got back on his horse and, with his command staff in tow, he moved toward the front of the column, commanding his troops to get up. Within ten minutes, Zerahemnah was close to his army's front lines and felt he was ready to push forward to the final objective. Yet, none of the soldiers were showing the same eager motivation they showed earlier that day. Some even sat back down.

"You want me to ride ahead and tell the Nephites to come here to fight you here; would that make you feel better?" Zerahemnah said sarcastically. "Pride of the Lamanite race ... you men disgust me. Your hated enemies, the Nephites, are around the next bend, outnumbered by us and defenseless. Yet, here you men sit crying like old women that it's too hot and you're so tired. Maybe I should go back to your lands and tell your wives and daughters to come and fight the Nephite dogs. Hopefully, your children and old ones will enjoy having Nephite slaves and Nephite gold because when I march them up here they will surely be more enthused to fight than what I see before me now."

Zerahemnah maneuvered his horse in and around the disadvantaged Lamanites as he shouted.

"Cowards, I brought you to the edge of victory and complete dominance over your enemies and, at the last possible moment, you shrink from the fight. Now get up and act like men."

Those who were sitting on the ground in front of Zerahemnah found some inner strength and got to their feet, rejoining the ranks of other Lamanite soldiers trying to stand up. Zerahemnah gave the order to advance and the Lamanite drums and horns sounded the command to move.

A while later, a Zoramite warrior rode up to Zerahemnah from the leading edge of the long column.

"My lord, we have reached the Nephite camp."

A broad smile broke across Zerahemnah's face, and he spurred his horse forward.

The young Zoramite pointed down the road with his sword. "Just beyond that last bend in the road, no more than a mile away, is the break in the jungle where the enemy camp is located, my lord. The enemy is attempting to set up a blocking force at the edge of the clearing. If we move now, sir, we can catch them in the open and crush them like bugs."

The Lamanite soldiers near Zerahemnah picked up on the report, and excitement rocketed as the news of the enemy sighting traveled through the ranks.

"What say you, men?" Zerahemnah shouted as he spun his horse in a full circle. "I go to drink the blood of the Nephite, to take his gold and his women as my slaves. Who is with me?"

A shout went up from the hundreds of Lamanites now gathered around Zerahemnah.

"Then pass the word back that your commander is leading the charge, and we are engaged with the enemy. Press forward into battle. Stop for nothing until all the vile Nephites are wiped from the earth!"

A second shout went up as the men readied themselves for the final rush to the battleground.

"Forward!" Zerahemnah shouted, as he spurred his horse down the wide, tree-lined dirt road toward the final bend and the Nephite camp beyond.

Zerahemnah trotted along, keeping pace with the jogging Lamanites next to him, all the while encouraging them to show no fear and press onward. After a few hundred yards, he gently pulled back on the reins of his mount to allow more Lamanites to pass him.

"I'll let a few more get ahead of me," he thought. He watched several more soldiers run past, shouting war cries. "I am much too important to get killed or wounded in the first engagement of the war. I'll just let those fools in front of me spring Moroni's trap, if, in fact, there is a Nephite blocking force set."

CHAPTER SIXTEEN

THE GHOST SOLDIERS

They had been riding at a light gallop for the better part of the afternoon, and the sun was starting its descent behind the mountains as the young corporal spurred his mount to move up next to Amiha.

"Sir, the horses need to rest," he said.

"Okay, we will stop so we can quickly eat something and switch out the horses. That looks like a good place." Amiha responded as he pointed to a small break in the tree line. Amiha knew they could not take long. He needed to get to the capital city and see the prophet, then get back to Moroni with an answer. The fate of the Nephite nation could very well rest in his hands.

They stopped along the wide, well-traveled road that led to the capital city of Zarahemla. A small natural spring was flowing just off the road, and they climbed down from their horses to let their animals drink. The hours of hard riding had restricted the soldiers' blood flow and made their legs and feet numb. Standing or walking around was difficult at first for the two warriors but, as they moved around, their tired legs started to gain circulation, Amiha spoke.

"We are more than halfway there, so get your saddle and pack off that horse and put it on one of the spares. We will move faster on fresh mounts."

"Yes, sir."

Without talking, the two moved around the horses, exchanging the saddles and fitting the fresh mounts for travel. When they were done setting up for the next leg of the journey, they refreshed themselves by splashing water on their faces and refilling the water skins from the spring.

"Sir, can I ask you a question?" young Corporal Phan inquired. He pulled the leather laces securely to tie the full water skins onto his saddle.

"Sure, anything." Amiha glanced at the young soldier, and then turned to pull a strip of dried beef out of his own saddle bag.

"How long have you known General Moroni?"

"The general is like a brother to me," Amiha said. "I was a child when my father was killed in battle while serving under Moroni's father. His father took pity on my family and raised me as one of his own sons. I was with Moroni at the battle of Jershon, and I was there when Chief Judge Nephihah gave Moroni command over all the people in matters of war. When Moroni was anointed by Alma the prophet, I stood as his second at the ceremony."

"So, it is true; he was given complete control over the people of Nephi to wage war. So, is he our king as well as the general of the army?"

"No, it's easy to explain but hard to understand. You see, by the voice and will of the people, through the chief judges, Moroni has been given the power to do whatever he thinks is necessary to defend us. He has complete power to compel the population to do what he needs them to do to help defend our lands."

"Compel? So, he could start a draft or arrest a Nephite without a warrant if he thinks that person is a spy or usurper?"

"Yes, he could. He could even tax the people or force them into hard labor if he wanted."

The young corporal paused for a second while the reality of that statement sunk in. Fussing with his saddle, he continued his questions.

"Sir, please don't think I'm a dissenter, but how is this wise? King Mosiah abolished that system of a monarchy style government years ago and gave us self-governance with the chief judges so we could avoid having one man with so much power and control of the people. Remember the stories of wicked King Noah?"

"I know, Corporal, on face value it might be hard to understand, but there are some things you need to know to help you understand why the chief judges and the prophet allowed this to happen. First, this war is like no other we have faced. After the battle of Jershon two years ago, our forces were so depleted that it would take at least a full generation to raise up and train another army able to stand toe to toe with the Lamanites. Remember, we did not beat them in open war; it was General Moroni and his daring assault on the Lamanite king's own camp that brought the battle of Jershon to a close. By the time the battle ended, our army had been pushed back past the river, and we were very close to defeat and a complete slaughter."

"I know. My father and older brother were there. But, I still don't understand …"

Amiha held up his hand, "Let me finish. We are not a savage people like the Lamanites. We do not have a large standing army, and we do not live in a state of constant conflict like the Lamanites. You know that old joke that the only thing that will stop the Lamanites from fighting among themselves is a good war against the Nephites?"

The corporal grinned and nodded his head in approval.

"A young Lamanite is taught from the time he can stand to hold and use a weapon. Our children are taught to be farmers and merchants and good citizens. They teach their young to fight, plunder and kill. We teach ours math, science, religion and history."

"I understand that, sir, but how is that different from any other time in our history?"

"Well, in the past, there has always been some time between wars to allow us to regroup and gather our strength. We also benefited from having a small professional cadre of soldiers like Captain Teancum and his ghost warriors to keep the peace and act as officers if and when the civilian militias were needed. Now, it's been only two years since the battle of Jershon where so many of our brave and valiant professional soldiers were killed, and we are lacking in everything—equipment, manpower, quality leadership and, most of all, time. Moroni understands better than anyone the situation we are in and what it will take to lead us out of the danger."

The young soldier's face took on an inquisitive look. "Sir, may I ask how that is?"

"Well," Amiha continued as he finished filling his own water skins and tying them to his saddle, "Moroni was raised in a military family. His father and grandfather were great and powerful military leaders. Moroni learned the arts and strategies of war and leadership from them at a very young age. He has been a soldier all of his life. Moroni and I worked as squires for his father from the time we were very young, and Moroni was given his first command at the age of sixteen. Also, aside from the prophet, Moroni is the most spiritual man I have ever met. He is always praying or reading the words of the old ones. It was his idea to have the chaplains assigned to travel with the army; did you know that?"

The soldier shook his head no.

"Yeah, he thought it would help these new and untrained recruits more easily adapt to military life if they could have the constant companionship of a holy man in camp with them."

"I know it helps me to be able to speak to the chaplain when I need some advice," the corporal said.

"Well, there you go," Amiha responded. He tugged on the saddle straps to make sure they were tight, and then rubbed his hand across the horse's flank. "You also need to know that Moroni was taught by his father that, to be a good leader of men, you must first and always be a servant of the people, not their master. He was taught to cherish freedom above all else. Moroni knows no other way. It is as if God set all these things in his past to prepare him for the task at hand. Like God knew all of this was going to take place and made it so General Moroni was prepared for it ahead of time."

"Prepared for what, sir?"

"To save us," Amiha said matter-of-factly. "Save us from the Lamanites and ourselves, if necessary."

Those words rained down on the young soldier like stones from heaven. "Sir, from ourselves?"

"The cycle of humanity has been the same from the time of father Adam. When a society falls into chaos like during a devastating war or national emergency, the opportunity for a strong leader to guide us through the crisis emerges. If that person has evil in his heart, he becomes a dictator or calls himself king. But if he is humble and a servant to God and the people around him, when the danger has passed, the leader returns his power to the people and takes his place back among society. The chief judges and the prophet all saw this danger coming. They all agreed that Moroni was the right man for the job. The great judges' council in Zarahemla was convened and the will of the people was made known. They elected Moroni by an overwhelming majority to lead and prepare this people for the greatest threat to our freedom we have ever faced."

Amiha mounted his fresh horse and Corporal Phan picked up the conversation. "I understand what you are saying, sir. It's just hard to comprehend the enormity of it all."

"It even scares me to think about it sometimes," Amiha said. "We'll be in the presence of the prophet in a few hours; tell me how you feel about General Moroni after meeting Alma the Great."

Amiha spurred his horse forward, and the corporal rushed to finish prepping his horse. Swinging up into the saddle he quickly caught up with Amiha for the final leg of their journey.

"I still can't believe I am going to meet Alma the Great. What is he like in person, sir?"

Amiha just smiled and said, "You'll see soon enough."

Moroni reacted to the new sounds of drums and horns coming from deep in the tree line. He turned to face the road that led out of the lush overgrowth and could almost feel the pounding of thousands of Lamanite feet moving toward his small army. The sun was just starting to set. The last of the archers and support units moved into place behind the two columns of soldiers, in the V formation lining the jungle road. Moroni could see that Lehi stood ready, commanding his ground forces at the point of the V formation, and had to trust that Teancum had deployed his special soldiers. Everywhere Moroni looked, he saw fear. Fear in the faces of those around him, and fear in the eyes of the men and boys standing shoulder to shoulder, waiting for the hordes of enemy soldiers to come spilling out of the darkening shade masking the road in front of them.

Moroni knew fear. He knew the power of fear. He learned very early in his career as a soldier that fear could be a dreadful nemeses or a powerful ally. Experience taught that the emotions from the anticipation of combat were sometimes more overpowering and damaging than the actual battle. Standing firm in the face of an overwhelming, charging enemy is an unnatural instinct, especially if you are not a seasoned, veteran soldier, which most of his forces were not. When facing the prospect of combat, every cell of your body is begging you to drop your weapons and run as fast as you can. But you hold fast. You hold fast because you are a good soldier and you trust the man next to you. You trust him because he is just as scared as you are, but he is standing firm. Moroni knew that it only took one to break that trust and fall out of rank for the whole line to collapse and retreat.

From deep in the dark shadows cast by the trees covering the road, the sounds of charging men echoed across the field. Moroni scanned his armored line of men for that one soldier who might be the one to break. To his horror, he saw several men back up off the line and look around as if plotting a course to make a break and run for safety. Moroni knew he had to do something or he was going to lose control of his army. If they turned and ran now, the Lamanites would slaughter them all. An army is at its most vulnerable when it is fleeing from the battlefield. Moroni knew this and he had to act quickly to make sure his men didn't panic. He ordered his security element to wait, and he spurred his horse forward. He commanded a group of soldiers to make a hole in the line so he could pass to the center of the V formation. Moroni rode out alone and positioned himself where all the men under his command could see him. Holding his spear high in the air and pulling back on the reins of his horse, Moroni let out a war cry that could be heard by all. The soldiers surrounding him instantly took courage from Moroni's defiant act and joined him in the shouting. Moroni nudged his horse forward and galloped up and down the lines of troops, looking into their eyes.

"We are the Lord's anointed and protectors of his flock. … Do not be afraid!" Moroni shouted as he rode on. "Today the God of our Fathers has led the enemies of freedom into our hands. Before this night is over, you will come to know who the God of this earth is. You will come to know that you and your families are under His protection, and we are the instruments …"

Sounds of shouting and clanking metal coming from the jungle cut Moroni's inspirational speech short. Moroni spun his horse to face the noise just as several wild-eyed Lamanites came bursting out from the shadows and onto open ground. Moroni felt beads of sweat run down his face. He had almost forgotten how intimidating Lamanite warriors could be with their shaved heads and painted faces.

Seeing a lone Nephite officer on horseback in front of them, the Lamanite soldiers let out a war cry and surged forward to attack the Nephite leader. They seemed oblivious to the fact that they were surrounded by a wall of armored Nephites. In an instant Moroni felt the swell of justified anger rise up within himself. He turned his horse around and faced the enemy. The Lamanite soldiers in the lead slowed their pace as they discovered they had just entered a death trap. Stopping completely, they looked around to see nothing but large, metal shields interlocked and Nephite soldiers with large spears and drawn swords standing several ranks deep. The Nephite military banners and command flags flapped in the evening breeze as the entire Nephite army held their positions, waiting for orders from their commanders.

As more Lamanite soldiers poured into the open ground from the darkness of the overgrown wilderness trail, the sounds of their war cries tapered off as they, too, began to comprehend what they were seeing. Even more Lamanites came out of the jungle and were stopped by the scene before them. Just as Moroni had predicted, the swelling ranks of Lamanites caused a jam of bodies at the tree line. They stood in puzzled confusion and fear, gaping at the Nephite trap they had run into.

The Lamanite assault fizzled out before it could even begin. Because Zerahemnah refused to lead from the front, the undisciplined Lamanites did not know how to react to the armored Nephite formations. Seeing that his inspired plan was working, Moroni smiled and dismounted. He pulled his large shield off the saddle bag and slowly drew the great Sword of Laban from its sheath. With the flat side of his massive sword, he gently smacked the hind end of his horse, urging it to trot off the field and out of danger. Moroni took two slow steps forward and, facing the ever-growing Lamanite army, he settled into a combat stance, like a massive stone. The entire Nephite army witnessed Moroni's act of valor as he stood alone, facing down the Lamanites in the center of the trap the Nephites had set. With renewed courage, faltering Nephite soldiers reformed their battle lines and stood shoulder to shoulder as unwavering as their young leader.

As more and more Lamanites were shouting and pushing forward from deep in the jungle, trying to move the stopped formation, word got back to Zerahemnah that his main force had made contact with the Nephites, but they were not attacking.

"Why are we not moving?" he shouted to the Zoramite who brought him the news.

"Sir, the soldiers in the front ranks aren't assaulting forward. They are stuck where the road spills out into the open, just staring at the Nephites' armored columns."

Zerahemnah was furious. "Go around those cowards," he shouted to the men next to him, "… through the trees; go around them!" Zerahemnah pointed to both sides of the jungle road. He directed his men to move through the thick growth and flank the incompetent, stalled soldiers at the front of the formation and attack the Nephites from the sides. A mass of Lamanites left the road in both directions, bursting through the jungle growth. They whooped and shouted as they went bounding around the massive trees and moved through the almost impassable array of large ferns and dense undergrowth.

Zerahemnah smirked and snorted with contempt as he watched hundreds of Lamanites rush into the jungle to flank both sides of the Nephite formations. He envisioned the hapless Nephites surrounded on all sides by his warriors and fighting for their lives.

"This will soon be over," he said in a cocky, matter of fact tone. He readjusted his position in his saddle and grabbed for his wine skin.

Suddenly, the sounds of a deep, hollow animal roar came from the right side of the jungle. Zerahemnah spun around in his saddle to see where the sound was coming from, and the rest of the Lamanite soldiers froze in fear.

Zerahemnah's horse, startled by the sudden roar, bucked up causing the Lamanite leader to spill a large amount of red liquor down his chest.

"What manner of beast was that?" Zerahemnah asked. He fought to regain control of his startled horse. An old Lamanite standing nearby shook his head to indicate that he did not know.

From the left side of the jungle growth, a second roar echoed from the trees. This one was high pitched and sounded almost like some great cat. Zerahemnah and those with him instantly turned to the left and several Lamanites held their weapons at the ready.

The Lamanites who were running through the dense undergrowth to outflank the Nephites were moving quickly and carelessly through the thick brush to get into position to attack. They showed no discipline in their efforts. They sent no advance party to flush out an ambush. They employed no tactical movements to support each other in case of attack. Instead, they ran wildly and let out war cries as they moved chaotically through and around the natural jungle obstacles.

When the strange and intimidating animal sounds again bellowed from the shadows, the Lamanites running in the jungle reacted in fear, some standing in shocked stillness, some dropping to their knees on the jungle floor. The roars coming from deep in the jungle echoed off the trees, making it very difficult to tell if whatever beast made the noise was close or far away.

Five Lamanites, who moved faster than the rest and had distanced themselves from the main party, now found themselves at the far edge of the Lamanite advance. Alerted by the horrible roars, they moved more carefully through the woods. They came to the edge of the trees and entered a small clearing. In the middle of the clearing, they saw a single large bush sticking out strangely in the middle of the open grassy area. Not wanting to come face to face with whatever made the dreadful roaring noise, the Lamanites, with spears at the ready, moved forward cautiously through the clearing and around the oddly located bush. The last man of this small squad trailed behind several paces, bringing up the rear. He was younger than his fellow soldiers and wanted so much to learn from their example. As he watched his four brother Lamanites walk past the strange-looking plant, he realized something.

"There is something odd about that bush," the young Lamanite thought. He stopped a few paces away and looked closely at it. "It almost looks like it's breathing," he whispered.

Then something moved inside the bush, and what the boy soldier saw next took his breath away.

"Eyes!" he gasped. The bush was looking at him and the horror of it froze the blood in his heart. "The bush has eyes!"

The plant suddenly moved and unfolded its branches, like a giant bird stretching its wings. The soldier watched, shocked into a panicked silence, as one of Teancum's well-camouflaged Ghost Soldiers instantly grew to the height of his own spear and changed from an odd-looking bush to a man. The Lamanite was petrified with pure fear as he saw this demon plant produce two short swords from inside its branches.

"It's smiling at me!" The frozen Lamanite tried to scream but barely a whisper escaped. His mind stopped working and his body locked in fear as he stared at the ghost soldier's painted face inside the camouflage cover.

Looking back from inside the bush, the ghost soldier had seen that look in the eyes of his enemies before. He knew the young Lamanite was too scared to move or defend himself, so the ghost soldier turned to attack the other Lamanites. The four other Lamanites, still walking together, were unaware of the unearthly menace behind them as it struck with lightning speed. The ghoulish Nephite nightmare spun and moved with the grace of a rhythmic dancer, severing the heads of each of the four Lamanites before turning back to face the lone straggler.

With blood dripping from the two short swords, the ghost soldier moved silently toward the last one in the Lamanite group. The sole survivor gasped with fear. He froze completely as all rational thought escaped him. His bladder emptied itself all over his loincloth and legs. He still held his spear out in front of him, but, with his arms shaking uncontrollably, the spear was useless. The Lamanite tried to step back but his feet would not work. The demon approached him, now showing even more of the shape and manner of a man.

"What?" The frightened Lamanite managed to choke out before the half man, half plant swung one of the small swords it held and knocked the Lamanite's spear out of his hand. The second sword held by the monstrous-looking Nephite came slashing up the side of the Lamanite's head, severing off his left ear. The pain of having his ear cut off instantly snapped the Lamanite soldier back into reality. He grabbed at the gushing wound and let out a panicked scream.

"Run!" the Nephite spoke. He pointed the swords at the Lamanite's chest. "I am coming after you!"

The wounded Lamanite screamed again, and then raced toward the safety of the rest of his army still on the road behind him. He ran several yards, screaming all the way and moving past other Lamanites still trying to get through the trees and undergrowth. "Stop!" one of the advancing Lamanites shouted. He reached out and caught the wounded soldier by the arms. Quickly inspecting the wound on the retreating boy's head, he asked, "Who did this to you? Where is your squad?"

"My squad?" the injured Lamanite responded choking back the tears. "A forest monster killed them all." Desperate to get further away from the nightmare he had just endured, the wounded Lamanite demanded, "Let me go!" He pulled his arms free from his comrades' grasp. "Monsters!" His high-pitched shouts sounded over and over. He continued running through the thick vegetation toward the safety of the road.

"What did he say?" a second Lamanite soldier asked.

"He said a forest monster attacked and killed his squad."

Some of the Lamanite soldiers with them started to chuckle, some imitated a child's voice and squealed, "Monster, monster" several times while dancing around and waving their arms in the air.

A loud, wooden crack, like the sound of a large tree branch snapping in two brought the merriment to a close. The Lamanites stopped what they were doing and readied their weapons. What had been, only seconds before, a jovial scene was now full of tension as hauntingly quiet Lamanites readied for action.

For several moments, the Lamanites silently scanned the trees for any signs of movement. Finally, an older Lamanite who was the ranking soldier lowered his weapon and turned to face the remaining soldiers.

"Monsters," he said with a smirk on his face. A nervous laugh rippled across the troops, and they lowered their weapons.

As soon as they relaxed, a flash of green and brown crossed the face and chest of their leader as the tree he was standing next to came alive. Wrapped in branches and limbs, he disappeared, sucked into the undergrowth. Muffled screams of panic and fear could be heard as the branches and limbs of the bushes and trees around him shook violently. Then there was silence. The remaining Lamanites stood in fear and astonishment, desperately trying to comprehend what they had just witnessed. They made nervous eye contact with each other as, all around them, Teancum's ghost warriors sprang into action. Jumping down from trees, coming up from the ground or crawling out from behind fallen logs, the well-camouflaged Nephite warriors sprang their trap. Their expert camouflage techniques hid them so well that Lamanites unknowingly walked right up to them. Using speed, surprise and violence of action, Teancum and his men managed in just a matter of moments to overwhelm a force that was far superior numerically. Teancum's troops were so efficient at killing the Lamanites that, just as quickly as this ambush began, it was over. Not one Nephite was injured, while more than thirty Lamanites now lay dead.

Those Lamanites who saw what happened, but were not close enough to be involved in the ambush, stood in motionless fear. Teancum had just finished bringing down a large Lamanite and was pulling his knife out of the man's back. He looked up and could see the remaining Lamanites who were not caught by the ambush.

"Poison darts!" Teancum signaled. Instantly the Ghost Soldiers around him stopped what they were doing, dropped to one knee and reached for the thin, hollow water reed attached to their weapons belts. From inside their satchels, they produced small gourds containing a black paste and a leather pouch with several darts made out of animal bone. Moving almost in unison, each soldier pulled open the top of his gourd. Taking out one of the bone darts, they rubbed the tip of it over the black paste. The poison black paste was one of Teancum's own discoveries as he had hunted down the criminals responsible for the murder of his family. Using his training as a physician, he was able to harness the potent toxin from local native plants and animals and make it into an efficient weapon. Carefully holding a finger over the mouthpiece end of the reed, they dropped a poison-covered dart into the other end, where it slid all the way down and rested against their finger. By loading the darts in this manner, there was no chance of accidentally rubbing any of the poison onto the part of the reed their mouths would be touching. Once the dart was loaded into the reed, they took in a giant breath, brought the loaded reeds to their mouths, found a target and then blew. The small, needle-shaped darts covered with poison were sent flying in unison through the air, heading for those Lamanites still frozen with fear and disbelief.

The darts struck several Lamanite targets and the poison instantly took effect. The first symptom, almost immediately upon contact with human flesh, was a severe burning sensation that radiated out from the dart wound. With the victim's heart racing from the intense burning pain, the bloodstream carried the poison throughout the body. Screaming in agony, the affected Lamanites dropped their weapons and tried in vain to find some way to stop the pain.

Teancum and his men knew the effects of the poison and how much time they had to take action. They knew the poison was not fatal in such small doses, but they did not envy the Lamanites who were suffering through the effects. Typically, the Ghost Soldiers used the poison to paralyze the enemy and keep them from attacking long enough to make their escape as they disappeared in the surroundings. Now, instead of retreating, the Ghost Soldiers moved quickly toward the poisoned Lamanites.

Within seconds, the Lamanites experienced the second effect of the poison—temporary loss of balance and muscle control. One by one, the Lamanites fell to the ground among the thick vegetation. Although hidden by thick jungle growth, their moans, screams of pain and thrashing about revealed their locations and the Nephites were able to find them. Teancum quickly moved to the closest Lamanite. He stopped just short of the enemy soldier and took a hurried assessment of the situation. He had an idea and he turned to his men.

"Bring the rest of the unit up on line and prepare to advance." He paused and looked around again. Pointing to where the first group of Lamanites had been killed he said, "And bring me the heads of those Lamanites." His faithful men quickly obeyed his commands and, once his men were on line, Teancum ordered the advance. They first killed the poisoned Lamanites around them, and then moved silently through the brush to face additional Lamanites advancing along the road.

More of his Lamanite soldiers joined Zerahemnah at that point in the road and readied themselves to follow the first few groups of Lamanites into the thick green wall of trees to try to outflank the Nephites. As they entered the jungle to follow their brother Lamanites, the blood curdling screams of poisoned and dying men could be heard coming from deep inside the thick vegetation on both sides of the road. Sounds of clashing metal and pleas for mercy echoed across the surrounding mountains. Those on the road backed away from the tree line with their spears pointing toward the sudden haunting screams. The screaming and commotion continued for several more seconds, and then a strange silence fell across the jungle. No sounds emerged from inside the trees and nothing was moving.

Then, from deep inside the trees, came the sound of crashing branches. The sound got louder and louder. Someone or something was moving through the brush very fast, heading right toward the road. Muffled moans and yelping came from the direction of the crashing sounds. As the noise got closer, the Lamanites braced themselves for whatever came rushing out of the trees. With spears and swords at the ready, the Lamanites backed farther away from the tree line and bunched together on the road as the sounds drew closer. Several wild eyed Lamanites, covered in blood and holding gashing wounds, came bursting out of the brush. Half crazed, the wounded Lamanites started shouting "Monsters, monsters!" and pointing back into the jungle where the crashing sounds were getting closer. They were such a fright that some of the fleeing Lamanites were almost stabbed by the spears of the Lamanites standing on the road. An older Lamanite with a scar on his cheek put down his spear and grabbed one of the injured by the shoulders.

"Calm down, lad," the older Lamanite shouted as he tried to control the hysterical young soldier.

"Run, run for your lives!" the injured soldier shouted and broke free of the older man's grasp. "Monsters, jungle monsters. They killed everyone; they're not stopping for anything and they're coming this way!" The shouting soldier and the other injured Lamanites ran past Zerahemnah and back up the trail, away from the battle.

"Jungle monsters?" the old scarred Lamanite spoke with a sarcastic tone. All who were around him started to laugh and point at the fleeing Lamanite. Suddenly, a haunting, high-pitched shriek came from deep in the jungle. A second shriek came from the opposite side of the jungle, startling the Lamanites.

"It's just a bunch of wild pigs," Zerahemnah shouted from atop his horse. "Kill them and move into the jungle and flank the Nephites, now!" he demanded.

"That was no pig." one Lamanite said to another. "I raise pigs, and they don't sound like that."

With the first wave of Lamanites retreating from the flanking maneuver, Zerahemnah tried desperately to get his men to either move forward on the road and face the Nephites or go around through the jungle.

Out of the woods came several hollow, chirping sounds, then a quick echo of the same noise from the other side. The Lamanites stopped and dared not get any closer to the trees than where they stood. With their weapons still out, they watched and listened for whatever was inside the shadows of the trees making that noise. Zerahemnah was hopping mad. He moved his horse up and down the road, kicking at his men and hitting them with his riding crop as he tried to get them to move into the jungle or press forward and fight the Nephites.

"Move, move," he shouted as he pushed his horse through the ranks of

Lamanites lining the road. From the tree line on the right, a large, round object flew out and struck Zerahemnah in the back. The object fell to the ground and landed with a loud thud, sounding like a watermelon hitting the ground.

"What was that?" Zerahemnah demanded, turning his horse to see what had hit him.

A tall Lamanite ran up and poked the object with his spear. The object rolled over and Zerahemnah gasped when he saw it was the head of one of the Lamanites who first entered the jungle to flank the Nephites. The tall Lamanite jumped back and shouted in horror. All the soldiers around him turned to see what it was.

"Forest monsters!" someone shouted from the Lamanite ranks. Suddenly, fifty more heads came raining out from the trees, landing all around the Lamanites. Panic broke out as the men shouted, pointed, and tried desperately to get out of the way of the heads crashing down around them.

That was the breaking point for the men with Zerahemnah. Like a stampede of spooked cattle, the Lamanites broke and ran back up the road in the direction from where came. The soldiers who were in the next wave, waiting their turn to move forward, saw the mass of retreating Lamanites coming back up the road and they, in turn, panicked. It was absolute chaos and Zerahemnah was powerless to stop it. The leader had to make a quick choice: To flee with his men or stay on the road alone to face whatever came out of the trees. For a coward, the choice was easy. Spurring his horse to a gallop, Zerahemnah quickly caught up to his panicked men fleeing up the road, away from the danger. What he did not consider was how to help the large group of Lamanites now trapped in the open ground between Moroni's well-armored forces.

ONE MAN ARMY

General Moroni, still holding his position in the center of the Nephite trap with his armored troops standing fast, heard the panic and confusion caused by his comrade Teancum and the ghost warriors he led. The screams of dying Lamanites echoed through the dark shadows and massive trees.

"Teancum must be giving them hell," he said to himself, smiling under his helmet. Turning around, he made eye contact with Captain Lehi, who was still holding his position at the point of the V. Lehi was holding his great axe in front of him and shifting his weight in anticipation of the order to attack. He could feel the fight coming and was eager to spill Lamanite blood. From the sounds coming out of the forest, Lehi could tell that Teancum was engaged in a pitched battle and Lehi did not want to miss out on all the fun. He was quietly mumbling under his breath to urge Moroni to signal the attack and nodded to his commander signaling that he was ready. Moroni nodded back and turned forward to face the remaining threat. Moroni could see the ranks of Lamanite soldiers in front of him were even more confused than when they had first came out of the jungle. With no viable leadership among the Lamanite ranks, many were turning their heads to look back down the tree-lined road from where they came. Others just left, moving back up the road or into the cover of the trees next to them.

"Now!" Moroni heard a voice echoing in his head that sounded just like his father's. Puzzled, Moroni quickly turned his head expecting to see the great Chief Captain Joshua standing next to him, but no one was there. He turned back to face the enemy. "Now, lad; attack," his father's voice was there again.

"Father?" Moroni whispered. His heart skipped a beat as he felt a surge of hot energy wash over his body. Before he realized what was happening, he was running toward the Lamanites, belting out a war cry and raising the great sword over his head. The front rank of Lamanite soldiers panicked when they saw this giant of a man charging at them. Grasping and clawing at those behind them, they desperately tried to move away but were stopped by the wall of Lamanite flesh behind them.

Moroni's muscular legs and great speed quickly propelled him forward. He closed the distance between him and the Lamanites before anyone on the Nephite side could react. Captain Lehi was momentarily stunned by what he was witnessing. Blinking several times, he barked "Where was the signal to advance?" He regained his composure and whispered, "Foolish boy." Holding his ax high in the air, he let out his own war cry and shouted, "Attack!" to the surrounding army. Lehi sprang forward and the Nephites with him collapsed onto the remaining trapped Lamanites.

Moroni, charging toward the enemy lines in his full armor, with his helmet, shield, crimson colored war cape flapping in the breeze, and that giant sword, looked more like a nightmare than a man to the unarmored Lamanites as he came crashing into their collapsing lines. The unlucky few who were in his path tried to put up a fight, but Moroni was just too powerful and too well trained. Using both his sword and shield as weapons, Moroni dodged and parried the Lamanite spear thrusts and cut a path of death right through the heart of the Lamanite lines. Before the hapless and bloodied Lamanites could adjust to Moroni's daring, lone assault the remaining Nephite army, led by Captain Lehi, was upon them. It was a blood bath. Moroni was spinning and striking with his sword in all directions. Using his might and the power of his huge sword, Moroni was cleaving grown men with one stroke. Weapons carried by his enemies shattered into pieces when Moroni hit them with his sword and every arm raised to attack was severed clean from its body. He not only used his shield to defend the feeble assaults of the Lamanites, he employed it in offensive moves as well. Swinging the shield as an extension of his own arm, Moroni knocked enemy soldiers to the ground with a stunning force. He struck them with the face of his shield to their bodies, or hit them with the rim of the shield, causing tremendous injuries and blood to spill. A ring of dead and cleaved Lamanite bodies was forming on the ground around Moroni as he engaged and struck at the enemy on all sides. Leaderless and demoralized, the Lamanite lines broke and they

fled back into the jungle from the lone Nephite madman before them. By the time Lehi caught up to the boy general, there was not much left to do but order his men to chase after the fleeing Lamanites.

With the enemy now in full retreat, Moroni stopped his dance of death. He was exhausted. The surge of adrenaline pumping through his veins had depleted the oxygen in his body and he was getting light headed. Dizzy and gasping for air, he pulled his helmet off and dropped to one knee. Bracing himself against his sword, he set the worn helmet on the ground and gently wiped sweat, blood, and his own hair from his face.

"Are you all right, lad?" Lehi asked. He extended his hand to help Moroni to his feet. Moroni reached up, took Lehi's hand, and pulled himself back to his feet.

"I will be okay," Moroni said, as he continued to gasp for air and did a quick inspection of himself looking for any wounds. Satisfied that he was not injured, the two commanders looked over the battlefield. Using his finger to point and counting to himself, Lehi took an account of the dead and wounded lying on the ground around Moroni. Shaking his head in approval and grunting, Lehi slapped the boy general on the back and continued to move forward with his men.

"Push them back as far as you can!" Moroni shouted to Lehi as he jogged off to join the chase. "Stop them before you get caught in the jungle after dark. I don't want anyone in the trees after the sun goes down!"

"Yes, sir!" Lehi shouted in return. He looked back, raised his ax in the air, and continued urging the Nephite soldiers toward the tree-lined path.

The wise and seasoned sergeant major calmly walked up to Moroni, who was continuing to inhale deeply, forcing oxygen into his body. The physical exertion of his one-man assault had taken its toll on the young soldier.

"You're not going to join Lehi and Teancum in the counterattack?" Moroni asked as he accepted and drank from the full water skin his old mentor handed him.

"No, sir," the sergeant major replied. "I'm too old to go running through the trees. If the Lamanites want to fight, they can come back … I'll be right here."

Moroni chuckled as he took a second drink from the water skin, and then poured a quantity of the cool liquid over his head. Brushing the wet hair out of his eyes, he handed the empty water skin back to his father's trusted friend. The sergeant major looked at the skin and wished he had taken a drink before he handed it to Moroni. Tossing the empty water skin to the ground, he turned and looked at the dead and wounded Lamanites behind him.

"What of the injured?" he asked his young commander.

"Get the wounded to the medical tent as soon as possible. Put a guard on them and feed those who can handle some food. Let's see if anyone is willing to talk." Moroni responded.

"Yes, sir … anything else?"

"Yes, Sergeant Major, there is one more thing … Try to smile; this was a good day."

"Just like your father." The old soldier grunted and walked off.

Moroni looked up to see the sun start its final descent behind the mountains in the west. He felt the gentle breeze cooling the sweat on his skin and closed his eyes to savor the moment. As Nephite support personel started to move around him to deal with the Lamanite wounded, Moroni took a long deep breath, and quickly left his short mental escape from reality. Moving out of the way of the medical personal, he walked off the battleground while signaling for his horse. A soldier guided the big animal up to Moroni, who pulled a rag from his saddle bag. Using the rag to wipe the blood from the blade of his sword, he put the great weapon back in its sheath. That's when he realized everyone around was staring at him. They all witnessed it but still could not believe what they had seen. How could one soldier do so much damage to so many of the enemy? Looking back at the shattered bodies and broken weapons that were left from his one-man assault, Moroni felt nothing but pity for the souls of the men he had killed and the suffering the families of those fallen Lamanites would endure. With a heavy heart, Moroni mounted his horse and spurred it away from the field of battle.

THY WILL BE DONE

It was just after sundown when Amiha and his young companion, Corporal Phan, reached the towering, armed gates of the capital city of Zarahemla. Their long trek had been uneventful but had taken its toll on the horses and, for the last few miles, the best speed they could muster was a slow walk. Dusty and worn out, the two messengers meandered down the wide and well-used dirt path that led up to Zarahemla's main entrance. The sight of the large, densely populated capital city always held wonder for Amiha. He had been here several times in the past and every visit had been an adventure for him. For the young soldier accompanying him, it was a first. The grandeur of it all was not lost on the young Nephite. With its array of tall buildings, spires and temples, the scene before them looked more like an oddly shaped mountain range surrounded by a massive stone wall and high guard towers.

"This is a dream. I did not know men could build cities like this," Phan gasped.

"Zarahemla is the center of our world," Amiha said. "It is inside that we will find the Prophet Alma."

The road leading to the main gate was lined on both sides with markets full of merchants' shops, food vendors and street bazaars. Even though it was getting dark, the activity in the marketplace was in full swing as people mingled and enjoyed the jovial environment the market provided. The smell of cooking meat and fresh bread greeted the two as they rode through the crowds. Music and laughter rang out from every corner. People drank intoxicating liquids from large goblets and young girls in flowing dresses with beads and other shiny embellishments danced in the street to the rhythmic beat of several drums. The scene before them looked more like dream than reality.

"Don't they know we are at war with the Lamanites?" Phan barked. He lifted his foot and used it to push away a drunken man who was trying to give Phan's horse a drink of wine.

"It is the way of things here in the capital, I'm afraid. With the troubles on the frontier so far away, unless it directly affects them personally, most people, including some of our leaders, simply do not care what happens outside those stone walls," Amiha said.

They continued working their way through the crowds to the main gate of the city.

The city gates were monstrous wooden double doors reinforced with iron bands that opened inward. For safety and security, the gates were closed at sundown and the only way in and out of the city after that was through a second smaller-sized door cut into the large gate. The entrance was protected by a contingent of soldiers standing guard outside the gate. Wooden pickets were set around the entrance, forming a perimeter around the gate and forcing all foot traffic to pass through an access point for inspection by the city guards. A stone guardhouse with a thatch roof stood just inside the perimeter of the pickets.

Amiha guided his horse to the back of the line that was forming just outside the pickets. People were already waiting to be inspected by the soldiers so they could pass through the smaller gate and go inside the city. As he dismounted from his horse, Amiha realized he was still wearing his armor. Not wanting to draw more attention, Amiha removed a large, dark-colored cloak from his saddle bag and covered his armor and the insignia that identified his rank as that of chief captain. Being one of the highest ranking officers in the Nephite army, Amiha knew it would require formal greetings, receptions, and inspections of the defenses and the troops if the local garrison commanders knew he was there. Following the lead from his commander, Phan did the same and covered up his uniform with his own blanket.

"Why are we covering up, sir?" he asked.

"This is not a formal event. I don't want anyone to know we are here. Get in, see the Prophet Alma, and get back to camp … that is our mission."

Amiha pulled the oversized hood of his cloak over his head and guided his horse slowly forward with those waiting in line to enter the city. Ahead at the checkpoint, they suddenly heard some shouting and a commotion. Amiha peeked out from his place in line in time to see three of the gate guards drag a man from the front of the line and take him kicking and screaming to the guard house.

"What's happening?" the young Nephite warrior asked. He tried to look past his commander at the commotion ahead of him.

"No money for the tax," the old man standing in front of Amiha said.

"What tax?" Amiha asked.

"What tax?" the old man's voice was indignant. He adjusted the bundle in his arms. "Why, the tax you must pay if you want to go inside after dark."

"There is no tax to enter Zarahemla!" Amiha snipped.

"Tell that to the bully guards. You just saw what happens to anyone who tries to get in without paying the tax. They drag you off into the guard shack."

"What happens there?" the young soldier asked.

"I don't know for sure, but I have been told you wake up the next morning in the trash pile behind the city, missing all of your property, and covered in bruises."

"Interesting," said Amiha. He watched the activities of the guards in front of him more closely.

"What is the fee?" Amiha asked as he observed the guards pushing and threatening the citizens.

"That depends on who is on guard duty," the old man whispered sarcastically. Waving Amiha and Phan closer, he looked around for eavesdroppers and continued. "I have a friend whose cousin works on the weekend at this gate. I only pay a few silver shiblums to get home after feasting in the open air market. For others, it depends on who is working. Sometimes it can be as high as one gold senine. When that is the case, most people just sleep on the ground outside the gate until dawn when they open the main gates."

Amiha felt anger swell up inside of him as the old stranger explained how the guards intimidated, mistreated and stole from the citizens. This was not the way the people should be treated by those who were there to protect the helpless and weak, but he kept his cool and remained silent as they got closer to the entry. He was almost near the boiling point as he watched the abuse of power by those who were supposed to protect the people of this city, not rob them.

The guard finally pushed the old man forward. "Next," he called, as he dropped a gold coin into his pouch.

Amiha, still fully covered by his hooded cloak, stepped forward and sized up the man before him. The guard was maybe ten years older, but his physical appearance made him look like he was thirty years older. He was just as tall as Amiha but slightly overweight and without the solid build Amiha had. He had the look of a man with a broken spirit. His teeth were rotten, and his long, black hair was greasy and unkempt. His uniform, if that is what he called it, was worn and unserviceable. His armor consisted of a thick leather vest covering a sweat-stained brown shirt. His leggings were dirty, and his only weapon was a long knife stuck in his belt.

"I need to enter the city. I have important business to attend to."

"Don't we all," the guard spoke impatiently, brushing his sweat-soaked hair out of his eyes. "It's one gold senine to enter."

"There is no fee to enter this Nephite city. Now stand aside and let me pass."

Insulted that this stranger was questioning his authority, the guard shouted, "There is a fee, and you will pay one way or another." He reached for his knife and stepped forward toward Amiha. The three other guards working the security checkpoint had come out of the guard shack and were standing a few paces off. The three stopped what they were doing when they heard their fellow guard shouting and started moving toward Amiha.

Seeing the first guard pull a knife and move toward his commander, Phan tried to move between Amiha and the guard. Amiha put up has hand to stop the soldier before he got too close.

"Oh, I see, you want to deal with me yourself. That was smart keeping your dog on a leash." The guard sneered as he looked at Amiha's companion. The young Nephite took two steps back and Amiha turned to face the guard.

"Well, tough guy, what are you going to do?" The guard spoke as he took his free hand and poked Amiha in the chest with his finger. Instead of hitting flesh and bone, the guard's finger hit the metal chest plate of Amiha's armor that was covered by his cloak. Hearing the dull, clanking sound, the guard was shocked and confused.

"What the …" he started to speak, quickly pulling his hand back. The guard's hesitation was the break Amiha was looking for. Slowly, Amiha moved both of his hands up to the hood covering his face. Lowering it, he looked the guard in the eyes. Then in one smooth, swift motion, he flung both of his arms up and to his sides, sending the ends of the cloak sailing outward and behind his shoulders, exposing his armor and sign of high rank. With lightning speed, he pulled his sword out and pointed its sharp tip at the guard's large stomach.

Phan followed his example and tossed his blanket behind him. Crossing under the picket, he drew his own sword and turned to face down the three advancing guards. Those three, not understanding what was happening, pulled their weapons out and stood ready to assist their corrupt comrade.

The first guard was stunned and confused, standing face to face with a chief captain in full body armor who was pointing a large sword at him.

There was an awkward silence as everyone involved stood motionless, wondering what would happen next. The three other guards, who now realized they faced two trained soldiers in body armor, dared not advance. Amiha let the moment play out as the corrupt guard in front of him continued to get more nervous.

Finally Amiha spoke, "I am Chief Captain Amiha, Army Field Commander and the personal aide to General Moroni. You remember him don't you, the Supreme Commander of all the Nephite armies? So that kind of makes me your boss, wouldn't you say?" He stared at the guards and continued in a slightly sarcastic tone, "So before I have you all whipped for assaulting your commanding officer, for theft, extortion of the public, dereliction of duty, and bad hygiene, how about you all drop your weapons and move over to the guard shack?"

The crowd of civilians standing behind Amiha realized they were now way too close to a possible sword fight and backed up several feet to avoid being hurt.

The dirty guards were completely frozen. With the combination of all the wine they had been drinking, the lateness of the hour, and the sudden arrival of two heavily armed soldiers, their bodies and minds were locked in place, not moving at all.

"Did you hear what your chief captain said? Now, move!" Phan shouted as he advanced toward the three guards.

Seeing the armored Nephite warrior advancing, the guards' survival instincts kicked in. They dropped their weapons. The big, dumpy guard standing in front of Amiha slowly turned his head back to see what his friends were doing. When he saw they had dropped their weapons, he slowly looked down at the long knife in his hand. Amiha raised his sword to remind him he was outmatched and that he would be wise not to try anything funny. The guard dropped the knife to the ground and took three steps back with his hands out in front of him.

"Move to the guard house, all of you," Amiha ordered, while pointing with his sword in the direction he wanted the four guards to go.

Phan looked at Amiha for instructions.

"Get the gate open," Amiha ordered. "Get these people inside where it's safe." He jerked his left thumb in the air and pointed it over his shoulder at the civilians behind him. A cheer went up from the crowd waiting behind Amiha. The people gathered up their belongings and started to move toward the access point that led through the city's walls and into the safety inside. Phan took several quick steps toward the city gate and then turned and jogged back to Amiha.

"Sir, are you going to be okay by yourself out here? There are four of them," Phan whispered.

"I'll be fine. The thing about bullies is that, nine times out of ten, they are just cowards. They abuse those they think are weak or who are just too good-natured to call their bluff. But when they run across someone who is not afraid or is willing to stand up to them, they are quickly put in their place."

"Nine out of ten, huh," the young soldier said, smiling. "What do you do about the other one?"

"Well, you just might need to kill the last one," Amiha responded, winking at Phan. The gate guards heard Amiha's remark and looked at each other in a panic.

The young soldier's smile spread even broader as he turned and ran back toward the city gate.

Amiha made his way to the guard shack, where the guards stood near the door. He put his sword back into its sheath and asked, "Where is your sergeant?"

The large guard responded sheepishly while pointing inside the shack, "He's in there, sir."

The shack was a well-made structure of stone walls and a thatched roof with a small, stone chimney sticking out of the top. It was built using the city wall as its back side. The only door leading inside faced away from the city wall. It had small windows with leather skins covering the openings on the other two sides. From a distance, the building gave the impression of being one large room but, as Amiha got closer, he could tell there were, in fact, two rooms inside. He also noticed that the closer he got, the worse it smelled. As he looked around for the source of the smell, he could see a large pile of rotten food, trash, and other garbage piled up on the side of the shack facing away from the main city gate. Amiha stopped and looked at the pile of trash for a few seconds out of sheer wonderment.

"There is only one reason that trash is piled up outside a military checkpoint," Amiha said, shaking his head in disgust. "No one in command has come out of the city to inspect the conditions here, have they?" he asked the guards who were waiting by the shack door.

"No, sir; not for some time now. We are pretty much on our own out here," one of the other guards responded.

"And the person in command of this checkpoint is not a very good soldier, is he?" Amiha continued, the anger he was feeling coming through in his voice.

"No, sir," a second guard replied and gestured toward the shack door. "But, he is inside if you would like to have a chat with him."

The big, overweight guard quickly whipped his head toward the one who just spoke and made an angry hissing sound at him. He was trying to keep the guard from saying anything else, but Amiha already had heard enough.

"Out of my way!" Amiha shouted, moving quickly toward the door. The guards near the door took several steps back. Amiha walked past them and burst through the opening.

The outrage Amiha felt as he gazed at the scene before him caused his hands to shake. There, passed out, with his feet up on the counter and leaning back in a wooden chair, was the sergeant of the guard. He was unarmed, out of uniform and had a large empty jug of wine in his lap. "Sarge," one of the guards loudly whispered from outside the door. "Sarge, we have company." The only response they got from the drunken man was his snoring and scratching.

"Sergeant, on your feet," Amiha said firmly.

The man didn't move. The entire shack stunk of human waste and rotten trash. Amiha had to breathe through his mouth to keep from gagging on the smell.

"Hmm, sir, we were gonna give this guard house a real good cleaning in the morning; weren't we boys?" the big guard spoke, looking at the other guards who were standing just outside the door.

"I'm sure you were planning that very thing." Amiha said in a low, sarcastic tone as he stood over the still sleeping sergeant. "I don't have time for this," he thought to himself. "But I can't just act like this is not happening right in front of me."

Amiha knew he could not just walk away from what he was witnessing. He was a chief captain, and these men had been charged with the defense of this great city. Convinced that he must do something, he looked around at his surroundings. Amiha spied just the thing he needed to make a quick example of the derelict leader passed out in front of him. Stepping back, Amiha grabbed the large metal bucket full of water that was sitting by the fireplace. He moved right up next to the sleeping man and, with one strong fluid kick, knocked one of the two legs of the chair still touching the ground out from underneath the drunken guard. With a terrified drunken yelp, the sleeping sergeant flew out of the chair as it went spinning out from underneath him. His legs and arms flailed wildly in the air in a desperate attempt to keep from falling. He landed on the ground, square on his back with a loud thud. He sat up almost instantly and, with an intoxicated slur, shouted, "Who dares …" Before he could finish his sentence, Amiha splashed the drunken man with the full contents of the bucket over his head and upper chest.

Setting the bucket down, Amiha took three steps back. The now completely furious guard tried to stand.

Gagging and choking from the deluge of water, the drenched sergeant started screaming at the top of his lungs every curse word and profanity ever conceived by man. Before he could right himself and face whoever had dared to splash him with water, Amiha spoke.

"Sergeant," Amiha said, "calm down and listen." The drunken guard was now on his feet, wiping water and his own hair out of his eyes. "I'll listen," he said. "I'll listen right after I run you through." He pulled a small knife from his waistband and thrust it wildly toward Amiha.

Being much better trained and more sober than the drunken soldier, Amiha easily sidestepped the attack as the knife sailed harmlessly past him, slicing nothing but air. Amiha caught the knife-wielding arm at the wrist with his right hand and brought his left fist crashing down on the soldier's upper forearm. Smashing the bundle of nerve endings in the arm with his fist, the blow sent shockwaves of spiking pain shooting across the sergeant's arm. The drunkard thought his arm had been broken and he screamed in pain. The hand that was holding the knife instantly went completely numb and he dropped the weapon. The knife stuck in the floor, blade first, directly between Amiha and the drunken soldier. Still in control of the soldier's right arm, Amiha twisted it back toward the solder's body with such force that the soldier flipped over himself and landed on the ground face down. The drunken soldier again screamed out in pain as Amiha locked the man's arm behind his back and rested all of his weight on top of him with both knees.

"I'll kill you for this insult," the trapped soldier shouted in a slurred angry tone as he tried to get to his feet.

"Stand down, soldier. That's an order," Amiha barked.

"Who are you to give me orders?"

"I am chief …" Amiha started, but he was interrupted as three well-armed and properly uniformed Nephite city guards forced their way into the confined space of the shack.

Amiha was now surrounded and out of options, he sprang to his feet, sword drawn and ready for a fight. As the three new guards looked on, an older and very distinguished-looking man wearing the uniform of a lower-ranking captain worked his way past the guards and stood in front of Amiha.

"Sir," the man spoke and saluted Amiha. "I am the Night Watch Commander. I understand you had some trouble with the gate guards."

"Do you know who I am?" Amiha questioned as he watched the drunken sergeant try to sit up.

"Yes, sir. Your assistant was very helpful." There was more movement in the room as Amiha's young companion came in, panting heavily, with a giant smile on his face.

"Captain, this man is under arrest. Have your men escort him and his squad to the brig."

The watch commander nodded to his soldiers behind him, and they all grabbed hold of the drunken sergeant at the same time. Amiha barely had time to get out of the way as the arrested soldier was brought to his feet and forced out of the shack.

"What are the charges, my captain?" The duty sergeant asked as the drunken sergeant was moved from inside the shack to the grassy area just outside.

"The charges, sir?" the watch commander asked Amiha as he was brushing himself off.

"Assaulting a superior officer, drunk on duty and dereliction for him," Amiha said, pointing to the drunken sergeant. "Theft, assault of a civilian and extortion for those men there," Amiha pointed to the guards he had dealt with earlier that night. They were trying to slowly back out of the area and avoid contact with the elite guards. Those men were also quickly taken into custody.

"They have been forcing civilians to pay a tax to enter the city through this gate," Amiha said to the watch commander.

"A tax? There is no tax to enter the city!" the guard commander barked as he looked at his disgraced men.

Amiha continued, "There is no way to know who or how many paid the tax. So search them and all their belongings. Seize whatever money you find on them. Give that to the church to help care for the poor and orphaned."

"What? You can't do that," one of the dirty guards shouted as his bags of coins were removed from his belt." He struggled a bit with the members of the elite guard who were holding him and searching his person, but eventually all his money was found.

"Take them away," the watch commander ordered, "and post a new set of guards at the gate."

"Yes sir," the sergeant responded. He, in turn, barked out a series of instructions to his men.

"Sir, are you alright?" Phan asked.

"I'm fine, but this has been a monumental waste of my time," he responded as he continued to brush off his uniform. "Captain, what is going on here?" Amiha spoke with disgust.

"I share your frustration, sir," the watch commander said. "When the bulk of the army left to support General Moroni, discipline dropped. It has been hard to establish or maintain control with these secondhand soldiers. Morale is low and it seems like we are quelling civilian uprisings on a weekly basis. Everything from the poor forgetting God's laws and demanding more social justice, to a bunch of rich snobs asserting their birthrights to be kings over us, these are trying times."

"Trying times, indeed," Amiha spoke back. "Keep the faith, Commander, all will be made right. Now I must see Alma the Great. I am on a mission from General Moroni himself."

"My chariot driver will take you and your aide wherever in the city you need to go." The guard commander whistled and waved for his personal chariot to pull up. "Your horses will be fed and bunked in the main army stables waiting for you when you are done. Do you require anything else, sir?"

"Yes," Amiha said as he climbed up into the chariot. "Have the chief military magistrate sign my name to the complaint and deal with these men accordingly. I cannot overlook what happened here."

"Yes, sir. I will see to this mess personally."

"Thank you, Commander. I will tell the general of your professionalism."

"Thank you sir," he responded as he snapped to attention and gave a hand salute.

Amiha returned the salute and then addressed the chariot driver. "I must meet with Alma the Great. Take me to where he is at all speed!"

The chariot driver said, "Yes, sir," and let out a shout as he slapped the leather reins down on the backs of the horses pulling the chariot. The young corporal almost missed his ride as he jumped into the moving chariot at the last moment. With everyone now safely on board, the chariot went speeding through the main gates of the capital city of Zarahemla.

ALMA THE GREAT

The thick, granite walls surrounding the large temple complex were lined with ivy, manicured shrubs, and fruit-bearing trees that greeted those who made their way up the cobbled path from the dirty city road to the main gate. The driver pulled the horse-drawn chariot to a quick stop, trying to let Amiha and his escort off as close as he could to the gate.

"I'll be waiting right over there for you, sir." The driver pointed to an open area several yards away from the temple gate, where some uncovered wagons were parked.

"Sir," Phan broke in. "They took our horses to the army stables. Maybe we should have our horses waiting for us here when we are done. That way, we can leave right away and not waste time going back to the stables in the chariot before leaving."

"An excellent idea, Phan. Driver, change of plans," Amiha said. He stepped down from the chariot and spoke to the driver. "Please have our horses here waiting when we're finished."

"Will do," the chariot driver said. He slapped the reins down and the big horses pulling the chariot jumped forward.

"Don't forget our saddles and packs," Amiha called out as the chariot whisked past him.

"Do you think he heard me?" he asked Phan.

"I hope so, sir. I still have some of that sweetbread in my saddle bags."

It was late in the evening, but the moon was high in the sky making it easier for Amiha to see the path and the gate. Waiting at the entrance to the temple grounds were two attendants who manned the gate at night.

They wore light leather armor over white tunics, and both were armed with spears and short swords.

"Who goes there?" one of the attendants called.

"Chief Captain Amiha, aide-de-camp to General Moroni. I come bearing personal correspondence from the general to Alma the Great. It is most urgent that I speak to the prophet."

"Come inside, Captain Amiha. We will inform the prophet you are here." A smaller door, framed inside the large wooden gate, opened from the inside and Amiha and his young friend were escorted inside the temple grounds.

Amiha had been there before, but not Phan. Nothing could have prepared him for what he was about to experience.

Once inside the temple grounds, it was as though they had stepped into a different world. As the small wooden door shut behind them, it seemed life outside the walls of the temple no longer existed. The temple itself was a large, single-standing structure in the middle of the walled grounds. Amiha could make out fine, decorative designs carved into the light-colored marble walls of the temple. The main door of the temple faced the gate, and two marble columns on each side of the door supported a marble canopy. A wide staircase led up from the ground to the door with two massive oil-burning pots stationed on the landing, giving off light for all to see. The grounds around the temple were covered with exquisitely maintained grass, along with all types of shade trees, fruit-bearing trees, palms, flowering bushes and plants. Well-worn gravel paths led through the grounds, around the temple and to the staircase. In the center of the grounds was a large pool with a fountain and swans swimming around it.

"Only in my dreams could I think such a place exists," the young Nephite corporal whispered.

"This is holy ground," he responded. "Great care is taken to make this as solemn as possible."

"This way, gentlemen," the armed attendant spoke and walked toward the main door of the temple.

Two more attendants, dressed in white, came out of the temple door and waited at the bottom of the stairs.

"Good evening, gentlemen," the older of the two said. "The ground you stand on is sacred. Please remove your shoes."

Without question, they bent over, untied their sandals and removed them from their feet. The second attendant held out his hands and took the sandals from them.

The older attendant smiled. "Your weapons and armor, gentlemen, are not needed inside the house of the Lord."

It took them several minutes to remove all of their armor and weapons. Once removed, the men gave the heavy metal pieces to the younger, slightly built attendant who was holding their shoes. It became a quiet joke between Amiha and his young assistant as they stacked, piece by piece, their armor, helmets, and swords in the young man's hands. They watched as the smaller framed attendant strained to hold the heavy gear as they put more and more weight in his hands.

"Your equipment will be cleaned and waiting for you upon the conclusion of your business," the older attendant said. He signaled for the junior attendant to leave. The young man strained to hold all the armor and maneuver his way around the group and to the side of the temple. The older attendant began, "We try to maintain a level of decorum here. It's …" but his words were cut off when the armor-bearing attendant tripped, spilling all of the armor on the ground. The clash of metal banging together echoed off the temple walls, followed by a frustrated outburst from the young attendant, who had tried in vain to catch some of the metal pieces before they hit the ground. Amiha looked the older attendant in the eyes and could not help but laugh. The attendant blushed and smiled back. "We try," he said. He gestured for the two soldiers to follow him up the stairs and led them to the great doors of the temple.

As Amiha crossed the threshold and stepped through the temple doors, he sensed a warm, calm feeling of peace. He had been in the temple many times before, and he was always amazed at the feeling of love that enveloped him in the temple. The room they stood in was a small waiting room separated from the inner sanctum of the temple by two more expertly carved wooden doors.

"Wait here and I will tell Alma you have arrived." The attendant made his way to the wooden doors. He opened one side by pulling on a large brass handle, closing the door behind him as he entered. Amiha and Phan were left alone.

"I should be dead tired, but I feel like I have the energy of three men."

"This place has that effect on you," Amiha agreed. They stood in silence for several seconds and marveled at how quiet it really was inside the room.

"It's so quiet," Amiha said. "I can hear my own heartbeat."

Phan closed his eyes and absorbed the energy flowing through the room. The temple door opened and the older attendant returned with two others.

"The Prophet will be with you momentarily. He asked that you enjoy some food and drink while you wait." The attendant waved his hand and two additional servants carried out a large basin of water from the inner room and moved to the doors leading outside.

"For washing before you dine. Please, gentlemen, join me outside?"

Amiha and Phan followed him out to the courtyard where the basin was set on a three-legged table. Two towels also were provided, with some aloe soap. The two washed their hands and faces, and then dried off with the clean towels. The two servants who brought the basin of water carried a larger table out from behind the temple and plates of food were placed on it.

"Water, some fruit juice, bread, and meat," said the attendant in charge. "I am sorry there is not more, but your visit was most unexpected. Enjoy. Alma the Great will be with you shortly." The man bowed and left them with the food.

The young Nephite looked at his commander. Amiha nodded in approval, and they both reached for the food.

"I think this is apple juice," Amiha said. He gulped down the liquid he had poured into his cup from a large jug. "You want some?"

"Yes, sir."

"Give me your cup."

Amiha reached out, took the cup from the young man and started to pour the juice into it. He filled it to the brim and handed it back to his assistant.

"Now, if only we had a set of chairs to sit on to enjoy our feast," Amiha said.

Amiha filled his plate and moved to the steps leading back up to the main doors of the temple and started to sit down. He stopped himself, remembering the attendant saying it was sacred, holy ground. "Maybe not," he whispered.

The two ate in silence for several minutes, until they saw the temple doors swing wide open and the older attendant step out into the burning lamp light.

"Gentlemen," he said. "Alma the Great." The attendant moved to one side of the doorway and bowed. Out of the shadows cast over the doorway by the oil lamps, a distinguished-looking elderly gentleman stepped into view. He was tall and wore a white, loose-fitting, one-piece robe, with a red sash tied around his waist. His silver hair hung loose down to his shoulders and his beard was trimmed and neat, but it was his eyes that always caught Amiha's attention. They were piercing blue and as clear and alert as an eagle's. He walked slowly with the aid of a large, wooden walking stick. Several attendants, all dressed alike, followed him at a distance. He stopped at the top of the stairs and looked at Amiha.

"Chief Captain Amiha, my dear friend, I am so pleased to see you again."

"I am honored to see you again, sir." Amiha bowed with respect to his religious leader. "The general sends his love and gratitude."

"Ah, young Moroni. The Lord is so very pleased with him. How is he?"

"He is troubled by events beyond his control," Amiha responded. "He sent me to you for advice and counsel."

"I am humbled that someone so favored by the Lord as General Moroni would have need of the advice of an old man like me." Alma paused. "I know little of military tactics, but counsel from the Lord is what we all must have in our lives. How may I serve our brave commander?"

"Sir, the counsel he seeks is of a sensitive nature. May I speak to you in private?"

"Of course, young captain. Walk with me in the gardens. I do enjoy the night air this time of year."

Out of respect, Amiha and his companion took several steps back and bowed as Alma the Great descended the stairs and walked slowly toward them.

"Come, Amiha; let us speak of the matter."

Amiha waited until Alma had walked past him. He turned to his young helper. "Wait here. We must be ready to ride as soon as I have the answer we seek."

"Yes, sir."

"I am so terribly rude," Alma said, turning to face Phan. "My name is Alma." He held out his hand for the young Nephite to shake.

"It's a pleasure to meet you, sir. I am called Phan." He took Alma's hand. As their flesh connected, a shock of energy shot up the young soldier's arm and filled his whole body with warmth. Speechless from the effect, Phan stood in silence, holding the prophet's hand and staring into his eyes.

Alma understood well what was happening to young Phan. He spoke as he winked and patted him on the cheek.

"Your Father in Heaven loves you very much."

"Thank you, sir," was all Phan could say before tears started to flow down his cheeks. Alma released his grip and turned to Amiha.

"Shall we walk a bit?"

"After you, sir." Amiha held out his arm for Alma to steady himself as they walked through the soft gravel.

They were several yards away from the others before Alma spoke.

"General Moroni has the weight of the world on his shoulders, doesn't he?"

"Yes sir, it would seem so, but he is the very best man for the job."

"Indeed," Alma said. "Very few men will ever possess all the skills, talents and moral courage needed to accomplish what we have asked him to do. Moroni is a great man with a great destiny, and the Lord is very mindful of him."

"Sir, you speak of other men. Are there others who can help us?"

"No, not for this challenge," Alma sighed. "Amiha, this land is choice and sacred above all others. As long as there is a band of Christians on this land, the Lord will not forsake us. But because this is sacred land, the father of all lies will rage against us with all of his might." Alma stopped. His eyes took on a faraway look as he paused in thought and continued.

"Sometime in the future, other men, like Moroni, will live on this land and will be challenged to fight for their freedom from a great power. They will be outnumbered, surrounded, and their own kin will turn on them. During this time of great trouble, one man, a great military leader like General Moroni, will hold the freedom-loving people together and lead them to victory. They will make a great nation from their victory and the word and laws of God will spread forth to all nations."

"A great day indeed. Will this happen in my lifetime?"

"No, Amiha, but you will live long enough to see our victory."

"We will win this war?"

"Good always will prevail over evil, young captain. Never fear."

"Yes, sir."

They walked for a bit longer in the gardens, and then took the path that led to the back of the temple.

"So, what is it the general needs of me?" Alma asked.

"Sir, Moroni has prepared the army the best he can, but we are still lacking proper manpower, equipment and supplies. We are not strong enough to face the enemy in open conflict and we lack the forces needed to reinforce all the cities on the frontier. The Lamanite army controls the north road and can strike at us at will."

Alma slowed his step and glanced over at Amiha. "What is your question, my son?" he asked with the tenderness of a loving father. Amiha took several seconds before he spoke. "Sir, what does the Lord want us to do?"

Alma raised his eyebrows and smiled.

"Do you have a map?" he asked.

"No, sir, my map is with my horse."

"Not to worry." Alma looked back at his attendants who were following at some distance.

"A map of the Nephite lands, please?" he asked in a loud voice.

Two of the younger attendants left and ran around the far side of the temple. Within a short time, they returned with a large map and a small table with a lit candle. They brought the items to Alma and set the table with the map and candle up in front of him.

"Thank you," Alma said to the young men. They bowed and moved quickly back to the others.

"All this fuss for one old man. Sometimes it embarrasses me that people respond in such a way."

"Sir, you are loved and respected by all. It is an honor to serve the prophet of God."

"I could still get it myself," Alma said. "But I move so slowly now it would take me an hour just to cross the gardens to get the table."

They had a quick laugh and Alma looked down at the map.

"Show me again where the army is camped."

"Here, sir." Amiha pointed to the Jershon valley.

"And, the Lamanite army?"

"Our scouts put them in this area near the crossroads." Amiha pointed to a second location.

Alma moved the candle across the map to see the terrain better. He studied the lines on the skin for several seconds, then stopped and stood up. Closing his eyes, he tilted his head up slightly and stood motionless for several seconds. He brought his chin back down, opened his eyes, and placed his hand on Amiha's shoulder. Speaking with conviction and power, the great prophet said. "Have your man fetch your horses. I will inquire of the Lord and learn what His wishes are. I will have an answer for you soon. I do know this. When I have an answer, you must ride with all haste back to General Moroni to give him the news. I fear time is not on our side."

Amiha looked back at the small crowd gathered behind them. He made eye contact with his assistant and waved him to come over. The young soldier ran up and reported.

"Yes, sir."

"We will be leaving sooner than expected. Get the horses ready and bring them back here. Take whatever you need from the garrison supply and get back here on the double."

"Yes, sir!" he responded. The young soldier turned to Alma the prophet and bowed very low before him. "With your permission, sir, I will take my leave."

"Go in peace, brave soldier."

"Thank you, sir," the young soldier said. He turned back to find his sandals.

Alma and Amiha watched as the Phan quickly lashed up his shoes and wrapped his weapons belt and sword around his waist as he ran for the main temple gates. Watching him leave, Alma let out a sigh and leaned on his walking staff. "I don't think I was ever that young."

"To him, war is still exciting and full of adventure," Amiha said matter-of-factly.

"He has not yet faced the enemy in combat?"

"No, sir, not yet."

"May God grant that he never will." Alma's heavy heart sounded in his voice. "I feel this war will be like no other we have ever faced. My thoughts continue to turn to the scriptures and the stories from the old country and how the twelve great tribes were divided after King Solomon died. At that time, brother fought against brother." Alma paused. "Amiha, we must not let Satan splinter this great nation. Tell the general he must do all in his power to keep our way of representative government and civil order intact. This enemy can defeat us only if we fail to stand together and, instead, fight amongst ourselves." Alma paused again and looked up to the heavens, then looked back down at Amiha with tears in his eyes.

"I can say no more concerning this matter. Just tell Moroni to be careful of those who would usurp the will of the people." Alma smiled and turned toward the main doors of the temple. Off in the distance, the sounds of thunder could be heard and a quick crack of lightning streaked across the sky.

"There is a storm coming, young captain. We should make for the safety of the temple. Don't you think so?

"Yes, sir." Amiha answered, and then wondered to himself if there was a dual meaning in that statement.

The wind blew in the rain faster than anyone expected and quickly changed a pleasant evening to a soaking mess. The swollen storm clouds blotted out the bright, full moon and the torches lighting the streets were suddenly extinguished, making the city even darker. Rolling explosions of thunder and cracking flashes of lightning startled the waiting animals, and both man and beast wished they were under cover. Amiha stood outside the temple gates, holding his horse's reins in his hand and trying to keep his mount calm. He had put on his large cloak in a vain attempt to stay dry. He sighed, knowing everything he owned would soon be soaking wet.

His metal armor was wrapped in treated leather pouches and attached to the saddle bags that were resting on his horse. Phan was sitting on his own horse and trying to maintain control of the two packhorses he had in tow.

"Sir," the young soldier shouted over the rain, "perhaps I should take the horses back to the stables and get them out of the weather."

"No, we were told the wait here, and wait here we will."

"It's been almost thirty minutes, sir. Maybe they forgot about us out here."

Amiha gave the young solder a stern look.

"Yes, sir," the young soldier awkwardly responded to the look from his commander. He settled back into his saddle and tried to cover more of his head with his own blanket.

The metal locks on the gate clanked together and Amiha turned to face the opening doors. Both sides of the gate opened and Alma walked out, escorted by several temple attendants who carried a large four-cornered umbrella over the old prophet to keep him dry. Alma had his arms folded across his chest, with his hands inside his sleeves. As the Lord's high priest moved toward him, Amiha could tell there was something different about the old man. He was walking unassisted, even without his walking staff. His skin and eyes were glowing, and he had an outward energy that transcended everything around him.

"The answer General Moroni seeks." Alma pulled a small, rolled parchment from inside his sleeve. The parchment was tied with a bit of twine and sealed with a red wax impression of the official seal of the high priest of the Church.

Amiha looked at the parchment he had been handed.

"For the general only?"

"Yes," Alma responded. "Now go with all haste, and may God protect and speed you on your errand."

Amiha bowed before Alma. "I am only in the service of my God." He put the sealed message under his cloak to keep it dry and pulled himself up into his saddle.

Alma stepped forward in between Amiha and Phan, as his assistants reacted quickly to keep him covered by the large umbrella.

"Give me your hands," the old prophet ordered.

They both held out their hands and Alma took them in his. Alma closed his eyes, bowed his head and said a quick prayer. As he spoke, Amiha and Phan felt waves of warm energy move up their arms and fill their entire bodies. All the pain, fatigue, cold and hunger they had felt were gone. Stunned by the experience, Amiha could not find words to express how he felt.

"That should see you through the hard ride ahead of you," Alma said and patted Amiha's leg. "Go. Quickly go." Alma ordered and he waved them away.

Still unable to give words to his feelings, Amiha simply bowed his head and spurred his horse on. The young Nephite with him didn't immediately follow. He just sat in the rain, with tears in his eyes, looking at Alma the Great.

"Go lad," Alma smiled with a soft laugh. "Go."

The soldier blinked several times and finally spurred his horse. He rode off, but kept looking behind him at Alma. Alma waved goodbye and watched until the two men were out of sight.

The soldiers disappeared down the darkened street and out of view. When they were out of sight, a sudden change quickly came over Alma. The light and energy that had surrounded him suddenly dissipated, and he wobbled and started to lose his balance. His attendants were not alarmed. Most of them had spent enough time around Alma the Great to recognize when he was filled with the Holy Spirit and what the aftermath was like. Such an experience always took its toll on him, but lately it had become even more tasking for Alma's tired body to handle. The men around him knew what was happening. Without a panic, they gently grabbed Alma's arms and propped him up until the old prophet regained his composure. They knew he was safe again when he asked for his walking staff. With staff in hand, Alma slowly turned toward the temple gate and, without looking back, walked through the open gate and back to the house of the Lord.

After riding nonstop from Zarahemla, the sun was once again starting to descend behind the mountains when Amiha arrived back at the main Nephite camp. Knowing that the Lamanite army had been approaching the camp when he left to meet with Alma, he was happy to see the camp still in one piece. After passing the guard force on the road, Amiha trotted his mount through the main camp toward Moroni's command tent. The camp was buzzing with activity. Most of the large tents had been taken down and loaded on wagons. The smaller tents and other camp supplies were being folded up and collected. As he passed the medical area, he saw several wounded Lamanites having their injuries tended to.

"What is this?" he asked a man who was moving quickly past him, carrying a large pot of boiling water and some fresh bandages.

"Sir?" the man asked.

"What are those Lamanites doing in the medical tent?"

A second Nephite, this one leaning on his spear and standing guard over the injured, tipped his head toward the forest. The Lamanites came out of the woods last night, and we had a battle right down there on the road."

"Why are we treating them?" Amiha inquired.

"General's orders." The medic moved around the wounded lying on the grass. "Which is kind of funny if you think about it, sir? Most of the dead and wounded Lamanites here were from his own sword." He shook his head. "If I had not witnessed it myself, I wouldn't have believed the stories. It was like the general was a dragon and could not be killed. He was cutting through them like a gardener pruning a hedge." The medic shook his head again and continued working.

"Teancum and his Ghost Soldiers pruned a few themselves," the young Nephite guard with the spear interjected.

"Yeah, I guess," the medic said. "But, what I do know is what I saw with my own eyes." The medic waved his blood-covered hands over the mass of wounded Lamanites. "One man did all this, and it was the general with his big sword."

"Where can I find the general and his big sword now?" Amiha asked.

The medic pointed with a bloody rag in his hand. "Up there, sir, in his tent. Can you tell him to save a few of these Lamanite dogs for us in the next battle?"

"I'll do my best." Amiha jumped back on his horse and galloped away.

Amiha reached the summit of the small hill and was greeted by Teancum outside the command tent. They saluted each other and Amiha spoke. "Did I miss all the fun?"

"We gave them a good scare, but the vast majority of the Lamanite army fled back up the forest road before we could do any real damage."

"Casualties on our side?"

"A few wounded, but nothing some rest and time can't heal."

"I saw several Lamanites being cared for in the medical area; what is that all about?"

"That was his call," Teancum said, poking a thumb over his shoulder toward the tent opening. "He thought we could get some good intel from the wounded if we patch them up and feed them."

"And?"

"Surprisingly, one or two are chattering like monkeys in a tree. I think what they are saying is solid information, but Lehi, as always, is skeptical. Any luck with Alma the Great?"

Amiha held up the sealed parchment for Teancum to see. "He inside?"

"Yes, and he is going to want to see that right away. Come on." Teancum moved toward the tent and held the flap open for Amiha. The Nephite guards posted at the tent opening saluted as the two chief captains walked in.

Moroni was still wearing his blood-stained, sweaty tunic from the battle the day before. He moved around the large open area inside the tent, giving orders and supervising the attendants who were packing his things. He looked like he had not slept in days.

"You're back," he exclaimed. His face registered joy at seeing his oldest friend. Shaking Amiha's hand, he continued, "I am glad you're safe. When did you arrive?"

"Just now, and I come bearing a gift." Amiha held up the parchment for Moroni to see. "He said, 'For your eyes only.'" Amiha wrinkled his brow and handed the message over.

"Sergeant Major, please clear the tent; command personnel only." Teancum ordered. Moroni moved to his desk, holding the parchment tightly.

"Out, all of you," the old soldier barked. The attending soldiers stopped what they were doing and headed for the opening. "You, too." The sergeant major pointed to Moroni's armed escorts. "Outside, and keep everyone out until I call."

"Yes, Sergeant Major!" The guards inside the tent responded in unison. As the last of the attending personnel exited, Moroni sat down behind the desk and carefully opened the rolled scroll. Teancum, Lehi, Amiha and the sergeant major stood a pace away from the table and waited as Moroni looked over the written message. After a minute of silence, Moroni stood up, looked at his staff and placed the scroll down on the tabletop. There was concern in his eyes.

"Moroni, tell us, what does it say?" Amiha asked.

Moroni rubbed his hand across the large map sitting next to the message from Alma the Great. Taking a small knife from his belt, Moroni stabbed at a point on the map. Stepping back and leaving the knife stuck in the wood, he looked his old mentor in the eyes and then motioned with his head for him to come and see the map. The sergeant major walked over to the table. He saw the location on the map where the knife was stuck, then picked up the message. Drawing a deep breath, the old warrior looked up at Moroni, then over at the other commanders.

"What? What does it say?" Lehi choked out.

The sergeant major spoke one word.

"Manti!"

They all turned to look at Moroni, who had moved to the corner of the tent. His back was to them, his head was bowed. "General?" Teancum spoke just louder than a whisper.

Moroni turned around to face his fellow leaders. He could see the concern on their faces. They all knew the stories about the City of Manti.

"Get your men ready to move. NOW!"

THE SHERIFF OF MANTI

Shem shifted nervously in his saddle. As he squinted under the hot midday sun, the lines around his sky blue eyes and the wrinkles on his weathered face gave away his age. Once again, he alone was the one having to face the ugly downside that came with the growth and prosperity of the great city of Manti. From its beginnings as a small Nephite trading post along the river Sidon, Manti had emerged into one of the largest cities on the frontier, where the economy was energized by the plentiful fishing, trapping and constant flow of river barges carrying trade goods and lumber from the river to the sea. The growth attracted thousands of families who yearned for a better life and migrated to Manti to take advantage of its open spaces to farm, raise cattle, and make their fortunes.

As Manti's chief law enforcement officer, Shem knew all too well that the city's expansion had attracted an ever-growing criminal element as well. Many of these were seedy, social outcasts who fled to the frontier when they ran up against the governing rule of law in places like the long-established capital city of Zarahemla. Some simply found it hard to conform to the norms of a religious people. Others were true predators, cowards who would not stand for freedom but, instead, fed on the weak and defenseless.

Today, Shem's task was to track down and arrest three such predators, who, just after dawn, had attacked a caravan loaded with goods being transported from the docks to the city market. One merchant was dead and his bag of gold was gone.

Shem gripped the reins of his horse in one hand and, with the other, wiped at the sweat forming on his brow. During his many years in the Nephite army, he had always been flanked by other soldiers. Since retiring and taking on this new appointment, as the Sheriff and Manti's chief magistrate, he often had to go it alone. With only Shem and his few deputies, there was never enough manpower to enforce the laws and properly protect everyone within his jurisdiction. As he had numerous times before, Shem wished he could count on some help from the handful of less than professional soldiers garrisoned in Manti to protect from Laminate invasion.

"Now would be a good time for Pachus to send men to help," he thought, but he knew Pachus, that fat, pompous army garrison commander and son of a rich nobleman from Zarahemla, had most likely been bribed to again look the other way while the bandits carried on their business.

Shem also knew that, unlike enemy soldiers who were trained to stand and fight, the bandits had run and were hiding from the arm of justice in some dark corner, most likely with a sharp dagger in hand. As the reigning Manti champion in both wrestling and sword fighting, Shem trusted his strength, quick reflexes and the advantage provided by his many years of combat experience, but hunting three murderous robbers alone was different than playing at sport or performing in battle with trained solders at your side.

"I sure would like some backup on this one," he thought.

He urged his horse into a fast trot, keeping an eye on the bandits' tracks that led toward a small farming village about two miles up the north mountain road.

"I hope the robbers passed through the village and did not bother the people there."

He crested a small hill and, from there, could see the village in the distance with its small family farms resting just on the edge of the forest. No flurry of activity stirred in the streets and no smoke billowed from any of the chimneys poking out of the thatched roofs of the wood and mud buildings.

Shem exhaled slowly and reached up to rub the back of his neck. "Looks good so far," he said aloud. He patted his horse on the side of the neck and gently tapped his heels into the animal's flanks to coax him forward.

The horse and rider dipped into a small valley and followed the road back up again. When the village came back into sight, Shem caught his breath and felt his palms grow wet against the reins. An old familiar feeling warning him of danger came over him. Shem looked again and, indeed, there was no flurry of activity. There was actually no activity at all. No one was outside. There was no one walking in the dirt streets, at the shops, in the town square or working in the many fields.

"It's too quiet," he whispered.

"Go slow." A still voice inside his head whispered.

He had learned long ago to trust his instincts and feelings. Shem swallowed hard, squared his shoulders, and spurred his horse forward. At the edge of the village, he dismounted and drew his sword. With his well-honed instincts continuing to warn of possible danger, he moved forward down the main road through the village, clutching the reins of his mount in one hand and, in the other, holding his sharp, well-used sword in front of him in a loose defensive posture.

"That's close enough, sheriff." A voice came from inside a small wood hut off to his left.

Shem ignored the lump that instantly filled his throat.

"Your issue is with me, not the villagers. ... Show yourself," Shem demanded while he quickly scanned the village for any additional threats. A young, crying girl, maybe ten years old and dressed in a homespun dress, was pushed through the doorway, and two men stumbled out directly behind her, one of them holding a large knife to her throat while his other arm was around her waist. The second man swayed from side to side, leaning first toward the short sword in his right hand, then toward the jug of liquid in his left. Both had unkempt hair and wore dirty rags for clothing. They looked more animal than human.

"Where's your other buddy?" Shem asked.

"Oh, he's around," the man holding the girl said, smiling and showing a mouthful of rotten teeth. "You tracked us faster than we thought you could. ... You're good."

The young girl bit her lip but couldn't hold back a whimper and a new flood of tears.

"Heesh you," her captor growled. He pressed the knife against the pale skin of her neck.

Shem clenched the hilt of his sword. "This is between you and me. Let the girl go," he said.

"I gotta better idea. How 'bout you drop that big sword of yers before I show you what I have in mind for this little lovely," the bandit leader barked. He pulled the girl close to his face and placed his slobbery lips on her cheek. She screamed and Shem lunged forward.

"Whoa there, big boy," the bandit holding the girl said, pushing the knife harder against the girl's neck. "One more step and she dies. Now, drop the sword!"

Shem's instincts kicked in and his senses were alive. He knew that if he dropped the sword the girl was going to die anyway. He knew that the only chance the young hostage had was for him to move faster than he ever had before and kill the leader before the second bandit could react.

"And the third one is probably off to my right with a bow and arrow aimed at me right now," he thought. He quickly scanned the surroundings again. "He is probably just as drunk as these two. If I move quickly enough, he will miss his first shot and I can free the girl and get her inside the hut before he nocks a second arrow."

"The sword … now!" the bandit shouted.

Shem tightened the grip on his weapon and carefully readjusted his stance, then slowly bent his knees and checked his balance to ensure the fastest propulsion possible. The second bandit was giggling and bringing the jug of wine up to his lips.

"Wait for it … two more seconds." Shem told himself to wait to strike until the bandit had the jug in front of his face.

Suddenly, the sound of thundering horse hoofs broke the tension. Within seconds, the entire village was filled with heavily armed Nephite cavalrymen. Five or six of the mounted soldiers formed a semi-circle around the bandits and moved in, spears pointed at them. The bandit with the wine, stunned and mouth open, staggered backward and dropped his container on the ground. It broke at his feet and what little liquid remained inside mixed with the dirt. He clumsily held his short sword out in front of him with both hands in a crazed and defiant act. The other bandit, still holding his young hostage, turned the long knife to point it at the cavalry in front of him.

"Stay back. I'll kill her. I mean it!" he shouted, waiving the knife in front of him.

Through the mass of soldiers, a path opened and a lone rider came forward. The bandit leader's eyes grew wider and he took another step backward as he watched the rider approach. True fear welled up inside of him. While the cavalry made way, the biggest man he had ever seen got off his massive warhorse and walked toward him. The red cloak that covered his body armor snapped in the breeze and the shiny metal helmet on his head shaded his eyes from view. It made the figure look even more monstrous and imposing.

"That's close enough. One more step and she dies," he snarled at the giant Nephite warrior.

The warrior moved steadily forward and stopped a few paces from the bandit. "My name is General Moroni," he said while taking off his helmet

and exposing his face to the hostage taker. "That is an innocent girl you have in your arms. Release her now, and you may live to see tomorrow."

"We're riding out of here, and, and, and she is coming with us," the bandit stuttered and shouted.

Moroni's jaw and neck muscles flexed and anger rose in his eyes. The bandit cowered under his stern look but refused to release the innocent girl.

"Teancum?" Moroni called over his right shoulder.

A mounted Nephite reacted by quickly jerking back and then forward to let fly a long, pointed javelin. At the last second, catching some movement out of the corner of his eye, the bandit turned his head slightly, just before the sharp javelin hit the bandit leader between his eyes, pinning his head to the mud wall. He died instantly, loosening his grip on the girl. The second bandit grabbed at her, but the girl broke free and ran screaming toward Shem. Shem saw his opportunity and, with one swift motion, pushed the girl out of the way and rammed his sword into the chest of the second bandit. The bandit fell to the ground, and Shim dropped onto his knees on the bandit's chest while holding the sword in place.

"There's one more out there. He's armed and loose in the village," Shem shouted to Moroni.

Just then the sound of splintering wood was followed by shouting and scuffling as an unkempt, scruffy-looking man crashed through the door of a hut on the opposite side of the street and landed face down in the mud. Captain Lehi and several Nephite warriors stepped through the now broken door, pushing the remaining pieces out of their way.

Lehi walked forward and pointed his own spear toward the stunned bandit, who had rolled over and was trying to scoot on his backside out of the mud. Unable to move fast enough, he curled his legs up to his chest, put both hands in front of his face and started to cry.

"Please don't hurt me. I surrender ... I surrender."

"Coward." Lehi grunted behind a half smile.

At a gesture from Lehi, two Nephite soldiers ran over to where their captain faced the criminal. They grabbed the blubbering bandit and stood him up, holding on to both of his arms. Still kneeling on the dead bandit, Shem pulled his sword out from the dead man's chest and wiped the blood off on the rags that covered the dead body. He put his weapon back into its sheath and walked over to where the young girl was. She was sitting on the ground sobbing and covering her face with her hands. Shem gently put his hand on her shoulder and spoke in a kind whisper. "It's over, child. You are safe now."

The girl uncovered her face and looked up into his eyes.

Now that it was safe, villagers started to come out of their simple houses, and one woman ran up to Shem crying, "My baby, my baby."

She scooped up the small girl and held her in her arms for several seconds.

"Thank you, sir. Thank you. Thank you," she repeated over and over, shaking Shem's hand up and down.

"Don't thank me. You should thank General Moroni. He and his men saved us all today," Shem responded as he gestured toward Moroni.

The mother put her child down and, holding on to her hand, moved past the gathered soldiers until she stood in front of the young general. She took his right hand and kissed it several times.

"Great One," she said, "how might a common woman thank you for saving the life of her only daughter?"

"Raise her to love and obey God. That will be thanks enough for me and my men. Now go, and tend to your child."

Moroni looked down at the young life that had just been saved. He winked at her and she produced a slight smile through her sobs and tears.

"My men and I are at your service, my princess." Moroni graciously spoke as he bowed before the young child. Taking a cue from their supreme leader, those Nephites around him also bowed respectfully before the mother and daughter. Moroni stood back up and asked the young girl, "With your permission, my lady, I will see to my men?"

The common village folk had never before been treated with such respect by someone with authority. The poor girl did not know what to do or how to answer the giant man before her. She simply curtsied and blushed. Moroni took that as a good sign and then bowed his head at her mother. As she wiped the tears from her eyes, she also smiled and respectfully bowed back.

"If you are feeling better tomorrow, I will need you and your mother to come to the court and swear before the chief judge about what happened here today," Shem said to the girl as he stepped around Moroni. She nodded in understanding and she and her child made their way past the Nephite soldiers and toward their home.

Moroni turned and faced Shem. "I am General Moroni," he said while extending his hand in friendship.

Shem blinked several times as he slowly reached for Moroni's hand. He was confused. Never before had someone who outranked him introduced himself and initiated a conversation. That was not the protocol. It has always been the other way around; the person deemed less important always sought the attention of those assumed to be above him. There was something different about this boy general, Shem thought. He saw Shem as an equal not a servant or lower class citizen.

"Yes sir, I know who you are. I served for a time under your father. I was sad to hear of his death at Jershon." Shem took his hand and shook it vigorously. "Thank you, sir, for helping me. I'm getting too old for this kind of thing."

"What about that one?" Moroni asked, indicating the bandit still being held by the soldiers.

"He's coming back with me to Manti to face justice," Shem answered.

"We, too, are on our way to Manti. My soldiers will escort you back."

"You're going to Manti?" Shem paused. "Why, is there a problem?"

"Yes," Moroni said. "But now is not the time to discuss it. I must meet with the chief judge and the city leaders as soon as possible." Moroni pointed to the remaining bandit "Bind his hands and put him on a horse." Indicating the two dead bandits, he said, "Let's get those bodies out of the street. Shem do you have some place to bury them?"

"Yes" he replied, "we have a pauper's gravesite behind the city."

Moroni dispatched some of his soldiers to retrieve the bodies of the two dead men.

"Just one minute," Shem said. He approached the body of the bandit leader still pinned to the wall by Teancum's javelin. The soldiers stepped back a pace from the body to let Shem by. Shem reached down and pulled a small leather bag full of gold coins off the dead man's belt. "This belonged to a merchant they robbed and killed this morning. I need to get it back to the merchant's family."

Teancum, a pace off from the dead bandit leader, caught Shem's eye as the lawman stood with the bag of coins in his hand.

"Was this your handiwork?" Shem asked Teancum, as he gestured back at the dead bandit pinned to the wall.

Teancum nodded and pulled his javelin out of the wall, letting the limp body slide down the wall and onto the ground.

"That was a great shot," Shem said as Teancum walked past him with his javelin in his hand.

"Thank you," Teancum nodded again and continued walking past Shem to his own horse.

Shem put his fists on his hips and tilted his head back, filling his lungs with air. This day turned out much differently than he had thought it would.

"Sheriff, what happened? Why are there so many soldiers here?" Shem slowly brought his chin back down. He stared blankly off into the distance, and then slowly looked back at the growing crowd of villagers.

"What happened, sheriff?" one of them asked again.

"You are all safe now. The bandits have been dealt with," Shem replied.

"But, the soldiers?"

Shem didn't quite know how to reply. Grateful for the impeccable timing, but still confused himself, Shem simply shrugged his shoulders.

He dropped his head and moved toward his horse that was still grazing on a small patch of grass right where he left him.

"All that excitement in town and you go for the fresh grass." Shem patted his mount on the neck and climbed up into the saddle. "All right, buddy, let's go home."

"Sheriff?" another villager called out. "What's going on? Why are there so many soldiers here?"

"I don't know," Shem replied. Trying not to hide his frustration, he quickly asked, "Did any of you see the bandits in the village take the girl?"

They all shook their heads. He knew they would be too scared to get involved. There were far more bandits in Manti than lawmen, but he had to ask. It was his duty.

"Your village elders will be fully briefed as soon as the chief judges and I know something. I promise," Shem told the villagers near him. Several of them nodded, and some even smiled. They knew he was one of the most trusted men in all of Manti. Shem was a man of honor.

Shem spurred his horse and rode up to where Moroni was waiting. Also waiting for Shem were two Nephites guarding the one bandit left alive. His hands were bound behind him and he was sitting on a pack horse. The two Nephites also had a second horse with the bodies of the two dead bandits lashed to it. Shem nodded his head to let Moroni know that he was ready to move out. Moroni raised his hand and waved it forward, signaling to the rest of the mounted soldiers to start moving. As the horse soldiers started to move down the dirt path through the small village, Moroni, Shem and several command staff officers trotted their horses up to the top of a small hill that overlooked the village. As Moroni twisted in his saddle to look back, Shem did the same and, for the first time, was able to witness the sea of humanity following General Moroni.

Shem let out a slow breath. "You bring an entire army to Manti," he said.

"This can mean only one thing." Shem had been a good soldier and some lessons you just never forget. He instantly knew well what was happening. "How much time do we have?" was all he asked.

"A few days, maybe a week at best," Moroni responded. Shem took a deep breath and pushed the air out of his lungs past his clinched teeth. "Manti is not prepared for war."

"I know," Moroni shot back. "That is why we are here."

DESPERATE TIMES

They spurred their horses onward and, in no time, were within sight of the gates and inferior walls of the city of Manti.

As the trail they traveled followed a bend in the river, Moroni pointed off to where more than a dozen young children were swimming in the shallows of the river to escape the heat of the midday sun. They splashed and played and jumped from a small dock into the cool water and dropped from a rope swing tied to a large tree branch overhanging to water.

"Look there," the general said to Shem, who was riding at his side. "Now, there is true happiness and wonder." A smile tugged at the corners of his mouth but faded before it was fully formed. "Do you ever think we will feel that young and happy again?"

"I hope, but it does seem that kind of joy is reserved for the young," Shem said.

As if on cue, the children's laughter stopped and they paused in their play to stare at the sight of an army marching toward their homes. One of the older boys, still dripping wet from the river water, stood ramrod straight, and brought his hand up in a child's attempt to salute. Two other young boys snapped to attention and mimicked their friend's gesture. Soon nearly all of the children had their hands pressed against their foreheads as the general passed.

Moroni returned the salute and, in a voice loud enough so only Shem could hear, said, "Brave boys. I wonder, when this is all over and they have seen firsthand the horror of war, if they will still want to salute as this army marches past."

Silence—like the death that was coming—fell between the two veteran soldiers. Moroni took a long, deep breath and held it for several seconds. He let it all come rushing out past his lips as he fought the urge to weep. He could feel the pain so many had suffered already because of Lamanite hatred. With frustration and anger in his voice, he spit out the words, "And for what—all because of the greed and hatred that only the father of all lies can create."

He could remember, like it was yesterday, his own childhood salute and the first time he watched his father kiss his mother goodbye, mount his war horse and ride off toward some unseen battlefield. He felt that old haunting pain in his chest. He felt again the sadness and confusing anger of wondering if he would ever see his hero again. "Where is he going?" he asked his mother. In his young, childlike way, he asked the question that troubled him most, "What for? What is he fighting for?" Moroni asked while he held his mother's neck, crying on her shoulder and hiding from the world in her red hair. His mother had told him about glory, honor and freedom, but at that age he did not care, he just wanted his dad to come back.

Moroni knew that the children playing on the river's edge would soon face that same pain and sorrow. War was coming to their doorsteps. He wanted to turn and look at them again, to shout reassurances, but the truth was that many of their mothers would soon be widows, many would lose their fathers, brothers—some of these children might even lose their own lives if he failed to protect them. He was heartbroken and ashamed.

The young general pulled his red cape tighter around his shoulders and held it with his fist against his chest. He bent forward as if pushed down by a heavy hand on his back. It was hard for him to force air into his lungs, and he felt moisture well up in his eyes. As he struggled with his own emotions and inner demons, his lips moved in a silent plea to a God he knew was their only hope.

"Father, I beg of you to give me the strength to do your will."

Just before reaching the next bend in the path, Moroni shifted his weight in the saddle, squared his shoulders and reined his horse to a stop. He suddenly felt it was important to recognize the children and make them feel respected. Hoping to convey encouragement and support, he drew out his great sword and brought the hilt up to his face to return the children's salute. Cheering, the children smiled and waved wildly in return.

The laughter instantly made Moroni feel better and a broad smile broke across his face. He looked over at Shem, who was looking back at the children. Shem glanced at Moroni and nodded in approval. The silent message of encouragement delivered, Moroni signaled his army to move around the bend and up a gentle slope toward the main gates of Manti.

To those at the front of the column, the city had been in view for several minutes, and they were close enough to see a farmer moving along his rows of crops and others working around the perimeter of the great city wall.

When most of the army was in full view of the city's watchtowers, the trumpeting of a great horn followed by drumming from inside the city walls signaled that the watchmen had finally spotted the Nephite army approaching. In response to the alarm, guards appeared and ran to their posts along the tops of Manti's walls.

Lehi, who had guided his horse up next to Moroni and Shem, said, "Well, they are finally awake. Seems like quite a slow reaction time to our arrival."

Teancum, bringing his horse up beside Shem to join the leaders at the front, agreed. "No roving patrols or any type of early warning, either. They just let an entire army walk right up to their front door before sounding the alarm."

"I think we are going to need to have a chat with the garrison commander," Moroni responded.

"Well," Shem said looking up at the sun. "It's almost noon, so our brave commander Pachus should be awake by now," he said sarcastically.

"Oh, look, here's someone now," Teancum continued.

The main gate had opened and a small contingent of riders came out at a gallop to greet the approaching army.

Moroni pulled up on his horse's reins and signaled the army to stop.

"Shem, perhaps if they see you out in front with us at the head of the column, they will know we come in peace."

"It's a good thing you do, since my city is obviously not prepared for war," Shem said and spurred his horse forward in response to Moroni's request.

When the riders from the city reached Shem, he was several yards in front of Moroni and his command staff. They pulled their mounts to a sudden stop several paces in front of Shem. Nervously, one of them spoke.

"Shem, what is the meaning of this?"

"Ask the general," Shem said matter-of-factly as he pointed over his shoulder at Moroni. Shem escorted the riders back to where Moroni and his captains waited.

Without waiting for an introduction, the lead rider growled, "I am called Kentle. I am a lieutenant of the garrison of the city of Manti. State your business here."

Shem cut in, "Slow down, Kentle. This is General Moroni, high commander of all the Nephite armies. Show some respect. He has come with his men to help us."

"Help us with what?" a second rider gasped.

Refusing to cow to the men's crass attitude and total lack of military respect, Moroni glanced at Teancum, then at Lehi, then spoke to Shem in an even, controlled voice.

"I'll explain myself to the chief judge of your city. Wake your commander Pachus and have him report to me with his command staff in one hour," Moroni ordered. He clicked his tongue and his mount moved forward toward the gates of the city.

The guards had no choice but to yield the way to General Moroni. They moved their horses off the road and watched as column after column of well-armed warriors marched past them.

Shem had resumed his position and was again riding next to Moroni.

"Sir, by your leave, may I excuse myself for a moment?"

"Certainly. Just don't be long. I have a feeling I will need your diplomacy again," Moroni said.

Shem rode back and pulled his horse next to Kentle's.

"You would be wise to be a little less hostile," Shem said.

"Why? What going on?" Kentle asked, this time with true interest.

"Real trouble. ... Lamanites, and from the looks of things, a great number of them, too." Shem said. He nodded at the soldiers moving past and added with a snort, "Upsetting a general—THE general—is not a career move I would recommend."

The lieutenant sighed. "How am I to know if Pachus does not tell us of such things? Speaking of Pachus, we had better get inside and find out which 'lady friend' he was with last night and get him up and ready to meet Moroni. I don't think the general is in a forgiving mood today."

Shem smiled. "This ought to be interesting. Good luck to you."

As Shem left the riders behind, he heard Kentle giving instructions to find Pachus before they galloped off toward the city gate.

Shem pulled his horse next to Moroni and his captains just outside the main gate. Moroni stopped his horse and signaled for the army to halt.

"Captain Lehi," he spoke.

"Sir."

"Garrison the army outside the walls. Set a watch and post a guard on the gate. I don't want any soldiers wandering in the city until we have met with the city's high council."

"Yes, sir" Lehi responded.

"Captain Teancum."

"Yes, my general."

"Send out mounted patrols to scout the countryside. I want detailed maps of the terrain and reconnaissance squads ready to deploy by nightfall."

"Yes, sir," Teancum replied.

"Shem?"

"Yes, General Moroni?"

"This army is hungry. We require food and drink from the city. Please advise the citizens to prepare a good dinner for all my men."

Shem shifted in his saddle as he looked back at the mass of soldiers along the road.

"Yes, sir," he replied with a bit of hesitation in his voice.

"Sergeant Major?"

"Yes, sir," the old soldier barked.

"I have a feeling we will need to make a good impression. I will need a detail of soldiers to act as my escort in the city. Please find a platoon of men suitable for the job."

"Sir?"

Moroni turned to his old friend and lowered his voice.

"I will need a group of soldiers to accompany me while I try to …" Moroni paused for dramatic effect "convince the elders of the city of the dangers we now face." He then winked at the old soldier.

The sergeant major had a puzzled look on his face as he paused to consider what Moroni had just said.

Then he brightened and said, "Oh, yes sir. Convincing looking soldiers, yes sir."

It took longer than the hour Moroni had allotted for the city leaders to assemble. In fact, it took nearly two hours for the meeting to begin, which only added to Moroni's first impression of the lack of readiness and the total disorganization of the city.

Once the meeting began, that impression changed only slightly. The gathering was held in a great reception hall lit by massive candles on stands as well as natural afternoon sunlight from windows high up in the stone walls. Several well-dressed men and women in colorful cloaks and bright jewelry stood in the center of the marble-floored room conversing, sipping drinks from bright metal cups and eating bits of fruit and meat delivered to them on trays carried by servants. Armored palace guards watched from the four corners of the room and the two large wooden doors that lead outside. Two more guards stood at each end of a raised platform at the far end of the room.

Idle conversation stopped when a man walked out of a door behind the platform and rapped three times with a mallet on the main table sitting on top of the raised platform.

"Ladies and gentlemen, the chief judges of Manti." The herald took two steps back and three elderly men walked through the doorway. All three men were wrapped in purple robes, but the chief judge also had a white sash draped around his neck and over his shoulders. The three men stood in front of the chairs behind the table, with the chief judge in the middle. The chief judge sat down first, in the center of the three high-backed chairs on the platform. His two vice judges sat down after him.

"Good people of Manti," the chief judge spoke. "Our honored guest, the great General Moroni, has asked to address the judges and city council regarding a very grave situation. Guard, please have the general come in."

The guards positioned beside the double doors at the far end of the hall pulled them open and stood at attention. General Moroni's imposing frame filled the doorway, lit from the back by afternoon sunshine. Moroni stepped through the doorway, followed by Lehi and Teancum, with the sergeant major and several very large, muscular, heavily-armed and dangerous-looking Nephite soldiers bringing up the rear. The sergeant major carried the Sword of Laban wrapped in a red cloth.

The entering guests caught only part of the whispered conversations that erupted at the sight of Moroni and his escorts. "… so young …" they heard one woman say. "… just a child …" another commented. "He's enormous," one man whispered. Another asked his neighbor, "Is that the Sword of Laban?" No one in the room had ever seen it before, but all knew stories about the spectacular weapon. The sergeant major had the scabbard covered with the red cloth, but he left the golden hilt exposed, which only added to the allure of the already mythical weapon.

The whispering did not go unnoticed by Moroni or his command staff, nor did the fact that the gathered citizens of Manti were overweight, overdressed and covered in fine jewels.

"Pompous fools," Lehi spoke out of the side of his mouth, loud enough for Moroni and Teancum to hear.

"Funny, I thought you would feel right at home among these plump and not-so pretty people," Teancum teased Lehi. A smile broke on his face.

Lehi turned his face toward Teancum, trying to maintain a stone-cold look of defiance, but he couldn't keep a smile from creeping across his lips and from breaking into a laugh. Teancum winked at his contemporary and Lehi nudged him back with his shoulder.

Moroni ignored the jostling behind him and maintained his stately composure as he moved forward until coming to a stop several feet in front of the judges' bench. Moroni bowed slightly at the waist, and the chief judge bowed his head in return.

"Who presents the general and his staff before the chief judges of the city of Manti?" the assistant judge sitting on the right hand of the chief judge asked to the crowd.

"I do," Shem responded as he stepped into the great hall from the door behind the judges.

"Come forward, Sheriff," the elderly chief judge requested.

Shem stepped around the judges' bench, stood to the right of Moroni and bowed to the elderly gentlemen sitting behind the bench.

"Honored gentlemen," Shem said facing the judges, "may I present General Moroni, the newly appointed high commander of all Nephite armed forces, and his command staff.

"Welcome General Moroni," the elderly and distinguished head judge spoke. "I knew your father well. He was a man of high honor and courage. Your presence in this hall is a great honor for us all. The city of Manti is at your service."

"Thank you, sir, for your warm welcome and honored hospitality. But it is I and my men who are here to serve you and the good people of this city," Moroni said as he bowed again. His staff and escorts followed his example, each of them bowing to the judges.

"Shem tells us you and your men are responsible for resolving the difficult and unfortunate problem with the bandits who attacked the trading caravans earlier," the judge sitting on the left said.

"The good sheriff had the matter well in hand. We just happened along in time to give him some moral support," Moroni said.

The crowd let out a quiet giggle in response to Moroni's humor and the judges all smiled and shook their heads. Shem blushed a bright red and gave Moroni a sarcastic look.

"I'm getting too old for this," Shem whispered. Moroni winked back at him.

"General, what brings you and your men to our fair city?" the old judge asked. Moroni took three steps forward before he spoke in serious, measured tones.

"Sir, the Lamanites are marching toward your city with a massive army. They could be as close as two days to a week away. If we don't start preparing now, your city will fall and the loss of life will be staggering."

At Moroni's words, an awkward silence fell in the great hall and no one moved for what seemed like an eternity. The gathered citizens of Manti slowly recovered, looking at each other with disbelief and shock. All at once, the entire room exploded with shouts of anger, concern, panic and demands for answers. Several of the people in the hall started to approach the bench, shouting at the judges. This caused the city guards to move into action. They quickly positioned their bodies in front of the bench. Holding their long spears parallel to the ground at chest height, they formed a barricade, forcing the citizens back and away from the bench.

"Order. There will be order in here," the old judge shouted as he pounded his gavel on the bench.

THE EMBARRASSMENT THAT IS PACHUS

Moroni and his men remained calm as the shouting and commotion around them reached a fever pitch. The chief judge, who was now standing, kept banging his gavel and demanding order. Slowly, the noise level lowered and the people in the great hall backed away from the judges' bench.

"General Moroni," said the chief judge, still standing and holding his gavel in a ready position, "this is most distressing news. What proof do you have that the Lamanites will attack us?"

Moroni patiently waited until the old judge sat down before he responded.

"Sir, we had reliable intelligence that the Zoramites had joined forces with several tribes from the Lamanites and formed a massive army to come into our lands and pillage. I moved what soldiers I could into the valley of Jershon to act as a blocking force until the militia could be called up to assist us. Several days ago, this Lamanite army, with the help of the traitorous Zoramites, came over the mountain pass and invaded our lands, killing several of our brave soldiers."

A collective gasp went up from the Manti citizens, who now were hanging on Moroni's every word.

"With the blessings of heaven and using the terrain to our advantage, we were able to inflect heavy damage and drive them back into the jungle. When they retreated, I sent scouts to follow them and watch where they went. My scouts reported the Lamanite army was moving through the jungle in the direction of this city. I also sent a messenger to Zarahemla to ask the Lord's Prophet, Alma the Great, to speak to God and plead for His divine intervention. The prophet gave my messenger this very scrap of paper with the answer to my prayers."

All eyes were on Moroni as he walked up to the bench and handed the piece of parchment paper to the chief judge. The old judge inspected the wax seal imprint on the outside of the parchment.

"This is the seal of the high priest of the church," he said, looking closely at the impressions on the seal.

The judge unfolded the scrap of paper and quickly scanned the one word written on it. Almost instantly, the judge slumped in his chair and let out a long breath. The assistant judge sitting on his left reached over to pick up the paper scrap that had fallen from the chief judge's hand. He unfolded it and held it up for the other assistant judge to read at the same time. They both sat back in their chairs, the color draining from their faces.

"What is it? What is written?" someone cried from the back of the room.

"Just one word is written on the message," the chief judge responded. "Manti. All it says is Manti."

Gasps of astonishment rose up from the gathered congregation.

"I know this is distressing news," Moroni spoke in an even, calming tone with his hands raised up to quiet the crowd. "But we are here to keep Manti safe from harm. Of course, we won't be able to do it without your help. We will need to coordinate our efforts with your local security forces."

"Of course," the head judge said. "Commander Pachus, please step forward."

No one stirred except Moroni, who curiously looked around the crowded room, expecting the commander to appear.

"Commander Pachus …?" The chief judge called out again.

"Sir … um … perhaps the commander is …" Moroni tried to make the moment more comfortable.

"Perhaps, young Moroni, Pachus has embarrassed me for the last time," the judge shot out. "Shem, do you know where we might find our missing garrison commander?"

"My men are searching for him now, sir," Shem hesitantly responded.

"You see, General Moroni," the old judge explained as he sat back in his chair. "Pachus is the commander of the city's forces, and he was sent to us by appointment from Zarahemla. I have asked several times to have him removed, and I even tried to replace him with Shem. But Pachus' father is a high-ranking bureaucrat within the national government, and I'm afraid we are stuck with him for the time being."

"Maybe I can help with that," Moroni said.

His offer was ignored at first as the chief judge's attention was drawn away. The distraction was caused by three well-dressed men speaking in loud whispers and pointing and shooting looks of distrust at Moroni.

"Uh, yes, about Pachus," the chief judge continued. "I wish he was our only problem. As I'm sure you have surmised from your initial observations, we are in no way prepared for an attack of any consequence."

The chief judge glanced again at the three men. Moroni followed his gaze and saw that the three were obviously arguing.

The chief judge went on. "Fortune favors us this day with the timely arrival of you and your men at arms. I'm sure with your help we can overcome any and all obstacles standing in the way of making this once-great city a safe place again." Casting another quick look at the arguing men, the old judge continued. "What is it we can do to assist you in the defense of our city?"

"I will need the city's militia called up. Every man and boy capable of bearing arms, every palace guard, temple security man, peace officer, even your personal escorts will need to report to my officers at five this evening outside the main gate for instructions. Every man or boy not capable of fighting, every woman and girl above the age of twelve will report to my officers in the morning at first light for instructions on helping shore up the defenses and preparing this city for a siege."

Upon hearing this, two of the whispering men faced the third. Both took a step forward, until their noses nearly touched the other man's. He looked over and made eye contact with Moroni. With real hatred on his face, he spat on the ground in front of his two opponents and turned to leave the room.

"Leaving so soon, Zacka?" The chief judge called, sarcasm dripping in his voice.

"Yes, your honor; I go to find Pachus." Zacka said. "If we are to discuss the city's defenses, by the law that you wrote," Zacka pointed an accusing finger at the old Judge, "we must have the city's garrison commander present."

"Don't snap at me boy. I know the laws of this city," the judge lashed back. "Your dear friend Pachus is drunk and up to his immoral antics again while a clear and present Lamanite danger confronts us."

"It's going to take more than the word of some would-be boy general to convince me that I should change the station of my life and consort with the unwashed outside the city gate like some common soldier. No, I do not work or do manual labor; I have servants for such things. You, soldier … Moroni is it?" Zacka flipped his hand at Moroni. "Well, Moroni, I have thirty servants, and they will be at the appointed place and time for your instructions. I, on the other hand, have an appointment with a nice lady at five this evening and shall not be attending your little gathering."

"Zacka, the council is still in session and you have not been excused," Shem shouted and moved to cut off Zacka's path to the door.

Zacka, who was younger and a bit shorter than Shem, with long black curly hair, pampered features, and a slight build, came face to face with Shem. Zacka's expensive robe and gold jewelry accented the smug grin on his face. Zacka intentionally avoided military service and hid behind his family's money whenever there was trouble, but he was not going to let anyone think he was afraid of Shem or anyone else.

"What are you going to do, Shem, arrest me? You and I both know how that will turn out." Zacka took a long drink from the wine cup in his hand and dropped the empty metal cup at Shem's feet. The cup bounced across the marble floor and the clanging echoed off the walls.

"No, I'm not going to arrest you, but if we come under attack and you interfere in the defense of the city or refuse to do your duty, I will have you hanged as a coward and a traitor."

Zacka smiled. "Pachus is in command of the city's forces, not you and not your new friend."

Shem started to reply but was interrupted by the crashing of dishes in the hallway outside the doors of the great hall, followed by a loud, drunken voice complaining and cursing about a table being left in his way. Everyone citizen of Manti knew that belligerent voice.

"Your commander has arrived," Shem said with an evil grin on his face.

Zacka's face turned a bright red.

The drunken voice cursed the tables again, screamed at the unseen servants for leaving the tables there, then flung open the door. Pachus was truly a sight to behold. When he burst into the room, he was off balance and it took him a moment to regain his composure while readjusting his lopsided helmet on his head. Standing no taller than an average man, Pachus weighed well over three hundred pounds. His thinning brown hair was a mess, eyes were bloodshot and his face was flush and covered with sweat. His tunic showed sweat stains under his arms and around his neck. Pachus's fat poked out from around the corners of his chest plate, and his flabby double chin jiggled as he moved. He held a wine goblet in one hand and used the other hand to help keep his balance.

"Your honor," he bellowed, holding the goblet high in the air. "You summoned me?"

The judges sitting behind the large table each had a look of utter disgust on their faces. One even tried to cover his face.

"Yes, Pachus," the chief judge said. "Thank you for responding in such a … such a timely manner."

Several people in the crowd giggled nervously under their breath.

"Pachus," the judge continued and motioned with his hand, "come forward so that I may speak to you without shouting."

Pachus took three slow and wobbly steps forward and then one step back to keep from falling as he tried to make his way past Moroni and his soldiers to the judges' bench. He even paused half way to take another drink from his wine goblet while bracing himself on Captain Lehi's shoulder. Wiping his face with the end of his crimson cloak and nodding to Lehi, he whispered, "Cheers," and continued forward. Lehi recoiled from the stink of Pachus's breath, very calmly picked up his massive battle ax, and moved to crush Pachus from behind. Teancum's hand caught Lehi's before he could raise the ax and he shook his head to tell Lehi "No." Lehi put down the ax and moved back with his men.

Pachus continued to shamble forward, passing by the gathered Manti citizens, who shook their heads in disgust as he made his way to the judge's bench.

"Commander Pachus of the garrison of Manti at your service," he spoke, sloshing back and forth in front of the judge's table. He rendered a sloppy hand salute.

"Commander, I would like you to meet General Moroni. He now commands all the Nephite military forces. He has been given power over the people to wage war on the Lamanites." Stumbling a bit, Pachus turned his face toward Moroni. Pachus took a second to look the young general over, then raised his goblet and slurred, "Young General Moraomie, welcome to Manti." He drained the remaining alcoholic contents of the goblet into his mouth.

Moroni did not return the salutation but stood as still as a stone with his jaw clenched, eyes burning and hands curled into tight fists. Pachus was a disgrace and Moroni was furious.

Belching out loud, Pachus turned back to the judges. "He's a big one. Not much for manners, though." Pachus next faced the gathered citizens. "One night in our fair city should wipe that frown off his face. Am I right?" he spouted in a drunken laugh and held the empty goblet high in the air. A chorus of moans, laughter and gasps of disgust came from the gathered people of Manti. Trying to drink from the empty cup, Pachus realized he was out of wine and called for more. "Bring me more wine!" he demanded. A young girl in rags, holding a large pitcher, moved toward him from the back of the room.

"You have had quite enough," Moroni barked in a commanding tone and jerked his head to the side, telling the girl to go back. Pachus was outraged.

"Come here, girl, and fill my cup!" The servant girl, her eyes wide and glistening with fear, turned back and moved toward Pachus. Moroni took two steps in her direction and held up his hand.

"Stop," he gently spoke. "What is your name, little one?" He bent over and kneeled in front of the now frightened servant girl.

"Please, my lord, let me pass and fill that man's cup. You are a guest here and, when you leave, my family and I will still be under his control. Please, I beg you, let me pass."

"Control? Do you mean his slave?" Moroni asked with anger building in his voice.

The girl blinked several times but said nothing.

"Boy, get out of the way. Wench, bring me my wine!" Pachus bellowed.

Moroni was still kneeling in front of the girl and had his back to Pachus. He stood up straight and closed his eyes, trying not to lose control of his emotions. The young girl darted around Moroni's dominating frame and ran to Pachus. She started to pour the red liquor into his goblet, but it was heavy and her hands were shaking. She spilled some on his shoes. In a rage, Pachus slapped the girl with the back of his hand, knocking her to the ground and spilling the remainder of the wine on the floor.

"Stupid, ignorant child," he shouted. "You ruined my new leather boots."

Bleeding from the mouth, the girl curled into the fetal position, covered her head and started to sob.

"You thought your family's debt to me was high before now," Pachus roared. He stood over her and raised his hand to strike her again. As his fist came down to deliver a second strike, it was caught, midflight, by Captain Lehi.

"That's quite enough, sonny boy," Lehi growled and kicked the back of Pachus's fat leg, knocking him to the ground. Pachus landed on his back, the impact knocking the air out of his lungs and leaving him gasping. Lehi, who still had a firm hold on Pachus's arm, twisted it into a painful wrestling joint lock. Pachus cried out in agony. The city guards started to move forward, but Teancum pointed his spear at the closest one and said,

"Back," while the remaining Nephite soldiers pulled their weapons and moved to strategic locations around their captains to keep anyone else from trying to come to Pachus's aid.

Moroni, who was positioned a few paces away from the sergeant major, motioned to the old soldier to let him know he wanted the sword. The sergeant major grabbed the scabbard of the mighty weapon with both hands and thrust it into the air. Rapidly jerking back, he held onto the scabbard as the sword flew out of its resting place and arced across the room toward Moroni. The general caught the sword with one hand in midflight and, with expert timing, made two full circles in front of him with the blade. Stopping next to Pachus, Moroni brought the sword of power up over his head. Pachus was still gasping for air. With two hands now holding the hilt, Moroni slashed the weapon down, striking the blade edge of the sword in the middle of Pachus's armored metal chest plate.

The sound of metal striking metal clanked through the air. Several onlookers gasped and some cried out. One woman fainted at the sight of the monster blade in Pachus's chest and the giant looming over him. Moroni held his position, standing over the plump, shallowly breathing commander. Suddenly, with the sound of popping metal, Pachus's chest armor broke in two pieces. The halves slid down opposite sides of his fat chest and clanked on the floor. Not a drop of blood showed on Pachus's now-panting chest. Only someone with an elite level of skill and strength, holding an expertly crafted weapon, could cleave body armor in two without injuring the one wearing it.

Looking Pachus in the eye, Moroni spoke. "This is the Sword of Laban, forged and crafted in old Jerusalem by the masters. I carry it now as a symbol of my authority and responsibility. I am the head of all the Nephite armies and this sword is only to be used to make men free." Moroni drew the sword carefully across Pachus's chest until the very tip was digging into his flabby chin. "Is there a dispute over this fact?" Moroni asked.

"No, no dispute, my general," Pachus said.

"Is there a dispute over this fact?" Moroni barked as he looked over the crowd of Manti's leading citizens. The only movement was Zacka and his two friends heading for the door. Before exiting, Zacka looked back at Moroni. Moroni caught the look and smiled at the retreating Zacka. Zacka quickly hissed air out through his closed teeth and was gone.

"That's not the last I am going to see of this Zacka character," Moroni thought.

THE OLD SERGEANT

Moroni stood and handed the sword back to the sergeant major. He bent down and held out his hand to the girl lying in the fetal position on the floor at his feet, sobbing quietly. She put her tiny hand in Moroni's massive palm and he helped her to her feet. He gently brushed her hair out of her eyes, took a quick look at the small cut on her lip and said, "Everything will be all right now, little one."

She started to smile but, instead, winced in pain when the cut on her mouth split open and started to bleed.

"Stand here next to me," Moroni said to her and guiding her to his side like a protective big brother.

Pachus, who was just getting his breath back, moaned loudly as he tried to roll to his side

"I have a wonderful idea," Moroni spoke as he turned to the crowd. "In light of today's events, I think it would only be right …" He stopped speaking, picked up his left foot and rested the sole of his sandal on Pachus's chest. Leaning forward, he put his forearms on his left knee and pushed his body weight down on his left foot.

"As I was saying, I think it would only be right if your brave commander released this poor girl and the rest of her family from their debt and obligations to him." Moroni pushed down a little harder as he leaned in closer to Pachus's face. "Yes?" Moroni asked in an inquisitive tone.

"Yes, yes," Pachus gasped and tried to nod his head in agreement.

"Wonderful," Moroni exclaimed. He took his foot off Pachus's chest and Lehi released his grip. "Now we truly have something to celebrate,"

Moroni said, smiling over at the table of judges. The chief judge was almost bouncing out of his seat with joy. All three of the judges smiled at Moroni and nodded their approval.

The young girl could not believe her ears. Her family was now free. She started to run out of the room to tell her family the exciting news but stopped half way. Turning around she ran back to Moroni and tried to wrap her arms around his waist.

The young girl looked up at Moroni, still quivering and fighting to hold back tears.

Moroni leaned over and said, "Well, young lady, I think you've got some exciting news to tell your family. You had better run along now. You're free. You and your family, too—free!"

"Thank you, my lord. Thank you," was all she could say. She ran toward the door, then changed her mind, and ran back to throw her arms again around Moroni's waist. "Thank you. Thank you."

Moroni lovingly patted her back in return and said, "No, it is I who should be thanking you. You showed great bravery, and I am at your service." He bowed before her and the rest of the Nephite soldiers followed.

The girl again started for the door, but turned back and bowed deeply before her new friend and deliverer. "Come here." Moroni smiled and knelt on one knee in front of the girl. "I want to give you one more thing. My gift to you was first expressed in the words of the great King Benjamin." He continued to kneel in front of the girl, but spoke louder so the entire crowd could hear. "Remember, 'when you are in the service of your fellow beings, you are only in the service of your God.' Again, I thank you for the opportunity to serve." Moroni tipped his head, and then lifted his chin again to look directly at the young girl. "Now, off you go."

This time she took off like an arrow, out the door and down the hallway.

"The rest of you men I will see promptly at five this evening for instruction and training," he said as he scanned the room. "Spread the word."

Pachus interrupted Moroni's instructions with, "General, what of ..." but his voice gave out. He tried to stand, but fell backwards into a small table.

At the pitiful sight of Pachus trying to stand up again, Lehi spoke. "He looks like a fat turtle trying to right itself." There was a collective chuckle among the Nephite warriors.

Moroni spoke without humor. "Sober up and make yourself presentable. Then you may address me." With that, General Moroni walked out the door, followed by his staff and officers.

Pachus continued to struggle to gain his footing. The chief judge shook his head in disgust. "Someone get him up." Two palace guards ran to Pachus's side. They strained as they helped him to his feet.

"Pachus, listen closely," the Chief Judge commanded with new found vigor. "I expect you to pull yourself together, now. You are to assemble the militia and open up the city's armory. Have those citizens who are without arms and armor draw what they need. Then, be ready by five to take your instruction from General Moroni. Do you understand?"

"Yessh, your honor." He swayed back and forth and tried to keep his helmet on his head but his attempt was in vain and it clattered to the floor. Someone in the crowd retrieved it and handed it back to Pachus who, between stumbling and swearing, made his way to the door.

At exactly five in the afternoon, uniformed soldiers, militia members and many of the male citizens of Manti were in place on the open ground outside the city's main gate. With General Moroni and the command leadership observing from several yards away, the sergeant major, with the help of some of Moroni's best warriors, was trying to get the men from Manti's militia into formation to participate in some simple marching practice, but the new recruits were failing miserably.

"I have seen cows move with more precision and discipline than this rabble." Lehi observed.

"I agree," Teancum said. "Their decadent, lazy lifestyles are certainly beginning to show. These men are pathetically soft and weak. I can see how common folks might not understand basic military movement and skills, but even the city's guard force and militia are inept."

"Like I said, Manti is not prepared for war," Shem added. Some of the gathered men tried to cover their lack of training and discipline by resorting to jokes and complaining. One pompous and well-dressed young man shoved his way to the front and began taunting and heckling the sergeant major. When the sergeant major told him to return to his post, he mimicked the sound and body movements of the old soldier, causing the other recruits to laugh and join in the disrespect.

As Moroni's soldiers tried to continue the training, the blatant disrespect and contempt steadily increased. The one who had been taunting the sergeant major earlier was now skipping about and imitating the soldiers around him who were trying to teach the men of Manti how to defend themselves and save their city.

"Soldiers, halt," the sergeant major yelled over the fray and most of the men came to attention. Some kept laughing and talking, including the one who had been leading the insubordination. The sergeant major spoke to him in a low tone that only a few around him could hear. The young man laughed in the old soldier's face and shouted, "What are you going to do about it, old man?" The sergeant major stood for several seconds with his fists clenched, facing the man who challenged him.

"Sergeant Major!" Moroni called out from his vantage point.

The old solder immediately marched up to where the general stood and saluted.

"Yes, sir?"

"Sergeant Major, it would seem there is a lack of focus with some of the new soldiers."

The sergeant major took a long breath and let it out slowly.

"Yes, sir, there is."

"Do you have any …" Moroni paused and winked as if wanting to make sure the message would sink in, "… any recommendations on how we can speed up the process of training and get those who are lacking in respect to fall in line with the others?"

"Yes, sir," the sergeant major responded with a slight smile. "I can think of one or two things I could do to get this moving along a bit faster."

"Good," Moroni smiled back. "Carry on, Sergeant Major."

"Yes, sir." He saluted, smiled and marched back to the waiting mass of untrained civilians.

"This should be interesting." Teancum said quietly as the officers around him giggled under their breath.

"What's happening?" Shem asked Lehi.

"You might want to get a medic over here," Lehi chuckled while gesturing with his head to have Shem look back at the old soldier.

"Or a priest," Teancum added in a jovial tone.

Shem was still confused and watched as the sergeant major walked right up to the man who had been challenging his authority.

The man smirked and raised his forearms, palms up, as if to question what the sergeant major was going to do about his disrespect. With lightning speed and the impact of a charging bull, the sergeant major punched the man squarely in the gut. Gasping, the man bent over and grabbed his belly. He dropped to his knees and vomited the entire contents of his stomach all over the grass in front of him. The three men closest to the sergeant major, who also had joined in the taunts, now moved to attack the old soldier.

None of them were prepared for the speed and viciousness of the sergeant major's defense. Kicking, punching, chopping, twisting and breaking those three men in a matter of seconds, the sergeant major hardly showed a sweat. When it was all over, four strong young men lay on the ground before him, crying out in anguish and pain.

The sergeant major stepped over the wounded men and spoke loudly enough for the assembled men to hear him.

"I am the Command Sergeant Major of the Nephite army and I answer only to General Moroni. It is my responsibility to train you and make you ready for the Lamanites. Does anyone else have a problem with this?"

The silence was almost tangible.

"Good. Then all of you, get back in your formations before you really start to upset me."

The men of Manti now moved with intensity and purpose in a mad dash to return to their places.

"Sergeant, take over training!" the sergeant major shouted to a young, but very large, Nephite warrior next to him.

"Yes, Sergeant Major. Move, you dogs. Forward march! Hut, two, three, four, move, two, three, four."

As the formation marched off behind him, the sergeant major leisurely walked back to Moroni and the rest of the command staff.

"I think I fixed the problem, sir. The training should run more smoothly now."

"That was outrageous," Pachus came running up the hill where Moroni was standing, snorting and panting as he went. "You saw him, Moroni. He assaulted my men. What are you going to do about it?"

"Nothing, Pachus. I am going to do nothing about it."

"Well, I am," Pachus barked. "If you are going to allow your cadre to assault my men, I am removing them from this field." Pachus started to move toward the training ground, but Moroni moved over and positioned himself in Pachus's path.

"If you do anything to disrupt the training in any way or try to weaken the defense of this city, I will behead you where you stand. Am I clear?" Moroni spoke calmly and clearly. "You are given annual allotments from the Nephite government to train and maintain an adequate defense force for this city. Explain this." Moroni angrily demanded, pointing to the folly unfolding before them.

"Well, General …" Pachus, who was only slightly more sober but much more congenial now, nervously cleared his throat. "It's really a matter of fiscal priority. When you take into consideration the earned interest of the last payment and add that to the rising cost of weapons manufacturing, you get...."

"Stop talking!" Moroni demanded. His face was flush with righteous anger.

"Sir?" Pachus inquired meekly.

"STOP TALKING!"

"Yes, sir." Pachus cowered before the massive man before him. Moroni was so furious that it took several seconds to compose himself. He could not lose control of his emotions in front of all those who were watching. He knew he was in charge and needed to set the standard of conduct for his men. He had to compose himself before he continued and took several deep breaths before he addressed Pachus further.

"Go stand over there," Moroni ordered Pachus while pointing away from himself.

"Me, sir?" Pachus asked.

"Yes, you, Pachus .... Go stand over there," Moroni pointed to a brown spot of grass several yards away from the rest of the command staff.

"Ah, right here?" Pachus asked, as he stepped toward the spot pointed out by Moroni.

"Yes, Pachus, right there. Now stand there and don't do or say anything."

Looking like a spoiled child sent to the corner, Pachus scanned the crowd of fellow citizens. When no one showed signs of support, Pachus huffed loudly, and cursed under his breath.

"Gentlemen," Moroni said to the gathered Nephite officers, "clearly there has been a failure of leadership in this city." As if carefully choreographed to do so, at the mention of his faulty leadership, Pachus felt the effects of the wine he'd been drinking all day and began wincing and crossing his legs to keep from wetting himself.

Moroni spoke again, immediately regaining his men's attention. "Dwelling on their incompetence or complaining about what they have failed to do will solve nothing. I will deal with Pachus in due time. God has set this challenge before us, and we will not fail Him. Is that clear?"

"Yes, sir!" they spoke in unison.

"Very well. Let's get to work. We know the enemy is coming; it's just a matter of time. Captain Lehi, I want patrols out, picket lines built and observation posts set. We don't need the Lamanites sneaking up on us and finding us unprepared to defend ourselves. Start a rotation for chow and sleep. Make sure everyone gets enough of both. Get all nonmilitary personnel who are living outside the walls of Manti inside, along with all the supplies and livestock. We don't need to make it any easier for the enemy if this turns into a siege."

"Yes, sir," Lehi responded. He made eye contact with one of his lieutenants and commanded "My horse." The young soldier ran off to obey the order to fetch Lehi's mount.

"Captain Teancum," General Moroni continued, "you and the sergeant major are to get this cluster of a guard force in line. Get them up to speed with our tactics and training. Once you have them moving, see to the city's armory supplies and defenses. Do whatever is necessary to get this city on a war footing. We will need food and medical supplies produced, arrows made, armor fitted … you know the drill. I'm not going to insult you by reciting all the things a city needs to produce for its army before a battle. Just make it happen."

"Yes, sir," Teancum acknowledged his orders.

"General Moroni, how can I help?" Shem asked.

"Thank you for volunteering, Sheriff." Moroni smiled "I am going to need all of my field commanders with the main body of the army, so I am giving you a promotion. You are now in command of all the city's defenses. Congratulations, Captain."

Overhearing the exchange, Pachus tightened his jaw and his eyes showed anger and offense at being demoted from his personal rank and responsibility. He managed to control his voice, saying, "General, a word with you in private, if I may?"

"No, Pachus, you're a drunkard and a disgrace to the uniform you wear. You're lucky I don't have you hung for dereliction of duty. Right now, I just don't have the time to deal with you. You're relieved of your command and on house arrest."

"Arrested?" Pachus gulped. "General, be reasonable," he begged as he moved closer to Moroni.

Moroni turned to the beefy young sergeant in command of his personal security detail. "Disarm him, then take him home and lock him in his house."

The sergeant saluted in response and signaled for three of his men to follow. They trotted over to Pachus and quickly grabbed his fat arms. Pachus resisted and tried to pull his arms free as he shouted, "This is not the last word on the matter, Moroni." He continued to bellow as the soldiers cut off his weapons belt and pulled him toward the main city gate.

"There is a history here with him, General." Shem paused as he watched the guards walk Pachus away. "You didn't see much support here today, but he has friends both here and in Zarahemla."

Moroni could hear the concern in Shem's voice and turned to look at Pachus again, just as the soldiers tasked to guard him recoiled from him as a wet urine stain spread down his pant leg. The guards held his fat arms tightly, but quickly danced their feet away from the puddle forming on the floor.

Moroni let out a snort of laughter.

"I'm not overly concerned right now over what Pachus might try to do to me, Captain. We will cross that bridge when we come to it. Right now I need you on point with command of the city's defenses. Are we clear?"

"Yes, sir," Shem replied. "And may I say how grateful I am to answer to the command of a true leader."

Lehi clapped Shem on the shoulder before moving to take the reins of his horse from the young soldier who had just returned.

"Lehi, before you go …" Moroni spoke again to all the gathered officers. "We will meet again after dinner in the chief judge's chambers for an update on our progress. Understood?"

"Yes, sir," they all said together.

"Questions?"

No one responded. "Good, let's move." Moroni commanded and everyone left to see to their assigned duties.

The food served to the soldiers by the ladies of Manti at dinner that night was simple but plentiful. There were hunks of broiled meat, squash, beans, and thickly sliced multigrain bread. As was the old custom, the officers ate after all the soldiers had been fed. It was well after nine before the command staff could meet in the judge's chambers for the war council.

"Gentlemen, thank you for coming." Moroni nodded to the members of his command staff, who had quickly come to attention as he entered the large room. He pulled maps out from under his arm. "Sit down, please. Did everyone get some chow?"

The combined "yes, sir" responses created a low rumble.

"Excellent," Moroni said. "So, all we need to begin are the chief judges."

"Here, General," the head judge called out as he and his two assistants walked in.

The staff members came to attention again, this time directing their respect to the three elderly judges. Moroni came around from the table to greet the leaders of Manti.

"Thank you, gentlemen for coming tonight," He spoke. "I felt it expedient that you be here as we discuss the defense of Manti."

"We are all in your debt and at your service, young General Moroni," the chief judge said and waved his hand toward the head table. "Please continue."

"Gentlemen …" Moroni gestured to his staff and they joined him around the table where Moroni had spread one of the maps.

"Captain Teancum has just provided me with the updated troop numbers." Moroni walked around the table covered with the map. "Even with the infusion of the city's defenses, we still are outnumbered by the Lamanites in both infantry and cavalry. We have set a watch on the towers and doubled the guard force on the walls. I have sent riders back to Zarahemla to requisition more troops, but I fear they will not get here in time to help."

Moroni felt a strange stirring as his own concerns came up against the wall of silence from his own strongest supporters. He waited for someone else to speak but knew it was his role to continue to take the lead, especially with the new direction he was about to propose. "Gentlemen, what I propose is a radical change in the way we fight. I have been in solemn prayer for hours, and I have asked the Lord what He wants us to do. My mind is taken back to the lessons Chief Captain Teancum gave on new tactics of using the terrain to our advantage and of splitting our forces to attack Lamanite weaknesses. It worked in Jershon, and I don't feel the Lamanites will be expecting it to happen again." Moroni walked over to a different large map hanging on the wall that showed the land around Manti. "Here is my plan."

THE BATTLE FOR MANTI

The first light of dawn broke across the eastern sky, spotlighting the strong shape of Lehi standing on the top of the hill Riplah. Lehi had kept a silent vigil all night, waiting for this moment in history to arrive. Before him was an open floodplain with the mighty river Sidon twisting through the land like a giant blue snake toward the horizon and the sea. On his right to the east were dark, jungle-covered mountains, with the merchant road breaking out of the mountain's green wall of trees and leading to the river's edge. To his left, and across the river, Lehi could see over the walls and into the interior of Manti and almost make out the movement on top of the walls and in the towers as the night watch was relieved by fresh guards, most of whom were still groggy from a restless sleep. Lehi blinked several times and squinted hard, trying to see clearly the movements on the wall. He muttered under his breath and shook his head in frustration at his failing vision.

"I'm getting too old for this."

The merchant road that led out of the jungle and to the river's edge continued on the far side of the river, thanks to the aid of a bridge made of wood and stone. The bridge had been built long ago by the people of that land, and it had survived flood and drought, famine and feast, good times and bad, and funeral and marriage precessions. Nothing had ever crossed the narrow path and wooden bridge that was anywhere near as sinister and dangerous as what was starting to emerge from the jungle tree line and travel down the merchant road.

A contrasting prelude to the emerging danger, Lehi had experienced peaceful, even surreal, moments throughout the early morning. Alone with his thoughts at the top of the dominant hill, Lehi had reflected on his family. He missed his wife and children. The last letter from his beloved wife, safely tucked inside his breast pocket, had mentioned that their oldest daughter, recently married, was now pregnant. Counting the moon cycles in his mind, he was thinking how close she must be to giving birth and how rewarding it would be to finally have grandchildren.

His peaceful thoughts were interrupted and replaced with watchfulness as the vanguard of the Lamanite army marched past the base of his hill in a giant, loose formation toward the bridge. Suddenly, he changed from a simple man awed by nature's grandeur and basking in the love of his family to a steel-eyed warrior with passion and intensity exuding from every part of his being. He took several deep breaths to calm the emotions building inside. He could feel the tension in the air and shook his hands as shockwaves of excitement ran across his shoulders and down his arms. He was a true warrior and the battleground was before him, but he had to be patient; he was the spring for the great trap that General Moroni had conceived.

"The timing must be exact to make this work." Lehi heard Moroni's voice in his head, repeating over and over again. After a solid week of training the militia and last night's final war counsel, the game was set and the pieces were moving.

The faint light in the eastern sky began to give way to streaks of yellow as the bulk of the Lamanite army emerged from the woods. Lehi could see the baggage wagons traveling with the main force, and there were no other units moving with the foot soldiers.

"Just infantry," he thought. "No cavalry units or chariots, and they do not leave their supplies with the reserves in the rear. Why would they do that?" he wondered, shrugging his muscular shoulders. "Oh well, be it audacity or stupidity, either way they have shown us their hand."

Like a thunderclap in his mind, he suddenly understood the reason for the Lamanites moving like they were.

"Those fools," he said to one of his lieutenants behind him. "They don't have anyone on their flanks or a reserve waiting behind the main body. They're sending everyone forward in one massive formation. They have no idea we are here. They think they are going to take Manti without a struggle."

"Now?" the soldier next to Lehi asked, almost begging.

"No, wait until the leading edge of their army is across the bridge and we have them trapped against the river."

Even though it was still fairly dark, it was clear that some among the Lamanites were on horseback. The mounted soldiers wore armor, but the rest of the Lamanite army only carried weapons. A few had small, wooden shields but no body armor of any kind. Perched on the hilltop, like a hawk watching his prey, Lehi could see that those on horseback were acting more like sheepherders than military leaders. Several of the leaders seemed more unruly than their men—shouting, pushing, and, in some cases, whipping the Lamanite soldiers forward toward the bridge.

The soldier at Lehi's side fidgeted nervously with his spear and spoke again. "Sir, they have reached the bridge; should we attack?"

Lehi held up his hand. "Hold!" he said. The men around him froze and time seemed to stand still as the first few Lamanites started to cross the bridge. Slowly, at first, the point men made their way across the bridge, stopping to scan for traps and inspecting the bridge to ensure the structure was such that it would be able to sustain the massive weight of the army about to cross over it. Once the scouts made it across the bridge, a few more soldiers stepped out and quickly moved across. The bridge itself was little more than a footpath built over the river. While it was big enough for a wagon, only one could cross at a time, and the troops had to break ranks and walk in a loose formation to cross. Shortly, the first sets of soldiers were carefully crossing the bridge. The closer to the other side they moved, the faster they ran and the more courage they gained. Before long, about a hundred enemy soldiers had reached the opposite side with several dozen more packed onto the bridge, forcing their way across. Those who had reached the far side shouted encouragement to their fellow Lamanites still waiting on the other side, urging them to quickly come across.

"It ends now," Lehi said. He stood upright and held out his hand. "Give me a torch."

A page handed Lehi a large, unlit wooden torch, stuffed with dried grass.

"Light it," he commanded.

A soldier positioned himself near the torch, struck flint to steel, and sent sparks across the head of the torch. The sparks instantly burst the grass into a glowing orange flame, and Lehi held it high above his head. Filling his lungs to capacity, Lehi let out a deafening war cry, and the whole of the Lamanite army turned to see a lone man on top of the hill, with a massive burning torch in his hand.

"I am Captain Lehi," he shouted loudly enough that nearly the entire Lamanite army could hear. "You are standing on sacred Nephite land. Leave now, or we will destroy you all."

The Lamanite soldiers had recoiled shock registering on their faces. Many had taken a step or two back. Zerahemnah spun his horse around to look up at Lehi on the top of the hill. Although surprise registered on Zerahemnah's face, he forced out a loud laugh and pointed at Lehi. Following their leader's example, the Lamanite soldiers joined in the laughter and in the finger pointing at Lehi.

From his post on the hill, Lehi simply smiled. He knew what awaited the men standing in the valley below him.

"You were warned," Lehi loudly whispered. Handing the still-burning torch to a soldier near him, the Nephite leader turned and looked south, down the back side of the hill. There, hidden from the Lamanite view and waiting with long bows in hand, were several hundred Nephite soldiers.

"On my command," Lehi announced, "volley fire; troops in the open, maximum distance."

The order was echoed by several sub-commanders standing among the archers.

On that command, each of the Nephite archers pulled an arrow from his quiver.

"NOCK!" Lehi continued.

Again, the order was echoed, and the archers loaded their bows, pulled their strings back and adjusted their aim upward to get the trajectory they needed to travel the necessary distance.

"LOOSE!" Lehi shouted and at once the mass of Nephite soldiers released their arrows. The sound of countless arrows all in flight was like a sudden rush of wind as they flew over Lehi's post in a high arc and headed for the sea of Lamanites below.

The Lamanites were still laughing, poking each other in the ribs and whispering about Lehi's words when they saw the giant black mass of Nephite arrows rise up in the morning sky over the top of the hill where Lehi was standing. Like a monstrous flock of birds, the arrows flew in formation, higher and higher, until they reached their zenith and began the deadly descent toward the Lamanite army below. Zerahemnah, still joining in the mirth that rippled through the ranks, suddenly stopped laughing when he saw the mass of arrows in flight. Some of the more seasoned Lamanite warriors had already realized what was happening and were trying to move out of the impact area. Zerahemnah stared blankly for a minute before panic set in.

"Incoming," he screamed as he tried to raise his shield to protect himself from the falling arrows. He managed to block the arrows and keep himself safe, but that was not the case for his defenseless army. Arrows rained down among his men. With no way to protect themselves, all they could do was try to dodge the falling arrows while struggling to maneuver around the wounded or dead who were falling everywhere, impaled by Nephite arrows. Although Zerahemnah had to have known that many more of his men would fall when a second volley of arrows hit, he was worried at the moment only about his own skin and about getting himself out of arrow range. He spurred his horse forward, hollering for his men to get out of his way.

"NOCK!" Lehi shouted and what followed was the haunting sound of hundreds of wood and steal bows creaking under the pressure of being pulled tight by the powerful arms of the Nephite archers.

"LOOSE!" The second volley of deadly arrows was sent flying.

The effect was even more dramatic than the first time around. This time, only slightly more prepared for an arrow strike, the Lamanite army had spread farther apart. While many were trying to get across the bridge, causing a logjam of bodies, the majority of the enemy soldiers were running along the sides of the river in a desperate attempt to get as far away from the hill as possible, hoping to get out of the impact zone of the arrows.

The chaos spooked the animals pulling the large baggage wagons, and the wagon teamsters fought to steady and control them enough to move the wagons out of the arrows' path. Some managed to get their wagons turned around and headed for the safety of the jungle behind them. Several of them drove their supply wagons toward the already dangerously overcrowded bridge, adding to the panic of those trying to cross. One wagon lost its driver to an arrow and was now being pulled by frightened, out of-control horses. The driverless team ran blindly across the valley, crushing already injured Lamanites.

"It's working!" Lehi gasped. "By the Maker's hand, it's working. Signal the cavalry to charge. Do it now!" he shouted.

A horn blew and Lehi saw his horse soldiers riding around the back side of the hill toward the scattering Lamanites.

Lehi picked up his large battle ax and turned to the soldiers who had been on the lines, shooting the arrows.

"Now, men, follow me!"

Lehi charged down the hill with his ax held above his head, shouting his war cry. The Nephites behind him slung their bows across their backs, picked up their shields and drew their swords. They, too, sounded their own war cries and charged over the hill to follow their leader into battle.

From his tree-covered position across the river, and north of the bridge, Moroni witnessed what was happening with Lehi and his men. Dawn was fully upon them as the sun began to peek over the distant mountains. Moroni, sitting on his horse, remained expressionless, watching his brave Nephite warriors spill over the top and around the sides of the hill Riplah like angry ants defending their home. The work of death had begun. He knew there was no going back now. It was open war and many of his brave men would die that day. The price for true freedom and true peace had always been paid with blood—the blood of those who fought and died knowing that the cost they paid was better than living in bondage and watching their families torn apart by slavery, their religion desecrated and their country destroyed.

"It's unfolding just as you had planned, General," the sergeant major said as he sat on his horse next to Moroni.

"See how they scatter and run on the far bank. They are trapped with their backs against the river," Moroni said. "They are out of rank, disorientated and unable to amass a proper defense against the charge."

"Sounds like you've got them just where you wanted them for your next move," the sergeant major continued.

"Almost, but not quite yet," Moroni spoke. "Lehi must force them into the river or across the bridge, and then, when they are most vulnerable, we will make our move."

Lehi and his men were working hard to wrap up their part of the trap. Following their arrow attack, Lehi's men moved quickly downhill at top speed. It took them more than a minute to reach the first of the Lamanites. His horse soldiers arrived at the battle site before him and began the work of death, running down any stragglers who broke away from the main Lamanite force. When Lehi reached level ground, he had to slow his pace and carefully pick his path to avoid tripping over the victims of the arrow attacks.

Because of added mobility and speed, the advantage in an open field attack always goes to the cavalry. They made quick work of the Lamanite foot soldiers who broke ranks and tried to flee. Lehi arrived at the edge of what was more like a mass brawl than a coordinated attack. There were Lamanites running in all directions, Nephite horsemen shouting war cries and killing at will, and Lamanite leaders trying in vain to organize some type of defense.

Lehi's eyes burned with intensity as he quickly surveyed the battle and coursed out his next move. Two half-crazed Lamanites, with their swords swinging wildly, dodged through the turmoil of the Nephite charge and lunged at Lehi. Lehi deflected the first sword strike with his ax and knocked the attacker to the ground with a hard body check. Lehi then sidestepped to the left to avoid the downward strike of the second aggressor. When his strike missed Lehi, the Lamanite fell off balance, exposing his back. Lehi made a quick step to his right and brought the blade of his great ax crashing down between the Lamanite's shoulder blades. The Lamanite was dead before he hit the ground.

Lehi turned back to face the first Lamanite, who had recovered from the deflection and was on the attack again. The Lamanite swung his sword at Lehi's head, but Lehi ducked out of the path of the blade at the last second. In the same movement, Lehi brought his ax up across his body and, in one fluid pass, struck the Lamanite in the neck, separating his head from his torso. The Lamanite's headless body fell to the earth, and Lehi stepped over him to ready himself for the next challenger.

Before another Lamanite could mount an assault, the Nephite troops caught up to their leader and were on alert for their orders. Lehi faced them and, still trying to recoup from the skirmish, managed to shout while gasping for air, "Form ranks, then move laterally and force them across the river!"

The bedlam continued in the Lamanite ranks. Lamanite soldiers who were already across the river or still on the bridge were trying to return to join in the fight. They were met and forced back by other Lamanites, who were trying to avoid the attacking Nephite army.

Nephite foot soldiers, breathless but boldly marching forward, charged past Lehi and engaged the still-disorientated and leaderless Lamanite army. The Lamanite army was without armor and the Nephites, well-protected with shields, helmets, and armor on their chests, arms and legs, slaughtered them. Nephite horse soldiers rode down any who tried to escape. The Nephite foot soldiers formed ranks and, using their spears and shields, drove the remainder back into the river. With wagons still taking up space on the bridge and more Lamanites packing in around them, the overcrowding became more than it could accommodate and some fell off and into the river. Others jumped off and tried to swim across to the safety of the opposite side.

Lehi, moving on foot with his men, calmly directed the battle lines. His courage and cool demeanor made a sharp contrast to the rider who came galloping up behind the mass of Lamanite soldiers near the bridge. The rider was shouting orders, trying to get the unruly men into some form of battle ranks. The rider wore metal armor and had a leopard-skin cloak covering his body. As Lehi looked closer, he could see that it was no Lamanite on the horse, but a Zoramite.

"Zerahemnah," Lehi shouted, "you traitorous Zoramite scum. Archers, I need two of you, front and center!"

Two Nephite archers ran up to Lehi and pulled out their bows.

"Shoot that man on the horse!" Lehi exclaimed, pointing at Zerahemnah across the battleground. The two archers loaded their bows, took aim, and let their arrows fly. The arrows missed their mark but struck Zerahemnah's horse in the front legs, just below the saddle. Reacting in pain, the horse reared up on its back legs. Caught off guard, Zerahemnah lost his grip on the horse and flipped backwards, falling off the back of the horse. He landed hard on the ground and the momentum of the fall sent him rolling off the edge of the river bank, down a steep slope, and into the water. The wounded horse reared up again and lost its footing on the crumbling river's edge. As the horse stumbled down the embankment, its legs gave out completely and the struggling animal tumbled directly toward Zerahemnah. Zerahemnah was forced to dive out into the river to avoid being crushed under his falling horse. Several of the Lamanites saw their leader swimming out in the river and, thinking he was retreating, they dove in the river after him. What started as a few confused and scared soldiers following Zerahemnah into the water grew as more and more Lamanites dove into the river. Without warning, there was complete panic as the entire Lamanite army instinctively followed. The calm, wide river turned into a boiling scene of madness as thousands of fleeing Lamanites swam for their lives toward the opposing bank.

Lehi and his men pursued the fleeing Lamanites to the water's edge, killing all who remained on their side of the river and capturing all of their supply wagons.

"Halt," Lehi breathlessly commanded as he reached the water's edge and held up his hand to give the signal for his men to advance no farther. Thousands of men swimming across the river all at the same time turned the peaceful flow of water into a raging torrent. Some drowned while attempting to cross the river, and their dead bodies were bobbing in the current, being carried away downstream.

"Company commanders, rally on me!" Lehi shouted. In no time, several men, still breathless and bloodied from the short but intense battle, were standing before him.

"Men," Lehi spoke, pointing to each ranking company officer as he addressed them, "I want 1st and 2nd Companies to form defensive ranks on the banks of the river, one company on each side of the bridge. 3rd Company, form a reserve behind the main lines. Give me archer support and secure the enemy wagons. Have your men collect the used arrows and spears from the battleground; we're going to need all we can find before this is over. Then start gathering up the dead Lamanites and toss them in the river. We don't know how long we are going to be here, and we don't need all the dead lying around us. 4th Company, send two platoons to the tree line and watch our backs. Tell them to be ready just in case the Lamanites have any remaining soldiers who survived the attack hiding in the woods. The other two platoons are to help the medics get our wounded off the field and to the aid stations, then round up whatever prisoners remain and place a guard on them."

"Yes, sir," was the united response as the sub-commanders scattered and began to organize the Nephites according to the command of Captain Lehi.

The men of the 1st and 2nd Companies reacted instantly. With the platoon sergeants as guides, each company formed in battle ranks on the Nephite side of the river. Standing shoulder to shoulder with their shields in front of them, the first rank acted as one giant blocking force to protect the men behind them. The second rank stood behind the first, with their columns slightly offset so they could see the battle by looking between the heads of the men to their front. The soldiers in the first and second ranks had long spears that they held in front of them. In a loose formation behind the second rank, archers were prepared to fire volleys of arrows at whatever target the commanders chose.

CHAPTER TWENTY-FIVE

THE TRAP IS SPRUNG

Lehi walked to the river's edge and looked across at the confusion happening on the other side. Disorientated and physically spent from a hard march and an intense battle, followed by a desperate swim to escape Lehi's surprise attack, the Lamanites were more a mob than an army. Most of them were lying on the ground trying to catch their breath. Some were aimlessly walking around waiting for instructions, and others were still in the water trying to reach the safety of dry ground. Lehi could see that the bulk of the Lamanite force survived his attack but he did enough damage to start General Moroni's master plan in motion.

"Come on, sir, let's go get them," one soldier shouted. "Look at them; they are like half-drowned rats. We can take them!" Several others in the ranks around Lehi urged their commander to give the order to attack.

"Easy lads," Lehi spoke. "There will be plenty more killing today. General Moroni ordered us to hold here. He has a little surprise for them waiting on the other side of the river. ... Right now we wait."

If his soldiers had been able to discern even a part of what Lehi was feeling, they would have known that their appeals weren't necessary. More than anything, Lehi wanted to continue the attack. His warrior instinct was telling him to march his troops across the defenseless bridge, secure it and engage the enemy on the other side before they had a chance to recover. Nonetheless, he had given his word that he would follow Moroni's orders. His job was to spring the trap, and now the master plan was underway. His duty was to trust in God and in his commanding general. Kicking a small rock into the water, Lehi took a deep breath and scanned the distant tree line behind the Lamanite troops.

"Okay, boy," Lehi spoke softly to himself as he looked across the river and north toward General Moroni's hidden position, "let's see what you've got."

The Nephites' execution of their well-planned attack continued to contrast with the sloppy response from the Lamanite troops. Zerahemnah came splashing out of the water, sloshed onto the muddy banks, and stood exhausted and water logged, his hands on his knees, trying to catch his breath. Looking around he found the bulk of his army was safe on this side of the river with him, but all of the supply wagons remained on the opposite side, now in Nephite hands, and many of the Lamanites had lost their weapons in the frantic swim. Groups of soldiers were lying on the ground; others walked around in a daze, trying to recover from the ordeal. None of them paid much attention to the Nephite soldiers who had surprised them. Only Zerahemnah seemed to notice that the small band of Nephites hadn't pursued them across the river, but were now setting up in a defensive position.

"What are they doing?" he said aloud. "Why did they not follow us?" A thought came to him as he tried to shake water from his clothing. "They are on the wrong side of the river. They think we will attack back across the bridge and not turn toward Manti, fools."

"Sir?" a voice spoke from behind him.

"What?" Zerahemnah barked as he turned to face the man speaking to him.

"My lord, what are your orders?" It was one of Zerahemnah's Zoramite lieutenants who asked the question.

Brushing wet hair out of his eyes, the soaked Lamanite leader responded, "Have the men report to their captains and make an accountability of what we have left to fight with. Get a group of men to set up a blocking position on this side of the bridge to keep the Nephites from coming across, and find me a horse. I am not walking to Manti!"

"Yes, my lord," the young lieutenant said. He ran off to relay the leader's commands.

Orders were shouted and the weary Lamanites began to move to their assigned positions. After checking his own weapons and personal belongings, Zerahemnah looked around to assess his situation. Down river, about 200 yards away, was a tree line of thick jungle growth. To his right an open, grassy area gradually sloped up from the river with the road to Manti running down the middle of it. Zerahemnah knew the road led right to the front gates of the city. He also knew Manti was less than two miles away and, as far as he could see, the city had been left unguarded.

"Those fools," he spat. "They tried to trap us against the river. They have left their city defenseless." He held his arms high in the air and shouted at Lehi's men on the opposite side.

"Young Moroni … you have made a fatal mistake. Your city will burn and your women will be our slaves." The Lamanites with Zerahemnah also turned to face the Nephites and shouted out war cries.

"Now," Moroni said under his breath.

The sergeant major held up his hand to catch the attention of the others with him.

"Archers, troops in the open, volley fire, on my command. NOCK!"

Hundreds of Nephites responded instantly to the commands and pulled back their mighty long bows.

Without taking his eyes off the mass of Lamanites, Moroni gave the command, "Loose."

The sergeant major relayed the command. "LOOSE!"

Again, a great rush of air sounded as hundreds of arrows flew out of the tree line and arced toward the wet and bedraggled enemy.

The Lamanites were still shouting and taunting Lehi and his men when the first volley of Moroni's arrows rained down on them. The outer edges of the Lamanite ranks were inundated with the pummeling barrage of arrows. Many of them went down, gravely wounded or dead from this latest strike.

"Again!" General Moroni shouted.

"LOOSE!" The old sergeant called, and a second volley came rushing out of the tree line.

The Lamanites made a mad dash, trampling each other and tripping over their dead, trying to get out of range of Moroni's inbound arrows. Some managed to move in time, but countless more were struck down by the second volley of arrows. Zerahemnah was thrashing his head around, trying in vain to understand what was happening. He thought the arrows had again come from Lehi's men but, looking across the river, saw Lehi's well-armored soldiers weren't engaging in battle but simply standing there, each holding his place in the well-disciplined formation.

It was then that a single trumpet sounded from the wood line, and a lone rider on a bulging warhorse emerged from the shadow of the trees. He held a large, green battle standard, with a golden sword on it. Even though the single Nephite was several hundred yards away, Zerahemnah could clearly see the markings on the battle standard as well as the soldier's massive frame, helmet, and his crimson red cloak.

"Moroni!" Zerahemnah hissed, with his teeth clenched tight. Pointing at Moroni with his sword, he shouted to his men, "There. Right there is the man that would make you all slaves to his false god. Your fathers were made to suffer because of Nephite tradition and religion, and now he comes to make you and your children suffer. Fight, men; fight with me and we will finally be rid of the cursed Nephites this day."

A great cry went up from the thousands of remaining Lamanites as they prepared themselves for the order to charge across the open ground and attack Moroni.

"Now, my brothers; now is the time for their blood," Zerahemnah yelled. The mass of Lamanite soldiers began to work themselves into a frenzied bloodlust.

Calmly, Moroni raised his standard high into the air. The sounds of several horns and drums came from the tree line. Hundreds of well-armored Nephite warriors ran out of the tree line. They quickly closed the distance from the trees to where their mighty leader waited on his horse. Orders were given, and the Nephites arranged themselves into two battle formations, one on each side of General Moroni.

The formations resembled two large squares with one hundred men each holding large metal shields, standing shoulder to shoulder on each of the four sides, forming the four outer edges. Inside the square were men wielding long spears and pikes as well as sword men, archers and older boys with stone slings. In the middle of each square stood the formation commanders as well as medics and lesser-ranked officers. Also inside the square, sergeants helped manage the formation.

The left square was commanded by the ranking sub-commanders with the aid of the sergeant major. Moroni slowly guided his horse forward toward the square on the right. The men stepped aside to allow Moroni's horse to pass through the outer edge. Once he was inside the battle formation, Moroni dismounted. A boy wearing leather armor took the reins and the battle standard from the Nephite leader and guided the horse off to a safer location.

General Moroni called as he walked among the men. "Steady men; let them come to us. Hold your ground and show no fear."

He ignored the curses and screaming coming from the unholy hoard of Lamanites a few hundred yards away, and continued,

"Remember your training. Follow your orders and trust in God to see you through this day."

Zerahemnah, still standing next to the river's edge, had a smug look on his face as he surveyed the Nephite formations. "What a wonderful target they make. Bow men, shoot at those dogs!"

At that command, several Lamanites brought their short hunting bows up and prepared to fire their arrows. When the Lamanites archers drew their bows back, several of the bow strings broke right off. Some of the Lamanite archers even sustained minor injuries when they were whipped in the face and across the arms by broken bows and strings.

"What's happening?" Zerahemnah shouted.

"My lord," one of his sub-commanders said, "the bows were soaked by the river water, many have lost their spring."

Zerahemnah was furious. He screeched in anger and punched his sub-commander in the mouth, knocking him to the ground.

"I don't want excuses," he shouted. "I said fire arrows at the Nephites! Do it now, or the next thing I throw at them will be your severed head!"

The sub-commander Zerahemnah had punched got sluggishly back on his feet. He wiped the blood from his nose.

"Ready your bows," he shouted. "Fire at them on my command!"

There were still several hundred Lamanites who had working bows. They each loaded an arrow, pulled back the string of the bow, and aimed at the soldiers in the two Nephite formations in front of them.

"Prepare for incoming arrows," Moroni shouted to the men in the first square formation. "Full shield coverage formation!" he commanded. A Nephite next to him sounded a small horn to advise all within the formation of the order and what the movement was to be.

Moroni looked to the second Nephite battle group at his left. He whistled loudly to draw the sergeant major's attention. When Moroni made eye contact with the old warrior, he formed a fist with his right hand and tapped the top of his helmet three times with his closed fist. The sergeant major gave thumbs up to acknowledge that he understood what Moroni was trying to tell him with the hand signal.

"What is it?" one of the young lieutenants asked.

"Arrows," the old sergeant responded. "Full shield coverage ... move!" he shouted to the men in his formation.

The men in the two Nephite formations understood what the command meant and instantly reacted to the order without question. The long days of training, discipline and preparations now paid off as each man knew his job and did it without question. The shield men on the outer edges all dropped to one knee and brought their large metal shields up to protect their bodies from the arrows falling from the sky. The second rank brought their shields up and placed them so the bottom of their shields overlapped the top edges of the shields of the men kneeling in front of the second rank. The third and fourth ranks of men held their shields above their heads and, in similar fashion, locked them in place with the shields to their front and sides. This created an almost seamless cover of overlapping metal, protecting the entire formation from falling arrows. The boys with slings and those without shields standing in the middle of the square found spaces near the men who were holding the shields above their heads.

All of this happened within seconds, so the Nephites were organized and in place before the Lamanite arrows were fired. As the arrows rained down on the two formations, only two or three of the hundreds of arrows made it past the shield wall. A few Nephites were wounded on their arms or legs. Those wounded were quickly helped off the line by the Nephite archers and older boys. To avoid leaving a hole in the ranks, the wounded men were quickly replaced by soldiers who picked up the shields of the wounded men.

The Lamanites let out a cheer as they sent the second volley of arrows toward the Nephites.

THE GENERAL'S MASTER PLAN

The second flight of Lamanite arrows followed a typical flight path, up, then arching back down toward the target. However, what came next was hardly typical. Rather than hit their marks, the arrows—every one of them—were deflected by the wall of shields covering the two Nephite formations. The Nephites had learned from the first flight of arrows and closed any gaps in the armored wall. Stunned and confused, Lamanite soldiers hung their heads, a look of disbelief in their eyes. Zerahemnah stood motionless, with his mouth gaping open for several seconds. All of them were dumbfounded at what they had just witnessed. As far as any of them knew, nothing like that had ever happened before—not in their own experience or in the history of warfare among their people.

Before they could recover their senses, a sudden and unexpected volley of arrows from Lehi's soldiers struck them from across the river. Unlike the Lamanite strike, the volley from the Nephites accomplished the intended result. Zerahemnah looked at his injured and dying men who were by the river bank and still within range of the Nephite arrows. He glanced back across the river his troops had just forded. On the other side, he could see Captain Lehi on his horse, casually waving to him. Lehi had moved his archers down to the river's edge, where they could get as close to the Lamanite army as possible.

They were near enough that Zerahemnah could make out their jeers and the looks of pleasure on the Nephite faces. He was almost blind with rage when the sub-commander he punched earlier came up to him.

"Sire, we're within range of their arrows," he said, pointing across the river.

"You think?" Zerahemnah responded sarcastically.

"What should we do, my lord?"

Zerahemnah held up his sword. "We attack!" he shouted and started to run toward General Moroni and the two battle formations on his side of the river. Caught up in the frenzy of the moment, those Lamanites tasked with keeping the bridge left their posts and joined in the assault. Many other Lamanites were dead or injured; some simply held back, others looked a bit wary about following Zerahemnah's command. Several of the Lamanite sub-commanders, as well as the other Zoramites, started to push and shove soldiers forward until a disheveled herd was charging headlong toward General Moroni and his men.

"Recover!" Moroni shouted. The two formations instantly returned to their original positions. "Stand by for movement orders!" he shouted. He surveyed to make sure all of his men were at their assigned positions. The sergeant major followed the same protocol from his position inside the second formation.

"Action front, enemy troops in the advance, archers at the ready!" Moroni yelled. The shield men dropped to one knee, and the ranks of armored soldiers behind them did the same. This gave the archers inside the two formations a clear view of the charging Lamanites. The archers fired their arrows over the tops of the heads of the men kneeling in front of them. Most of the arrows found their marks and many Lamanites fell from arrow strikes to their unprotected bodies.

"Slings," Moroni commanded. This time, the archers dropped to one knee to reload their bows while the boys in the formations stood up and let fly a mass of stones from their slings. Although the stones were not as accurate or deadly as the arrows, several were expertly placed and more Lamanites dropped as they charged forward, quickly closing the distance between them and the Nephite formations.

"Recover!" Moroni shouted again. The soldiers who had been kneeling stood up again. "Close ranks and prepare to repel attackers!" The shield men moved as close to each other as they could and braced themselves behind their large shields for the human wave of Lamanites that would soon impact against them.

"Steady," Moroni urged them. "Steady!" The Lamanites were closing the distance between them at a dead run, shouting their war cries. "Steady men. Have faith. For freedom … for liberty!"

The Lamanites crashed against the wall of shields and pushed forward until the soldiers in front were smashed up against the shields of the Nephites. The Nephite shield men groaned under the weight of the onslaught but, with the help of the soldiers bracing behind them, they held their ground. The Lamanites tried in vain to strike at the Nephites with their swords and cimeters but, with the crush of bodies behind them, they were so compacted against the Nephite shields that they could not properly swing their weapons to inflect any real injury. Even if they had been able to move more freely, they couldn't have done much damage. The Nephites were too well protected with their metal helmets, chest plates and armor on their arms and legs. When the Lamanites realized they were unsuccessful attacking the front of the formation, several of them began to move around to the other sides, hoping to find and exploit a weak point. All they found was an interlocking wall of shields.

"Spears and swords!" Moroni shouted, and the men in the second and third ranks thrust their spears and long pikes out through the gaps in the lines and over the tops of the large Nephite shields. They slashed with their swords at the exposed Lamanite flesh. Whatever Lamanite body parts they could see, the Nephites stuck with the metal tips of their spears or slashed with swords. They cut off arms, sliced open legs, crushed heads, and pierced chests. This caused tremendous injuries and death to those Lamanites unlucky enough to be trapped between the shields of the Nephites and the pressing mass of their fellow Lamanite soldiers. The dead and injured Lamanites fell to the ground at the feet of the first rank of Nephites, only to be replaced by more Lamanites, who were pushed to the front by the surge of soldiers from behind. The work of death continued as the Nephites behind the shields stabbed and sliced at any Lamanite flesh exposed to them. In less than one minute, the dead and wounded Lamanite bodies were stacking up at the feet of each shield man, and the ground turned slippery and muddy from all the spilled blood. In addition to the shields, the ever growing mass of dead bodies surrounding the Nephites was making it difficult for the Lamanites to get close enough to engage the Nephites in combat. Lamanite soldiers who managed to rush past the dead were cut down themselves by a Nephite spear or sword. The Lamanites who tried to back away from the slaughter had no chance of doing so but were continually pushed forward by the crushing mass behind them. If a Lamanite soldier happened to distance himself from the deadly strikes of the Nephite weapons, a Nephite archer stepped up to the armored wall and fired his arrows point blank into the enemy's chest.

"Get them to encircle the Nephites," Zerahemnah shouted to his Lamanite sub-commanders and Zoramite lieutenants, but the noise and confusion of battle was too much for the Zoramite commander to effectively give orders to his men. Things were not going well for Zerahemnah, and he knew it. He had suffered a major setback when he was attacked and forced across the river by Lehi's troops, only to be hit by Moroni's arrows and again by Lehi's arrows. Now, to have his men slaughtered and stacked like firewood at the feet of a much smaller but more disciplined and better armed force, was nearly too much for him. He could see his men starting to back away from the Nephite lines. Nothing they did was effective against the armored wall that Moroni had created, and no one wanted to be the next to die in an obviously useless cause.

Zerahemnah kicked angrily at the ground. He paced, scratching his head and pursing his lips in frustration. He rubbed his hands together, trying to gather some hope of coming up with a plan that would save the day and keep his army from being destroyed or deserting him en masse. In the distance, he saw the tops of the buildings behind the walls of Manti. He knew the city was not far. A plan began to come clear as he realized that, on foot, his men could easily outrun the Nephites, who were wearing heavy metal armor. He turned to look at the bridge and was dumbfounded to see that Lehi's small force remained on the other side of the river.

"They still did not cross," he thought out loud. "Those fools kept all of their cavalry and reserves on the other side of the river. They will never get them all across in time."

A smile broke across his face as the strategic move that he thought would save the day came together in his mind.

"Commanders, rally on me," Zerahemnah yelled over the noise of battle. In seconds, several of the remaining Zoramites and Lamanite leaders were at his side. "Our Nephite friends have left the city undefended. My orders are this: when the command is given, all the men will turn and run at full speed for the gates of Manti. It lies only a short distance across the valley and over the rise behind us. We will take and hold the city with the force we have remaining. They will never be able to retake it with the small number of men they have. We can then bargain for our wounded and captured men with the women and children inside the city and ransom the rest before Moroni can raise an army large enough to retake the city. The wealth and women of Manti are yours for the taking men. Just get your soldiers to run when I give the signal. Is that understood?"

The men around him murmured and cheered, and clapped each other on the back, showing their excitement at the prospect of pillaging the city of Manti. The sub-commanders understood the orders and moved back to where they had left their men.

"My lord," a young Lamanite exclaimed as he ran up to Zerahemnah with a horse in tow, "I found you a horse, my lord."

"Well done," Zerahemnah said, climbing up on the horse. "Now I don't have to run." He jerked the reins out of the hands of the young Lamanite and spun his horse around, knocking the boy to the ground. He galloped off several yards behind the mass of Lamanites still trying in vain to assault Moroni's armored formations. He rode up next to a man with a trumpet and ordered him to sound the signal for a change of orders. The horn blew, and the Lamanite soldiers stopped the attack and turned to see where the sound had come from. In the distance, they could see Zerahemnah sitting on a horse with his sword in his hands.

"Follow me, men," he called. "Manti is the prize we came for and it's left undefended." A shout went up from the Lamanites as they turned and ran after their leader. The other Zoramite and Lamanite sub-commanders urged them on as the Lamanite army moved in mass away from Moroni and his armored formations. The ground shook as the entire Lamanite army ran toward Manti, leaving their dead and wounded behind.

Zerahemnah dared not move his horse any faster than his men were running. He wasn't about to take a chance of being caught alone without his army close by.

"Let them go, men," Moroni shouted, as the Lamanites ran from the battleground toward Manti. "It's all part of the plan. Get our wounded back to the medics in the tree line. Gather the Lamanite wounded and put them under guard. Archers, scavenge up your arrows. Sergeant Major!"

"Sir?" the old soldier responded from the second formation.

"Refit the lines. Distribute water and prepare these men for the move to Manti."

"Yes," Lehi shouted. He shook his head in joyful disbelief at the sight the Lamanites pulling back from Moroni's formations and moving toward Manti. Hundreds of dead and wounded bodies of the enemy were lying on the ground, outlining the two Nephite armored formations. Lehi was not often amazed, but, at that moment, he was completely taken aback. He galloped his horse along his side of the river's edge and cheered with his men as they watched the grand battle plans of General Moroni play out before them. It was as if, even when Moroni was making the plans, he already knew the outcome.

A MOMENT OF CLARITY

From the center tower above the sally port of Manti's main gate, Teancum, Shem and the other leaders of the city's garrison and militia strained to watch as the battle unfolded. It was early morning now, with the sun fully exposed above the mountains.

From their vantage point, Teancum thought the Lamanites looked like ants. He smirked as the scurrying enemy disengaged from around Moroni's battle formations and turned to move on the city.

"Here they come, just like Moroni said they would," he thought to himself. He spoke calmly to Shem. "Ready the men to move to the walls." Shem looked over the back side of the tower and into the courtyard behind the main gate. There, the men of the city, as well as the army garrison, waited, ready to climb the stairs to the ramparts and towers or to defend the large wooden gate and repel the oncoming charge of the enemy. Every man knew his assignment and was alone with his thoughts of the coming battle. Most had never faced an armed enemy. Even from where he was, Shem could feel the tension among the men. They shifted nervously, looking at the gate or up at Shem, waiting for the orders to assume their battle positions. Shem noticed one of the soldiers became sick and vomited, which sent another man's stomach into heaving up his latest meal. Although he couldn't see it, Shem could smell there were others among this group of first-time soldiers who had lost control of their bowels.

One among the group took a different approach. Pachus, with his ever-present goblet of wine, walked around laughing and trying to joke with the men standing ready to fight. When the Nephite guards who held him on house arrest left to join back up with Moroni, they left some of the city militia to watch over him. A quick bribe was offered and Pachus was free to roam the streets again.

He wore armor that was clearly too small for his blubbered frame and his jovial attempt was almost as inadequate as his too-small armor. Since his defrocking and public humiliation at the hands of the "Boy General" Moroni, few of the men regarded him with much respect. No one seemed to be in the mood to make nice with the man who was personally responsible for their lack of readiness for the emergency they now faced. His commands were ignored by most of the gathered men. Only a few ranking city leaders and his paid help remained outwardly loyal to Pachus as he demanded a refill of his wine.

"House arrest," Pachus giggled to those around him as his wine was replenished by one of his staff. He held his full goblet up toward Shem in a taunting toast and shouted, "To your health."

Shem's face turned a bright shade of red with anger.

"Not the time for this," he spoke quietly, and then he called to the gathered men below him. "Make ready."

The men picked up their shields and weapons. Pachus lifted his cup in the air a second time and, with a drunken voice, shouted, "To victory." He gulped the remaining fluid in the cup, spilling some down his chin and cheeks. Burping loudly, he worked his way to the back of the formation and climbed aboard his personal chariot. Taking the reins from his chariot driver, he shouted, "Follow me, men, I will lead you to victory!"

Pachus slapped the reins on the backs of the horses drawing his chariot, but the way forward was blocked by men in front of him. Not wanting to be trampled by the agitated horses, the men of Manti shifted as best they could to get out of the way as Pachus slowly moved forward toward the main city gate.

"What are you doing?" Shem shouted at Pachus from the top of the battlement. Pachus stubbornly ignored Shem and drove his chariot to the edge of the gate.

"Open the gate," Pachus yelled to the gatekeeper. The man moved toward the large metal latch and stout wooden beam that held the gate closed.

"No, don't open the gate, you fool. Keep it locked," Shem called out.

"I am Pachus, the commander of the city's defenses. I order you to open the gate!"

Not knowing whose orders to follow, the gatekeeper looked around for some guidance, but no one spoke up to counter Pachus's command.

"I said, 'Open the gate,'" Pachus shouted, red faced from anger and wine.

The hapless gatekeeper unlatched the large lock and pulled open one side of the gate to expose the outside world.

"We will see who the great war hero is this day," Pachus said. He took one last, long gulp of his wine and tossed the goblet to the ground. He then slapped his horses again with the reins and moved his chariot forward past the gate and onto the road.

"No, you fool. Come back … shut the gate," Teancum demanded, as he looked over the edge of the tower. With the enemy approaching, the actions taking place below were inconceivable to Teancum. He turned to face Shem.

"It's too soon, the trap is not set. Shem, get the archers to the wall and prepare them to fire," Teancum ordered. He moved toward the trap door that covered the stairs leading out of the tower and down to the ground.

"Where are you going?" Shem shouted back.

"I'm going to get the gate shut and the men back inside before the Lamanites overrun us!"

Driven by nervous emotion and lack of experience, many of the men in the garrison instinctively followed Pachus out of the gate. Before Teancum could reach the open gate, many of the armored troops had followed Pachus and were well outside the walls, moving in a loose formation toward the river. Pachus, who was at least 50 yards ahead of them, was oblivious and had a giant, drunken smile on his face as he drove his chariot with his horse at a slight trot down the rise and toward the advancing Lamanite army.

"Archers to the wall," Shem shouted, but most had already left the protection of the city and joined the ground forces that were spilling out of the gate and moving in the direction of the river. Some of the archers managed to hear Shem's orders and moved to the top of the walls and covered towers. They formed into a line and prepared to fire down on the enemy they could see rapidly advancing toward them.

As Zerahemnah and his army moved toward the walled city, they saw the gate open and a lone chariot exit from inside.

"What fool would open the gate to the city when the enemy is advancing toward it?" Zerahemnah thought out loud.

He was even more surprised to see armored troops following the chariot out of the gate. Unlike the well-trained and motivated forces they had just faced, these troops moved in an undisciplined manner. They were not crack troops but the rag tag remains of the city's defenses. It looked like they were mobilizing for a final fight outside the protection of the city's walls.

"But why would they come out on the open ground when they have the advantage defending from behind the walls? And why would they come out when Moroni's army is coming up on our rear?"

An idea suddenly hit him, and he smiled as he contemplated the thought that he had just figured out Moroni's master plan. "That's it," he thought. "They are hoping that we delay our attack and give Moroni enough time to move his army into place to attack us from behind."

"What are your orders?" a Zoramite asked, riding up next to Zerahemnah.

"Have all of our brother Zoramites form at the center of our lines. We will show these Lamanite cowards how to fight. Order the Zoramites to smash through the lines of Nephites defending the city and rush the gate while the Lamanites deal with the remainder outside. We will take and hold the city and, if need be, close the gate behind us. We can still ransom the lives of those inside for our freedom with Moroni if we need to or counterattack from the walls as they try to retake the city."

"But, sir, won't that trap the Lamanites outside to deal with the Nephites alone?"

"So, what? Let them hack away at each other while we remain safe inside the walls. When it is all over, we Zoramites will be a stronger force than whoever remains alive after the battle outside the walls, and we can either hold out against the remaining Nephites or let the Lamanites in to enjoy the spoils of war with us."

The young Zoramite stopped for a moment and, with a blank expression, stared for several seconds at his leader. Then a broad smile crossed his face.

"You're a mad man," he shouted.

"Yes, I am. Now do as you're told."

"Yes, sir," he replied as he rode off.

The order was given and the Lamanite army halted while the Zoramites reformed at the center of the mass of humanity. The Lamanites gained courage from seeing the well-armored and experienced Zoramites form ranks and take hold of the center of the battle formation.

Wanting to get his eyes on the enemy that was advancing toward the city, General Moroni had moved ahead of his forces and, for several minutes, had perched on a hilltop southwest of the city. He watched the scene unfold before him like slow-moving pieces of a chess game. Horrified, he saw the city gate open while Pachus, in his chariot, and the city's undisciplined garrison spilled onto the open ground. Feelings of dread welled up inside him as he watched the Lamanite army stop and reform, with the mighty Zoramite warriors at the center. This was not part of his plan and he could see in his mind's eye that it was a disaster in the making. All of the planning and preparations, the sacrifice, the lives of his brave men that had already been lost this day—all of the good they had accomplished was about to be undone because of someone's drunken, reckless behavior.

"Why did Teancum order the troops out of the protection of the city?" the sergeant major asked.

"Teancum would not do that. Something has happened. Look." Moroni pointed to the chariot moving away from the protection of Manti's walls and toward the Lamanite lines. "Pachus!"

"What in the blazes is he doing?" the old soldier barked.

"I don't know, but we need to move quickly to keep this from becoming a slaughter."

A dark feeling came over Moroni as surveyed the scene before him.

"You knew this would happen," a voice deep in his mind crept in. "You are not the man to lead these men. You are not your father."

Moroni whispered to himself as he tried to calm down.

"I am not my father?" he choked, turning his back to the battleground and starting to hyperventilate. Emotions welled up inside—failure, dread, hopelessness, and, most of all fear.

"Sir?" The sergeant major wondered if Moroni was okay when he turned away from the battleground.

"I am not my father," he said a bit louder, sucking air into his lungs. "What have I done?" he repeated several times in a panicked whisper.

"General, your orders?" came a second more forceful question for the seasoned soldier.

The evil presence seemed to be shouting in Moroni's mind, "Yes, what have you done? Your men will be slaughtered, and the city will fall. This is all your fault because you were not strong enough."

"MORONI?" The old mentor barked like a stern taskmaster.

Moroni snapped back to reality. "No," he shouted aloud in a moment of clarity. "I am the Lord's servant. I am anointed to lead, and I trust in God. It does not matter how strong I am. It only matters how much I trust in God to guide my actions."

The words of his father echoed in his mind. "Good will always prevail over evil."

His strength and resolve renewed, Moroni spun around to face the enemy again.

"Sergeant Major, I need a runner to take an urgent message to Lehi."

"Yes, sir. RUNNER!" he yelled with a bit of relief in his voice. The sergeant major was very concerned. He had seen Moroni's emotion and personal conflict. This was not the time for Moroni to doubt his abilities, and he was glad to see that Moroni was acting like a leader again.

Instantly, a young Nephite wearing only a tunic and leggings came up to the side of Moroni.

Without taking his eyes from the scene before him, Moroni spoke.

"Go make contact with Chief Captain Lehi. Give him my compliments on this morning's attack. Tell him I am ordering a change to the battle plans. Tell him to cross the river with his army, but leave a strong rear guard on the opposite side of the bridge. He is to take his remaining forces and, staying in the lowland and out of sight, skirt the river's edge. He is to follow the river upstream and move north of the city." Moroni pointed while he spoke so the runner could understand the direction he wanted Lehi to travel. "When he is parallel with the city walls, have his army form ranks and advance eastward on the Lamanites. We will smash them between our two armies in a pincer move and force them back to the river. Is that clear?"

"Sir, yes sir."

"Go as fast as you can, and report back to me when you have delivered the message."

"Yes, sir," the young Nephite exclaimed. He took off running toward the bridge.

"Sergeant Major, we need to leave the wounded and the supplies in the wood line. Form a security detachment and have them move our wounded and baggage wagons down to the river and join with Captain Lehi's detachment on the other side. Get the rest of the army ready to move. We must advance toward the city with haste, or all will be lost."

"Yes, sir." The old soldier turned to the crowd of officers gathering behind them.

"Fall in, formation now!" he shouted, as he pushed the Nephites into ranks and moved up and down the lines of soldiers, squaring them away for the movement to the city. Everyone, regardless of rank, responded instantly to the orders. The sergeant major was both a harsh presence and father figure for most of the young Nephites. No one had been in the army longer or fought in more battles than the sergeant major, and the young and inexperienced soldiers he was now trying to line up gave him instant and genuine respect.

THE PLAN IS FALLING APART

The young runner made quick work of traveling the several hundred yards to the bridge to deliver the important message to Captain Lehi. He had to sidestep a few dead Lamanites whose bodies were littering the ground, but he managed to make it to the bridge and across with little trouble. When he reached the opposite side, he was stopped and challenged by the heavily armored forces from Lehi's infantry guarding the bridge.

"Halt. Who goes there?" a voice demanded from behind the wall of large metal shields and pointed spears, blocking the bridge's far edge.

"I have an urgent message from General Moroni for Captain Lehi. Let me pass," the messenger shouted breathlessly.

A command was given, and two soldiers in the front rank moved their shields out of the way, allowing the young messenger to cross from the bridge onto dry land. A large sergeant, holding his helmet in his hand, walked up to the runner who was looking around for Captain Lehi.

"He is back there," the sergeant spoke, pointing behind the ranks of soldiers guarding the bridge. Captain Lehi, with his command group and standard bearer, was moving around the battlefield on horseback. Lehi examined the carnage before him caused by the ambush he set. His soldiers worked to clear the field of the hundreds of dead and wounded Lamanites who lay across the wide expanse of open ground from the base of the hill Riplah to the river's edge. They stacked the dead on carts pulled by donkeys, which carried them to the river where their bodies were dumped and washed downstream. The wounded were gathered into small groups and, under guard, given first aid and water.

"Sir. Sir," the young Nephite called out while running toward Lehi.

Lehi turned his horse toward the approaching messenger.

"Yes, what is it?"

"Sir," he panted, "I have an urgent message from General Moroni!"

"Well, catch your breath and give me the message."

The young Nephite bent over and took a few seconds to force some much needed air into his overused lungs.

"Sir," he said still partly gasping for air, "the battle has taken a turn for the unexpected."

Lehi searched the young man's face.

The messenger continued, "With his compliments, General Moroni sends word that the Lamanites are moving against the city. Something has happened to cause the city's garrison to leave the safety of the walls and move to meet the Lamanites in open ground." Panic raced across the faces of those with Lehi as he remained motionless in his saddle listening to the message. "The general has ordered your forces to move across the river. You are to leave an armored detachment to secure the bridge, then move along the low area of the river north and then toward the city." The messenger, still breathing heavily, pointed upriver. "When you are aligned with the city walls, you are to form ranks and move against the Lamanites. General Moroni will move his army on the opposite side of you and, together, you and he will catch the Lamanites in the middle."

"Is that all?"

"Yes, sir, but … it's just that the general had a sense of urgency in his tone when he gave me the message to deliver."

"There must be urgency if he has ordered a sudden change of this magnitude," Lehi said. "Very well. Inform the general that the message was delivered and understood. I compliment him on the management of the battle so far, and I will move with all speed to the new position and attack when ready. Are we clear?"

"Crystal clear, sir." The messenger saluted and asked, "Anything else, sir?"

"No. Now go and tell the general I am coming."

Without another word, the messenger was off at top speed toward the bridge and beyond. Moving to catch up with his supreme commander, he knew the message he carried could very well mean the difference between victory and defeat for his people.

At a dead run, it took Teancum little time to catch up with the garrison and militia units moving away from the protection of the city walls.

"Get back inside the gate. ... Move!" Teancum shouted. One after another, he grabbed the arms of garrison soldiers and militia men at the rear of the loose and disorganized formation, pushing them back toward the gate. The bulk of the city's garrison had only gone about a hundred yards when it became clear that Pachus was going to outdistance them in his war chariot. They stopped and, without a commander to lead them, shuffled their feet, watching their drunken, defiant leader move unprotected toward the Lamanite lines.

The chariot driver, now just a passenger with Pachus at the reins, grew more concerned every time he looked behind to see where the army was and forward to see how fast the Lamanites closed the distance. He could see that the Lamanite lines had stopped moving forward and had shifted their forces. Now, instead of Lamanites foot soldiers at the center of the battle lines, armored Zoramites made up the core. Finally, he could take it no more.

"Sir, I think there is a problem."

"What is it?" Pachus replied, his jolly drunken mood showing how completely unaware he was of the extreme danger they were in.

"The soldiers have stopped moving forward. We are alone out here."

"Nonsense! My soldiers will follow me. I am their commander, and I ordered them to fight for me." Pachus laughed.

At that moment, a large arrow struck Pachus's passenger dead center in the chest. The force knocked him out of the back of the chariot and onto the dusty road, killing him instantly. Pachus, with a stunned expression on his face, stared at the dead body of his attendant lying on the ground. It took several seconds for Pachus's intoxicated mind to catch up with reality. He was now alone on the battlefield and, when he turned to face the front of his chariot, he saw, charging at him at a full gallop, several dozen of the most dangerous and ferocious looking mounted warriors he had ever seen. The Zoramites were advancing. The shock and horror of it all were too much for his mind to process. All he could do was run away, and fast. He pulled hard on the left rein and slapped the other rein on the backs of the horses drawing his chariot. The chariot turned hard to the left, almost tipping over from the quick shift in direction. Terrified beyond rational thought, Pachus wailed like a child and slapped the horses with all of his might. Two more arrows smacked against the side of the chariot, causing him to scream even louder as he drove his horses back toward the safety of the garrison and the city walls.

Teancum, now standing in front of the garrison with his back to the Lamanites, was trying to get the undisciplined soldiers to form into battle ranks. One of the soldiers in the front row called out, "Sir!" and pointed with his spear. Teancum turned around to see Pachus driving his chariot toward the lines of Nephites at breakneck speed. Teancum could tell that Pachus was screaming something, but he was still too far away to make out what was being said. Behind Pachus, mounted Zoramites and the entire Lamanite army were chasing after him. Teancum knew the only thing he could do now was to try to get his soldiers back behind the walls of the city before the Lamanites reached them.

"Run ... get to the city," Teancum shouted, but most of the men had already figured it out for themselves. The entire group of Nephite soldiers was now on the move, running as fast as they could toward the gate. Those not wearing metal armor or who were in better physical shape outdistanced those wearing the heavy protection, causing the formation to spread out along the road leading to the gate. Pachus caught up with the fleeing soldiers and, with complete disregard for the safety of his panicked soldiers, drove his chariot through the formation, running over the top of three of his own men and causing several more to jump out of the way.

"Run for your lives, we're all doomed," Pachus screamed as he continued driving his chariot on toward Manti's main gate. Teancum stopped to help one of the victims of Pachus's negligence and heard the demoted leader scream again.

"Shut the gate," Pachus hollered. He jumped off his still-moving chariot. Unable to get his feet under him after the jump, Pachus lost his balance and plowed into several soldiers standing inside the sally port, knocking them over like bowling pins. Pachus came to rest on his back. His fat frame and drunken state made it almost impossible for him to get up. After several attempts, Pachus was able to roll over and get to his feet. Fixing his helmet back on his head and staggering toward the gate, he shouted, "Shut the gate or we will all die!"

The gatekeeper would not budge. He held the gate open as the fastest runners from the retreating garrison returned inside the safety of the walled city. Pachus moved to the open gate and, using his massive weight advantage, pushed the gatekeeper out of the way and forced the gate closed, trapping the bulk of the garrison and militia outside the walls, with the Lamanites quickly approaching.

"No," Teancum screamed. He was sprinting for his life toward the closing gate, but it was no use. He was just steps away from the gate when Pachus pushed the gate the last few inches closed and clanked the locks in place. The two men had made eye contact as Pachus pushed the gate closed. Teancum had seen the devilish grin on Pachus's face as he slammed the gate shut, trapping him outside with the Lamanites.

The soldiers inside the city, rattled by Pachus's wild actions, lost what little discipline they had remaining and started running in every direction. They knew there were men trapped outside the gate, but they were afraid to counter Pachus's orders.

Teancum and the Nephites trapped outside the safety of the walls frantically pounded on the gate, begging to have it opened, while others screamed up at the archers on the wall to open the gate.

Teancum stepped out from the sally port and scanned the tops of the walls for Shem, but he was nowhere to be found and, by the looks of things, it was too late anyway. The Lamanite arrows were starting to make their impact. Two soldiers next to Teancum fell instantly and another was wounded.

"Form a horseshoe around the gate; shields up!" Teancum yelled. According to Teancum's quick assessment, the Lamanites were less than 50 yards away, but they had stopped their charge. Teancum could see why. The archers from the tops of the walls were firing back at the Lamanites, killing a few but holding the remainder at bay. Teancum knew they wouldn't be able to stave them off for long. Teancum took advantage of the pause in the Lamanite charge to get the men remaining outside of the gate into a solid defensive position. They formed a semicircle around the gate, and Teancum put the best of his armored soldiers in the front ranks.

"Open the gate. Let them in." Teancum was relieved to hear Shem's voice and to see him running along the top of the wall shouting down to the inner courtyard.

What Teancum couldn't see was that his pleas were drowned out by the utter chaos taking place in the sally port just inside the gate. Pachus, in his drunken panic, had run his chariot into a stack of crates and kegs of liquid, killing one of the horses pulling the chariot and injuring the other. The injured horse reared up and tried to stomp or kick at anyone who came close to it. No one could get close enough to the gate to unlock the massive locks and allow the remaining Nephites to come inside.

Shem was furious. He quickly made his was down the stone steps leading from the wall to the ground. Grabbing a lit torch, he waved it in front of the spooked horse and shouted several times in an attempt to get the animal to move away from the gate. After a few tense moments, the half-crazed horse made a break for it and ran at full speed down the cobbled road that was the main passageway to the middle of the city. Shem threw open the lock and tried to move the large, wooden beam that spanned the gate. Pachus grabbed him on the shoulder from behind.

"What are you doing … you fool, don't open the gate," Pachus screamed. Shem shoved Pachus away and returned to the gate to let the trapped Nephites in. Pachus recovered from the shove, staggered back and drew out his sword.

"I am your commanding officer, and I am ordering you to move away from the gate," he said in a drunken slur.

Shem gave Pachus a look of disgust, held his hands out to his side, and stepped away from the gate.

"Now, be a good boy and go gather up my personal belongings. We are abandoning the city and fleeing to Zarahemla," the drunken fool continued, adding indignantly, "I want to personally inform my father of the debacle today caused by the upstart boy general."

"What about your chariot?" Shem calmly asked, pointing at the overturned vehicle and the dead horse next to it.

Pachus took a long look at the mess he had created. "Well…" the words sloshed out of his mouth, "get me a fresh set of …" That was all that came out. Before Pachus could finish, Shem pulled out his faithful old weapon and slashed at Pachus's sword hand, slicing the top of it wide open. Then, before Pachus could react, Shem slashed again at the cloth ties that attached Pachus's cloak to his armor, cutting them both and causing Pachus's cloak to fall off. Pachus let out a painful scream and dropped his sword. He grabbed the fallen cloak and wrapped it around his wounded hand. Pachus, with tears in his eyes, looked up at Shem.

"I'll have you hanged for this." He winched in pain and drew his wounded hand close to his fat chest. "I … I'm telling my father!" He stumbled away from the sally port and weaved down the street toward the center of the city, stammering and crying in agony.

The soldiers in the sally port watched Pachus's retreating figure in disbelief. "Don't just stand there," Shem yelled at the soldiers. "Reassemble the garrison for a counterattack. Archers to the walls. Defend our brothers until we can get the gate open."

"Yes, sir," the soldiers uniformly responded. They moved about like disorganized school children, trying to reassemble and prepare for the counterattack.

"I am too old for this," Shem barked as he put his sword back into its sheath and moved back to the gate.

The sergeant major made quick work of reforming the remaining ground troops for movement to the city. Most of his cavalry was on the other side of the river with Captain Lehi, only Moroni and his staff were on horseback, so the pace was slow but steady as the first elements of the Nephite soldiers started toward Manti.

General Moroni was leading from the front of the formation as the young messenger came dashing up to him with the return message from Lehi.

"Sir ... sir," he gasped, "I have a response from Captain Lehi!"

Moroni moved off to the left of the formation to allow it to continue marching forward while he spoke to the runner. The young Nephite was fighting for air, and it took him a moment to compose himself to the point that he could deliver his message.

Moroni was patient but eager to hear the reply from his chief captain.

"Sir, Captain Lehi sends his compliments and is, with all speed, moving to attack the Lamanites from this side of the river."

"Excellent. Well done. Stay close ... I may need your services again."

"Yes, sir," the runner exclaimed. It was an honor to be the personal messenger for the general and the young runner was doing everything he could not to blow this chance. With fresh lungs, the messenger ran to a supply wagon that was moving toward the wood line. He grabbed a spear and long knife from the supply master, then ran back to the front of the formation and assumed his position behind Moroni, ready to sprint off with whatever important information he was given.

"We don't want to take a straight line to the city. We will move along the tree line to the west and come down on them from the far side of the city's walls. When we attack, we will act as the hammer driving them into Lehi's anvil," Moroni said to the staff members riding behind him. They agreed with his battle plan and the formation took a slightly western course away from the main road.

Lehi, at the head of his forces, had finally crossed the footbridge. He stood off to the right of the bridge foundations and watched as his men ran across and reformed their ranks. Knowing that the cavalry could easily catch up to the foot soldiers, he ordered his infantry to move up river toward the city first while the horses finished crossing. When the horse soldiers had all gathered, Lehi, made contact with the commander of the two platoons of infantry he ordered to stay and secure the bridge.

"Lieutenant Joffa, your orders are to stay here, hold the bridge, and keep an eye on the wounded Lamanites and their supply wagons on the other side," Captain Lehi said to a young lieutenant he had assigned to head the contingent.

"Yes, sir," the Nephite officer responded. Lehi caught a hint of sadness in the officer's voice.

"Don't worry, lad," Lehi reassured him. "You may think this assignment is far less honorable than charging into the enemy lines, but I have a feeling you will see plenty more fighting this day."

Lehi smiled at the young Nephite.

"Take your post, and lead with honor," he said.

"Yes sir." Joffa responded with disappointment in his voice. "I will do my duty."

Lehi left the bridge and spurred his horse along the riverbank, joining his men as they moved toward the city.

Several Lamanite soldiers shifted nervously as their entire army stared at the small band of soldiers defending the main gate to Manti. Still fresh in their memories were the devastating arrows from Lehi and Moroni's forces, as well as the shocking results from attacking the small, well-armored formations of Nephite infantry in open battle. No one in the Lamanite ranks was in any hurry to find out if the archers on the city walls were as deadly accurate or if these well-armored soldiers waiting at the front of the gate were as well-trained as the last Nephite elements they faced. All of the Lamanites were exhausted, some were wounded, and most had been demoralized by a much smaller army that had exacted so much damage with little consequence to itself. The Zoramites and the Lamanite captains urged their men forward, but no one was budging.

Zerahemnah could feel the momentum change. He had lost the advantage of the attack when his forces stopped to assess the defense of the city gate. Looking back at Moroni and his army, Zerahemnah could see they were moving around to try to outflank his army from the west.

"We cannot effect an assault on the city with Moroni attacking from our flank," he shouted to the fellow Zoramites surrounding him. "We must get inside the city walls and regroup. Attack…attack now!"

Zerahemnah pulled out his sword and, with a chilling war cry, spurred his horse forward, pushing past his troops and forcing them out of his way. Like wild animals, his fellow Zoramites surged forward after him out of the massive Lamanite formation and charged toward the band of Nephites holding the gate.

Teancum held a strong defensive point, but he knew he was vastly outnumbered, with his back to the now-locked city gate. With his Ghost Soldiers, he might have had a chance of surviving this, but inside the perimeter created by the poorly trained soldiers of the city's garrison, he was quickly losing faith.

"Hold fast, men … keep together, shields up," he shouted as the Lamanites moved more soldiers around to his flanks. But that was not his biggest concern. To his front, less than one hundred yards away, were the dreaded Zoramites. Teancum knew that, at any moment, those large and wild-looking men were going to crash right through his line of Nephites and rush the gate. He could see his men were losing their nerve and starting to back up.

"Hold the line," he ordered as he pushed his men from behind to keep them in formation. "Stand fast, do not back up."

Teancum watched as the mounted leader of the Zoramites pulled out his sword and shouted, "Attack, attack now!" He charged forward with the other Zoramites following close behind.

A volley of arrows was fired from the city wall, but there were too few archers, and most overshot the rushing hoard of Zoramites. The soldiers with Teancum shifted in fear, and large holes formed in the defensive perimeter.

"Close the gaps," Teancum shouted, as he pushed soldiers back into place. Kicking and screaming, he tried in vain to maintain some sort of control over the men, but these were not disciplined warriors. One of the Nephite soldiers dropped his weapons and ran toward Zerahemnah, and then a second and a third followed, all with their hands held high in the air as a sign of surrender.

Zerahemnah moved his horse close to the first Nephite and, with one quick motion, slashed his large sword across the neck of the surrendering Nephite. The Nephite clutched at his mortal wound and spun completely around before falling to the ground. For the two remaining cowards who abandoned their friends and tried to surrender, it was too late to run back to the Nephite lines. Enveloped by the charging Zoramites, they were cut to pieces.

SHEM AND TEANCUM DEFEND THE GATE

Shem had been able to muster only about fifty men when a guard from on top of the wall interrupted his efforts, calling to him to come up and see what was taking place. Shem took a moment to order the fifty men to be ready to rush out of the gate to assist the trapped Nephites on his command. He ran to the top of the wall. From there, he looked out and saw the new positions of the charging Lamanites and the Zoramites.

"Gather stones, boiling water, burning oil, anything we can throw down on their heads to keep them from getting inside," Shem said. Several of the guards standing next to him began to move toward the stairs.

"Not you ..." Shem jumped in, "you need to stay and fight. Call to the women and children to help." The guards and archers, realizing their tactical blunder, sheepishly moved back to their positions

"Captain Shem, they are attacking," one of the archers called out.

"Fire your arrows," he shouted. He ran along the rampart, urging the few archers there to fire down on the charging Zoramites. The archers' inexperience immediately showed. Most of the arrows shot were off target because the archers did not know how to make adjustments for the movement of the charging horses.

"Reload and keep shooting," Shem ordered. He worked his way back to the main tower over the gate. There he grabbed a sergeant and said, "Take charge and keep firing; hold them back until we get everyone back inside."

"Yes, sir!"

Shem ran back down the stairs to the gate. He drew his sword and moved to the front of the gathered men.

"We will hold the line until everyone is back inside," he said. He turned to face the gatekeeper. "Open one side," he shouted.

The gatekeeper unlocked the right side gate and started to pull at the handle to open it. The soldiers trapped outside the wall heard the sound of the gate being unlocked and opening. Already panicked at the prospect of facing the charging enemy, the men were now in complete chaos. They dropped their weapons and rushed to get back inside the city. The gate was flung open by the mass of men running back into the city. Shem fought his way against the pounding current of bodies being forced through the open gate. He finally got outside the wall, only to find Teancum standing alone facing down the advancing enemy. Shem grabbed Teancum's shoulder and shouted, "Come on, get inside!" They both started to back step, holding their weapons out in front of them, but it was useless. The Zoramites were moving too fast, and there was no time to get the gate shut before they got everyone safely inside. The two leaders knew they were out of options. Without speaking, the two sheathed their swords and picked up long spears that had been left on the ground by the fleeing militia members. Holding the spears in front of them in a defensive posture, they moved shoulder to shoulder, attempting to hold off the charging horses as long as they could, while the remaining Nephites struggled to get back inside the gate.

The advancing Lamanite ground forces closed the distance to the city walls and started firing their arrows and shooting their slings at the defending archers on the wall. Some of the defenders were hit. One fell backward off the catwalk and landed in the courtyard at the same time some of the city's women and older boys arrived with baskets of stones and pots of hot liquid to assist with defending the wall.

Zerahemnah was only ten yards from the gate when he pulled up on the reins to avoid driving his horse into the spears held by Teancum and Shem. Teancum lunged forward and stabbed at Zerahemnah's horse, causing the animal to suddenly rise up and toss Zerahemnah off. For the second time within a few hours, Zerahemnah did a complete backward roll off his horse. As luck would have it, this time he landed squarely on his feet with his sword still in hand. A second Zoramite charged and Shem thrust his spear into the center of the soldier's chest, killing him instantly and knocking him off his horse. Shem lost his grip on the spear, and the weapon dropped to the ground. Shem quickly drew his old sword and turned to face the next enemy soldier who advanced. Both Teancum and Shem kept moving

and fighting as they backed up into the sally port and tried to hold off the charging hoard. A few arrows from the Nephite guard towers were landing around Zerahemnah but, for the most part, the Lamanites were keeping the defenders' heads down with their own arrows and stones.

Shem and Teancum had their backs against the gate and were locked in mortal combat with overwhelming odds as Lamanites and Zoramites closed in from all sides. Several Lamanites with short bows worked their way forward to shoot arrows at the two Nephites.

"We've got to get inside," Shem shouted as Teancum stabbed at another enemy soldier who tried to close the distance. Shem banged on the gate with the hilt of his sword, and the door cracked open. Several large hands shot out from inside the gate and grabbed Shem by his tunic. He, in turn, grabbed Teancum's arm, and they were both sucked back inside the safety of the gate.

"Don't let them lock the gate," Zerahemnah shouted. Several of his warriors tried to push open the closing gate. As more and more Lamanites arrived at the gate to help push it open, the sally port filled up with bodies. The Nephites inside the city struggled with all their might to force the gate the rest of the way closed. It was just a matter of time now as the Lamanites trying to push the gate open were quickly outnumbering the Nephites holding it closed. Some of the defenders gave in, fleeing from their posts to save themselves and their families. The gate was slowly giving way. Horrified, the Nephites who were still fighting at the gate desperately pushed as more light began to appear in the crease between the left and right gate doors. A few more inches was all Zerahemnah needed as he urged his men to push with all their might. He could see the gap getting wider, and he could hear the screams from inside.

"We have them men. Keep pushing," he shouted. "Keep pushing!"

Moroni had reached the crest of a tall rise of ground where the tree line opened up to the valley below. This position gave a closer and more panoramic view of the city of Manti, as well as the river and valley beyond. The sergeant major, with several junior officers, made up an advance party, with the bulk of his soldiers about one hundred yards behind him. They had quickly moved through the tree line, hoping to keep the Lamanites from detecting their flanking maneuver. Moroni pulled up on the reins of his horse and stared at the scene below him.

"They're breaching the gate," the old sergeant major gasped. "If they get inside all is lost."

Moroni clenched his teeth, his large jaw rippling and hardening as a result. He focused on his troops coming out of the tree line and made quick calculations in his head of the time it would take to regroup the Nephites for a charge, and how long it would take to move his soldiers down the hill to the gate of the city. He looked across the valley to the river's tree-lined bank. Lehi was nowhere in sight.

"We are out of options and out of time," he said.

The general dismounted, swinging his right leg up and sliding out of his saddle. He moved to the left side of his mount, pulled the massive Sword of Laban off the horse and fastened it to his side. He unbuckled the round, metal shield off his saddle bags and fixed it to his left hand. The soldiers with Moroni followed his example and dismounted from their horses and were making ready their weapons and shields when the sergeant major rode up.

"Get the men into formation for a charge down the hill," Moroni said to his old friend. "Hurry, we are out of time."

"Yes, sir," the old sergeant responded as he rode back to where the soldiers were gathering.

Moroni turned to his security detail and the young officers who were riding with him. "My intention is to run down this hill and engage the enemy in a fight. Who is with me?" A shout went up from the gathered soldiers, and they raised their swords and spears in the air.

"Excellent, you officers join your men. Form the ranks and get them ready for the charge. You men …" Moroni said, nodding to the security detail, "You men stay with me. We are going to punch our way right through the Lamanite lines and clear them away from the main gate, understood?"

They shook their heads in agreement.

"We are with you, sir, for freedom, to the death," one of the young soldiers shouted.

Another cheer came up from the small group. Moroni smiled back at them and nodded his head in acknowledgement.

He knew and understood what must be going on inside the minds of each of these soldiers. He had been in their shoes before and knew what a great honor it was for a young soldier to be assigned to protect their leader. These men not only had that honor, they also had a chance to join him in what many would call an audacious battle tactic. Moroni could see himself in these young men.

"This moment in time is the stuff of legend," Moroni thought, like the heroes of old: General Joshua, young David and the giant, father Nephi,

Gideon and the wicked King Noah. History was full of men who stood for right and freedom. They paid the price for liberty and now are remembered forever as the Champions of God's kingdom. "The people of that city need our help and we will not fail them!" A second shout went up as Moroni gave encouragement to his men.

The sergeant major made quick work of reforming the lines and getting the men ready for the final charge.

"All is ready, sir," he shouted back to his general. Moroni acknowledged the old soldier and ordered the trumpeters to sound the advance.

The sergeant of the security detail questioned the order. "Are trumpets such a good idea, sir? The enemy is still far away, and they will be ready for our attack if they hear the trumpets."

Instead of getting mad at a subordinate questioning his orders, Moroni used it as a teaching moment.

"I want them to fix on our advance and stop trying to breach the gate," Moroni explained.

"What of Captain Lehi, sir? Do we wait for him to get into place?" a second officer asked.

"No, we are out of time. We will just trust in God that Captain Lehi is also ready to attack." Moroni faced the men under his command. He held his massive sword in the air and shouted, "For liberty!"

The men were wildly enthusiastic as they repeated, "For liberty!"

Moroni turned his attention back to the valley below. Pausing for a few seconds to whisper a quick prayer, he looked over his left shoulder and called, "Forward!" The movement command was echoed by his officers and the trumpeter, too, sounded his horn to alert the army of the movement.

Moroni shouted "March!" as he took one giant step with his left foot to begin the final descent to the valley below. The men behind him followed in step and marched down the hill to the rhythmic drum beat keeping cadence. "At the double time … March!" Moroni commanded and led the men downhill at a fast jog.

Shem pushed with all of his might against the wooden gate. He could feel the ground under his feet giving way as the force of the pushing Zoramites and Lamanites slowly overpowered the efforts of the city defenders to secure the gate. Teancum shouted for more men to come and help, but only a few responded. Most had already run away to hide from the advancing enemy, but among the responders were two large boys, who dashed up to help. Teancum moved out of the way to allow fresh legs and arms to push in his place. Instead, Teancum grabbed a spear that was leaning against the wall just past the sally port, and, moving quickly back to the partially open gate, he stabbed through the gap in the gate at whatever Lamanite body parts were exposed. Again and again Teancum's spear went thrusting rapidly through the gap. In one of those thrusts, he stabbed three Lamanites in their legs or the sides of their chests. The wounded soldiers fell to the ground, causing several other Lamanites to trip over their bodies as they tried to push on the gate. Teancum stabbed two more Lamanites, and that was the break the Nephites needed. As the Lamanites lost traction, tripping over the wounded bodies of their comrades, the Nephite defenders were able to surge forward and force the gate nearly closed. In a stroke of bad timing, however, Teancum's spear caught in the gate as it closed. He pulled on the spear's shaft several times but, with the pressure of the Nephites pushing against it, he was unable to dislodge it. At that same moment, a Lamanite soldier, holding a small sword, stuck his arm through the gap. As the Lamanite's arm slashed back and forth, Teancum let go of the spear and quickly stepped back, dodging the sword. He pulled out his own sword and, with one mighty stroke, cut off the Lamanite's arm and split the wooden spear shaft in two, freeing it from the pressure of the gate. With one last valiant effort, the Nephite defenders pushed the gate closed and the large metal brace was moved into place, locking the gate. Exhausted almost to the point of collapse, Shem dropped to his knees and gasped for air. Teancum moved through the crowd of tired Nephites.

"Brace the gate," he shouted. He pushed and pulled soldiers in the direction he wanted them to move. A large, wooden beam was placed into the gate's metal brackets, locking the two sides in place. Teancum moved over to Shem and grabbed him by the shoulders and tried helping him to his feet.

"Get the men to the walls!" he said to Shem, and, to the dazed men around him, he added, "Some of you grab weapons and move to the walls. The rest of you muster here, and be ready to defend the gate if they breach it again."

The men of Manti moved in all directions, looking for their weapons of war. Some who had managed to gather bows and quivers of arrows left to find the quickest way to reach the tops of the walls.

"Come on, brother; on your feet." Teancum said in a more gentle tone as he helped Shem stand. From the other side of the gate, they could hear Lamanites cursing and pounding on the wooden gate with their fists, as well as the screams of the wounded. Shem pointed to the severed Lamanite arm on the ground, still holding a sword.

"A bad day for him," he said.

Teancum snorted and tried to hold back a laugh. Together, Teancum and Shem turned away from the gate. They had only gone three paces when the sound of distant Nephite horns could be heard outside the walls. The two warriors stopped in their tracks and turned to look at each other.

Teancum smiled, "General Moroni is here and has begun his final assault. Get what militia we have left lined up in the sally port, ready to advance out of the gate in support of the attack. We might still recover from this debacle!" Teancum clapped Shem on the shoulder and ran for the closest stairs leading up to the ramparts.

Shem saw about two dozen armed men in the area sitting or wandering around in a daze after what they had just witnessed. From his life of combat, Shem understood that war is hard for trained and experienced fighters. For common folk living through such dangerous times, war could be completely disabling. His own experience had taught him how to respond and how to inspire the men of the city to rally and to prepare to advance on the enemy just outside the gates.

"General Moroni is coming," he yelled as he ran up to the dazed men. "Do you hear the trumpets? We must rally our remaining forces at the gate. We must be ready to avenge our dead. Go, move, get every able-bodied man and assemble at the main gate!" He shoved the lifeless men into action. "Gather what men we have left for the assault. Now is the time for our vengeance!" The men took confidence from their leader. Some moved toward the assembly point, while the rest took up the cause of sounding the rally cry throughout the city. Shem continued to push the stragglers forward, shouting encouragement to them to join the fight. Standing off to the side were the two large boys who had come to help push the gate closed.

"Captain Shem, we want to fight," one of the boys exclaimed.

"My brave lads," Shem responded, he grabbing them both by the shoulders, "run through the streets of the city and call for the men to come and fight. Help gather what forces still remain find their weapons and rally them at the main gate. Together, we will all go out and face the enemy."

"Yes, sir!" they said enthusiastically. The two ran off in different directions, shouting for all able men to come to the gate and join up with the city's defenders.

Teancum, with a fresh burst of energy, flew to the top of the stairs and looked out over the wall. He could tell that, unchallenged, it would only be a matter of time until the Lamanites laid siege to the city and found a way to batter down the main gate. With the gate now secured, the main body of the Lamanite army started to move away from the walls and out of arrow range. A number of Lamanites were trapped in the enclave of the sally port, just under the main tower overlooking the ground in front of the main gate. Those Lamanites were safe from the Nephite arrows that were now raining down on them with increasing intensity, but they were cut off from the support of their army. Teancum watched as four Lamanites attempted to run from the cover of the sally port back to their lines. Three of the hapless Lamanites were cut down by the defenders' arrows, while the last made it back safely to his fellow soldiers. As Teancum scanned the scene before him, his military mind made a quick assessment. He noticed the Lamanites did not have any of their baggage or equipment wagons, no siege equipment, battering rams or ladders.

Teancum had not been there during Captain Lehi's early morning surprise attack on the other side of the river. He did not know of the stunning victory or that all of the baggage wagons had been captured. He wasn't aware of how Lehi had forced the Lamanite army across the river only to face General Moroni and the ingenious battle formations Moroni had concocted. What Teancum did know was that, given enough time, the Lamanites could easily use the large trees found in the surrounding countryside to fashion what they would need to properly assault the city. Teancum tried to scan the horizon for any sign of where the distant Nephite trumpeting came from. Just then he heard a second trumpet coming from the direction of the hillside to his left. There he spotted the battle standards of General Moroni's army, carried at the front of the formation marching at the top of the ridge line.

Teancum, in a very uncharacteristic moment, shouted with joy at the top of his lungs and jumped up and down at the sight of the city's rescue coming. As he was celebrating, two Lamanite arrows impacted the wall next to him and he was forced to duck down behind the stone ramparts. Embarrassed that he allowed himself to make such a rookie mistake and expose himself to enemy archers, Teancum laughed at himself under his breath and looked around for the city's defenders who were posted on the wall. He saw that no one was shooting back. Lying on the catwalk were the bodies of three dead Nephites with arrows sticking out of them but no soldiers standing up to defend the city. Most of the original archers were dead or had fled their posts. Now that the Lamanite army had pushed back out of range, the rest were cowering down behind the top of the wall to avoid being hit by a random Lamanite arrow or stone. Teancum could see the bulk of the Nephite army massing at the top of the hill, preparing for the assault.

"They will need a distraction," he thought, "And I need those remaining Lamanites to move back from the gate." Teancum looked at the other soldiers who were cowering and hiding behind the walls. He knew instantly they were useless to him. Quickly forming a battle plan in his mind, he moved carefully back to where he could look down at the sally port below him and where the remnants of the city's militia were assembling. There he could see the exact items he would need.

"You men," he called out from the top of the wall to the men of the city who were gathering below. When he had the attention of most of them, Teancum continued, "Gather up all of the straw bales in the stable over there and bring them to where you stand." He pointed to several jars of liquid the women and children of the city had brought when Shem called for help. "And those jars of oil … bring them also."

A COWARD'S DEATH

Captain Lehi was making great time moving his army along the river's edge toward the east end of the city.

"Keep moving boys. The city is in danger!" he urged them as he rode up and down the river bank on his horse, encouraging his men to move on.

"Sir," a young rider called out. He pulled on the reins and stopped his horse next to his captain.

"Report," Lehi said.

"Sir, about a quarter of a mile upstream, the river bank becomes rocky with cliffs forming on both sides; we cannot follow the river any farther on foot."

"Show me," Lehi responded and spurred his horse into a light gallop.

Eons before, the river had forged a path through the mountains and hills, carving its way downstream to the sea. Over the years, the river had been fed by countless mountain streams and plentiful rain. Not even giant rock formations could withstand the relentless erosion of the large swath of water. Lehi galloped along the river's edge for several hundred yards until the river made a sharp bend to the left and the gentle slope formed by the constant motion of the water gave way to a strong current flowing over jagged rocks inside high cliffs. Here, a large mill with stone walls and a thatched roof, along with several smaller buildings and some simple homes, had been built near the water's edge. Four small, wooden boats, with fishing nets strung along ropes attached to large wood poles, were anchored to the shoreline. The mill had a large wooden waterwheel to harness the power of the river and turn the grinding stones inside. There was also a unique conveyer of large buckets made of skins tied to ropes that went from the river to the top of the gentle rise. This was set up to help bring water from the river to the farmsteads springing up outside of Manti's walls.

Lehi dismounted and was met by several civilians who had been hiding inside the mill. They had armed themselves with rakes, hoes and other farming tools, but were visibly frightened.

"Thank the Maker you are here," one of the older men and spokesman for the group exclaimed as he walked up to Lehi and bowed. He was dressed like a farming peasant, in simple handspun clothing and a leather skull cap.

"Forgive us, my lord, it was wrong of us not to heed Moroni's command to barricade inside the city. Please, our wives and children are still inside the mill, will you protect us?"

"I cannot spare any men to watch over your village. We must attack the Lamanites as soon as I have reassembled my men," Lehi said calmly, "and it is not safe for you to flee to the city." The great warrior's shoulders dropped slightly and the hard features on his face softened as he moved his horse closer to the old man. He bent down and spoke in a gentle tone. The last thing he needed was a village full of panicked civilians. "Have all the women take what boats you have here and ferry themselves and the children to the other side of the river. Tell them to hide in the trees until the battle is over, and then you will come and get them."

The old farmer looked at the villager next to him and then at another young farmer. They shared a puzzled expression.

One of them spoke. "What of us? Why would we need to come back? Aren't we going to hide with them?"

"No, my brother," Lehi laughed kindly, "you and these men here will not be hiding. You are going to join my army and fight for your freedom and the lives of your families."

"But, we are not soldiers," one of the civilians spoke.

"Ah, but very soon you will be." Again Lehi's tone was calm and kind, but the civilian's comeback was curt and disrespectful.

"Well, I'm not going up there to face the Lamanites. That's your job, not mine."

Lehi's eyes narrowed slightly, the softer demeanor he was trying to display changed instantly to the hard warrior. He spurred his horse forward toward the defiant peasant, drew out his sword, and pointed it at the face of the rebellious man. He felt a twinge in his chest, like his heart had suddenly gained a few pounds and was now extra heavy. He knew the man was speaking more from fear than anything, but it was no time for insubordination, even from a civilian.

Lehi answered sternly, "No one in my army will die for you and your family or their freedom if you are not willing to do the same."

"So, you're saying you're surrendering and going home now?" the civilian taunted.

Lehi's eyes burned with anger at the audacity of the man. He pushed his horse forward a little more and nearly spat in the man's face. "I curse you as a coward and have a mind to put you out of your sorry misery right now. To expect these men to save you when you will not fight for yourself is insult to the lives of all the Nephites who already died today fighting for your freedom."

The obstinate man blinked several times but held his stiff posture. He looked around for some backing from the other civilians around him. When he saw none, his face turned red with embarrassment, and he started to take several steps backward. The coward dropped his shovel, turned and ran to the water's edge, where the small fishing boats were tied up.

"Baca, no!" the old leader of the group shouted. A young and very pregnant woman, who held another small child in her arms, came running out of the mill, screaming his name. Baca didn't even pause. He continued to push a boat into the water and started to paddle away from the shore.

As the one defector was leaving, the bulk of Lehi's army was catching up and gathered several paces away from their leader. Hundreds of foot soldiers now stood just a few yards behind him, breathing heavily from their run up the river's bank.

The young pregnant woman had become completely hysterical. Crying and shouting her husband's name, she tried to wade into the river, pursuing her cowardly spouse while still holding the small child in her arms.

"Get her out of there," Lehi ordered the small group of soldiers standing watch behind him. Six of them dropped their spears and shields and went into the chest-deep water after the woman. They forcibly took the baby from the woman's arms and tried to bring her back safely to land by wrapping her in the strong arms of two soldiers. The sobbing woman refused to comply. Pushing and twisting, she fought against the men as they tried to get her to come out of the water, all while screaming out Baca's name. The Nephite soldiers finally grabbed her, hoisted her up over their heads, and carried her out of the water and back to shore. She was still screaming and thrashing, calling out to her deserting husband as the soldiers gently set her down on dry land.

"Get your women to tend to her, and keep her quiet! We don't need the Lamanites hearing her scream!" Lehi said to the fishermen and farmers who were now waiting for their orders. With their heads poking out of the mill door, several additional women of all ages were watching the commotion. The leader of the village waved for them to come out and tend to the pregnant woman. Three of the women ran up and knelt down next to the young mother, who was now lying on the ground in complete despair and anguish. A fourth woman came for the child who was in the soldier's care.

"He left me; he left me," she repeated over and over between sobs of gasping air. As the women were trying to pick up the young mother, she suddenly grabbed at her stomach at let out a painful cry.

"It's the baby," one of the older women tending to her said. The women worked together to help the mother lie back down on the ground.

"Lieutenant …" Lehi called over his shoulder. His face again registered a soft kindness and sympathy. Only a slight wrinkle across his forehead showed that his mind was reeling with a mixture of thoughts. He was eager to move his army forward but now was caught in the curious position of knowing they would soon be witnesses to a birth in the middle of this day of death. His thoughts raced back to the letter in his pocket and his own daughter who was great with child and due any day.

"Yes, sir," the lieutenant answered.

"Lieutenant, find the surgeon, have him attend to this woman," Lehi ordered with a resolute tone.

"My captain, the battle is upon us; shouldn't the surgeon stay with the army?"

"I need soldiers more than I need surgeons now, young Lieutenant. The Doc can catch up when he is finished. Besides, it's not the baby's fault the father is a coward and there is war all around us. I have spent my life ordering men to their death. I will see to this child and, for once, order my men to bring life into this world.

The young leader blinked several times in disbelief. "This is Captain Lehi I am speaking to?" he thought to himself. "The bane of the Lamanites has gone soft." He smiled to himself, saluted and turned to find the medical staff.

"Sir, I have archers ready to take care of the coward in the boat," a second officer pointing to three archers with loaded longbows.

Lehi looked from the archers to the man wildly rowing away in the boat. "No," he said, sighing deeply, "let him live his cowardly life." The man was well away from the shore, paddling with all his might to get to the other side of the river.

Lehi continued. "The coward will die a little every day knowing he abandoned his family.

Lehi again addressed the old fisherman. "My scouts say I am not far from Manti."

"Yes, sir," The old one responded. "Manti is just over that rise." The old man indicated a slight elevation lined with trees.

"Show me," Lehi ordered.

With several senior officers following, Lehi crept up the grassy slope to the edge of the tree line. As they got closer to the top of the rise, they could hear the sounds of battle. Not wanting to give away his position, Lehi held up his hand to signal to his men to stop. He then dropped to his belly and crawled the last few yards in the high grass to a point where he could just peek over the top of the rise without exposing his head.

What he saw was almost incomprehensible. In the distance, about half a mile away, was the city of Manti. From that distance, he could make out the thousands of Lamanites clamoring around the gates of the city and columns of dark smoke rising from inside the walls of the city. With his years of military experience, he understood the situation almost instantly.

"Come and look," he spoke in almost a whisper to the soldiers waiting behind him. He waved at them to tell them to move up the rise and, in the same motion, indicated to them to lower their bodies to the ground. Within seconds, the soldiers with Captain Lehi were lying at the top of the slight rise next to him.

"Look," Lehi pointed to the city. "The gates remain closed. That is a good sign, especially since those Lamanite fools have no other way in. They abandoned their ladders and siege equipment with the baggage trains back at the bridge."

Lehi made a quick decision about what their next move should be.

"When I give the word," he said, "I want the lead companies to form up just in front of that large stump out there in the clearing. And I want the remaining companies to dress and form the lines right off of them."

"Yes sir," was the response.

"Then I want …" Lehi started, but he paused mid-sentence when he saw the sudden movement of the Lamanites backing away from the gate. This was followed by the sounds of distant war trumpets coming from the opposite side of the valley.

"What in the world?" Lehi asked.

"Look there," one of the soldiers exclaimed, pointing to the top of the hill on the opposite side of the valley. Lehi could just make out Moroni's battle flags and his small but well-armored army forming at the top of the gentle grassy hill overlooking Manti.

"Moroni!" Lehi said. A broad smile spread across his face. "Bring them up on line men. Quickly now or we are going to miss the battle."

"Fall in," one of the officers shouted as he jumped up and turned to face the lines of soldiers waiting back at the river's edge. "1st Company rally on me." The officer drew his sword, ran out into the clearing and stood next to the large stump Lehi had pointed out just moments ago.

"Sound formation. The rest of you fall in on 1st Company," Lehi said as he waved them up from the bank.

The trumpets sounded for the men to assemble as shouts of excitement and war cries went up from the mass of humanity that was Lehi's army. They crested the gentle rise of the riverbank and formed into their battle groups in the freshly plowed clearing.

Zerahemnah was exhausted. He was in desperate need of food, a drink of water, a good rest, and a lucky break, but none of that was going to happen anytime soon. The gate was secured and he was falling back, hoping to move his army out of the range of the Nephite arrows. Looking around at the men with him, Zerahemnah knew he had lost the momentum. The surge of energy his men showed just a few moments before was quickly replaced by fatigue and frustration. No one in his army had slept in over twenty-four hours and their last meal had been well before dawn. His army had been in almost constant combat for the entire day. The trail behind him was littered with dead and wounded Lamanites. His entire supply train had been captured by Moroni's men during the first engagement at the river this morning. He had just now lost his only opportunity of getting inside the city walls without a battering ram or any of his siege equipment. He knew that Moroni and his small, but surprisingly effective army, was somewhere behind him, closing ground fast.

Zerahemnah could sense he was close to losing all control over his army. "This is not good," he thought. "One more setback and these dumb goat-herding Lamanites just might give my head to Moroni as a peace offering."

"What now, sir?"

Zerahemnah turned to see who dared to question him. He found himself face to face with a young and bloodied Lamanite soldier, holding a spear.

"Who are you speaking to?" Zerahemnah demanded. Out of pure instinct, Zerahemnah struck the questioning Lamanite face with the back of his right hand, knocking him to the ground. "I give the orders here, and you obey. How dare you question me regarding the battle?"

It was at that moment that Zerahemnah realized he had made a giant mistake. The Lamanite he just hit had friends … lots of friends. Those friends seemed to materialize instantly, and they now were standing around him, breathing hard and clenching and unclenching their fists. After suffering defeat after humiliating defeat under this Zoramite's command, they had seen him assault their comrade, and they were done. They were done following his orders. They were done being half-starved and walking for days at a time, done facing the inferior Nephites and being defeated by them over and over again. They were done being treated like lower class people by Zoramites who looked and sounded a lot more like Nephites than their brother Lamanites.

"Get back," Zerahemnah shouted. "Get back. That is an order." The Lamanites nearest him started to circle him with weapons drawn.

"I lost six kinsmen on this war path, and I have yet to kill a Nephite. So maybe I will just kill you instead," one of the bigger Lamanites hissed as he positioned himself to attack Zerahemnah.

"I'll kill you and burn your village to the ground," Zerahemnah shouted. He pointed his sword at the challenging Lamanite warrior. "Now, stand down, all of you."

Zerahemnah could see that his verbal threats were having no effect. The biggest soldier was taking several deep breaths and repositioning his feet to get the angle that would give him the greatest advantage over Zerahemnah. Zerahemnah moved to counter the big warrior while frantically scanning the growing crowd. Lamanite soldiers had stopped trying to assault the city and, instead, turned to watch the showdown. Zerahemnah continued to search the crowd, looking for any of his fellow Zoramites who might be willing to assist him in quelling this mini rebellion before it boiled over to the entire Lamanite army.

A few tense seconds passed and Zerahemnah all but convinced himself he was going to need to fight his way out of this mutiny. Suddenly, sounds of the Nephite war trumpets echoed across the valley. The standoff ended as quickly as it had begun as every Lamanite soldier stopped to look in the direction of the trumpet sounds. They saw General Moroni and his small band of well-armored soldiers forming at the top of the hill.

271

"Move away from the wall and form ranks," Zerahemnah shouted to the Lamanites around him.

"No, we are done with you," the big Lamanite shouted back.

"Look," Zerahemnah said in a soft tone. He lowered his sword, smiled and walked toward the angry Lamanite. "I think we had a real misunderstanding over this issue."

The defiant Lamanite, caught off guard by his commander's change of tone, lowered his own sword. The instant the big warrior put down his weapon, Zerahemnah attacked. With one powerful backhand swing of his sword, Zerahemnah struck the head of the Lamanite clean off his body. The head flew off and rolled on the ground several times, causing the gathered crowd to back up. The headless body stood motionless for several seconds, and then fell forward and hit the ground with a loud thud.

With fire in his eyes, Zerahemnah screamed, "I said, 'Form ranks!'" The remaining Lamanites jumped at the order and ran to rejoin their own units to form the defensive ranks.

Three Zoramites ran up to Zerahemnah, who was still standing over the headless body.

"What happened?" one of them asked.

"A slight misunderstanding over who was in charge," Zerahemnah said.

A second Zoramite tipped his head toward the advancing Nephite army, which was now coming down the hill toward them. "Your orders, sir?" he said.

"We still outnumber them at least three to one," Zerahemnah answered. "It looks like they want to face us in an open fight, those fools. Form the men into three groups, have the center element face them head on and the other two attack their flanks. We will make quick work of them and then we can lay siege to the city at our leisure. Go and pass the word to our brother Zoramites. GO!"

Most of the Lamanite army had moved out of range of the remaining archers on the city wall and started to form up to face the charge from Moroni's men. The three Zoramites who just left Zerahemnah started to move back to form the ranks when the sounds of more trumpets came from the direction of the river. As if on cue, the entire Lamanite army turned to the sounds of the trumpets coming from behind them. The impossible was happening; a second Nephite army was forming out of the tree line by the river, almost out of thin air.

Zerahemnah could not see Lehi's army through the mass of Lamanites between him and the Nephites by the river.

"What is it; what is happening?" Zerahemnah pushed and shoved through the ranks, working his way to the back of the formations. Forcing his way past the last few men of the Lamanite ranks, Zerahemnah stepped out into the clear and saw for himself the impossible.

"A second army? You have two armies? What devilry is this Moroni?" Zerahemnah shouted. The reality of his position suddenly dawned on him "I have a city wall to my rear and an army on each of my flanks. ... I am trapped!"

"Get Pachus's chariot, turn it upright and lash as much hay to it as you can. Then soak it with the oil!" Teancum called from the top of the wall down to the courtyard below. "Bring the rest of the oil up here. Quickly now, before we lose our chance."

Most of the city's militiamen had recovered from the shock of the day's events and, under the direction of Shem and Teancum, were moving quickly to make the final preparations for the counterassault.

The sounds of a second set of trumpets coming from the river caused Teancum to look back over the wall.

"Lehi!" he said, a smile crossing his face as he recognized Captain Lehi's battle standards.

The Nephite soldiers under Captain Lehi's command formed up and prepared to attack from the opposite side of the valley.

"I see your plan now, Moroni," Teancum exclaimed. He hollered down to the men gathering in the courtyard, "Quickly, men, we have no time to spare!"

Teancum searched for Shem among the men and, when he didn't see him, called his name.

"Here," Shem replied, stepping forward so Teancum could see him.

"Meet me at the stairs!"

Shem waved and moved quickly to the bottom of the stairs that led up to the wall.

"Shem," Teancum spoke when he met up with his comrade in arms, "the timing must be perfect for this to work. On my command, have your strongest men push the chariot full of oil-soaked hay out the gate and into the Lamanites that are still crowding the gate. We will set it on fire with a flaming arrow from up here. At the same time, the men on the walls will throw down buckets of the remaining oil onto the Lamanites that move to get out of the way of the burning chariot. The burning chariot will ignite the vapors from the oil and cause a giant flashover. This will kill or burn all the enemy soldiers near the gate. Then we regroup and advance to face the Lamanites when General Moroni engages them." Teancum looked Shem in the eyes searching for understanding. "Any questions?"

"Sounds like fun." Shem said smiling back.

No one had a question for Captain Teancum.

FIRE

"Right, where are the rest of my archers?" Several men raised their hands. "Come up here with me, and bring all the arrows you can find. Leave two buckets of oil and bring the remaining containers, a bucket of tar pitch for your flaming arrows, and a fire-starting kit."

The archers moved quickly to gather the needed items and made their way to the stairs.

"Shem, set the chariot at the gate and stand by!"

"Right," Shem replied. To the men tending to the chariot, he asked, "Is it ready, men?"

"Just finishing now, Shem," one of the men said. He poured the last drops of oil from his bucket on the stacks of hay stuffed in the chariot. He moved out of the way as others pushed the oil-soaked chariot into position.

"Move it over by the gate and get ready to push it out. Make sure when you push it out it goes far enough that we can close the gate behind to keep the fire from coming back inside the walls."

Teancum went back to the wall and looked out over the Lamanite hordes below. While most of the Lamanites had moved their attention from breaching the gate to preparing for the advancing armies of General Moroni and Captain Lehi, not all had lost focus on trying to get inside the city. Several more soldiers had moved close to the gate where they were safe from the arrows. The Nephite archers could not lean out far enough to shoot the Lamanites standing against the wall below them without exposing themselves to the Lamanites' own arrows and stones, and there was still a large group of enemy soldiers huddled in the sally port.

"We can't open the gate with all those men standing so close," Teancum said to some of the archers who had assembled next to him. "They will rush the gate when they see it opening, and we might not be able to get it closed before the other Lamanites see what is happening and charge inside." Teancum paused as he assessed the situation. "Okay, change of plans. We pour the oil first on the soldiers hiding against the wall. Fire your flaming arrows at the soldiers to get them back from the gate, and then we push the chariot out." Teancum looked at the two dozen archers now with him on the wall. "You men each get a bucket of oil and spread out along the wall. When I signal, pour the oil out over as many as you can. I want it to affect as many of them as possible, understand?" They all shook their heads in agreement. "Go," he commanded.

The men spread out along the top of the wall over the main gate, carrying the large buckets of cooking oil with them. Teancum found a small iron cooking pot and filled it with fire-starting tinder. He grabbed a handful of arrows and set the tips in a bowl of tar pitch. He pulled out his fire kit from his shoulder bag and grabbed his flint and steel. Striking the flint with the steel, he showered burning sparks over the iron pot full of tinder. After three strikes, he was able to get a small line of smoke coming out of the pot. With one gentle, well-placed breath of air, a fire quickly started.

Teancum surveyed the courtyard to check on Shem's progress. The chariot was in place and several large men were ready to push it out into the Lamanite crowd. A group of assigned men were standing behind the chariot, fully armored and ready to advance behind the flaming chariot and exact their revenge. All that was needed now was for the timing to be just right.

"Shem," Teancum shouted down at his comrade in arms. Shem waved to acknowledge he could hear Teancum. "Change of plans," Teancum said. Doing some quick calculations in his head, he smiled and said at Shem. "When I give the word, set fire to the chariot and push it out the gate as far as your men can. Have your militia follow the chariot out and engage the Lamanites that remain near the outside of the gate. The archers will cover you from here. Understand?"

Shem waved again to let Teancum know he understood his orders.

"Get ready, boys," Shem said. He spoke to two men next to him, "You two, ready a torch."

The two armed militiamen quickly complied and Shem was handed a freshly lit torch. Shem had nearly two hundred men at arms now. He felt confident that, with that many men, he could easily clear away any straggling Lamanites and hold the gate until General Moroni finished off the remainder.

"Spear men to the front," Shem ordered. He moved closer to the oil-soaked chariot, and the men assigned to carry the large spears repositioned themselves toward the front of the formation. "When the gate opens, stab at anything that moves. Push forward and clear away the enemy from the sally port and from both sides of the gate. You men pushing the chariot," he called back to the men waiting at ready, "use it as a battering ram and plow into the Lamanites without mercy. Be strong; be without fear!"

"Captain Lehi, we are formed up and ready to advance."

"Very well, lieutenant, stand by to sound the charge," Lehi said. Holding his massive battle ax with both hands, he started to walk through the formations of soldiers. He reached the front of the lines and held his intimidating weapon high above his head. Every man in the lines before him held his weapon in the air and let out a war cry.

Lehi, at the head of his troops, turned to face the Lamanite battle lines and called over his shoulder, "Follow me, men." The war trumpets blared their haunting notes and Lehi started marching, his personal command staff and flag detail following closely behind. The ranks of Nephites behind him took courage from their brave captain and moved toward the enemy.

With armored soldiers closing in fast from both sides and a city wall at their rear, some of the less courageous Lamanites started to shrink back. Several looked dazed and confused. Others looked pale, their eyes wide and darting from one side of the battlefield to the other.

No one, who had seen even a small part of what those Lamanite soldiers had seen the last several weeks, would blame them for being afraid. First, they had faced the boy general in their encounter on the jungle road in the Jershon valley, where he single handedly stopped their advance and killed dozens of men. They still couldn't understand what had happened to all the men who went into the jungle growth to outflank the Nephites. The stories they heard from those who had escaped were tales of plants coming alive and ghosts with swords. Those hearing the stories tried to ignore them as nonsense, but they couldn't come up with any logical explanation of how so many died.

Then there was the surprise attack at the river this morning and the strange formations of well-armored and disciplined men that held the much larger Lamanite army at bay. The formations had been invincible to their arrows and spears and quite deadly for the assaulting Lamanites.

Now, they had been unable to destroy the militia guarding the city, or even breach the gate, and the same Nephite army that had just beaten them twice had reemerged almost out of thin air and was attacking from both flanks.

With all that had happened to them—the forced marches, sickness, defeat at the hands of a smaller force, the lack of rest, food and, most importantly, water—the mighty Lamanite army commanded by Zerahemnah the Zoramite was falling apart. Loyalty to, or fear of, their leader was starting to wane as soldiers, alone or in small groups, started to break ranks and run back toward the river. Some of the Lamanites kept their weapons but most dropped what they had and ran. The officers within the Lamanite formations were trying to keep discipline and order, but they were overwhelmed by the numbers of soldiers who were trying to flee for their lives.

"Stop those cowards," Zerahemnah shouted as he worked his way back among the formations. "Kill the deserters!" Two Zoramite archers followed his orders and fired arrows at some of the Lamanites running from the ranks. Two were hit, but the rest managed to avoid the arrows and continued to run back toward the river.

Confusion and frustration among the Lamanites was quickly changing to shear panic as the Nephites continued to advance from both directions and their own leader was busy killing his own men who were running away. The Lamanite soldiers who remained firm and stood their ground did so only with extreme strength of will. The man they had pledged to serve was now killing his own men—their companions—right before their eyes. With everything else that had happened to them, now their own leader was willing to kill them rather than see his men escape from a very precarious situation.

With his trained eye, Teancum could also see what was happening to the Lamanites below him. He knew that loyalty to their leader had to be fading fast.

"One more push and the enemy will break," Teancum said under his breath. "Now is the time." He stood and looked down the catwalk in both directions at the men who were ready to spill the oil over the sides of the walls onto the Lamanites below. Teancum grabbed up his bow and pulled out one of the arrows soaking in the small bowl of pitch. Using the flame from the small fire in the cooking pot, he lit the arrow and set it in the bow string. "Go, now. Throw the oil," he shouted.

The men with the oil buckets stood up and, in unison, flung several gallons of flammable liquid over the side of the wall onto the hapless Lamanites below. Teancum did not want to give the oil-soaked Lamanites a chance to escape. He quickly moved to the edge of the wall and leaned over, aiming his arrow at a Lamanite who was trying to wipe oil out of his eyes. The arrow struck the enemy soldier with incredible force, right in the center of his chest, knocking him flat on his back. He almost instantly burst into a giant ball of flames. Teancum watched as the oil and fire mixture had the effect he was hoping for. The flames went racing across the ground where the oil had been spilled and ignited every man who had even a few drops of oil on him. The fire was spreading so fast and had so much energy that it erupted across the entire front of the main gate, engulfing any of the Lamanites who were anywhere near the gate. Dozens of Lamanite soldiers, covered in fire, ran in every direction, screaming in unimaginable pain. The screams were punctuated by the rushing windstorm-like sounds of the exploding fire as a massive black cloud rose into the air. From his vantage point, Teancum could see several soldiers trapped by the fire in the sally port just outside of the gate. Others soldiers, who had some oil on them and did not get burned from the first flashover, were backing far away from the gate to keep from catching on fire.

"Archers, shoot them," Teancum shouted. The Nephite soldiers, frozen in shock at witnessing the fire attack, snapped back to reality and engaged the fleeing enemy with their own burning arrows. That brought more eruptions of flames and screams of burning pain among the Lamanite soldiers.

"What happened? Where did the fire come from?" one of the Zoramites asked Zerahemnah.

"How should I know?" Zerahemnah shouted back. "Move those soldiers back." He pointed to the soldiers who were trying to extinguish the fires and help their burning friends. "Get them back into formations."

The sudden rush of heat, the massive black cloud rising in the air, the screaming from the burning soldiers, others running for their lives, still others deserting and being shot by their leaders, the charging Nephites getting ever closer—it was all too much for the Lamanite army. Like a strong breeze over a wheat field, the momentum caused the entire Lamanite army to sway and shift away from the fire and start moving back toward the river.

Then someone shouted, "Dragon ... Moroni has a dragon!"

It was a trickle at first, starting with the soldiers on the edges of the formation farthest from the city. In the beginning, just a few took off running back toward the bridge, then a few more. Suddenly, the entire Lamanite army was moving without direction or command—wild, panic-filled running, without discipline or order.

Teancum saw it happen but could not believe his eyes. The militia on the wall with him started shouting for joy, dancing and hugging each other. Teancum looked back over the side of the wall at the outer part of the sally port. He could see the fire that had trapped the Lamanites was quickly dying down. He moved back to where he could see Shem on the ground.

"The Lamanites are in full retreat, clear the stragglers from the sally port!" As Teancum spoke those words, a shout went up from the armed men waiting to advance back out the gate.

"Open the gate," Shem commanded, as he dropped the burning torch in his hand on top of the oil-soaked hay in the chariot.

The sounds of the locks being opened and the brace being removed gave the Lamanites trapped outside renewed hope that they could escape the horror of burning alive. They started to bang on the doors of the gate, pleading with the Nephites inside to let them in.

"Make ready." Shem said. The men assigned to help with the chariot positioned themselves to push it through the gate, while the rest readied their weapons to attack the Lamanites who were trying to get inside.

"Push out the chariot!"

The final brace was removed from the gate and the large wooden double doors started to swing inward. The Lamanites pushed on the doors, using all their might to get away from the burning bodies and oil-soaked ground around them. The doors opened and the Lamanites spilled into the inner sally port, tripping over themselves, coughing and charred from the fire.

"Now," Shem shouted, and the chariot was pushed forward. The chariot gained power and momentum as it moved. The men, with their weapons drawn, moved in behind the flaming chariot as it passed by them.

The Lamanites were still trying to recover from the smoke and flames, still trying to push their way inside the gate, when they looked up to see a massive burning ball of fire barreling down on them. Some had the wherewithal to get out of the way by sucking up to the sides of the sally port walls, but most of them just froze in fear. The burning chariot hit the group of scrambling Lamanites with full force, knocking many of them to the ground and setting some on fire. Some were crushed by the weight of the chariot, others sustained broken bones or were burned alive.

Teancum's flaming chariot worked. It punched a hole right in the middle of the only group of enemy soldiers left to threaten the city. The momentum of the rolling chariot carried it past the injured and dead Lamanites on the outside of the wall and into the open field.

"Charge," Shem yelled as he waved his sword in the air. The armed men with him cried out and moved at once toward the open gate. The Lamanites who had managed to avoid the burning chariot were cut down by stabbing spears and sword strikes as the gathered Nephite militia overwhelmed them when they rushed out of the gate, through the sally port and out into the open ground.

The Lamanite army was two hundred yards away from the city gate and in full retreat. Shem and his city guards had made such quick work of the few Lamanites remaining behind that, once they cleared the gate, there was a bit of confusion as what to do now. Shem quickly assessed the problem and ordered half of the men with him to form a skirmish line facing the Lamanites. The rest he put to work dealing with any wounded Lamanites, gathering up all the dropped weapons and picking up any arrows fired down at the Lamanites from the city defenders. Looking back on the wall, Shem waved his sword high in the air to signal Teancum all was clear. Teancum returned the wave and ordered the archers to gather up all their remaining arrows and follow him. Teancum bolted down the stairs and out past the burned bodies of the Lamanites to Shem's position.

Shem smiled at Teancum and asked, "Now what?" Teancum took a quick look around and saw the still-burning chariot with charred Lamanite bodies around it.

"Are these the only soldiers left from the city?" Teancum asked as he turned back to face Shem. Shem made a quick calculation in his mind as he looked over the men with him and Teancum.

"No, but how long do you want to wait for the rest to find their courage and muster?"

Teancum looked at the fleeing Lamanites and back at the city.

"We are about to witness a Nephite victory of historical proportions, and I don't want to miss it, do you?"

"No," Shem said with a laugh and giant smile.

"Pick some men to remain and have them lock the gate behind us. Have them organize the stragglers into a defense on the walls and wait for our return."

"Yes, sir," Shem said. "You and you," Shem commanded as he pointed to two older men gasping for air. "Fall back and shut the gate behind us. Get those who are still in the city up to the wall as security and wait for our return."

"Yes, sir," the two responded breathlessly.

As the two old men turned to leave, several others walked up to Teancum and Shem with their arms full of arrows, spears and other weapons left by the Lamanites.

"Give a spear to every man who does not have one. Have the archers carry as many arrows as they can, and get the men into formation. We have a date with some Lamanites!" Teancum shouted to the men standing close by. The men of the city let out a shout of joy and moved to comply with their commander's orders.

At seeing the giant flash of fire coming from in front of the city gate, the troops marching toward Manti with Moroni and across the field with Lehi let out a collective gasp. Moroni and Lehi halted their separate advancing forces to assess what was happening before them. They witnessed the Lamanites on the ground in front of the gate running and scattering from the fire. They saw the burning chariot crashing through the group of Lamanite soldiers hiding inside the sally port. Finally, they watched as the entire Lamanite army turned and headed back toward the river.

Moroni could see Lehi's forces across the valley and Teancum's small band forming outside the city walls. "We can't let them get back to the river and reorganize," Moroni said as he turned to face his cavalry officers. "Take the horses, run down the stragglers and cut into their left flank," he said.

The horse soldiers leaped at the chance to take the fight to the Lamanites and bolted off at an angle to cut off the fleeing Lamanite stragglers. General Moroni held his massive sword in the air. He looked down the line of soldiers with him and shouted as he took off toward the fleeing Lamanites at a full sprint. His army followed his example and ran after him, shouting and waving their weapons in the air, chasing after the retreating enemy only a few hundred yards away.

Lehi saw Moroni's tactic and urged his own men to follow him as he sprinted after the retreating Lamanites. "Come on, lads. Do you want to live forever?" he shouted as he ran toward the enemy. Lehi's cavalrymen took off at a full gallop to engage the retreating Lamanites on the right flank.

As Moroni and Lehi made their advances, Shem and Teancum smiled at each other and shrugged their shoulders. They both held their weapons in the air and shouted as they started at full run, leading the men toward the Lamanites.

The Lamanites who were first to fall victim to the charging Nephite cavalry were those who were wounded, too slow, or too old and tired to escape. Unable to keep up with the main body of retreating Lamanites, they were quickly cut down by the horse soldiers.

The few mounted soldiers remaining in the Lamanite army were Zoramites, and they were now riding as fast as they could to get away from Moroni and his men. The Nephite cavalry made quick work of Lamanite stragglers and left a trail of dead bodies behind them. Soon, there were so many dead that Moroni and his men had to hurtle and sidestep bodies lying on the ground as they charged forward in pursuit of the retreating enemy forces.

THE BRIDGE

The young Nephite lieutenant who had been left to guard the bridge hated his first command.

"Left behind to watch the wounded and baggage, this is an insult," he thought as he walked. He left a small contingent of fully armed men at the ready on the Manti side of the bridge, while the remainder was making quick work of rounding up the wounded Lamanites and tending to the few wounded Nephite soldiers from the early morning fight. He also linked up with the wounded Nephites and supply wagons from General Moroni's army and brought them safely across the river.

The several Lamanite supply wagons captured by Lehi's surprise assault had been rummaged through by the Nephites and food and kegs of wine were found. A fire had been built and an older, shirtless Nephite soldier tended to a large pot of boiling food and a giant hunk of roasting meat. The young lieutenant had removed his armor and was inspecting the work being done by his men. Dressed only in his tunic and with his sword strapped to his side, he walked around the stacks of equipment removed from the supply wagons and surveyed the groups of wounded men. With the many wounded and captured Lamanites, the lieutenant knew that he and his men would be outnumbered if they should start to rise up.

"Put all the confiscated weapons in one wagon and move that wagon by the bridge where we can keep an eye on it," he ordered. A wagon was quickly emptied and refilled with the spears and swords left behind by the wounded and dead Lamanites.

"Sergeant," he called, signaling to a young Nephite soldier walking past him.

"Yes, sir," the soldier replied.

"Position the wagon with the Lamanite weapons in it at an angle facing downhill by the river's edge. Place a log under the wheel to keep it from rolling into the water. That way, if the Lamanite prisoners start an uprising, we can kick out the log and sink the wagon in the river before they can get to their arms."

"Good idea, sir. I'll see to it personally," the soldier saluted and moved toward the wagon, calling to several others to help him with the wagon.

The young lieutenant spent the rest of the morning organizing the medical facilities and trying to separate the Lamanite officers from the common soldiers. He wanted to be ready when General Moroni returned in case there were to be interrogations or prisoner exchanges.

At noon, he directed his men to take turns eating lunch, courtesy of the captured Lamanite food. Like a good leader, the lieutenant waited until all of his men had their food and, finally, with a grumbling stomach, he approached the mess area. He licked his lips as he held his bowl out for the cook to scoop a heaping ladle full of food into it. The aroma of the steaming pile of meat, potatoes and carrots swimming in brown, thick gravy being poured into his bowl was almost intoxicating. He licked some spilled gravy off his hands and was walking toward a shade awning when someone called out his name. One of his soldiers pointed toward the tree line at the far edge of the clearing opposite of the river. The young Nephite officer stepped out from behind a wagon to get a better view of what his soldier was trying to show him. Coming out of the tree line was a long, single-file line of Nephite soldiers riding horses. The young officer strained to see the insignia on the battle standard carried by one of the horsemen in the front of the column. He smiled when he finally identified the markings.

"Cook," he called out to the Nephite who had taken charge of the noon meal. "Put another pot of food on; they will be hungry."

"Yes, sir," the old cook responded. He sounded tired but moved with swift precision as he cut into a giant side of beef with a meat cleaver.

The young officer gulped down his food like a famished dog and was still chewing and swallowing when the lead elements of the Nephite formation reached him. The lieutenant smartly rendered a salute to Captain Amiha, who was leading the column of Ghost Soldiers. Amiha saluted back and held up his hand to halt the soldiers following. The column responded in disciplined unity and all the horses stopped moving forward.

The lieutenant, still chewing his food, stepped out to greet the party.

"Where is the army?" Amiha asked the young officer.

"Sir, they have crossed the river and are chasing the Lamanites to the netherworld for all I know." He swallowed his mouthful of food and cocked his head toward the bridge.

"How long ago did they cross?" Amiha asked. He dismounted and stood facing the lieutenant.

"Sir, we engaged them at dawn on this side of the river and made quite a good showing for ourselves." The young officer pointed to the area where the dead Lamanite bodies had been gathered. The two slowly walked together, away from the kitchen area and toward the bridge. The lieutenant continued, "We pushed them across and that's where they met the general." He indicated the spot across the river where the piles of dead Lamanites were already bloating in the noonday sun and being ravished by birds of prey.

"Outstanding!"

"Yes, sir. It was a well-executed plan. What remained of the Lamanite forces broke and ran from the general and his men and raced toward the city over that rise. General Moroni and Captain Lehi split up and gave chase. Lehi went by way of the river and the general took the route over the hills there."

"What are your orders?" Amiha asked.

"Sir, my orders are to hold security on the bridge, secure the prisoners and wait for General Moroni's return."

"It looks to me like you have about one hundred prisoners," Amiha said.

"Eighty-two to be exact. They are being pretty mellow now. I made them dig graves for our soldiers and then pick up all their dead friends. After that, I lashed them together with cords and assigned a guard to stand over them."

The young soldier looked at Amiha and asked, "Sir, why are you here? I thought you and the Ghost Soldiers were to stay at Jershon in case the Lamanites came back."

"We are scouting ahead for our baggage and supply wagons from Jershon. A large contingent of troops and equipment arrived a few days ago from Zarahemla. I left a strong element to garrison Jershon and brought the rest, along with Teancum's Ghost Soldiers, to bring supplies to the army. We picked up the Lamanites' trail on the road a few days ago, and we are moving ahead of the main party to sniff out any ambushes. That reminds me … Sergeant," he called out, looking back to the Ghost Soldiers who arrived with him.

"Yes, sir," a mounted soldier responded.

"Send two riders back to our main body and supply wagons. Tell them the path is clear and bring them here as quickly as they can."

"Yes sir." The sergeant pointed to two men, who turned their horses around and galloped back toward the trees.

"Hungry?" the young officer asked Amiha.

"I'm starving."

"The cook will have something for you and your men shortly. Until then, I will have my men take some tarps from the Lamanite wagon and make some shade for you. When you are rested, I am going to scout the other side of the river a bit. Would you like to join me?"

"Absolutely, and my soldiers are available to relieve yours for a rotation at the guard posts on the river."

"Thank you, sir. Let's see if we can rig up some kind of corral for your horses."

The two leaders started to walk back toward those Ghost Soldiers who were still waiting on their horses when the sergeant of the guard at the bridge sounded the alarm. He waved his arms and shouted for assistance. They immediately saw why. Coming over the rise from the direction of the city was the first wave of Lamanites running from Moroni, some alone and some in small groups, running wildly toward his bridge.

The two young officers instantly sprang into action, running in different directions and shouting orders. The lieutenant called, "To arms, men, to arms!" as he moved quickly to retrieve his armor and spear. Stopping just long enough to put on his breastplate and armguards, he scooped up his helmet and spear and ran toward his soldiers forming up at the bridge. The men assigned to him all dropped what they were doing and ran for their armor and weapons.

The sergeant of the guard at the bridge made quick work of putting his men in a strong, defensive position. He moved them back toward the middle of the bridge, over the water. This kept them from being flanked by the Lamanite force advancing toward them. Because the bridge itself was not wide, the sergeant lined them up behind a wall of shields with spearmen ready to gouge the few Lamanites who could cross the bridge at the same time. The lieutenant, seeing the defensive position his squad took, moved the remaining men onto the bridge, lining both sides of the bridge with shields to keep the Lamanites from hitting his men with arrows. The first of the retreating Lamanites reached the edge of the river but dared not try to cross and face the Nephites waiting for them in the middle. They had seen an armored formation like this before and knew the folly of a direct attack.

AMIHA JOINS THE BATTLE

Lieutenant Joffa reached his men on the bridge and could hear the insults and challenges the Lamanites were shouting at them.

"Steady men. Let them come to us."

A Lamanite arrow bounced harmlessly off one of the shields at the front of the formation.

"Keep your shields up and your eyes open. Watch for their archers," Joffa nervously shouted as he scanned the ever-growing number of enemy soldiers before him. Hundreds now gathered at the far edge of the bridge. Desperate to get away from Moroni, some were wading out chest deep into the river.

The river barges, which the people of Manti used for transport and commerce, had been removed days before by Moroni in preparation for the battle. Now, the small wooden docks on the downstream side of the bridge used to moor the big boats were covered with men trying to find a way across the wide river to avoid the Nephites.

Two more arrows struck the shields of the Nephites lining the sides of the bridge. Joffa looked out at the large, disorderly mob of Lamanites. He took a quick assessment of his men and the strong position he held. As long as he held the bridge and the Lamanites did not swim across to flank them, he could hold against them for a very long time. The remaining Nephite soldiers who were not on duty guarding the bridge arrived quickly with their armor and weapons. Joffa positioned them at the edge of the bridge as reserves to respond when needed to fill any gaps.

When fleeing Lamanites started to appear on the opposite shore, the demeanor of the wounded Lamanite prisoners on the Nephite side of the river suddenly changed. They became belligerent, defiant and animated, reacting to the sudden arrival of their comrades on the far side of the river. Braver now with this backup, the prisoners hollered at the Nephite guards stationed to watch over them. Some of the captive men stood, cursing and shaking their fists at the guards. The guards backed away from the prisoners and formed a line between the Lamanites and the water, pointing their spears at the prisoners.

"You animals, back off and sit down," one guard yelled.

"Are you crazy?" another called. "Back down. You're safer here than with your Lamanite brothers, who will soon be used for our target practice. Settle down, you fools."

Suddenly, one of the Nephite soldiers pointed back across the river. "More Lamanites are coming!"

A wave of Lamanite humanity came pouring over the top of the rise.

Joffa stiffened at first, then immediately relaxed, realizing the Lamanites were not attacking, but running and screaming in sheer terror. He knew the thousands of soldiers running blindly toward the river weren't charging, they were trying to escape, which had to mean the combined Nephite forces were in pursuit. Splashes from men now trying to swim across the river were coming from both sides of the bridge. The young lieutenant looked in both directions and saw men in the water. Several fleeing Lamanites, entering the water upstream from the bridge were swept along by the current and pushed up against the bridge. They grabbed the wooden planks of the bridge, trying to climb out of the water, but the Nephites quickly killed them with rapid spear thrusts into exposed chests and necks. More and more enemy soldiers jumped into the water and Joffa could see that hasty plans for a direct assault by the Lamanites across the bridge were slowly forming.

The young security commander made a quick calculation and decided to move his men back to the near edge of the bridge. There, he could refit the line and form a stronger defensive perimeter against the ever-increasing horde of desperate Lamanites.

"Archers," he shouted, "fall back and cover us as we pull back." Four Nephites, carrying their large bows, quickly moved back across the bridge and set up to fire, two men on each side of the bridge.

In what his men on the bridge would later describe as an impressive and courageous move, the young Nephite officer skillfully commanded his small group of bridge defenders to back step off the bridge, and to do so without ever losing their tactical advantage and shield coverage. Inspired by their leader's calm demeanor, the men responded with uncanny professionalism. Performing a move they had never practiced before, and even under the overwhelming pressure brought down on them by the threatening Lamanite army, they worked together without panicking.

"Now, men," the lieutenant continued, "on my command, keep your shields up and back step to our end of the bridge. Ready, step! Ready, step! Ready, step!" With each command, the men forming the small, armored wall took one step backward, moving as a single unit.

Seeing the Nephites stepping back, Lamanites slowly moved forward on the bridge. They didn't charge headlong into the armored wall, but moved up as close as they could without exposing themselves to the spears and swords of the Nephites.

Amiha, hearing the alarm and seeing Lamanites coming over the rise, ran back to the Ghost Soldiers still waiting on their horses.

"Dismount and prepare to reinforce the line at the choke point there at the edge of the bridge," Amiha barked, pointing to the Nephites who were already lined up.

As the Ghost Soldiers climbed down from their horses, Amiha noticed several things happening at the same time. He saw that young lieutenant Joffa was fully occupied, focused on directing the Nephites who were moving their defensive line back, while keeping a close watch on the Lamanites who were slowly advancing toward them on the bridge.

At the same time, Amiha saw twenty or so Lamanite prisoners charge the Nephite guards. The rest of the prisoners, some hobbling, others holding their bleeding wounds, moved toward the large wagon full of confiscated Lamanite weapons parked at the river's edge.

He also could see Lamanites trying to swim across the river Sidon.

"If those Lamanites make it across the river and join with the prisoners, we could be outflanked and lose the bridge!"

Amiha pulled his shield and helmet off the saddle bags tied to the back of his horse. "Sergeant, take six men and aid those guards. The rest of you, come with me; full charge."

Having supreme confidence in the Ghost Soldiers' professionalism, Amiha knew they would respond without question. Without even waiting for them to move, Amiha drew his own sword and sprinted toward those Lamanites who were now trying to dig weapons out of the wagon.

Joffa, managing the soldiers on the bridge, was not aware that the prisoners were loose and his guards were in a desperate fight for their lives as dozens of enemy soldiers tried to grab them and take away their weapons.

The Nephite archers, who had taken up positions near the bridge, attempted to pick off lone Lamanite swimmers making their way closer to the Nephite side of the river. They also had been too distracted to notice that the prisoners had escaped. Each now had three or four of the wounded Lamanite escapees jumping on them, trying to disarm them or push them into the water.

As they slowly advanced on the bridge toward the Nephite armored line, the Lamanites started to shout and cheer. They were looking and pointing at something going on behind the Nephites on the bridge. Joffa saw this and quickly turned his head to check on his men behind him. He gasped when he saw the chaos behind him. He was about to redeploy his men when he saw Amiha and the Ghost Soldiers running toward the bridge. He instantly relaxed, knowing he was going to be safe from attack. The Ghost Soldiers could easily handle a few wounded Lamanites.

Two of the guards attacked by escaping Lamanites were on the ground. The other guards were immersed in a brutal battle, each trying to ward off eight or ten Lamanites. Finally, seven Ghost Soldiers arrived to aid them. Teancum's warriors were so well-trained in the art of war that they were able to fire several arrows while on the run. Six Lamanites fell from arrow strikes. The remaining Lamanites turned to see where the arrows came from but were too late to react to the charging Ghost Soldiers. Teancum's special soldiers, with their amazing fighting skills, cut through the rioting Lamanite prisoners like wind through a pile of leaves, piercing bodies, hacking off limbs, and removing heads from necks. It was over in a matter of seconds. Spinning, jumping, and using unspoken coordination developed from countless hours of training and combat together, those seven elite warriors killed thirty dangerous men.

The sergeant of the Ghost Soldiers made a quick assessment. None of his men was wounded. Two fallen Nephite guards were dead, and the remaining Nephites were too wounded to continue the fight.

"Quickly bind the wounds of our men," he instructed. "Gather up your arrows and weapons. We must make for the bridge at full speed." Any remaining wounded Lamanite on the Nephite side of the river was quickly killed by Amiha and the rest of the Ghost Soldiers. Killing a wounded man was not generally something approved by General Moroni, but these Lamanites chose to continue the fight and not submit to their capture. There was no honor in fighting injured Lamanites, but the Ghost Soldiers knew they could not leave them alive. With somber efficiency the uprising of the captured Lamanites was put down and the dead left where they fell. There was no time to bury or move them, and the Ghost Soldiers made the ground behind the Nephites safe before moving on to the bridge.

Up river, in the far distance, thunder could be heard coming from storm clouds gathering around the tops of the jungle-covered mountains.

General Moroni called his men to a halt as he and the Nephite warriors with him met Captain Lehi, Captain Teancum, Shem and their men in the middle of the battleground. It was a grand reunion of brothers, friends and comrades as they celebrated their accomplishments and the gains they had made to that point.

"It's a fine morning for a parade, general!" Lehi exclaimed, with a broad smile on his face as he, along with the other ranking Nephite officers, saluted General Moroni.

"Gentlemen, well done." Breathing heavily, Moroni acknowledged the men around him and returned Lehi's salute. "Is the city safe?" he asked Teancum.

"Yes, sir. No one got inside the gate, and the walls still stand. The gate was locked behind us, and a force remains to secure the civilians."

"Why the lone chariot charge? It completely foiled the original plan of pinning them against the walls," Moroni asked with a bit of confusion.

"Pachus," Shem replied.

"Pachus," Moroni said with disgust and spit on the ground. "Please tell me he is dead."

"No, sir. Not yet," Shem said.

"There will be time for that soon enough," Moroni responded, with anger in his voice. "Now, the problem at hand ...," he continued as he turned to look at the remaining Lamanites, now running for their lives.

"Sir ..." Lehi interrupted, "we can't stop now; I left only a small contingent of my men to hold the bridge. They will be slaughtered and the remaining Lamanites will escape over the bridge and into the mountains if we do not advance." Lehi's tone, the look in his eyes and the beads of sweat that formed on his forehead revealed the concern and urgency he felt.

"We will advance old friend. We will merge our forces together and move as one against the Lamanites at the river's edge. Sergeant Major?" Moroni called out.

"Yes, General?" The old soldier responded. He worked his way through the growing crowd of men and officers around Moroni.

"Sergeant Major, two minutes, and then we move. Refit the lines. Tell them to drink water and prepare for the charge. Infantry in front, archers and support personnel behind. Everyone moves, everyone fights, is that clear?"

"Yes, sir," the sergeant major responded and turned to do what he did best—manage an army.

"Sir, what of the cavalry?" Teancum asked.

Moroni turned to look at the trail of death left by the cavalry as they chased the fleeing Lamanites toward the river. He then looked down at a dead Lamanite near where he was standing. "I just hope they leave a few for us." There was a quick laugh from the gathered soldiers. As Moroni looked back out over the sloping plain before him and scanned the littered bodies of fallen Lamanites, he was hit with a sudden sadness. Each of the dead was someone's father, son, or brother ... now they were dead, and for what? There would be great weeping and mourning because of the evil intentions of a few men. "Curse you, Zerahemnah." Moroni whispered as he wiped sweat from his brow.

A sudden vision came to him as he stood looking at the dead. As though he were an eagle soaring over the land, Moroni could see the Lamanites gathering at the bridge. He could see the danger faced by the guard force left to man the bridge, and battle plans were laid out before him by the hand of God. He instantly knew what to do. "Thank you, Father. ... This needs to end now!"

Asserting his control, Moroni raised his hand for his officers' silence and attention. "Gentlemen, here is the plan." Moroni took a large knife out of his belt and knelt down. Using the knife, he drew a long S-shaped line in the dirt. "This is the river Sidon." He drew a small box and said, "The city Manti." He made a slash across the river line. "This is the footbridge where we fought this morning." Looking up to ensure everyone understood his crude drawings and was following his plan, he saw nods of understanding from his men. "Lehi," Moroni spoke while looking up at his captain, "this is the tree-lined riverbank to our right where you came up." Moroni drew some broken lines in the dirt next to the river. Lehi nodded in understanding. Then, Moroni drew a large oval. "This is the ridge line to our left where I came from." He pointed to the hills with his knife. Do you all understand my map?"

There was a unison, "Yes, sir!"

"Good. We will split the infantry into three elements of equal size. Teancum, take whatever companies you need from my army and Lehi's army. Make a new command and fold your militia in to it."

Moroni drew three small hash marks in a row on the dirt map to show their location.

"Lehi, you command the right flank, Teancum, the left. I lead from the middle. Captain Shem, you are to follow with the archers and support us with volley fire."

"Sir, if I may," Shem interrupted. "I would like to stay with my men from the city garrison and fight under Captain Teancum."

Moroni looked at Shem for several seconds in silence and smiled. "Very well, Shem. I guess you have earned the right to fight with your brothers from Manti. Pick your replacement to command the support element and report back to Teancum."

"Yes, sir; thank you, sir," Shem said as he smiled back.

General Moroni continued, "We will break up the archers into three groups, one for each infantry element. All support personnel are to arm themselves and join in the fight as the reserve force. We don't need cooks and clerks right now; we need warriors. We advance together and come at them from three different angles, pinning them with their backs to the river. Are we clear?"

"Yes, sir," the answer came again in unison from his men.

"Outstanding," Moroni responded as he stood and put his knife back into its sheath. "Form up your infantry companies on my banner, and let's end this once and for all." His imposing frame and decisive leadership gave inspiration to all who stood near him. "All right men; let's move before we lose the advantage."

The army leaders moved away to reorganize their units for the final charge, shouting commands to their men based on what Moroni had just outlined.

Moroni paused to take a long drink of water from a small water skin tied to his belt. The water was warm and tasted like dirt, but it quenched his thirst. He smiled to himself as he thought how something as simple as a cold glass of clean water would mean so much to him right now.

He looked out over the grassy plain before him. There were some wounded Lamanites who moaned and moved about, and many more who were dead or injured too badly to move under their own power. He looked out past the dead and thought about his cavalry chasing the Lamanites to the river. With that thought came another feeling and Lehi's words from just a few moments ago came to his mind, "Men on the bridge." A strong feeling of urgency suddenly came over him. He replaced the cap on the water skin and turned back to his army.

"Let's move, men; the Lord has put our enemy in our hands. We must move quickly. For justice, for peace, for our families, for our God---move, move, move!"

General Moroni walked forward several paces and called out for his battle standard. A large soldier on a horse came galloping up with Moroni's flag attached to a wooden pole.

"Dismount," Moroni ordered. The young soldier climbed off the horse and stood next to his commander. "We are on foot the rest of the way. Have the honor guard form up on you and prepare to move on my command."

CHAPTER THIRTY-FOUR

LEHI REPENTS

"Yes, sir," the flag bearer responded. He waved to a cluster of soldiers standing a bit off from the main element. The soldiers came running up and formed a line, with the flag bearer in the middle. The sergeant of the honor guard called them to attention and the men of the detail stood ramrod straight, holding their spears and shields perfectly still. From their formation, the honor guard had a panoramic view of the carnage left by the attacking Nephite horse soldiers. Had they been able to see over the rise and down to the river's edge, they would have seen the trail of death continue back to where they first battled with the Lamanites that morning.

"Wow, so many dead," one of the soldiers in the detail said under his breath.

"Steady," the sergeant hissed.

"Yes, but there are still way too many left to fight," a second soldier responded.

"Quiet, I said," the sergeant spoke again and, this time, he continued his reprimand. "You are an honor guard; it is a privilege to be here. Now, show some discipline, and be still."

With their discipline and honor called into question, the men of the flag detail quickly complied, standing even straighter and tightening their lips against the temptation to whisper. Their stillness was now in sharp contrast to the controlled chaos that raged around them, as thousands of Nephite men quickly moved and lined up for battle.

The Lamanites were now in a full and panicked retreat. They looked more like a giant herd of scared deer running from a pack of pursuing wolves than a mighty army.

The Nephite cavalry was making quick work of the slower and wounded Lamanite stragglers, cutting them down and charging forward. This kept the Lamanites moving toward the river to avoid the Nephite pursuit. The Lamanite soldiers were not being guided by commands or leadership, only by panic and fear. Zerahemnah and his staff were running as fast as they could toward the river's edge with Zerahemnah in the center of the group and his Zoramites brothers all around him, pushing the slower or wounded Lamanites out of their way. When he and his group of faithful Zoramites reached the gentle slope leading to the river's edge, Zerahemnah shouted, "Make for the bridge!" As they moved toward the only path across the river and away from Moroni, they saw the jam of Lamanite bodies on the bridge and the Nephite detachment defending the opposite end.

"Blast!" he shouted as he realized his escape plan was foiled. Slowing his pace, Zerahemnah looked over his shoulder to try to figure out what General Moroni's army was doing. To his surprise, he could see only cavalry and even they were slowing their attack now that the bulk of the Lamanite army was gathered at the river's edge.

"Why is Moroni not continuing his infantry attack on us? We are in a full retreat and he has the advantage," Zerahemnah thought. The small force of Nephites left holding the bridge was hardly enough manpower to do much good against the Lamanites.

"Moroni, you idiot," Zerahemnah scoffed. "You have left only a handful behind to guard the bridge. The sheer numbers of our army will overwhelm your silly bridge defenses within minutes."

Zerahemnah chuckled, and then released his tension with a huge belly laugh. "You are even more foolish than you look, mighty Moroni."

Zerahemnah's laughter was drowned out by deep, rolling thunder coming from the distant mountains where a tremendous rainstorm was drowning the jungle with torrents of water. The mountain streams were quickly swelling to overflowing, sending the runoff racing down the mountain gullies. The river Sidon was already beginning to rise.

Ignoring the rising waters, more Lamanites moved down the riverbank and threw themselves into the river to swim across. Nephite archers on the opposite side tried to stop them from crossing, but they were quickly running out of arrows. It was difficult to hit a target as small as the head and upper body of a human, even when the target was motionless. Trying to hit that small of a target when it was in constant movement from water currents or swimming was proving almost impossible. It could take several arrows before an archer found the range and hit one Lamanite swimmer.

"Don't waste your shots!" Amiha shouted as he ran up to the Nephite side of the bridge. "Volley into the mass on the other side, or wait until the swimmers rise out of the river and shoot them point blank." Amiha looked out onto the bridge and could see the Lamanites were still a good distance away from the armored wall of soldiers defending the Nephite side. The Lamanites cursed, shouted and waved their weapons in the air but refused to move any closer or charge headlong into the Nephite defense.

More and more Lamanites were making attempts at swimming across the river. Those who got into the river upstream from the bridge were swept along by the increasing current. Most were slammed into the wooden bridge before they could make it safely across. Those hapless Lamanites, pinned up against the bridge by the fast-moving waters, were easy prey for Nephite defenders, who leaned over the rail to stab at them with their spears. Some Lamanites tried to swim under the bridge to avoid the Nephite swords and spears. Holding their breath, most who tried that escape route got lost in the dark, murky rain water and drowned, tangled among the pylons and reeds under the bridge. As bodies piled up under the bridge, it became even more difficult for others to try to swim under. A few made it under the bridge safely, only to be swept farther down river before they could climb out on the other side. The lucky few Lamanites who finally did make it to the other bank lost all of their equipment in the boiling river. Separated from their fellow soldiers and completely beaten by the raging waters, they simply ran away.

The storm runoff continued to feed the now-raging waters. Lines of Lamanites, still wanting to cross, could see it would be a fruitless endeavor. Anyone who tried to swim across now was swept away, drowned or killed outright by the soldiers on the bridge. The churning river continued to rise until it finally crept over the top of the footbridge. It seemed everyone, both Nephite and Lamanite, immediately came to the same conclusion: the only way across now was over the bridge.

Amiha ran up to the commander of the bridge defenses. "A small miracle," he said matter-of-factly.

"Yes, sir," the lieutenant said, trying to hold his attention on the threat across the river. "We'll take any size of miracle right now. Your orders, sir?"

"I don't think we need to worry about them trying to swim across anytime soon," Amiha smiled. "But they will reorganize and either follow the river downstream to find a different crossing point or make a frontal assault on your little garrison here. As soon as they realize we are stationary targets on this bridge, we will be enveloped by their arrows."

Amiha glanced back at the Ghost Soldiers waiting on the shoreline for his command.

"Hold your position here, Lieutenant. There is a reason they came running toward us like they did. It must be that General Moroni is behind them, and they are fleeing for their lives," Amiha said. Overhearing these words, a nervous buzz went up from the Nephites on the bridge. "Listen up, all of you," Amiha continued speaking to Joffa but loud enough for every Nephite on the bridge to hear. "When the Lamanite arrows come, use your shields to cover each other the best you can, but you must hold the line. The bridge is a natural choke point. If they attack across the bridge, we can funnel them into a kill zone at the edge of the bridge behind us. I will set up fighting positions, using the supply wagons as cover and blockades. When the ghost solders are in place and ready to support you, I will give the order to withdraw, then tactically fall back and get your men behind the wagons."

"Yes, sir. Shield men," the young commander shouted, "close any gaps, watch for arrows, hold steady, men, and be ready on my command to back step to cover."

Amiha sprinted back to the Ghost Soldiers as two Lamanite arrows bounced off the bridge and skidded past him on the water.

"Get those wagons over here," he shouted to the Ghost Soldiers. "Line them up on their sides along the bank and set up fighting positions. Make a choke point here for the enemy when they come across the bridge."

The Ghost Soldiers understood instantly what Amiha was asking them to do. Their efficiency surprised even Amiha and, within minutes, the wagons were in position along the river's bank. The Ghost Soldiers blocked off the end of the bridge in such a way as to create a funnel effect if the Lamanites tried to come across. Only a few enemy soldiers at a time could exit the bridge and, from there, they would be forced into a Nephite kill zone. They layered the wagons in defensive rows to allow both close contact with the enemy and archer support if any Lamanites tried to jump into the river and swim around their blockade.

A few of the Lamanites, seeing what the Nephites were doing at the far end of the bridge, tried to shoot arrows at them, but the short hunting bows the Lamanites carried did not have the power to get an arrow all the way across the river accurately. Most of the arrows fell harmlessly into the water or stuck in the ground on the far bank. The Ghost Soldiers quickly moved into place behind the overturned wagons and got ready to slaughter any Lamanite who entered the kill zone. Using the same back step maneuver they had tried earlier, Joffa's soldiers slowly moved off the bridge and took their places behind the barriers alongside their brother warriors.

The tactic worked as planned. Seeing the Nephite defenders slowly giving ground on the bridge, the Lamanites gained courage. Several raised their swords in the air and others shouted threats at the Nephites. Several more even surged forward on the bridge, coming dangerously close to the Nephite side, but they were forced back at the points of the Nephite spears.

Zerahemnah rubbed his clenched fist under his chin, and his eyes narrowed in anger and concern. He had watched the Nephites move the wagons and set up a quick but surprisingly strong defensive position. He needed to get his own army across the river quickly or, at least, into some form of defensive perimeter of its own. He knew that Moroni would not miss the chance of attacking the Lamanite army while it was pinned against the river. He was learning very quickly that Moroni was not a fool after all but a brilliant commander who had planned this outcome from the very start.

"He played me like a pawn in a game of chess. How did this happen?" Zerahemnah gulped. "My army outnumbered Moroni's army at least three to one." He spun on his heels and did a complete circle, looking at the remains of his once-mighty military force. "Now, after only one day of fighting, I have lost all of my supplies and so many men we are evenly matched with Moroni's strength."

For the first time in a very long time, real fear began to well up inside of Zerahemnah. Moroni now had the advantage in battle. Moroni had the advantage of troop morale, motivation, position, and the high ground. Moroni and his men had won every encounter that day and had inflected tremendous damage to his army.

Now, Zerahemnah and his men were trapped against the river with Nephite forces on both sides. He was left without any more options and could only wait and react to Moroni's next move.

"This fight is over," he thought. His mind raced to find a way out of the disaster with his honor and pride intact, but nothing was going to work. He no longer cared about the welfare of his army; the only thing that mattered now to Zerahemnah was getting out of this alive.

"Do we make for the far shore or stand and fight Moroni?" he asked several of the Zoramites with him.

"We should push across the bridge with all our might," one of his Zoramite brothers suggested also gasping for air from the hasty retreat.

"I agree," a second warrior sounded up. "They have fresh horses and our supplies on the other side. We can push these coward Lamanites across the bridge and overwhelm the Nephite defenses with our greater numbers."

"Yes," Zerahemnah responded enthusiastically. "Once across, we can resupply and regroup. Then we can hold the bridge and trap Moroni and his army on the opposite side. That will give us time to figure out what our next move will be, agreed?"

"Agreed!" Zerahemnah's men said in unison.

"We must act fast," Zerahemnah continued. "Moroni will attack as soon as he gets word that we are stalled on this side of the river. Go, and get those Lamanite dogs on their feet and get them to attack across the bridge. I don't care how many Lamanites are killed; just get me across!"

The Zoramites moved out and started to shout and push the mass of Lamanites around them forward toward the bridge.

A nagging feeling of dread made Moroni's chest ache. He couldn't keep his mind from conjuring up all kinds of horrors that may be happening to Lehi's men who had been left alone to guard the bridge. Not wanting his worry to affect or distract his sub-commanders, Moroni moved back toward his troops. He paced up and down the lines, urging his men to move faster.

Finally, after several moments walking among his men, feeling their energy and the love they had for him, he regained his composure and moved back to the front to confer with Teancum and Lehi.

"Are we ready to move to the final objective?"

"Yes, sir," the two men said.

"Well done," Moroni said. "Take your places in front of your men and follow me." They both saluted and Teancum jogged off, but Lehi remained.

"Yes, Captain Lehi, is there something else?" Moroni asked

"Yes, sir, there is." Lehi's tone was sober, and Moroni could see the seriousness in Lehi's eyes.

"Speak."

"General I ... I owe you an apology."

"For what?" Moroni asked, puzzled by the apology.

"For having doubted your ability to lead this army."

Moroni blinked several times and waited in silence for Lehi to continue.

"Sir, your father was a great captain, and he was my friend."

"Yes, Captain Lehi, he was both of those things."

"Moroni ..." Lehi began to speak, but stopped again as he grappled for the right words to say. "I thought your victory at the battle of Jershon two years ago was just dumb luck. I also thought your ascension to the rank of chief captain over the legions commanded by your father was out of opportunity, not merit. My pride would also not let me see that the way you led the attack against the Lamanite king's camp the night your father was killed, and the way you fought at the jungle road those many days ago, was divinely inspired. But now I am standing here, with you, on the brink of defeating a vastly superior Lamanite army. I watched as we beat them over and over again in combat. It was your execution of battle plans, your training and your leadership abilities that got us through and brought us to this point. I see the ground all around us littered with the dead of our enemies; yet, I have made an account of my own troops and found so few had been killed or wounded that I still cannot believe it." Lehi paused, not for dramatic effect, but because he was genuinely emotional. "You, Moroni, have been chosen by God to lead this army. I doubted that, and I was wrong. I beg for your forgiveness, my general, and I will accept whatever punishment you have for me."

"Punishment?" Moroni was astonished. "Why would I punish one of my finest chief captains and closest advisors? I demand the truth, not only from myself but from all those I command. You spoke your true feelings to me even though you knew it might offend me." Moroni smiled and had a twinkle in his eye. "No, Captain Lehi, I cannot punish a man with such integrity and moral courage. And there is nothing to forgive. You were my father's dear and trusted friend," he said. "Now I know I can trust you to be mine."

Moroni extended his right hand and Lehi shook it vigorously. Smiling at each other they both turned to look down the road in the direction they must go.

"Well," Moroni said, gesturing toward the Lamanites location, "shall we?"

"After you, lad," Lehi responded jokingly while saluting again.

"Try to keep up, old man," Moroni cracked back.

Lehi let out a deep, barking laugh and nodded in approval at Moroni's quick humor.

As Lehi turned to run back to his own formation, a lone Nephite horseman galloped toward them from the direction of the river. He rode up to Moroni and saluted.

"Report!" Moroni shouted and Lehi turned back to hear the message.

"Sir..." the messenger spoke breathlessly as he tried to maintain control of his excited horse. "We have the enemy pinned against the river. We have corralled them like dogs herding sheep, but it is only a matter of time before they regroup. Our defenses on the bridge are holding, but not for long. There are too many Lamanites for us to ride through and give aid to the defenders. My commander humbly requests that you attack with all speed before the Lamanites overpower the blocking force on the bridge and find a way to escape across the river."

"Tell your commander we are coming," Moroni responded. "Instruct him that when he sees us descend down the rise, he is to break off and bring the cavalry around to our rear. There he is to act as a rear guard and be prepared to exploit any weakness in the Lamanite lines. Is that clear?"

"Yes, sir."

"Good, then go and give the orders."

"Yes, sir!" the messenger shouted with a giant smile on his face. He pulled hard on the reins of his horse and galloped back to the river.

Moroni turned back and faced the sea of Nephite soldiers under his command. The humanity of bloodied men and boys standing shoulder to shoulder was awe inspiring. This was not a fight for personal vendetta or for some nobleman's land grab. There was no money to be gained, no chance for plunder. This was honor at its purest. Regardless of status or wealth, these men were willing to fight for their freedom, for the safety of their families and for the right to worship as they chose.

"Remember this day, Moroni," Lehi counseled. "They all know you brought us to this point. Now, victory is at hand. Your father would be proud." Lehi put his big hand on Moroni's shoulder and smiled. "What are your orders, my general?"

Holding back his emotions, Moroni blinked several times, and nodded. "Let's get them moving."

"Runner!" Moroni shouted to his command staff. The same boy who took the last message shot out of the group of men and ran up to the general.

"Sir, you called for a messenger?" The boy spoke while saluting.

"Yes, stand by and listen to my instructions," Moroni said. "Captain Lehi, a slight change in plans. Keep your formation as close to mine as you can. I now want to hit the Lamanites with a wall of shields and spears. We're going to move at double time, so have your men keep in ranks."

"Yes, sir," Lehi responded.

"We will fight now as one; do you understand"? Moroni asked.

"Yes, sir!"

Moroni turned to the runner. "Did you understand my instructions to

Captain Lehi?" he asked the boy.

"Every word, sir."

"Good. Tell Captain Teancum the exact same thing."

"Yes, sir. Is that all, sir?"

"Yes that is all. Now, off you go."

The boy took off like a stone shot from a sling.

Moroni finished adjusting his armor and looked in the direction of Teancum. Moroni could see the runner covering the distance between him and Teancum very quickly.

"Wow, he's fast," Moroni snorted under his breath.

Teancum got the orders and held his spear high in the air. Looking at the boy general, he pumped his spear two times in the air to tell Moroni he understood his instructions.

Moroni looked back at his command staff and made eye contact with the old sergeant major.

"All is ready, general," the old soldier exclaimed with an almost bored look on his face. It was as if he knew what Moroni was going to ask before he spoke the words. To him, this was just one more day in the life of a man who had seen more battles than anyone else in the army. The sergeant major was older than most of the fathers of the soldiers around him, but he was truly a lion among the sheep. A stoic and lone figure standing calmly as the storm of humanity raged around him. Just his presence demanded respected and order from the young men and boys working for him.

Moroni knew these were the final moments of peace before the last charge. The outcome of this war would now be decided.

A hush fell over the army, and they all stopped what they were doing and looked back at their leader. The moment was accented by Moroni's regal appearance, with his red war cloak and black hair blowing in the gentle breeze. Moroni could see the faces of his men. They were faces he knew well. This was going to be the final battle charge for some of his brave soldiers. The matter would be settled once and for all. No more tricks or allowing the enemy to withdraw. Enough Nephite blood had already been shed that day. He was either going to crush the enemies of freedom or make them pay such a dear price for their victory that they would not have the strength or the will to go on.

"Victory or death!" he shouted as he held the sword of power high in the air.

"Victory or death," the mass of soldiers responded.

Moroni could see into the eyes of the men in the front ranks. The look on their faces was the same he had seen other men give his father before the final battle of Jershon, so long ago. The look revealed a mixture of trust, love and devotion for their commander.

Moroni looked down at the massive sword in his hand. The Sword of Laban felt almost weightless to him. He brought the sword up to his face and looked closely at the polished metal blade. Even after all the battles it had fought, the sword was still flawless and razor sharp.

"It was true master craftsmanship at work so long ago and so far away," he thought. "Now, this holy weapon is in my hands and it falls to me to wield it once again for the defense of God's people. Am I worthy, and have I done all I could to make these men ready for battle?"

He lowered the great sword and looked down the line of men. Captain Lehi stood in front of his men on the right flank of the formation. Lehi nodded his head and shook his big ax several times to tell Moroni he was ready. Moroni nodded back and shifted his attention to Teancum. Teancum was standing in front of the left flank of men and showing no emotion at all. Teancum nodded once at Moroni and pounded the bottom of his spear into the ground next to his right foot. A slight smile broke across his face as Moroni nodded back at him. They were ready.

Moroni put on his helmet, took one last full breath of peaceful air, and held his sword up over his head. He looked over his right shoulder and shouted, "For liberty!"

"For liberty!" the mass of Nephites responded.

Moroni lowered the sword until it pointed toward the Lamanites, and he shouted, "Forward!"

The drums and horns sounded the advance as he took off at a slight jog down the well-worn path that led to the river crossing and his destiny. The Nephite army responded to his command. Letting out a mighty war cry, the army lurched forward to follow their general toward the final battle.

END GAME

Zerahemnah struggled to regain some sort of military control over the mob of Lamanites. He and his Zoramite brothers in arms desperately tried to reassemble the ranks of their tattered Lamanite army when the sounds of the Nephite war drums and trumpets echoed through the air. Everything happening on both sides of the river stopped as the great war banner of General Moroni, chief captain and commander of all the Nephite forces appeared over the rise.

A cheer rose up from Amiha and the Nephite men defending the far side of the bridge as Moroni stopped jogging at the top of the rise and stood next to his standard long enough to scan the scene below at the river's edge. His army followed his example and stopped behind him where they could also see that the trapped Lamanite army was backed up against the river and cornered on all sides.

Moroni pointed to Teancum and shouted, "Left side!"

Teancum nodded.

Moroni then pointed to Lehi. "Right side," he said.

Lehi nodded and shook his battle ax in the air. Moroni turned to face the formations behind him. "You men are to follow me right down the middle."

Another shout went up, and Moroni turned back to face the Lamanites. Taking in a large amount of air, Moroni filled his lungs and then let it out in a long, slow breath. He shook the fatigue out of his tired legs, then readjusted his grip on his shield and spun the sword hilt in his hand. Raising the sword high into the air, Moroni shouted, "Forward!"

Teancum and Lehi followed exactly the orders they had been given.

When Moroni moved, they both moved, taking their men with them. Lehi went to the right of the Lamanite army and Teancum to the left, while Moroni, in command of the center, plunged headlong into the middle of the trapped Lamanites.

Zerahemnah watched from the river's edge as the Nephites advanced. Looking left and right, he realized he was now truly trapped. Moroni had deployed his forces so expertly that Zerahemnah knew that he now had only two options: Fight to the death or suffer the humiliation of defeat.

Zerahemnah's mind raced between the two options, until, suddenly, a third idea struck him. He knew that the Nephites were given to press for peace if the slaughter during combat is great on both sides. "I might just have a chance here if my timing is perfect," Zerahemnah thought. "I will force these dog Lamanites to fight until the body count is so high that Moroni takes pity on them and asks for a pledge of peace. Then I lie to him about surrendering, escape and live to fight another day." Zerahemnah rubbed his hands together, and then clapped his hands. "Brilliant," he said aloud. One of the ranking Lamanites near Zerahemnah stopped in his tracks while another asked sarcastically.

"What is brilliant, my lord? Is it how you have so carelessly led us into a trap, or is it how Moroni has taken a smaller, weaker army, defeated us at every turn, and now moves to surrounded us?"

Zerahemnah knew he had to act quickly if he was going to maintain some semblance of order and command over the Lamanites. He did not care if they lived or died. He needed them to stay in the fight just long enough so he could to make his escape. "Surround us?" he snorted. "He has not surrounded us."

Zerahemnah began to move around the Lamanites with a bit of theatrical flair. "No, my dear Lamanite brothers, the boy general has blundered and shown us his hand." The Zoramite looked around nervously to see if anyone was buying his lies. When no one seemed suspicious, he went on. "He is committing his entire force to this assault, with no units in reserve." Pointing toward the advancing Nephites, Zerahemnah continued, "See how he is dividing his forces? He has taken his weaker, smaller army and broken it into three parts, hoping to scare us into surrender. He knows he can't face us, so he is trying to trick us into giving up. What an insult to the great sons of Laman and Lemuel!" He paused to let the words sink in. Invoking the hallowed names of the great fathers of old struck a primal cord in the minds of those around him. Every Lamanite knew you only spoke the names of the old ones if you were serious. It was blasphemy to do less.

Zerahemnah sensed that he had struck a nerve, and he quickly acted to exploit the moment. "Form ranks!"

The Lamanite leaders around him echoed Zerahemnah's order as they moved among their exhausted soldiers. Each of the Lamanite soldiers stirred and shuffled forward to find his place. Just then, a Zoramite ran up to Zerahemnah. "Zerahemnah," he shouted, "what of the bridge and the Nephite garrison on the other side?"

Zerahemnah took a quick look at the bridge, pointed his sword toward it, and shouted, "You must take the bridge at all costs!"

He next turned back to the Zoramite, grabbed his tunic and pulled the man close. Looking into his eyes he whispered, "We need a way out if this goes bad. Take every Zoramite left with a horse who can fight and spill every last drop of Lamanite blood taking that bridge if necessary, but we must be able to cross before Moroni completely routes this army!"

They both understood the message. Like all evil men with plans of domination, Zerahemnah never really cared about the soldiers under his command, and he had no qualms about the inflammatory and false causes he and his men used to rally those soldiers to battle. This was about greed and power, nothing more. If they lost every Lamanite soldier in battle, he wouldn't care, as long as the Zoramites were protected from harm and their evil ambitions were realized. The Zoramite responded with an evil grin and moved toward the Lamanite side of the bridge.

The runoff from the mountain rains continued to swell the river. It now raged over the disputed footbridge and tore violently at the river's banks, which were starting to give way. Large sections of earth were breaking off under the strain of the rushing water, sending huge chunks flowing downstream.

"Look at this," Amiha whispered to those closest to him as he pointed to the water. Some of the Lamanites who were still standing on the bridge were suddenly swept off by the powerful current flowing over the footbridge. They tumbled downstream into the now raging torrents. This caused a panic as the rest of the Lamanite soldiers still on the bridge stampeded back to their side of the river to avoid the same fate.

Watching nature's influence on the outcome of the war, the little band of Nephite defenders holding the far side of the bridge cheered. The longer they held the river crossing, the more time General Moroni had to envelop the Lamanites and destroy the enemies of freedom.

"The Lord is truly on our side this day!" a Nephite soldier exclaimed.

"Yes, yes He is," Amiha responded. They shouted with joy watching as the God of Heaven and Earth intervened in the battle.

Amiha regained his composure and did a quick assessment. Moroni's army was rapidly descending toward the trapped Lamanites. "They will be desperate to cross before General Moroni reaches them," he shouted. "Stand ready for a mass charge!"

The soldiers with Amiha refocused on the task before them and readied themselves for battle.

"No … get across the bridge!" Zerahemnah shouted as he witnessed some of his soldiers get swept away and the rest move away from the bridge.

"You," he demanded, pointing with his sword to one of the few Zoramites on a horse. "Lead the charge across the bridge. Take every horseman left and smash through their defenses. Go now!"

There was desperation and terror in his voice as Zerahemnah commanded his mounted horsemen to retake the bridge. The Lamanite foot soldiers around him were unraveling and disorganized.

"You cowards," Zerahemnah cried as he pushed men forward toward the Nephites and toward the river crossing at the same time. "Stand your ground and fight!" he shouted at those closest to Moroni's charge. He looked behind him at the soldiers standing near the edge of the bridge. "You men follow the horses across and destroy the Nephites!"

The Lamanites moved away from the bridge to give room for the Zoramite cavalrymen to cross. The leader of the mounted Zoramites looked back at Zerahemnah, while trying to control his animal. The horse clearly did not want to cross over the footbridge with raging water cascading over it.

"What are you waiting for? Go!" Zerahemnah demanded. The remaining mounted Zoramite riders urged their horses into a gallop and charged across the river with a surge of foot soldiers following behind.

"Cavalry charge, ready your spears!" Amiha ordered. The bridge defenders brought up their spears to defend against a charge of horses.

The sounds were quiet at first, almost inaudible, but the longer the weight of the horses and men moved on the bridge, the louder the creaking became. The sound of the wood braces snapping caused the lead rider to slow his horse and come to a stop right in the middle of the bridge. Those on the bridge could feel it vibrate and shake. There was a second very loud snap, and the bridge shuddered. The lead rider knew what was about to happen, and he turned in his saddle to those behind him. He tried to shout out a warning to get off the bridge but, before the first words came out, the entire middle section of the bridge broke free and all the horses and men fell into the river.

There was stunned silence as soldiers on both sides of the river watched the bridge collapse and those on it disappear in the wreckage and water.

Seeing his last escape route disintegrate before his eyes and most of his Zoramite brothers drown, Zerahemnah screamed out, "No!"

Amiha and his men on the opposite side shouted and cheered when they saw the disaster happen to the bridge.

"General Moroni will need our assistance!" Amiha shouted over the noise of his excited soldiers. "Find every long bow you can and prepare to fire across the river into the Lamanite mass."

The soldiers did as they were told and searched the area for any of the large Nephite bows left behind. Several were found, along with the last bundles of arrows. A firing line was formed. Amiha walked up to the closest soldier holding a long bow.

"Test the distance," he ordered.

A bowman drew back and let fly one arrow across the river. Amiha watched as it landed harmlessly into the muddy riverbank on the opposite side.

"Close, but not good enough. Change the trajectory."

The bowman quickly set a second arrow and raised the bow higher into the air. He let the second arrow fly, and they all watched as it arced across the sky and impacted somewhere inside the mass of Lamanite soldiers.

"That's it!" Amiha said. "Good angle. Now line the rest up with you and stand by to shoot."

"Yes sir," the bowman responded. He gathered the remaining Nephite archers around him and demonstrated the needed angle for arrow flight to reach the opposing army across the river.

An older Lamanite man with an eagle's feather tied to his hair was one who was well-respected among his kin and clan. He was a Lamanite who was seen as a leader and village elder. One of those very Lamanites was trying in vain to get those around him to assemble in some sort of line to prepare for battle. Suddenly a Nephite arrow dropped out of the sky and struck him square in the chest. It was the same arrow just launched from Amiha's men on the Nephite side of the river. He was dead on impact and fell backward hard. Blood spat out of his mouth when he hit the ground and those around him stared in silence for several seconds, trying to process what had just happened right in front of them.

"It came from across the river," one Lamanite spoke. Several others turned to look and saw Amiha and the Nephites lining up to fire volleys of arrows at them. One big Lamanite holding a spear looked down at his dead friend and leader, back at the soldiers across the river, then up at Moroni and his army marching toward them. He dropped his spear and unbuckled his weapons belt and dropped it to the ground. Without saying a word, he bolted through the crowd and ran downriver as fast as he could away from the rest of the doomed Lamanite army. As if responding to a silent order, more Lamanites followed his example. They dropped their weapons of war and ran parallel to the river, trying to get away from Moroni's army. First by tens, then twenties, then by the hundreds, Lamanites were deserting and fleeing from Moroni and his men. Others, in surrender posture, started walking with their hands up toward the advancing Nephite lines.

Moroni saw the bridge collapse and knew the Lamanites were trapped. He could also see deserters running from the Lamanite formation.

"Let them go. Advance toward the main body!" Moroni shouted to his men. "If they drop their weapons, they are not our enemy!" He could feel the terror and the tension in the air, wishing there was time to stop and reassure his men and to explain his actions. He simply whispered a prayer, his lips moving rapidly, and his eyes never leaving the goal ahead. His intent was not to deal harshly with deserting Lamanites, or to take in the prisoners who were turning themselves over. They were no longer a threat. Instead, his focus was on reaching the center of the Lamanite mass, where their Zoramite leadership huddled safely, at least for now. "Zerahemnah is the cause of all of this death. He is the prize!" He lifted his chin and pushed forward, picking up his speed and rushing toward the main body of Lamanites.

The Nephite army charged headlong toward the Lamanites. They were close enough now that they could make out the scared faces of their enemies. Some of the Lamanites tried to form a defensive line of men. They even shot a few arrows at the charging Nephites, but their attempts were in vain. Moroni and his men crushed the first line of Lamanites with their overwhelming force of men and armor. The three separate Nephite units struck the Lamanite army at the same time and the carnage was unspeakable.

Zerahemnah, now drunk with rage, rushed toward the Nephites. With the strength of his madness and hate, he cut his way through the charging Nephites, killing several before they could adjust to his berserk tactics. Inspired by their leader's sudden demonstration of courage and daring, several of the Lamanites, and the few Zoramites that were left, joined Zerahemnah and began to push the Nephites back. Even the metal and heavy leather armor worn by the Nephites was no match for Zerahemnah and his raging, out-of-control men. They moved like mad men with power fueled by the fear and hate only desperate men feel, easily cleaving men in two and piercing the heaviest armor plating. A large semi-circle of dead Nephites started to form around Zerahemnah and his men, who were attacking in all directions, moving outward and defeating any Nephite who dared to challenge them.

Moroni was busily engaged in directing the battle right in front of him, so he was unaware of Zerahemnah's conquests until a Nephite soldier ran up to him.

"General, we are about to lose the left flank. The Lamanites are fighting like dragons, we cannot hold!"

Moroni looked across the battleground and saw Zerahemnah and his men dealing death with every strike of their sword and thrust of their spears.

Seeing the leader of the Lamanites in the open, Moroni seized on the opportunity to face him personally. "Follow me," Moroni called to all those around him. Moroni charged across the outer edge of the battle line, cutting his way through the Lamanites that were between him and Zerahemnah. Moroni was not going to be denied the chance to kill the one responsible for all the death he had witnessed.

The Nephites facing Zerahemnah and his men were in panic mode. Most of the sub-commanders for that section of the army were dead or wounded, and men were fighting alone or in small groups for their very survival. Zerahemnah looked like a demonic butcher with blood covering his uniform, shield and sword. He wildly fought his way around the ground before him, screaming and cursing the Nephites, their God, and, most of all, General Moroni.

Moroni and his men drove their way through the Lamanite lines and burst into Zerahemnah's kill zone.

"You want me, Zerahemnah? Here I am!" Moroni demanded.

Two Zoramite soldiers turned to challenge Moroni and attacked him directly. The closest Zoramite tried to stab Moroni with the tip of his spear, but Moroni blocked it with his shield. Knocking the spear tip away from his body, Moroni countered with an overhead chop of the great sword severing the Zoramite's arm from his body at the shoulder. With a follow up slash across his body, Moroni took the head clean off the spearman and turned to move toward Zerahemnah. The second Zoramite tried to strike Moroni with his sword, but Moroni, still looking at Zerahemnah, quickly sidestepped the swordsman's attack. The blade passed harmlessly by Moroni and pulled the Zoramite off balance. Moroni chopped down and away from his body with his own sword and severed the right leg of the second Zoramite at the knee. Moroni gave the second Zoramite a quick sidekick to his left knee, destroying the ligaments and tendons holding the enemy's knee to his leg. The Zoramite dropped like a stone and let out a scream of pain.

Moroni continued toward Zerahemnah, brushing aside or slicing through any Lamanite who got in his way. With every step toward Zerahemnah, Moroni could feel blinding hate well up inside him. Zerahemnah moved back and forth like a caged animal, shouting insults at Moroni and daring him to move in closer and fight him.

Moroni's blood was boiling as he closed the distance to Zerahemnah. He was still too far away and contending with other Lamanites when he saw Zerahemnah smile at him while ruthlessly cutting the throat of a wounded Nephite who haplessly stumbled in front of the Lamanite leader. Seeing Zerahemnah's complete lack of humanity, Moroni's thoughts turned dark and a feeling of hate began to rise within him. He let out a war cry and felt pure anger pulse through his veins. After smashing the face of one more Lamanite with his shield, Moroni was finally within striking distance of Zerahemnah. The two great warriors started to circle each other, each trying to gain the advantage of the best attacking angle. Nephites and Lamanites who were fighting each other around the two leaders saw what was happening and stopped fighting to watch.

"Ready to fight with a real man, boy?" Zerahemnah taunted Moroni.

"These are your last moments!" Moroni spat back as he shook his shoulders and arms to loosen them up for the fight.

Moroni was almost blind with anger and rage. Before this moment, he had felt raw determination to defeat the Lamanites and righteous indignation toward the enemies of freedom. Now his dark emotions controlled his actions and his lust to kill mixed with sheer hate. This man before him had been the cause of so much suffering and death. He must be destroyed. Moroni knew that killing him would immediately end the war. He was eager to spill his blood, and to do it now.

Moroni crouched into a powerful fighting stance, like a wild predator ready to strike. His sword and shield at the ready, he continued circling Zerahemnah. While trying to control his breathing, Moroni waited for the right moment to attack.

Suddenly, like the breaking of the first light of dawn after a cold, dark night, a wave of calming emotions cascaded over Moroni. It was so all-encompassing and powerful it caused Moroni's throat to catch and he choked on his own breath.

"Peace," was the one word he heard echo in his mind. It was as gentle as a breeze and as powerful as a thunderclap.

Moroni stopped circling, silently questioning what he had just felt and heard.

"Know that I am God, and be at peace." It came again, only louder and clearer.

A flash from his childhood crossed his mind as Moroni remembered the words of his mother as she taught him to walk uprightly before God.

"When the Lord commands us, we do not question; we obey."

"But how will I know if it is of God?" the young boy had questioned, while looking up into the soft eyes and strong, but beautiful, face of his mother.

"The Spirit of God will fill you with warmth and light," she replied, and then asked, "Do you understand?" as she took his little head into her hands and looked into his young eyes.

"Yes, Mother."

Moroni instantly flashed back to reality and realized what had happened. He had allowed the spirit of hate and destruction to fill his mind and control his actions. He had lost control of his emotions and was blinded by his rage. He stood up straight and, in a dreamlike moment, looked around at the soldiers who surrounded him, both Lamanite and Nephite. Those closest to him had stopped fighting and had moved back to watch and cheer as the two leaders fought each other. Moroni could see the bloodlust in the eyes of his men as they urged him to kill the mighty Lamanite leader. They chanted and screamed for Moroni to "Kill, kill, kill!"

The young general recognized what was happening. After all, he had just seen it in himself. Now he could see that the Spirit of God was departing from his entire army, only to be replaced by evil. He knew he was responsible for that. He was in charge, and, in losing control of himself, he was about to lose control of the entire Nephite army as well, and then the soul of his country. He was the General, and he set the example for his men to follow. If he was filled with hatred and an evil lust for blood, his men would be the same. To Moroni's horror, he looked around again and saw it was almost too late to stop a massacre.

"I am to blame if this army fails to honor its responsibility to God," he thought.

He relaxed his posture, stepped back a pace and took some deep breaths.

All around, the battle raged on. The Lamanites were trapped with their backs to the river. They were leaderless and panicking. Now they were being butchered by the well-positioned Nephites. This was no longer an honorable fight. It was now something horrible. It was a slaughter and the killing was not going to stop unless Moroni acted.

Out of the midst of pandemonium, a young Lamanite boy with a head wound broke through the circle of soldiers surrounding Moroni and Zerahemnah

"Mercy, great one; have mercy!" he cried as he fell at Moroni's feet. "I surrender; I surrender to you. Please don't kill me. Please stop killing my brothers," he begged.

Moroni looked down at the crying wounded boy pleading for his life and the scene of battle and death before him. That was it, he had had enough.

"Yes, my Lord." He looked up to the sky. "Peace, I understand; and Thy will be done."

The words, though spoken aloud, were only a whisper. What Moroni said next came out in a thunderous shout to his command staff.

"Halt the attack," he ordered. "Sound the halt," he commanded the trumpeter standing near him. The young trumpeter blinked several times out of confusion. He was young, but he knew enough about battle to know that the enemy was about to be utterly destroyed, and he couldn't believe they were going to stop now. He was also a good soldier and did as commanded. General Moroni was in charge and he had not let the army down yet. He blew into his brass horn to sound the signal to halt the attack. Instinctively, the other trumpeters in the Nephite army picked up the signal and blew into their own horns to echo the command to all the troops to stop the attack. Quickly, and without question, most of the soldiers in the Nephite army responded to the command and disengaged with the Lamanites. Some of the less disciplined militia from Manti's security force, still overwhelmed with emotion and bloodlust, either did not hear or ignored the order to halt the attack. They were not professional soldiers. Consumed by blood lust after the assault on their city, several of the militiamen continued to advance. They were quickly brought back in line by Shem, who ran up and down the field of battle, moving his forces back to the Nephite lines.

"What are you doing?" Zerahemnah snarled. "Coward ... fight me!" he barked at Moroni as he lunged forward to strike. Several Nephite soldiers jumped in front of Moroni and formed a protective wall of metal and wooden shields between their general and the Zoramite. With dozens of spears and swords pointed at him, Zerahemnah drew back and took a moment to consider his position. He was almost completely surrounded and personally outnumbered ten to one. There were several spears pointed at him and none of his soldiers were fighting back. They were taking advantage of the fact that the Nephite army had stopped attacking, using the break from battle to drag their wounded past Zerahemnah and to regroup behind him.

Moroni gave Zerahemnah several seconds to take it all in. He stood rock solid still as Zerahemnah paced back and forth cursing and frothing at the mouth. After Zerahemnah stopped pacing, Moroni called out,

"Sergeant Major."

"Yes, sir," the old and exhausted soldier responded from a distance. It looked like he had been in the thick of the battle; he had blood all over his armor and sword.

"Have the army step back a pace and reform the lines. Assemble my command staff on me. Set my standard right here, and move our wounded to the rear of the formations."

"Yes, sir."

The old soldier started barking orders. The Nephites responded and started to move back without lowering their defenses.

"What madness is this, Moroni?" Zerahemnah lamented. "Are you afraid to fight me, coward?"

"Zerahemnah," Moroni shouted back. "Stand down so we may talk."

"I knew it," Zerahemnah muttered to himself. "He wants peace." Then, to Moroni, he said, "Move your army back to the city, and then we will talk."

"Zerahemnah, you are in no position to be giving demands," Moroni called back. "We have trapped your army against the river. It's over. Look around you, look at all the dead Lamanites that lay before you."

Moroni paused while Zerahemnah turned to look at what remained of his army. "Zerahemnah, you are beaten. I do not want to kill any more Lamanites. I grant you twenty minutes of peace so you can collect what remains of your command staff and see to your wounded. Then meet me here at my standard so we can parlay."

"I will never treaty with you or any dog Nephite," Zerahemnah spat back. That was a lie. "Moroni is falling for it," he thought to himself. He almost gave it away with a smile breaking across his lips.

"If that is so, in twenty minutes, every Lamanite who will not make an oath of peace with me will die," Moroni calmly responded. He looked over

319

the Lamanites who were within earshot of the exchange he was having with Zerahemnah to ensure they also had heard what he had promised.

They stood for several seconds staring at each other. Moroni finally made the next move and turned his back to Zerahemnah.

"Where are you going, coward?" Zerahemnah taunted.

With his cloak flapping in the breeze, Moroni looked back over his shoulder and glared at Zerahemnah. "I go to see to my wounded men and to pray to my God for guidance. I suggest you do the same, because in nineteen minutes," he paused, "I will return and you will surrender or be killed." Moroni made his way through his men and walked to where his battle flag was now posted. The sergeant major was waiting there with a water skin full of cool liquid. He handed it to Moroni, who took off his helmet and drew a long drink. Handing the water skin back, he asked, "The wounded?"

"They are being cared for as we speak, general," the old soldier responded.

"Where are my captains? Where are Teancum, Lehi and Shem, are they alive?"

"They have been summoned, sir. They are coming."

Moroni nodded his head and looked around. He was proud of his men. They had won the day with their bravery and loyalty. He had given them the order to stop fighting when the moment the bloodlust was greatest, and they followed his order. Moroni knew that only a well-disciplined force, with complete respect for their leaders, would stop advancing on a routed enemy when commanded to. His thoughts drifted back to the love and respect he saw in the men at arms who served his father those many years ago. He remembered how he and those who served under him had so much love and respect for their great chief captain. He understood that the love and respect came from knowing that their leader cared more for them than for his own life and safety. It came from knowing that the man who led them into battle was moral, just, and feared God. He now felt that same emotion directed at him as he looked into the eyes of the men standing around him.

Moroni drifted back to that moment in the wagon where his father lay mortally wounded.

"Now is your time. You must be a man and lead these men!"

Those words echoed in his mind as Moroni felt the great sword in his hand. He knew he had fulfilled his destiny. He was his father's son, a great leader and true warrior for freedom.

Zerahemnah was infuriated.

"How dare he announce his intentions to my army!" he grumbled under his breath. "They do not get to make the choice to surrender. I am their commander and I will decide. If they surrender against my will, my plans to escape will be destroyed." When the bridge collapsed it left him with few Zoramite allies, and his Laminate soldiers were deserting by the hundreds. After hearing Moroni speak, those who remained loyal to him were starting to second guess their choices. Zerahemnah could see and hear open dissention and doubt in the ranks.

Zerahemnah's mind became cloudy and his thoughts became confused. He could almost hear voices in his head saying, "Kill him, kill Moroni." They whispered it over and over again.

He shook his head violently and slapped his own face to clear his thoughts. He barked out to his soldiers. "He wants to trick us into lowering our weapons so he can attack and slaughter us all!"

As Zerahemnah spoke, many Lamanites walked past him toward Moroni's flag, holding their weapons in their arms like they were carrying bundles of wood. The oldest among them called out to Moroni, saying, "Great one, we wish to make peace."

Moroni turned toward the voice calling out to surrender and ordered his men to stand down. He worked his way through his men until he came face to face with the surrendering enemy.

CHAPTER THIRTY-SIX

THE FALL OF ZERAHEMNAH

"Great one," the spokesman for the surrendering group bowed his head slightly as he addressed Moroni, "we wish to make peace with you." He dropped his sword, bow, and war club at Moroni's feet and signaled the others to do the same.

"I know of the treaty you made with Captain Lehonti and our Queen after the defeat and death of the king two years ago. You are a man of honor, and we will fight you no more."

Moroni's gaze took in the large group of surrendering men.

"You all wish to pledge peace with me?" he asked.

The surrendering men responded in unison, "Yes."

"Stop them!" The voice in Zerahemnah's head got louder and more demanding. "Stop them from surrendering. You are the leader!"

Zerahemnah gasped and rushed forward pushing his way to the front of the group of men. "You are fools, stupid fools," he screamed. "Don't you see that he will kill you all?"

Moroni ignored Zerahemnah's ranting and continued speaking in a low and even tone.

"Raise your right hands and take this oath," he said.

The defeated Lamanites standing before him all raised their arms to the square.

"Do you swear, on your honor and before almighty God, to never again take up arms against the Nephite people in anger? Do you swear it?"

The Lamanites all answered, "Yes," and lowered their arms.

"If you break your oath, you will find no mercy from me or from God;

do you understand?"

They all looked blankly at Moroni until their spokesman again took the lead, saying,

"We do not know your God, but we do know you. We will swear to you that we will never again fight the Nephites."

Moroni put his hand on the shoulder of the older Lamanite who was acting as the voice of the group and looked him in the eye. "You may not know of the God of this earth, but He knows you. Swear to Him and you may go in peace."

"Lies, all he speaks are lies," Zerahemnah yelled in a crazed rant. "He will preach words of peace from his false God and kill you all when you turn your backs to him!"

Moroni moved past the old Lamanite and addressed Zerahemnah, but spoke loudly enough for all the Lamanites standing close by to hear.

"I am a man of honor, Zerahemnah. You know that we did not start this war," Moroni said. "We have kept our word and our Nephite nation has held its treaty with your queen these many years. It is you who has brought this horror upon us all. May you be cursed for that, Zerahemnah." Moroni looked around at the gathered soldiers, both his and Zerahemnah's, who were listening to his words. "Zerahemnah, we do not desire to spill any more blood. We are men of peace, but you must understand that we have beaten you. I need only to give the word and my men will fall upon you and continue the slaughter until nothing remains of your army but your broken carcasses. We are not here for power or to gain advantage over our brother Lamanites. We do not want to take you or your men as slaves. We do not seek to impose our will on you or force you to worship our God. We do not lust after your property or want to harm your families. Yet, these are the very reasons you have come against us and attacked the city of Manti."

There was a commotion from behind the Nephite ranks and Moroni turned to see Lehi, Teancum and Shem work their way through the lines of Nephite soldiers. The three moved forward to stand next to their leader. Moroni was relieved to see his friends alive and again at his side. Gaining courage from his captains' support, he continued.

"Can you not see the events of this day? Do you not wonder how a smaller force could, at every turn, defeat you so soundly? It is because of the power of our God, the God of all of our fathers, the God of this land, and the God of liberty. Our God has blessed us and delivered you into our hands. Your army cannot and will not win. Your army will not shake our faith in our God. Make peace with me, Zerahemnah, here and now. I want to go home and live a long, boring life. I want to marry and have children. I do not delight in the shedding of blood. I want all men to be free and enjoy the fruits of their own labors. Make peace with me, Zerahemnah, I beg you. Swear to the God of freedom that you will fight no more, or you and your men will all die."

Zerahemnah looked around at his soldiers. As any observer would have easily been able to see that the Lamanite army had been beaten, there was no more fight in them.

Still, Zerahemnah's face showed stubborn resolve. His unyielding determination was born of pride and greed. Moroni knew he was the kind of man who would rather die than surrender, especially here, especially now when his rank and credibility were in question.

"Zerahemnah, what else do you need to see? How many more ..."

"Stop. Enough." Zerahemnah interrupted. "I don't need to hear any more. I will surrender to you, Moroni."

Moroni narrowed his eyes and swallowed hard. He didn't know what to make of Zerahemnah's turnabout and still didn't trust him, even though Zerahemnah was now walking toward Moroni, removing his weapons and dropping them at Moroni's feet. He looked up at Moroni. A smile flashed across his face but was quickly replaced with a snarl.

"You ..." he said, spitting the words out in rapid succession, "...yes, you have beaten us, Moroni, but only because you used trickery and deception to gain an advantage over my army. You are a coward. You could not face us in open war, so you snuck around like a snake and nipped at our heels until we could no longer walk."

Zerahemnah faced his soldiers while continuing to address Moroni.

"Your false God had nothing to do with your victory. You hide behind your metal armor and then claim divine power has protected you. You killed hundreds of my soldiers, all while claiming you wanted peace. Your fathers betrayed their fathers and tried to make my brother Lamanites slaves to your false religion. I will surrender to you, Moroni, but I will not make peace with you. I will not swear to your false God, and I will not swear to be a peaceful farmer like you. I am a warrior and I fight for the Lamanite people."

Zerahemnah looked over what remained of his army. "I will learn from this day and prepare my soldiers for the next battle. Then we will see about your claims of divine protection from your false God. So here, mighty General Moroni." He snorted as he kicked his weapons with his foot. "Here are my weapons of war. You claim to not want to shed my blood if I lay down my sword. Let's see if you are a man of your word. There is my sword. I am leaving with my army, and we will meet again."

Moroni was outraged. "Zerahemnah, make an oath of peace with me here and now, or you will be destroyed."

"You see," Zerahemnah shouted to his army. "He is a liar and a deceiver. He said we could go free if we laid down our weapons, and I did. Now he wants to fight. We cannot trust anything this man says!"

Shem, standing behind Moroni and watching all of this unfold, tightened his hands into fists. That old but trusted feeling came over him again as it had in the village when he faced the robbers. Something was wrong. Like a good sheep dog on watch, he was reacting on sheer instinct to a threat he couldn't even see and didn't really even know was there. He just felt something was wrong. He straightened his shoulders and his eyes darted around the gathered Lamanites.

His gaze paused to examine each man, watching closely for anything that looked awry. Lehi, too, shifted nervously. "What's up?" he whispered to Shem.

"Something's wrong," Shem whispered back.

"Indeed …"

"But I don't see what yet. Do you?"

"No, but I'm afraid we will soon enough," Lehi said, then fell silent again, scanning the Lamanites standing several yards in front of them as Zerahemnah continued with his inflammatory speech.

"Watch him!" A calm voice burst into Shem's mind. Instinctively, Shem put his right hand on the hilt of his trusty sword and focused on Zerahemnah's every movement.

"So, what is it general, are you a man of your word?" Zerahemnah was saying, sneering at Moroni as he spoke. "What's it going to be? I have surrendered; are we free to go?"

Moroni handed his helmet and shield to a Nephite attendant standing behind him. He bent down and picked Zerahemnah's sword up off the ground.

"If you do not make an oath with me before God to never again take up arms against the Nephite people, I will order my men to fall upon you and destroy you," Moroni repeated.

"See how he twists his own words?" Zerahemnah shouted to his men. "You have my sword, you don't need my oath. No oath to you boy, or to your God. You let us go or we will resume the fight and conquer or perish!"

Some of Zerahemnah's men nodded in approval. Most, however, looked concerned and unsure. One yelled from the ranks, "Swear and get this over with."

Zerahemnah held up his hand to silence his men "What will it be, my boy? Peace or death?" Zerahemnah chided again.

Moroni flipped Zerahemnah's sword over in his hands. He drew the sword out of the scabbard and examined the blade. "How many innocent lives have been taken by this weapon?" he asked. He looked back up at Zerahemnah, who just stood and smirked. Moroni continued. "I cannot take back the words I have said, Zerahemnah. I ask you one last time. Will you make peace with me? Swear to the God of heaven and earth to go and never return."

"You and your God can go to hell!" Zerahemnah cursed back.

Moroni shoved Zerahemnah's sword back into the sheath and threw it at Zerahemnah so hard that it hit his chest and almost knocked him over. Catching the sword in his hands, Zerahemnah's face flickered with a look of worry. His little ruse had not worked, and Moroni had shown again that he was far from a "boy" and not a coward.

"This ends now!" Moroni commanded.

Zerahemnah was stuck between his soldiers, who wanted him to surrender, and Moroni's, who wanted him destroyed. Refusing to back down, he walked in a small circle, glaring at all of the men standing around him.

Shem tightened his grip when the voice in his head again whispered, "Watch him!" Acting on an automatic, ingrained response to protect his leader, Shem found himself moving toward Moroni.

Zerahemnah's face turned dark and brooding, as if his evil thoughts were showing through. He had long been steeped in his own evil designs and lust for power and glory. His foolish ranting had shown how desperate he was. Now, without any hope or chance of escape, he still was not willing to yield. His eyes were dark and hollow, filled only with hatred and disdain. The dark thoughts in his mind screamed, "It's all Moroni's fault! Kill him, kill him now!"

Screaming, Zerahemnah lunged forward, pulling his sword out of its scabbard as he ran. Without his shield to deflect the sword attack, Moroni tried to get his sword out in time to defend himself, but Zerahemnah was too close.

Like a flash of lightning, Shem was there before anyone else could react. With his own sword out, he jumped in front of Moroni and brought his weapon up.

With all the strength he had left, Zerahemnah wildly swung his sword at

Moroni's neck. So focused was he on killing Moroni, he did not see Shem move into position to deflect the blow.

Zerahemnah's sword was within inches of Moroni's neck when Shem's sword came crashing down in an overhead chop. Shem's blow hit Zerahemnah's sword near the hilt, exploding the sword into two pieces.

Zerahemnah, thrown off balance by the force of his swing and the impact of Shem's sword, took two steps to his left to regain his balance. With the expertise that only comes from years of combat, Shem made a powerful back stroke with his sword, striking Zerahemnah on the top of his skull, severing a large section of his scalp.

Zerahemnah cried out in agony as he dropped his broken weapon and grabbed the top of his head. Falling to the ground, he thrashed in pain as blood poured from the gaping wound and covered his hands and face. Several Lamanites came forward and dragged Zerahemnah behind their lines.

Everything stopped as Shem bent over and picked up the piece of Zerahemnah's severed scalp. He put the bloody hunk of hair and flesh on the tip of his sword and held it out for all to see.

"Just as the scalp of your leader fell to earth, you will all fall here today if you do not now swear before the God of this earth an oath of peace with General Moroni."

Shem held the scalp above him for several moments to let his words sink in with the remaining Lamanites. He then dropped the scalp to the ground and turned to face Moroni. Moroni, with a look of gratitude and wonderment in his eyes, held out his hand to Shem and said, "Thank you." The two embraced briefly, and Shem returned to his place by Lehi.

Lehi patted Shem on the shoulder and said, "Well done, Captain Shem."

Teancum leaned over and whispered, "Nice shot." Shem and Teancum locked eyes and enjoyed the private joke, both remembering the scene when they first met in the village after Teancum killed the bandit with the javelin.

All of a sudden, Shem realized he was shaking. He chuckled to himself and shook his head. He was surprised by what he had just done and, with tears in his eyes, said a quick prayer of gratitude.

Slowly at first, a few Lamanites came forward and left their weapons of war at Moroni's feet. Then a rush of Lamanites came forward, each swearing an oath, each making their pledge of peace, and moving off to return to their homes. It took almost an hour for the many Lamanite soldiers who wanted to surrender to come forward and make their pledge to never again attack the Nephites.

At the same time, Zerahemnah was moved by his closest advisors to the river's edge and his head wound was bound tightly with a cloth. He had already suffered so much blood loss that he was delirious and babbling with hate. Those few in the Lamanite army who remained loyal to him gathered around him as the bulk of the Lamanite army surrendered. They formed a tight perimeter around their wounded leader with their backs to the river.

Amiha and the Nephites on the opposite side of the river could see what was happening, but they were too far away to hear what was being said.

"What do you think is happening?" a soldier asked Amiha.

They could see a long line of unarmed Lamanites heading for the bridge, but the men still could not cross. The bridge had been damaged and water still raged over the sides, making it impossible to cross.

"I think they have all surrendered and are trying to leave," Amiha said. "But look, the water is still too high."

No sooner did Amiha say that than the water calmed. Within only a few seconds, the river went from a raging torrent to the lazy flow that was typical for the river Sidon. Seeing that the flash flood was over, the Lamanites who had surrendered now attempted to cross the broken bridge.

"You see," one Lamanite said. "Even the Great Spirit wants the Nephites to win."

"The Lamanites are attacking us; make ready," someone shouted from behind Amiha. Several soldiers readied their weapons.

"Stand down," Amiha ordered. "They are unarmed and have surrendered!"

"How can you be sure?" the young lieutenant asked.

"The water stopped raging. God wants them to cross and to go in peace," Amiha whispered. "Let's be prudent, though, and be ready if one of them has a change of heart." He stood up from behind the makeshift barricade and shouted to his men, "Form single columns on both sides of the road next to the bridge. Let's make sure they get the message to leave in peace."

The soldiers with Amiha jumped up and formed armored walls on both sides of the well-worn road, their shields up and spears at the ready. They stood for what seemed to be an hour and watched as surrendering Lamanites worked their way around the shattered and broken parts of the bridge and made their way across.

Only a few hundred Lamanites and a handful of Zoramites remained with Zerahemnah. In his wounded and dazed condition, he was making no sense as he gave commands to his men not to surrender. It didn't really matter, though. Those who remained were completely loyal to Zerahemnah and were caught up in the greed and darkness that drove their leader. Like Zerahemnah, they refused to surrender to Moroni. They knew the final fight was coming, and they worked themselves into a frenzy. They started to taunt the Nephites and dare them to attack. Zerahemnah, in his crazed stupor, was shouting insults at the Nephites and at the surrendering Lamanites as well, urging the soldiers who remained to stand and fight to the end.

"We will die before we submit to the Nephites and their false God," he said over and over.

Moroni looked over to the bridge and could see that the Lamanites who had surrendered had all crossed over. Only the defiant enemy soldiers remained.

Moroni turned to face his command staff.

"Get the men back into formations and make ready!"

"Yes, sir," they all responded.

From his vantage point, Amiha could see the Lamanites preparing themselves for a fight and the responding movement among the Nephite ranks.

"This isn't over yet, boys! Lock down the bridge so they can't escape. Archers, get ready to fire on the remaining Lamanites. You and you," he said, pointing to two soldiers standing next to him, "keep an eye on the tree line. Let us know if any of those Lamanites who left change their minds and come back."

The Nephites took their long bows and as many arrows as they could find and moved back to the edge of the riverbank or to where the section of bridge had broken free. The rest moved to the bridge and reformed their shield wall.

Moroni moved forward a pace ahead of his army and shouted to the remaining Lamanites, "Surrender!"

They replied with cursing and vulgar gestures.

"I'm asking one last time—surrender. Do it now!"

Moroni got the same reply.

He turned back to the attendant who was holding his helmet and shield and gestured with his hand for the soldier to give them back. He put the helmet on his head once again and looked down into the eyes of the man who had been holding it. The soldier locked eyes with his commander and nodded, telling Moroni he was ready for the final fight.

Moroni looked at his chief captains and they, too, signaled that they and their men were ready.

He dropped his head, closed his eyes and said a prayer to his Father in Heaven.

"Forgive us, Father. We tried to make peace with our brothers the Lamanites. Many were spared, but some still refuse to follow your wishes. What I command your army to do now, I only do for the protection and safety of your children, the welfare of your church, and for the liberty of all mankind. Please, Father, continue to look upon us with favor. In your Son's name, I pray, amen."

Moroni lifted his chin and looked out at the enemy.

"May God forgive us," he said with sadness in his voice and pain in his heart at what he must now do.

He raised his sword and let out a war cry. The entire Nephite army joined him and their cries drowned out the Lamanite's cursing.

Without giving an order to advance, Moroni surged forward toward the group of belligerent Lamanites. The whole of the Nephite army raced after him, eager to end this war.

Amiha saw General Moroni's sudden advance and ordered his few archers to fire. Because Zerahemnah was so close to the river's edge, arrows started to fall all around where he was lying. Some of the Lamanites attending him were struck and mortally wounded by the arrows and fell to the ground. One dead Lamanite fell on top of Zerahemnah, pinning the gravely wounded leader to the ground. The soldier falling on him was more than his already-damaged mind could handle. Zerahemnah completely lost control and screamed like a scared child.

Moroni locked on Zerahemnah's position and nothing was going to stop him from reaching the Lamanite leader. Moroni hit the wall of defending Lamanites like a whirlwind. Spinning, jumping, slashing, kicking, he used every part of his body as a weapon. With his massive sword tearing through flesh and bone and his large metal shield swatting and pounding the enemy, Moroni cut a path of death through the front lines of the Lamanites for his men to follow.

For the first time since the encounter in the valley of Jershon, the Lamanites were now the numerically weaker force. Second by second, they were losing more and more men as the Nephite soldiers poured over them, following their leader to victory.

Amiha saw the Nephites spilling into the perimeter the Lamanites had created around their wounded leader and ordered his men to stop shooting for fear of hitting one of their own. He was satisfied they had done all they could to aid their general without abandoning their position.

As the attack intensified, more Lamanites panicked and broke ranks. They ran for the bridge and tried to cross but were stopped by the broken pathway across the water and the armored wall of shields created by Amiha and his men on the other side. Seeing that there was no escape for them now, those Lamanites on the bridge stopped. One of them standing at the edge of the broken bridge made an overt gesture with his sword to the Nephites on the far side. He raised it up into the air and then dropped his weapon into the river, sat down on the planks of the undamaged part of the bridge and put his hands on top of his head as a sign of surrender. The other Lamanites on the bridge soon followed, and a cheer went up from the Nephite defenders with Amiha.

Moroni continued to fight his way inside the Lamanite perimeter, cleaving bodies and shattering bones as he tried to find Zerahemnah among the wounded and dead. Several Nephites, including Captain Lehi, caught up to Moroni and formed a protective wall around him. They fought off any Lamanites as Moroni personally searched for the body of Zerahemnah.

Moroni heard the screaming before he could see who was making the noise. He stepped over two dead bodies and found Zerahemnah lying face up with a dead Lamanite on top of him. Zerahemnah was crying and screaming, and fresh blood was oozing from his head wound.

"Zerahemnah … you coward dog!" Moroni shouted as he pulled the dead Lamanite off the gravely wounded Zoramite. Moroni held up the sword of power over his head and readied himself to deliver the final victorious blow.

Zerahemnah felt the dead weight of the Lamanite come off him. In a moment of clarity, looked up to see who was standing over him and saw the great sword positioned to deliver the fatal strike. "Moroni, I surrender, I surrender. I pledge peace. Please don't kill me!" he begged over and over again with his hands out in front of him. Zerahemnah curled into the fetal position and started to sob uncontrollability.

Moroni saw Zerahemnah in this helpless state and took pity on the man. He lowered his sword and looked around at the fighting still raging around him. The slaughter of the Lamanites was unbelievable.

"I am done killing," he said and ordered the trumpeters to sound a halt to the fighting.

The trumpeters sounded the halt and, almost instantly, the battle was over. Very few Lamanites remained standing. An eerie silence broke over the battleground, and all that could be heard were bellowing sobs from the once-great Lamanite war chief, Zerahemnah. When the remaining Lamanites saw and heard Zerahemnah, they knew the battle was finally over. They dropped their weapons and sat down like the Lamanites on the bridge, with their hands on top of their heads.

Moroni took the stained and dirty leopard skin cloak from around Zerahemnah's neck and wiped the blood off his sword. What was once Zerahemnah's symbol of power and leadership was now no better than a rag, and Moroni made sure all who were around him saw what he was doing. This silent, simplistic act spoke volumes to both Nephite and Lamanite warriors. This was a complete and unconditional surrender. When he finished, he dropped the skin on the ground and looked up at his brother soldiers. For as far as he could see, his victorious countrymen stood looking back at him. Battered and bloody, but full of pride, this ragtag army of citizen soldiers had just defeated a massive Lamanite army. With a wave of emotion, Moroni held up his sword high over his head and shouted, "Victory!"

The entire Nephite army erupted in celebration and shouted back, "Victory!"

As the army shouted for joy, Moroni held out the Sword of Laban for all to see. He put the tip of the sword in the sheath and, very dramatically, slammed the sword of power back into its resting place, a move that signaled to all that the war was finally over. The Nephite warriors went into a frenzy of celebration as Moroni stepped off the field of battle.

One week after the battle, Moroni sat in his command tent, just outside of the gates of Manti. The work continued of disposing of the thousands of dead Lamanite bodies. At first, the thought was to bury them all but, by the time graves could be dug for all of the bodies; they would be rotten and covered with pestilence-bearing flies. Shem proposed that the bodies be tossed into the river and buried at sea. He knew that the river Sidon was wide and had a strong current past the bridge, all the way to the ocean.

It was a hard and gruesome job to gather up all the dead from the battlefield. Captain Lehi recommended they have the captured Lamanites do the deed, and General Moroni agreed. Under a heavy guard, the Lamanites who survived the final battle were compelled to spend the next few days filling wagons with the dead and putting them in the river.

"The river creatures will be feasting for days," Amiha said as he walked into the command tent. "It's a win-win for everyone today."

Moroni looked up from his paperwork and handed a dispatch to the young Nephite courier who carried the general's messages during the battle.

"My orders for Captain Lehi," Moroni told the runner, "Stay until he gives you a response and return with it here right away.

"Yes, sir," the young Nephite boy responded as he took the sealed message and bolted out of the tent.

"Report," Moroni said with a smile as he watched the boy race away. Shaking his head, he laughed, sat back in his chair and said to Amiha, "He is really fast."

Amiha looked back out the tent opening and watched as the young boy ran toward Lehi's tent. "You should sign him up for the games next year."

"The games." Moroni snorted. "After this battle I don't think I will ever take something as simple as watching sports for granted again."

Amiha agreed with a nod and smile. Moroni gestured for Amiha to come closer and sit by his side.

Amiha continued his report while he walked closer to Moroni. "All of the captured Lamanite weapons have been distributed to the city's garrison. The weapons they have no need for are now warehoused for the militia. Captain Shem and his men are still hunting for Pachus and any of Manti's citizens who would not fight for their freedom. Lehi is almost ready to move his army back to Zarahemla, and Teancum and his Ghost Soldiers are working on the bandit problem along the merchant road."

"Outstanding. And what of our wounded?" Moroni asked.

"They are in the personal care of the chief judges. They have ordered open some of the wealthy homes inside Manti and our wounded are convalescing there. When they are fit to travel, they will be escorted back to their own cities by some of Shem's men."

"What of the Lamanite prisoners?"

"Their work is almost done. The one who calls himself their leader now wants to make their surrender and peace pledge official. They have asked you to come at sunset to the bridge so they can officially swear their oath of peace to you, in person."

Moroni nodded his head in approval and gathered his thoughts.

"I want a strong presence at the river tonight when they pledge peace. I don't need anyone having second thoughts and ruining it for the rest of us."

'Yes, sir," Amiha spoke back. "I thought so. It just so happens that we have arranged for you to conduct a full dress inspection of Manti's new well-armored garrison at the same time by the river."

Moroni chuckled lightly. "Funny how it worked out like that."

They shared a quick laugh.

"Still no sign of Pachus?" Moroni asked while getting up out his chair.

"No, sir," Amiha said as Moroni looked over a hanging map of the area around Manti. "Shem and his men are combing the countryside. If anyone can find him, he will."

"I hope so," Moroni said, while taking a deep breath. "I have a bad feeling we have not seen the last of him."

Pachus was crashing through the thick underbrush like a drunken bear. He had a day's head start on Shem and his men, but he was taking no chances and moving as fast as his fat, pathetic body could go. Cursing and holding the bandage covering his wounded hand, he made his way around some large boulders and through a flowing stream bed that led toward an old smugglers' path he knew about from his interaction with the criminals of Manti. The path continued over the mountains and down to the crossroads of Zarahemla.

"Curse you, Moroni!" he spat as he gulped for air and rested against a large tree, rubbing his wounded hand. Pachus was a weak and pampered man. He was in no condition for a cross-country trek. Resting under the cool shade of an old tree, he was suddenly taken by how alone he was in this vast wilderness. Closing his eyes, he sat quietly daydreaming of sweet bread, broiled meat and fine women pouring his wine. Suddenly, there was a crack of twigs off in the distance. Frightened, Pachus turned in the direction of the sound.

"Who is there? Show yourself!" he pleaded as he tried in vain to pull a small dagger from his belt.

Out of the shadows stepped a cloaked man, covered in dirt and grime.

"Who are you?" Pachus commanded, as he finally retrieved the weapon and held it out in front of himself.

"My name is Baca," the hooded figure replied

"Do you know who I am?" Pachus questioned.

"Your name is Pachus; you were the garrison commander of Manti," Baca replied, looking Pachus over with contempt. "What are you now?"

"Just a man trying to get to Zarahemla, so that I can have my revenge."

"I heard you curse someone called Moroni. Is that the same Moroni who is the commander of the armies at Manti?" Baca asked as he slowly moved toward Pachus.

"The very same," Pachus whined like a spoiled child. "He usurped my authority and ordered his men to attack me." Pachus held up his wounded hand. "I tried to organize the defense of the city when his lackey, the sheriff, assaulted me." Pachus continued with a bit more theatrical flair. "I barely escaped with my life."

"That same Moroni ordered his men to drive me from my fishing village as they took my wife and child as slaves. I have cursed him many times. I, too, am trying to get to Zarahemla to find my justice."

"Well, my friend, this looks like the start of a unique friendship," Pachus said, as he put the small knife back in its sheath. "We will travel together and, when we get to Zarahemla, you can stay with my family while we plot the demise of this upstart boy general."

Baca smiled and started to walk toward the mountain trail.

"I see," Pachus said under his breath as Baca walked past him. "The strong silent type. I like that."

END OF BOOK ONE.

INSPIRATIONAL ART

Invite true Christian heroes
to serve as role models in your home with
these full-color, fine art prints.

Each full-color print includes the heroe's key virtue,
a scripture reference, and their symbol. Across the top are the words
Honor • Strength • Courage • Discipline.

Print sizes:
5"x7" • 8"x10" • 18"x24"

Available at your local LDS bookstore or online at
TheWarChapters.com

HONOR

HONOR · COURAGE · STRENGTH · DISCIPLINE

MORONI

HONOR

"...a strong and...mighty man;
...a man of a perfect understanding;...
that did not delight in bloodshed;
...whose soul did joy in...liberty
and...freedom" ALMA 48:11

THE WAR CHAPTERS .COM

© 2014 - Ethos Productions, LLC

COURAGE

STRENGTH